MW01526720

"You

"David's gorgeous, isn't he?" said Posy.

I didn't look at her. "I suppose he is."

"Don't worry," she said indulgently to my back. "You're sure to meet some nice, quiet little man in a few years' time. I expect you'll be terribly devoted."

I treated her to the patronizing smile I'd been practicing all week. "As a matter of fact, I've already met a man," I drawled. "He's not quiet, but he's certainly experienced."

Posy stared. "You mean you've kissed him?"

I laughed as if the possibility that I hadn't was absurd. "Of course."

"Oh. Is that all?"

"Of course it's not all," I said.

The Bantley-Brown mouth gaped most satisfactorily. "You don't mean...you haven't *slept* with him? You couldn't have."

"Well, there hasn't been much sleeping about it," I admitted with a smirk.

"Janey!"

If I'd wanted to I could have seen her tonsils...

To Kathleen,

Great to meet you again.

Happy Writing

Kay Gregory

What readers are saying about A Woman of Experience

"Wonderfully written, a nostagic experience for anyone who grew up insecure and 'outside' the popular/rich/beautiful group. Janey's experiences as she moves from insecure girl to confident woman are frequently confused, often painful, as she searches for happiness and success. She struggles to understand love and honour, both in herself and others, as she falls in love, finds the right career, makes friends, all while learning what is truly important to her and in life. Her relationships with the men she loves and with her family and friends resonate in the reader's heart. All the characters are so real, you could swear you'd met them in your own life. Anyone who likes Maeve Binchy's books will love this one."

~Judy Jackson, author of FIND HER KEEP HER

"Kay Gregory's delightful coming of age novel A WOMAN OF EXPERIENCE will tickle your funny bone and warm your heart. With wit, keen insight and an eye for detail, Gregory draws the reader in to the world of her courageous, yet vulnerable heroine. Impossible to put down, Gregory's latest novel is quite simply unforgettable."

~Gael Morrison, bestselling author of HEART OF A WOMAN

A WOMAN OF EXPERIENCE

by

Kay Gregory

NBI
NovelBooks, Inc.
Douglas, Massachusetts

NBI

Published by
NovelBooks, Inc.
P.O. Box 661
Douglas, MA 01516

NovelBooks Inc. publishes books online and in trade paperback. For more information, check our website: www.novelbooksinc.com or email publisher@novelbooksinc.com

Produced in the United States of America.

Cover illustration by Linnea Sinclair
Edited by Nancy Bishaw

ISBN 1-931696-39-X for electronic version
ISBN 1-931696-60-8 for trade paperback

DEDICATION

With love and gratitude to:

My husband, **Bob**, without whose love,
support and computer skills
I might never have written this book of of my heart.

And to **NovelBooks, Inc**. who published it.

1954—1956

I did not know
That heydays fade and go,
But deemed that what was would be always so.

From *Regret Not Me* by Thomas Hardy

CHAPTER ONE

"Lord dismiss us with Thy blessing,
Thanks for mercies past receive."

The moment I opened my mouth to join the off-key chorus, Posy Bantley-Brown put her hand behind my back to unfasten the top button on my ugly gray uniform skirt.

"Beast!" I delivered a sharp kick to Posy's shin as I scrabbled to refasten the button. Behind us, someone giggled. From the scuffed stage at the front of the gym, Miss Barclay delivered her power glower.

Thank heaven the one great mercy, which wasn't 'past receive,' was that after today I would never have to set eyes on Posy B-B's saucer-smug face again—certainly not first thing on a perfectly good summer morning.

I twisted to the right to get a better view of her permed blonde head uplifted in virtuous piety. Her face was a bit redder than usual, but otherwise she looked as innocent as an angel. *Phony little cat.* Her lips were moving—those rosebud lips that had opened so often to deliver hurtful barbs at my expense—but she wasn't actually singing. I watched the fair curls dancing on her short white neck and thought of my mother's half-hearted strictures about charity, tolerance and compassion.

All very well for Mother. She hadn't had to put up with Posy day and in and day out for twelve years—or almost twelve years. There had been time off in the long summer holidays, of course, when I had fantasized about the autumn term beginning with the miraculous news that the Bantley-Brown had succumbed to some mysterious and fatal holiday virus with a long name. Needless to say, she never succumbed to

1

anything more useful than the occasional day off school to attend Ascot, Wimbledon, or something county to do with cricket.

Pardon all their faults confessing;
Time that's lost may all retrieve....

Oh no, I wasn't going to pardon all Posy's faults. God might. That was up to Him. I said a quick, guilty prayer just in case He was paying attention, then eased my conscience with the reflection that the plump little snob wasn't likely to confess her faults anyway. She didn't think she had any. I saw her fingers edge towards my waist again and grabbed them before they could do any damage. "Leave me alone," I hissed.

Miss Barclay heard me and frowned. Posy smiled sweetly and raised her voice in song.

Around us, the chorus reached a crescendo of enthusiasm never achieved when a dispirited "Lord Behold Us," was sung at the start of each year.

Sanctify our every pleasure;
Pure and blameless may it be....

Pure and blameless? I closed my mouth in mid-verse. Did I want my every pleasure sanctified? Distracted, I stopped brooding about Posy and thought about life as I hoped to live it once I escaped the strict clutches of Chantersley Private School for Girls.

The pleasures I had in mind were of a romantic and, doubtless, unsanctified nature. Not that I planned to go as far as actual sex—a mysterious and frightening enigma that sounded more messy than pleasant. For now, kisses and flirtation would do nicely. I ran a discreet finger over my tiresomely crooked mouth. If only someone—anyone—would attempt to kiss me. Of course, there had been that man who'd put his hand up my skirt on the train to London last year...I'd known I was meant to be indignant, and I hadn't liked it much. But there had been a svelte and mascaraed brunette on his other side, and he'd chosen me.....

An elbow smacked against my ribs, making me jump. But it wasn't Posy this time. Glancing to my left, I met Allison Campbell's wickedly laughing gaze.

Beautiful Allison, pretending to sing lustily, had noticed my inattention and understood it.

May all taint of evil perish
By Thy mightier power restrained;
Seek we ever, seek we ever
Knowledge pure and love unfeigned....

"Love unfeigned sounds all right," whispered Allison.

"Yes, but I've had enough of 'knowledge pure' for a while," I whispered back.

She giggled. "I know. And I'm not sure about 'all taint of evil' either. I mean a little bit of evil might be..." She subsided hastily, nailed by Miss Barclay's repressive glare. Not that there was any need for either of us to cringe from our headmistress anymore. In another half-hour Miss Barclay's dominion over us would be ended. Forever and ever, amen.

It didn't seem possible. Wasn't possible yet. Twelve years of, "Yes, Miss Barclay, no, Miss Barclay," and, "I'm terribly sorry, Miss Barclay," had so conditioned all of us that even on this, our very last day of school, we couldn't defy the Head.

Both of us fixed our eyes on the row of tired teachers standing on the creaky wooden stage and lifted our heads to carol a rousing conclusion to the last hymn we would ever sing at Chantersley.

Those returning, those returning
Make more faithful than before.

But we weren't returning. It was a strange thought. Unbelievable really.

Allison had her "A" levels and could have gone on to college, but she'd chosen drama school instead. I had an "A" level in English, and another, as Miss Barclay had frequently warned me, in daydreaming, which meant I would have to find a job.

An expectant silence followed the last notes of "Lord Dismiss Us," and after a suitably reverend pause, Miss Cleethorpe, our long-faced music mistress, began to plunk out a melancholy march on the ancient piano. At once all three hundred of us turned right to file solemnly out of the gym.

As soon as we were through the door and free of Miss Barclay's quelling scrutiny, solemnity was discarded like wet clothing.

"No more Latin, no more French," the familiar chant started up, even though half of us had never taken Latin. Funny, now that the term was really over, nobody seemed all that anxious to leave. We hung about in the hall chattering, exchanging addresses, and taking pictures of everything from the ornate Victorian fireplace to self-conscious mistresses and the school cat. It was as if we had suddenly realized that in the years to come we would want to remember this turning point in our lives and were trying to record it in slow motion.

"Did I tell you we're off to the Riviera for our holidays, Janey?" Posy's exaggerated county accent cooed into my ear as she sauntered up beside Allison and me.

"Frequently," said Allison.

"Oh. Did I? Where are you going, Vanda?" Posy turned to a mousy little blonde whose father, we all knew, was threatened with bankruptcy.

Vanda's eyes filled with tears, and she didn't answer as she pushed her way through the crowd of milling girls and hurried off to cry in the lavatory.

"You are a pig, Posy," said Allison matter-of-factly.

Posy had always been a pig, but no one besides me seemed to think much about it anymore.

"I don't see why." Posy's baby-blue eyes widened. "I only asked her—"

"We know what you asked her," snapped Allison.

I wished I had been the one to puncture Posy's spiteful balloon.

My mother said I ought to feel sorry for Posy, who didn't have the advantage of good breeding. That always set me giggling because it made Posy sound like a horse. Mother had once sat next to Mrs. Bantley-Brown on Sports Day. She said Mrs. B-B wore silk and jangle-bangles when everyone else was wearing tweed and that all she talked about was Posy's younger sister, Jasmine, a gorgeous dark-haired gypsy of a girl with a lot more brain than plump and pretty Posy.

Jasmine never went around saying things like, "Oh, do you mean you only have two bathrooms?"

I had once heard Mother murmur to Dad, "Nouveau riche, poor things. No background, you see."

I often felt we could have done with less background and more riche ourselves, so that Posy wouldn't be able to sneer at my secondhand school uniforms and the Victorian row house on the wrong side of Willbury that, to Mother's eternal chagrin, was the best my parents could afford. Their resources had been strained to the limit to send me to Chantersley, and because of that, I'd started school a year late. Since Posy Bantley-Brown was the price I'd had to pay for their sacrifice, I wasn't sure the whole thing had been worth it. Oh, I'd made a few friends, of course, but no special friend. I was too quiet and I wasn't good at games. Still, nobody minded me, and if it hadn't been for Posy, my schooldays would have been no worse than anyone else's.

It had been easier this last year though, because Allison, who was good at everything, had offered me a casual sort of friendship.

Allison was the only girl in the school who had the courage to admit to voting Labour in the school's mock elections. I was lost in admiration—and demonstrated my own individuality by standing firmly in the middle and voting Liberal.

A crowd of fourth-formers jostled past and Posy was pushed aside. "Have a lovely time in Eastbourne," she called to Allison. "It was Eastbourne, wasn't it? Or Brighton?"

"Scotland, actually," drawled Allison, as Posy was wafted out of sight.

"That was supposed to put you in your rightful place," I told her. "You should have said you were going for the shooting or something."

Allison shrugged. "Who cares? I don't suppose we'll ever see her again."

"I know. Hard to believe, isn't it?"

"Mm. Come on, let's get out of here."

As we made our way to the cloakroom, I wondered, with premature nostalgia, how much I would see of Allison after today. She was the closest thing I had to a friend, but our lives were set to run on different tracks.

Allison was lucky. Her father was sending her to drama school in the autumn because, of all the things she was good at, acting was the one she loved best. I watched her beautiful, confident face as she waved to a friend I couldn't see, and all at once the future seemed less thrilling and more intimidating.

I might dream of romance in some handsome suitor's arms, but there were times when even I had to face the fact that romance didn't sit well with a tendency to spots. And although my hair was a rather dramatic red, my nose was snub, and my chin too pointed to be easily ignored.

There was also the small matter of my need to find a job.

Ten minutes later Allison and I were standing on the gravelled driveway listening to shouted goodbyes as we looked back at the squat brick building, mellowed today by a kindly sun, where we had spent the last twelve years of our lives. Funny, next time we came back—if we came back—we would be "old girls." And Miss Barclay wouldn't be able to tell us what to do.

My momentary anxiety faded, and I gave a little skip, grabbed Allison by the arm and began to run down the driveway.

"Watch out world!" I crowed to the accompaniment of Allison's giggles. "Janey Blackman is about to take you by storm."

When I reached the heavy, wrought iron gates, my toe hit a loose pebble and I stumbled and fell to my knees. At the same moment, Posy's family Rolls swept past in a swirl of gravel.

Miss Barclay was right. I had always been a dreamer.

~*~

No. 48 Willbury Road was the only home I'd ever known, but it wasn't until I was sent to Chantersley and encountered Posy that I discovered we didn't have a 'good' address. Oh, I knew the posh part of town featured separate houses with bigger gardens than our little patch full of cabbage. But I also knew that some of the newer houses were called townhouses and were supposed to be very chic. Not ours, Posy hastened to assure me.

My footsteps slowed as I approached No. 48. By now Mother—I'd never been permitted to call her Mum—would be home from her part-time job at Curry and Coles, the Estate Agents. She was sure to be in one of her 'tell-me-all-about-it' moods, and I didn't want to tell her all about it. Partly because there was nothing to tell, but also because my confident, excited feeling had gone flat, and I wanted to be by myself—to think about what I'd left behind as much as what lay ahead. I'd never taken endings lightly. Goodbyes were to be savoured and stored away for future nostalgic reminiscing.

I climbed the steps bracing myself for Mother's eager questions but she wasn't in the kitchen as I'd expected, nor was she in the sitting room with its square brown furniture and the yellow curtains that were supposed to distinguish our windows from those of our neighbours. Most of the neighbours favoured white net. We didn't associate with them much although I knew a lot of them by name, and sometimes I caught Dad chatting over the back fence when Mother wasn't looking.

To my surprise, there were voices coming from upstairs—raised voices, or rather voice, my mother's, with my father's as a kind of protesting background hum.

What was this? Dad wasn't supposed to be home until this evening.

"Frank, how could you? Of all the stupid, selfish, inconsiderate things you've ever done—"

The hum grew a little louder but was overridden.

"How could you?" Mother repeated. "Didn't you even think of me and Jane? How are we supposed to manage with no steady income coming in? What?" She paused as Dad, who hadn't a selfish or inconsiderate bone in his body, tried to make some sort of objection. "Yes, I know Jane has finished school, but she has no job yet and no particular training." Mother's voice was high-pitched, as persistent as the whine of a gnat. "I suppose that doesn't matter to you, does it? All you care about is your silly dream of playing shop. And a fishmonger's shop at that—"

"I thought you liked fish, Edith." Dad at last succeeded in making himself heard.

I stood with my foot on the bottom step and closed my right hand over the banister. I couldn't remember the last time I'd heard my parents argue. They had no need to because Dad almost always did exactly as Mother told him. It was hard not to. She operated like a sugar-coated tank blithely icing over opposition—not that sugar seemed much in evidence today.

What could Dad possibly have done to upset her so? It seemed to have something to do with fish....

"Of course, I like fish," I heard her wail. "To eat, you silly man. I don't want to be associated with selling them. Horrid, smelly things."

"Somebody has to," Dad murmured.

"Yes, but not people like us. What's got into you, Frank? You had a perfectly good job—well, it could have been better, of course. You don't—didn't make a lot of money. But at least insurance is respectable."

"So are fish," said my amazing father. I'd never heard him sound so assured and I too wondered what had gotten into him. His voice was louder now too, firm and quietly convinced.

On the other hand, I'd never heard Mother sound so out of her depth. She had always been the one in charge of "those things that ought to be done"—and her family had dutifully done them.

Dad said something else I didn't catch, so I heaved my satchel off my shoulder and holding it in one hand, started to creep up the stairs in a slow, furtive slither. I had to know what Dad had been up to, and if I interrupted them now, they'd probably clam up and pretend nothing had happened. They did that sometimes, usually when the problem was money.

"Fish," said Mother. She made the word sound like an obscenity.

"Don't worry, Edith. I've looked over the books and the shop's been doing very nicely. There's no other fishmonger in that part of town—"

"Then why are they selling out?" Mother didn't mean to be placated. "What if their customers have all switched to chicken because of the pollution from the oil during the war?"

I reached the top of the stairs but was so intent on catching Dad's reply, I forgot to watch out for the squeaky board. When I stepped on it, it gave its usual impersonation of an alley cat making passionate love to a pampered Persian.

Silence hissed from my parents' bedroom.

"Jane? Is that you?" Mother called.

I froze, flattening my satchel and myself against the wall, and tried not to breathe. If I kept very still they might think they'd imagined the squeak.

"Jane?"

I went on imitating a pancake.

"It's nothing, Edith." Dad's voice again, brisk, anxious to get whatever it was settled.

"What do you mean, nothing? Jane—?"

If I didn't move, in the next few seconds I was going to be found out. I searched frantically for a place of concealment, spotted it, and without wasting further precious time, darted across the landing and edged behind the partially opened door. It had never fit well, and when I put my eye to the space where it met the wall I found I could see into most of my parents' bedroom. Like the sitting room, it was decorated in Mother's idea of 'simple good taste.'

She was sitting on the brown and black striped bedspread. Dad was standing by the window with his moustache sucked in. He had a small mouth and right now it wasn't visible at all. He seemed to be all wide forehead and pale blue eyes. But he wore a look of determination I'd never seen on his amiable face before.

"Jane?" my mother repeated.

Dad sighed and came over to the door. "Janey's not home yet. There's no one here," he said patiently.

"Oh. I thought...never mind." It sounded, to my astonishment, as though my managing mother was actually on the brink of tears.

"Now, Edith, you mustn't upset yourself." Dad took his place by the window again and gave her a bracing smile, which had no visible effect. Mother's shoulders continued to slump and she looked as despondent as I had ever seen her.

"Upset! Of course, I'm upset," she moaned. "Have you no idea what you've done, Frank?"

"Well, I haven't committed any crime—not in the eyes of the law, at any rate.

Mother and the law were not of the same mind. "No crime!" she exclaimed. "You call it no crime to throw away the job you've had for twenty years and use all the money Hilda left you to buy a fish shop? Thank God Jane isn't going back to school."

I blinked, not seeing the connection at first. Then I realized she was right. Imagine what Posy would have said about a fish shop!

"Hilda was my sister," Dad said mildly. "She wanted me to use the money as I pleased. It wasn't all that much—"

"Enough," muttered Mother, plucking at the bedspread with long, work-worn fingers. "It was enough. You could have told me, Frank."

"But I couldn't, Edith. I saw the shop was for sale and I knew at once I wanted to buy it. Only I didn't think..." He paused to brush a hand over his thinning wisps of hair. "I didn't think I could manage it. Then today at the office, when Munnings told me off for leaving my desk to pay a call of nature, I knew this was meant to be my chance. Maybe my only chance. Destiny, if you like. And that if I didn't make the move now, I'd regret it for the rest of my life. Edith, you know I've always wanted to own a shop—"

"Destiny? Fish?" Mother's voice began to rise again. "And what about me? What about Jane? You didn't even think about us, did you?"

I swivelled my head to get a better view of my father. He still looked the same, but there was something about him that was different. A sort of glow, a resolute way of standing that hadn't been there before—as if he'd had a message from an angel.

Then I looked at my mother. If she'd received any message, it could only have come from the devil—presumably in the shape of my harmless father. She was hunched over as if she expected coals of fire to descend on her mouse-coloured head. Her straight, determined mouth was actually quivering.

"Yes, Edith, I did think of you," Dad said. "And I'm convinced we'll do very nicely with the shop. We may even end up better off—"

"Better off? With a fish shop?" Mother was a needle stuck in a groove.

My easy-going father finally lost patience. "There's nothing wrong with fish. If it's good enough to eat, it's damn well good enough to sell. And whatever you may think, Edith, we're no better than anybody else in this town, or in this country for that matter. I know my dad was a grocer and yours was a solicitor who brought you up to think you were a cut above the mob. But you weren't always so particular, were you?"

He stopped abruptly, pale eyes staring, and suddenly I wished I hadn't taken up my station behind the door. I couldn't bear to see my parents, my boringly predictable, safe parents, turning into people I didn't know. But it was too late. I had to hear what Mother would say next.

She was staring at Dad as if he'd slapped her in the face. "What do you mean by that?" she asked. "You wanted to marry me, didn't you?"

"Yes, Edith, I did." Dad swallowed as if he had a golf ball stuck in his narrow throat. "I did indeed. Now there's no need to fret. Everything's going to be all right...."

That was when my mother, my calm, church-going mother, seemed to fall apart in front of my eyes. Eye anyway. I shifted my position to get a better view.

"Everything is not going to be all right," she wailed. "It never was and I don't suppose it ever will be. I knew that when I married you, Frank. But what else could I do?" She pressed her knuckles against her eyelids, and her long face turned an ugly, mottled pink.

"I suppose you could have married Marlowe," said my father, looking straight at me instead of at my mother. Thank heavens he couldn't really see me.

Mother's hand clutched the front of her yellow print blouse. "What?" she asked. The mottled pink became mottled beige. "John Marlowe? I couldn't have married John."

"Why not? He owed it to you, didn't he?"

"Owed it...? What—what do you mean?"

"What do you think I mean? Did you really imagine that all these years I haven't known—?" He stopped to put a hand to his shirt pocket, and I knew he was reaching for the cigarettes Mother had made him give up after he fell asleep and burned a hole in the carpet. Finding no cigarettes, he pulled out a greying handkerchief and wiped it round the back of his neck. "Never mind. It doesn't matter."

Mother was dead white now, her eyes cagey, darting from side to side as if she was looking for a way to escape. "Known what, Frank?" she asked.

I didn't believe she really wanted an answer. But I did. I held my breath.

Dad shook his head. "I said it doesn't matter."

"Frank!" Mother lifted her head and fixed him with her no-nonsense eye.

I breathed a private prayer of thanks. This, at least, was the mother I was used to.

"All right," Dad said, responding to the eye as he always had. "All right, Edith. If you must know, I was talking about you and Marlowe." He hesitated before he added, "And Janey."

"Jane? What about Jane? John and I were friends, of course, but that was before—"

"Before I asked you to marry me? I know it was. But not before you and he had..." He stopped, cleared his throat, and adjusted his mud-coloured tie. "Edith, you don't really want to talk about this now, do you?"

Mother's grip tightened on the front of her blouse. "I think we have to."

Dad shrugged, and after a pause Mother said, "Frank, are you telling me you proposed to me, knowing all the time that Jane—that Jane...?" She stopped, as if someone had grabbed her by the throat.

I moistened my lips and leaned forward. My heart was thumping so loudly it was hard to believe it hadn't already given me away.

Dad passed the back of his hand across his eyes. "Edith," he said, "I'm sorry. I shouldn't have—this isn't the right time..." He gestured vaguely at the window.

Mother sat up, jerking her shoulders back and linking her hands in her lap. "Maybe this is the right time. Maybe it's time we both told the truth."

"Edith, don't. There's no need—"

"No need for what, Frank?" She turned towards him and smiled. It was a strange smile. Not at all the controlled flick of the lips I was used to.

"Edith—"

She stood up then and began to move towards him, but he shifted sideways into the shadows, and after that I couldn't see them anymore. I could hear them though.

"Have you always known?" Mother asked.

Known what? "Why can't you just come out and say it?" I wanted to shout. *There's nothing wrong with me, is there? I don't have some horrible hereditary disease...?*

Dad must have nodded, because Mother's voice came again, quietly now. "I had to do what was best for Jane, Frank. I had no choice. That's why I married you."

"I know that, Edith."

Oh. I drew a great breath that was only partly relief. Was that what this was all about? I'd been conceived before my parents were married. It seemed indecent, the thought of Mother and Dad engaged in that faintly obscene act, and although I knew just enough not to be surprised, I certainly didn't want to hear about it.

"I knew Janey was his." My father was speaking now, words that at first made no sense. When they did, I shut my eyes, as though that could block out the words I didn't want to hear. *No. It couldn't be true. It couldn't. I must have misheard. Or misunderstood.* I put a hand to my mouth to stop the peculiar sound erupting from my throat and discovered I was still holding my satchel. It was heavy with end-of-term debris and books I would never open again. School things.

For no good reason, the thought of school made me want to laugh and laugh and laugh—as if school had happened in another century. In reality it was barely an hour since Janey Blackman had called on the world to watch out and promptly fallen on her face—or, more accurately, her knees. They were still sore.

All at once the satchel was an unbearable burden. I opened my fingers and allowed it to drop onto the faded yellow carpet.

"Jane? That is you, isn't it?" Mother's voice was shrill with what sounded like panic—or guilt.

I didn't have time to decide what to do because before I could pick up the satchel, the door was pulled back and I was gazing into Dad's shattered face.

We stared at each other for what felt like an eon.

"Janey? How long have you been here?" He sounded more sad than angry.

"Only a minute," I lied.

He let out his breath. "Come on in then. You know you shouldn't listen at doors."

No. No, I shouldn't. If I'd known, I wouldn't have. But now it was done, and there was nothing I could do to purge the knowledge that I would have given anything not to possess.

Dad took my arm and urged me into their bedroom.

Mother was standing in the middle of the floor, but as soon as she saw me, she sank back onto the bed. For one crazy moment I half-expected her to say, "Tell us all about it then, Jane."

But she didn't. Instead she said, "Come in, Jane. Your father has something to tell you."

I stood in the doorway, looking from one stiff face to the other. Dad had gone back to his place by the window.

"It's all right, Janey." He made a valiant effort to sound hearty. "Your mother's just a wee bit upset. You see, today I did something I've always wanted to do, and she's afraid it may not work out."

"What?" I looked at him blankly. *What was he talking about? Had both of them gone mad?*

"The thing is, Janey, I've—"

"He's bought a fish shop," Mother said dully.

Yes, I knew that. But what had fish to do with what I'd just heard?

"Your mother is worried I won't make a go of it," Dad went on. "She's not keen on my being a fishmonger—"

"Of course, I'm not keen," Mother interrupted, giving me a smile that made her look as if she were coming down with the plague. "Such smelly things, fish."

"You'll come round to it," Dad said. "What do you think, Janey?"

I opened my mouth but couldn't seem to speak. I had just heard something so shocking it made me want to scream. Yet here were my parents, my dull, but presumably sane parents, calmly discussing fish. Was I the one who was going mad? Or had I totally misunderstood everything?

"Who's John Marlowe?" I whispered.

Mother went white. Dad turned a waxy yellow.

"You heard," he said.

I nodded.

"You'd better tell her, Edith." Even his moustache seemed to droop.

Mother ran her tongue around her lips. "Jane," she said, in a funny sort of croak. "You know I always tried to do my best for you."

It was a statement, not a question. I wondered if she expected me to answer.

In the end it didn't matter, because I couldn't.

For a while Mother too was silent. Then she straightened her back and carried on quite calmly, as if she were discussing what to have for dinner. "That's why I agreed to marry your father."

My legs felt so woolly I had to lean against the doorframe for support. "You mean because—because..." I couldn't go on.

"Because I was going to have you." Mother's breath, coming out on the "you," reminded me of air rushing out of a balloon.

I wanted to say it didn't matter, that I knew some people didn't wait for marriage. But Mother had always insisted it did matter. Anyway, this wasn't about premarital sex and my parents. It was about someone I had never heard of until today.

"Who is John Marlowe?" I asked again. I had to hear her say it. Just in case the answer wasn't what I feared. Just in case I had heard wrong.

"He—John was—is—your father." She looked me straight in the eye and didn't even blink, though her skin was still as white as the freshly bleached pillowcase she had pulled onto her knees and was kneading fiercely with her fists.

13

Dad made a sound that wasn't quite a groan, and the golf ball in his throat moved down further.

"Oh," I said when I was able to speak. There didn't seem much else to say. At least not just at this minute while my world fell apart around me, came together again, then quietly turned upside down.

It was true what I'd heard. Dad wasn't my father.

"Tell her all of it, Edith. Nothing's ever quite so bad once it's in the open." Dad sounded desperately tired.

"Very well." Mother folded her hands on the pillow. "Jane, you've heard of Marlowe and Jermaine, the shipping people?" She threw Dad a look that spoke volumes. I guessed that in spite of her embarrassment and her genuine concern for my feelings, she was, in her own way, paying him back for the fish shop, for not being one of 'the shipping people'—and for having known all along that I wasn't his.

I didn't care. My chest hurt, I felt sick, and hammers were pounding in my head. But gradually, the truth was sinking in.

My mother, my coolly unflappable, faintly superior mother, was sitting there telling me, as though I ought to be pleased, that I was connected to Marlowe and Jermaine, the shipping people—and that the kind and gentle man who had brought me up was not my father.

But he was my father. He was, he was!

"Dad," I cried. "Oh, please, Dad, it's okay. Really it is. John Marlowe, whoever he is, isn't my dad. You are."

I knew he loved me. It was written in all the sagging lines of his face.

"Thank you, Janey, thank you. I..." He took a half-step towards me, then changed his mind and turned to face my mother. "You'd better finish it. Tell her the rest." He seemed defeated, and although his face was partly in shadow, I thought I saw the glassy sheen of moisture on his cheek.

Mother nodded. "Yes. Yes, all right." She patted the bed. "Do you want to sit down, Jane?"

I shook my head. No, I didn't want to sit down. I wanted to run away and hide in a cupboard and not come out until the nightmare was over. But it wasn't going to be over, and I knew I wouldn't run because deep down, along with the shock, outrage and feelings of betrayal and hurt, lurked a horrible fascination with the drama of which I had reluctantly become a part.

I wasn't, after all, plain Janey Blackman of 48 Willbury Road. I was a changeling, a family secret, a love child. I looked at Mother, her face all blotchy and long. Okay, maybe I wasn't a love child—more like a foolish girl's mistake. I'd read about lots of those in the historical novels I so loved, as well as in the magazines prohibited by Miss Barclay that someone was always smuggling into school. It was strange though, almost incomprehensible, to think of Mother being foolish.

I shifted my shoulders against the doorframe and tried to look nonchalant and worldly. It seemed important not to be shocked.

"I didn't know your father," Mother began. "I mean..." She stopped, apparently at a loss.

"She means me," Dad said. "She didn't know I knew about John Marlowe."

"Why didn't you tell me, Frank?" Mother's attention was once again on Dad. It was as if she'd forgotten I was there.

"You didn't want me to know." His voice came out of the shadows. "And I wanted to make it easy for you to accept me. I loved you, you see."

I felt like crying. How like Dad to take responsibility for another man's child yet let the woman he loved hang onto the pride to which she had so little right.

Mother stared at the window, her eyes following the path of a passing swallow with its wings tipped silver by the sun. "Yes," she said. "Yes, I know you did, but I thought—"

"You thought I was a patsy, didn't you?" He sighed. "Maybe I was."

"No," said Mother. "No, I—" She held up her hand as if to stave off an invisible blow.

"Why didn't you marry my-my other father?" I interrupted, saving her the trouble of finding words. I didn't try to soften the way I said it. I'd never really thought about it before, but I wasn't sure I liked my mother much.

"John couldn't marry me. He was engaged to Marian Dalby. He married her before you were born, and I never told him you were his."

"But if he was engaged, what was he doing sl—what was he doing with you?" I asked her, even though it was pretty obvious what he'd been doing. I knew I didn't like my real father much.

She didn't answer, and after a while Dad said gruffly, "Marlowe's fiancèe was in France that summer. Nineteen thirty-five, it was. He happened to go into the office where your mother worked, and that was it. She didn't know he was engaged at the time."

"You didn't live in Willbury then, did you?"

"No, in Richmond. We both grew up there."

Thank goodness for that. I couldn't have born it if half the older people in Willbury already knew I wasn't Dad's.

"I don't understand," I said, glaring at the dull beige carpet. "What about you, Dad? Where do you come in?"

How little I knew about my parents when they'd been young. I was aware that Dad hadn't fought in the war because of his flat feet, but whenever I tried to probe further, they changed the subject.

"I'd known your mother for some time," Dad said heavily. "We both belonged to the Young Conservatives, but she wasn't much interested in me. I was only a dull insurance clerk. Not much to look at either, was I, Edith?" He poked his face into the light and gave her a smile that nearly broke my heart. "Your mother was very pretty, Janey." He cleared his throat. "She still is."

"No," said Mother. "I used to be. Frank, I did like you. It wasn't my fault I couldn't—"

"Of course, it wasn't," Dad agreed. "I never thought it was. Besides, it was common knowledge that John Marlowe always got all the pretty girls. You weren't his only victim by a long shot." He lifted a corner of the curtain, let it drop back against the wall and turned to me. "You mustn't blame your mother, Janey. I never did and—well, when I saw she was in a bit of a fix, I thought there might be a chance for me after all. And there was. Marlowe got married and moved away, and—"

"Mother didn't need to have me," I interrupted, grinding my toe into the carpet. "I know people did—that—even in those days."

"Oh, Jane. Of course, I had to have you! How could you think...?" Mother broke off and put her hands over her face.

"Your mother was respectable," Dad said, frowning at me, not recognizing the irony. "She wasn't one of those girls in tight skirts and cheap makeup who were always getting into trouble. Naturally, when she made a mistake, she wanted to do the right thing."

That, I guessed, was as close as he would come to telling me not to take my hurt out on my mother.

"Didn't you mind about me, Dad?" I couldn't believe all this. Mother in tight skirts and flashy makeup? Even the idea was ridiculous. Surely at any moment I would wake up and burst out laughing at the improbability of it all. I wanted to laugh. It seemed so much better than crying.

"No, Janey, I didn't mind a bit," Dad said softly. "You've always been my little girl."

The tears I'd been fighting back stopped pricking at my eyelids and started to trickle down my face. I couldn't stand here any longer pretending to be sophisticated when I wasn't. My dear father, my sweet, kind Dad, who had been so happy about his fish shop, was hurting—because of Mother. I could hear it in his voice. It was all her fault. He'd been good to her, worked hard for her, and just because he'd bought a fish shop she thought was beneath her, she'd taken all his pleasure away. I wasn't John Marlowe's daughter. I belonged to Frank Blackman, who had lovingly and gently brought me up. It wasn't exciting anymore. I wasn't important and different.

I was Janey Blackman.

"Dad," I cried, hurling myself across the room to throw my arms around his neck. "Dad, please don't be sad. I'm glad you're my father, and you've been lovely to me, and I know your new shop will be a huge success and everyone will come to buy your fish, and, and—oh, Dad!" I buried my face in his shoulder and allowed the dam holding back my tears to burst into flood and soak his shirt.

Dad patted my back and murmured, "It's all right, Janey, it's all right. I'm sorry—all my fault...."

"No. No, it's not," Mother's voice interrupted from behind us. She sounded all creaky and funny. "Frank, I should have seen that fish shop coming the day Hilda left you the money." The bed gave a squeak as she stood up. "And now I suppose we'll have to make the best of it. I'll just go and make us a cup of tea."

I lifted my head. Dad, oblivious to the damp stain on his clean white shirt, was staring after Mother with a look I couldn't quite believe was admiration.

"That's my Edith," he said. "Can't keep that one down for long."

My mouth fell open. Only seconds ago I'd been sure their marriage was over. But Mother had gone to make tea. And Dad—Dad was smiling.

I let out a moan and pulled away from him to search for a hankie. When I couldn't find one, I muttered something about needing to wash my hands and dashed across the landing to my bedroom—my familiar blue and white, cluttered bedroom with its overflowing drawers, shiny white washbasin and books piled on every flat surface.

I leaned over the washbasin and retched, but nothing came up. Eventually, I dragged myself over to the bed to gaze blearily at the periwinkle blue of the quilt.

I was the daughter of a man called John Marlowe who was 'one of the shipping people,' and who always got all the pretty girls. That was all I knew about my-my father.

It was enough. I didn't want to know any more.

Bending down, I scooped a worn, one-eyed teddy bear from my pillow and held him tightly against my chest. I knew he sympathized. His tattered plush body was all loving consolation and comfort and his fur smelled of dust and the past.

Darling Teddy. He had been my friend and confidante for so long. Yet teddies were supposed to be for children and I had just been catapulted into the disturbing, ugly, frightening, slightly ludicrous world of adults.

I didn't like it. I didn't like it a bit. But the girl I had been that morning was the old Janey Blackman. I wasn't yet familiar with the new one, but I was fairly sure she didn't play with toys.

Sadly, I laid Teddy on the bed. His one eye looked up at me reproachfully.

After a while I sank down beside him and cried my eyes out.

Early the next morning, I left home.

I hadn't exactly meant to. My plan had been to live with my parents after I left school and make pots of money doing something glamorous that would make Posy turn green. Then, once I could afford it, I expected to move to a fabulous flat of my own.

But home wasn't home anymore, and my parents weren't the parents I'd always known.

When I woke, baggy-eyed and exhausted after a fitful, unsatisfactory sleep, I realized I wasn't going to forgive Mother for John Marlowe. Not yet. It was too soon, the secret too raw. To add to my sense of grievance, when I went down to breakfast, Mother wouldn't look me in the eye. She was unusually attentive to Dad though, and the way she fussed over his eggs and fried tomatoes and plied him with extra milk for his tea, made me uncomfortable and horribly embarrassed.

Dad responded to her fussing as if he were a puppy being stroked, and when they started eyeing each other like couples did in films just before the kissing broke out, I couldn't stand it and scurried back upstairs.

My satchel was lying on the floor beside the bed. I picked it up and went to find the suitcase Dad had bought me years ago for our annual holiday in Cornwall. In less than half an hour I was packed.

My parents' voices, engaged in bewilderingly amicable conversation, reached me as I hesitated in the hallway, and for a moment I was tempted to sneak away without a word. Then Dad said something about 'Janey,' and my conscience wouldn't let me.

Mother and Dad were still sitting at the kitchen table surrounded by jam pots and toast crumbs. Dad was holding Mother's hand. As soon as he saw the suitcase, he started to protest, but I cut him off with a hug. Then I gave Mother a dry peck on the cheek and hurried out.

It must have taken a few seconds for it to register on them that I'd gone, but I hadn't reached the gate before Dad came running after me. He wasn't used to running and he was panting.

"Janey," he gasped. "Janey, where are you going?"

"London," I said. *Where else did girls go to make their fortunes?*

"But you can't. You haven't any money, you're too young..." He put a detaining hand on my arm. It was shaking a little. Behind him, Mother hovered in the doorway looking pale.

"I have the money Aunt Hilda left me. And I've been saving some of my allowance."

"That's nothing. Janey, you can't leave. Your mum and I want you here—"

Yes, they probably did, both of them—though Mother wouldn't say it. Now that I knew about John Marlowe she didn't seem to know how to talk to me.

"I'm sorry, Dad," I said, meaning it. "Don't worry. I'll come back to visit." I would too, when I felt ready to face them again.

"You've no job." His voice had never been deep, but now it was even higher, cracked.

"I'll find one. Dad, please...."

He must have seen something in my face then that told him I didn't mean to change my mind. I almost wanted to when I saw the bewilderment in his eyes. But I couldn't stay. This house I had always taken for granted no longer felt like my home, and if I didn't make the move now, I soon would. Better to get it over with at once.

"I have to go," I said doggedly.

His shoulders slumped, and I knew he wouldn't fight me anymore. "All right, Janey." In the bright light of the morning sun every wrinkle showed and he looked old. "You'll call us, won't you? Let us know where you are? Do you have a place to stay?"

"Yes," I lied quickly. "Allison's aunt has a friend who runs a rooming house." She did, but I had no idea where the rooming house was.

"That's good, that's good." Dad patted my arm. "You will call?"

I nodded.

"Here." He put his hand in his pocket and pulled out a wad of notes. "Take these. And if you need more, you let us know."

I nodded again. "Thanks, Dad." Turning to look back at my mother, I saw she hadn't moved from the steps. But she raised her hand when I picked up the suitcase. "Bye, Mum," I called.

She winced.

I knew they were watching me as I walked down the street and that they would go on watching until I turned the corner.

CHAPTER TWO

The outside of Number Fifteen Wrenbert Terrace, Mill Hill, didn't look much different from the house I'd left that morning, except that it was taller and the brick a little greyer. "Clean rooms, use of kitchen, low rents. Call Mrs. Carmody," advertised the paper I'd picked up at Victoria. What more could I ask?

I rang the bell and waited, and after some shuffling and throat clearing, the door was opened by a faded little woman in black whose white hair tumbling around her shoulders made her look like a fairytale witch. She waved a smouldering cigarette under my nose and said, "You've come about the room."

I said I had and was she Mrs. Carmody?

She nodded and ran an unexpectedly brisk eye over my plain blue dress and unpretentious luggage. I knew I'd passed inspection when she jerked her head at the narrow flight of stairs directly behind her and said, "Come on up then."

I followed her up to the first landing. "Bathroom," she said, waving a trail of smoke at an open door through which I caught a glimpse of a cracked mirror and damp towels hanging on pegs. "Hot water."

Well, I should hope so. This wasn't the eighteenth century. If the landlady regarded hot water as a selling point, what would the "clean room" be like?

After following a puffing Mrs. Carmody up three more flights of stairs, I found out.

The top story must originally have been the servants' attic, and it didn't look as though much had been done to improve its status since. An uncarpeted wooden floor slanted towards the ill-fitting door that Mrs. Carmody flung open to the accompaniment of a chorus of protesting creaks from tired hinges. "Here we are then," she announced. "Couldn't do better now, could you?"

Well, yes. One could. I took in the cramped little room with its low, sloped ceiling and only just succeeded in stifling a groan. A single brass bed was pressed against the wall next to a small chest of drawers. The remaining furnishings were a scratched table supporting a bilious yellow glass ashtray and a straight-backed chair that bore a disturbing resemblance to a medieval torture rack. A worn piece of brown carpet beside the bed looked as though it housed a tribe of gluttonous moths. Other then that, the floor was bare and even more scratched than the table.

"Suit you?" asked Mrs. Carmody.

It didn't, but I was tired; it was getting late and I'd already looked at six other rooms. In spite of the strong possibility of moths, this was the best I'd seen yet.

"Where would I hang my clothes?" I asked glumly.

Mrs. Carmody waved her cigarette at three pegs on the back of the door. "Low rent," she said, as though that excused the lack of a wardrobe—as indeed it would have to. The room was dingy and depressing, but it had the advantage of being close to the Underground. Besides, it was all I could afford.

"Yes," I said. "I think it will suit me. That is...the advertisement mentioned a kitchen?"

"Downstairs. First floor. You'll share it with the rest of 'em, of course. Pots and pans provided." She beamed me a proud smile that revealed three blackened teeth.

"Oh. Yes. Thank you. Um—how many other tenants are there?" I had visions of waiting in line to boil an egg, which was about the extent of my cooking skills. Mother didn't like anyone messing about in her kitchen, and she had been impatient with my half-hearted attempts to help her bake biscuits or buns. Anyway, I'd always preferred reading to anything domestic and was quite happy to exchange biscuits and buns for my books.

"Well," said Mrs. Carmody, clamping her cigarette between her lips and counting deliberately on her fingers. "There's Miss Lavender and Mrs. Garcia on the second floor, but they don't cook, and Mr. & Mrs. Ash below you—and Mr. Bozelli. And you are Miss...?

"I'm Jane. Janey Blackman."

"Miss Blackman," said Mrs. Carmody firmly, and I understood there would be no unseemly informality in her house.

"Yes," I agreed weakly. "That's right."

"Well then?" She raised her eyebrows expectantly.

I scrabbled in my bag and pulled out the correct number of notes. "Thank you. I'll take it," I said.

Mrs. Carmody's right hand shot out to snatch the notes before I changed my mind. With her left hand she butted her cigarette in the ashtray.

"I'll leave you to settle in," she said. "You can fetch the door keys when you come down. My flat's in the basement. No visitors after eleven, no parties and no immoral behaviour." She eyed me sternly. "You have red hair."

"Yes, I..." I stopped myself before I could start apologizing for my curly red locks. "Yes, I have."

"Hm." Mrs. Carmody nodded, and I thought she was about to tell me I wouldn't do after all. But she didn't, and as soon as she had shuffled off downstairs, I shut the door and took possession of my drab little room.

The first thing I did was pull back the thin white curtains. It didn't help. A cloud obscured the sun and in its leftover light the view was unrelentingly cheerless. Grey backs of houses like this one, dustbins and a couple of skinny cats. So different from the neat rows of vegetables at home....

Home. Lord, what on earth had I done? My throat began to tighten and I sank onto the hard edge of the bed and fixed my eyes on the moth-eaten carpet. I was used to being alone, but this was worse than alone. This was lonely. And frightening. It was also all my devious mother's fault. She was the one responsible for my plight. But, oh, I did miss my dad. It didn't matter that he wasn't really my dad.

The cloud across the sun drifted away and was instantly replaced by another. Then two of the cats began to fight and when somebody swore at them, I put my hands over my ears. If only I could sit here shutting the world out forever.

For a while the thought of permanent oblivion seduced me, but eventually self-pity became boring, so I got up and arranged the few clothes I'd brought with me in the drawers. Three historical novels by Margaret Irwin placed squarely in the centre of the table completed the business of unpacking. Now all I had to do was fetch my keys.

With a certain reluctance, I abandoned my grotty penthouse and made my way down four flights of stairs to the basement.

"Remember now, no parties." Mrs. Carmody stood in her doorway dangling my keys off the end of her little finger.

"No, of course not." I grabbed the keys in case she decided to change her mind, and forestalled further strictures by adding, "There wouldn't be room, would there? And no visitors after eleven."

Mrs. Carmody shut the door in my face.

I shrugged and, without much optimism, went up to investigate the kitchen.

As I had more or less expected, it came equipped with chairs and a bargain basement table covered in oilcloth, a cupboard which had once been pea-green but was now more peel than paint, an ancient gas cooker and a sink with half the enamel chipped off. As I definitely hadn't expected, it also contained a young man with an athletic physique nicely set off by curling black hair and matching black shirt and trousers. He was standing in front of a dilapidated draining board doing brisk things with an eggbeater.

I started to back out. Other than in my dreams, I hadn't had much to do with young men, and I couldn't think of anything to say. But he heard my feet sliding on the lino and turned around.

"Hello there. Be out of your way in a minute. You Mrs. C's new victim?" His eyes were very dark, and they were looking me over in a way that made me feel self-conscious and awkwardly flattered at the same time. I wasn't used to being looked over.

He grinned—a wide, white grin in a smooth, olive-skinned face. He was very handsome.

"You're blushing. I didn't think girls did that these days." He grinned some more. "Don't worry, I won't jump you. What's your name?"

"Janey Blackman." I put a hand up to my face to cool the blush and encountered a spot on my chin.

"Carlo Bozelli. Pleased to meet you, Janey. Want to use the cooker?"

"No, I don't have any food to cook yet. I was just looking. At the kitchen," I added hastily, when I saw his lips begin to slant up.

He laughed. "Too bad. Want some eggs?"

"No. Thank you. It's all right. I mean I'll buy my own. Where's the nearest grocer's?"

"Nanji's. Out the front, turn left and it's on the corner. He's open quite late. But you can borrow some of mine if you like."

"Oh, no I—"

"I'm harmless, I promise," he jeered softly.

He thought I was scared of him. I was. Not physically, but I just didn't know how to talk to boys, and there was something very confident and sophisticated about this dark stranger with the knowing black eyes. He looked at least twenty-five. But he was being helpful, and I was alone in a city that, in spite of the fact that I'd visited it often, had become frighteningly unfamiliar overnight.

"I know you're harmless," I said quickly. "If you're sure it won't be any trouble...?"

"I'm sure." He gave me the white smile again, and this time, shyly, I smiled back.

Carlo slid an omelette onto a plate and told me I could eat it. I started to argue, but he was already preparing another one for himself.

"You're a good cook," I told him, swallowing a savory mouthful as I listened to butter sizzle in the pan.

"I should be. It's what I do for a living. Tonight's my night off."

"Oh. Where do you work?"

"Coffee bar near Leicester Square. What about you?"

I watched him being competent with a spatula. He had a lovely, slim back. "I don't work. I mean I'm looking for a job," I explained.

"What kind of job?"

"I don't know. Anything."

"What are you good at?" He plunked his plate on the table, sat down across from me and started to eat with the enthusiastic air of a man for whom food is one of life's lustier pleasures.

I told him I wasn't good at anything special.

"You'd better get a job with the government then," he suggested through a mouthful of egg. When I frowned, he added. "That was a joke."

"Yes, I know." I hadn't known, not being in any mood for jokes this evening. Besides, the Conservatives ran the government and my parents said they were all right.

Carlo put down his knife and fork and rested his forearms on the table. To my astonishment, he was wearing a gold watch. "You must be good at something," he said.

"Only if you count reading."

"Aha!" He snapped his fingers. "That's it! There's a book shop off Charing Cross Road..."

"There are lots of them." I had to show him I knew that much.

He cocked an eyebrow, unimpressed. "Yes, but this one has a "Help Wanted" sign in the window. It's been there for days. The shop's called Inspirational Books."

"Maybe no one feels inspired," I said, trying to sound clever.

He grinned obligingly and said he'd take me over there in the morning.

"Oh, there's no need. I'll find it."

"Don't be so independent." Carlo suddenly turned masterful. "I said I'd take you. Now let's get the kitchen cleared up before the Ashes come down."

"The Ashes?" *What kind of place had I got myself into?*

"The couple upstairs. They fight a lot while they're making supper, then they go upstairs and tear each other's clothes off." He flashed his eyes at me, and I wondered if that was another joke or if he wanted to see if I'd be shocked.

I was. I blushed. "What about the other people who live here?" I asked hastily, lowering my head and pretending to concentrate on the remains of my omelette. "Mrs. Carmody said they don't cook."

"Lavender and Garcia? Oh, they tear each other's clothes off too, but they're quiet about it."

I had my skin under control now. "I meant is it true they don't cook?"

Carlo shrugged. "Most of the time. I think Garcia has a husband somewhere."

What on earth was he talking about? I laughed, so he wouldn't think I was embarrassed. "How amusing." Sophisticated people often seemed to say that in books.

Carlo didn't respond, so I got up and began to run water into the sink. That way he couldn't see my face.

I washed the dishes while Carlo dried, and it would all have been very comfortable and domestic if the kitchen had been bigger and he hadn't stood so close to me that every now and then his fingers brushed up against my breast.

The moment the dishes were done, I told Carlo I was going up to my room to settle in. What I really planned to do was fetch groceries, but I wanted to go by myself so he wouldn't see me stocking up on peanut butter, crackers, chocolate biscuits and tins of fruit I wouldn't need to cook.

Carlo followed me out of the kitchen, but the moment we reached the landing Mrs. Carmody popped up from behind a wilted aspidistra. I guessed its purpose was more to provide adequate cover for lurking than to please the eyes of her tenants.

"Evening, Mrs. C," said Carlo. "You're looking very well today."

"Hm." Mrs. Carmody wasn't disarmed.

I smiled at her nervously, and as we headed up the stairs, she called after us, "Remember now, no parties, no immoral behaviour."

Carlo promptly put his hand on my bottom. I wriggled away, half-wishing I didn't have to. "Don't," I whispered. "You'll get me thrown out."

"No, I won't. Mrs. C loves a bit of immorality. Minding her tenants' business is what keeps her going."

His hand was back on my bottom. It felt nice, but when I glanced up at him and saw the way he was looking at me, I was anxious to get away.

"Goodnight," I said when we reached the second landing. "And thank you for all your help."

Carlo tipped his head to one side, crinkled his eyes at me and said he'd see me in the morning first thing.

My room looked even bleaker now that the sun was definitely down. The overhead light shone directly onto the faded brown blanket on the bed and I could no longer avoid focusing on its tatty, frayed binding and bleach stains. I glanced at the strip of carpet. At least the moths hadn't yet come out to party. Perhaps they had moved on to more luxurious quarters. Or perhaps they didn't care for the strong smell of tobacco in the room. I didn't either. It meant Mrs. Carmody had been poking through my things.

Although it wasn't cold, I found myself shivering.

Was I crazy to think I'd be able to manage on my own? Shouldn't I give up now, go back to Willbury and tell my parents I was sorry? That I didn't want to leave them after all? Maybe Dad could use an assistant in the fish shop....

Oh, but I wasn't sorry, not really. Mother was the one who should be sorry. She, with all her pious talk of tolerance and compassion, had for years attempted to deceive my self-effacing father—the father who had never been in shipping. Because of her, home would never be the same. Besides, I wasn't Janey Blackman anymore. I was—I was...who was I? Janey Marlowe? No, never that.

I pulled off my blue summer dress and flung it over the torture-rack chair. I was plain Janey. Janey-whoever-she-wanted-to-be. Janey, who had just been intimately touched by a man. Not just any man either. Carlo Bozelli was every woman's fantasy come true. I hugged myself, swaying my hips in voluptuous remembrance.

By the time I turned off the light and climbed beneath the bleach-stained blanket, I was telling myself the day had been an adventure. A real-life adventure. And I absolutely wasn't going to cry just because for the first time in my life I was alone.

I turned on my side and forced myself to think of black so I'd fall asleep. But the spot on my face began to itch and when the thumping noises started below, I jumped as though the crack of doom had sounded under my bed.

What was happening? Was the house on fire? I sat up—and just as my feet hit the floor someone gave a weird, gurgling shriek. The shriek was followed by a man's voice growling a word whose meaning was clear to me even though I'd never heard it before. I closed my gaping mouth as it dawned on me that what I was probably hearing was the Ashes tearing each other's clothes off.

I had a sudden vision of Posy-Bantley Brown's rosebud mouth curved in an 'oh' of shocked disapproval. Not that she wouldn't be listening just as hard as I was to every frenzied shriek and gurgle coming from below. Posy was fascinated by sex. But I was the one who, in only two days, had seen three times as much of life as she had.

Posy wouldn't like that if she knew.

I lay down again, already feeling a bit less lonely and depressed.

~*~

"Janey? Are you ready?"

Ready? I wasn't even awake. I struggled through jumbled layers of receding dreams and made myself open my eyes. Where was I? There was an unshaded lightbulb above my head....

"Janey! Come on, love, it's almost ten o'clock. I told you to be down by half-past nine."

Carlo. Mrs. Carmody's. This was the first full day of my new life. Reluctantly, I pushed back the blanket and sat up. "I won't be long," I said. Then belatedly, "Thank you."

"Open the door."

"I'm not dressed."

"Even better. Come on, Janey. You do want that job, don't you?"

What job? I rubbed my eyes, trying to remember. Oh. Yes, of course. The book shop near Charing Cross Road. Carlo had insisted he would take me.

"All right," I called. "I'll meet you in the kitchen in ten minutes." I couldn't let him in. It wasn't modesty or my mother's warnings that stopped me either, but the fact that the straps of my blue cotton nightgown were held together with big, ugly pins. Mother had given up doing my mending when I was fifteen and I rarely got around to doing it myself.

Carlo laughed. "I told you last night I wouldn't jump you," he coaxed."

"I know. I'd still rather meet you in the kitchen."

He gave up, probably pulling a face at my prudery. "Okay. Suit yourself."

I suited myself, and fifteen minutes later, after a quick wash in the sour-smelling bathroom, I hurried into the kitchen munching crackers.

Carlo closed the magazine he was reading—I caught a glimpse of bare flesh on the cover—and stuffed it into the pocket of his black leather jacket. He frowned when he saw me.

"You look like the warden of a girls' reformatory in that suit," he mocked. "And why scrape all that wonderful flaming hair into a bun?"

"Miss Barclay said I should put it up for interviews," I said firmly, not wanting him to guess how pleased I was that he liked my hair.

Carlo stood up. "Not if I was the one doing the interviewing. Miss Barclay must be some frustrated old bag."

I giggled. "She probably is. But I think she's right about my hair."

He shrugged. "Your funeral. Okay, let's go." He took my arm possessively, and I gave a little shiver of pleasure.

On the way to the station, Carlo looped his arm around my waist. No one had ever done that before, and I tried hard to look as though I thought nothing of it. Maybe passersby would think this good-looking man was my boyfriend.

It didn't occur to me that passersby might not care.

The Underground was crowded, and we had to stand so close together that my face was jammed up against Carlo's chest. He smelled faintly of sweat camouflaged by cologne. It wasn't unpleasant, but the man next to him smelled of bacon and garlic, and by the time we arrived at Leicester Square I was glad to escape into the hot, muggy air of a London morning.

Inspirational Books was at the end of a row of shops in a narrow street just behind Charing Cross Road. Carlo left me at the door with a wink and a thumbs-up sign. I waited until he had disappeared around the corner, then tugged at the hem of my suit jacket, patted my hair and stepped through the open door onto a pockmarked floor that looked as though termites had been at it.

Two walls of the dark, rectangular room were taken up by floor-to-ceiling bookshelves. Another half dozen or so lower shelves formed narrow aisles in the centre of the floor, and a high, varnished counter that might have come from Dickens' Old Curiosity Shop took up the far end of the room.

Behind the counter, a big man with a beard was eating fruitcake.

He eyed me over the top of tortoiseshell glasses and went on chewing. The smell of old books wafted to meet me as I stumbled over a chipped oak footstool and made my way towards him. It seemed an awfully long walk from the door.

"I've come about the job," I mumbled when the man didn't speak.

"Ah." He swallowed the rest of his mouthful and coughed. "Monday to Saturday noon. Duties to include selling, stacking, sorting, inventory, and letters. Can you write letters?"

"Yes. But I'm afraid I don't type very fast." There wasn't much point in pretending I could do what I couldn't.

He shrugged. "How's your handwriting?"

"It's quite good, I think. Shall I show you?"

He waved at a lined yellow pad beside the cash register. "Go ahead."

I pulled a pen out of my handbag and wrote my name.

The man shoved another mouthful of cake between his lips, ate it, then said, "Not bad, Jane Blackman. Now write, "Unfortunately we have not yet received your invoice."

I wrote it and he actually smiled. "Excellent." He groped in a drawer beneath the counter and handed me a rumpled letter. "Now write me an answer to this."

I studied the single sheet of cream bond stationery. It was printed with a terse message from a book wholesaler demanding payment on an overdue account. I wanted to ask the odd man behind the counter how he normally handled this type of problem, but he was chewing doggedly and looking at me with a tricky sort of stare. Given the hint he had already dropped, it seemed probable that Inspirational Books wasn't inspired to pay this bill. I decided to handle the letter the way we'd been taught in school—politely.

On a fresh sheet of paper, I wrote that since the wholesaler's invoice had undoubtedly been lost in the mail, perhaps they would be good enough to send us another. When we received it, we would, of course, expedite payment in full. With a flourish, I added that it was a pleasure doing business with their firm.

The man behind the counter scanned my effort quickly and nodded. "Splendid." He held out his hand. "I'm Ivan Reid. You're hired. When can you start?"

"I—um—right away," I said dazedly. "But..." I couldn't afford to give him time to change his mind, but I needed to know if he intended to pay me.

He waved his cake at me. "Ah. Money. Standard rate. All right?"

"Yes," I said doubtfully. "Um—what is the standard rate?"

He named a figure, not over-generous, but acceptable.

"That will be fine," I agreed.

"Good. You can begin by transferring that letter to my letterhead. There's a typewriter in my office, but you can write it by hand if you like."

"That's all right. I can manage a typewriter if you don't mind my taking it slowly."

"No hurry. The slower the better." He opened a drawer, took out a crumpled square of wax paper, and started to unwrap a fresh piece of cake. I blinked at him and he waved impatiently at a heavy mahogany door behind the counter.

Taking his wave to mean my job training was over, I scuttled into the small office to type his letter.

It was the first of many I wrote for Mr. Reid with the sole purpose of putting off paying his bills.

~*~

The kettle was just coming to the boil when Carlo found me in the kitchen of Number Fifteen at the end of my first day on the job.

"Well?" he asked. "How did it go?"

"I got the job." I tried to sound nonchalant, as if there had never been any doubt about the matter, but in the end I couldn't quite suppress a grin. "The work doesn't seem hard. Mostly not paying bills."

Carlo grinned back, and it was such a pleased, attractive grin that I hastened to add, "Thank you. If it hadn't been for you, I'd still be looking for work."

"I know. So how are you going to repay me?" He perched on the edge of the table and swung a leg.

I blinked. "I-I don't know. I mean, I haven't had a paycheck yet—"

"And when you do, it won't be much," he guessed accurately. "I was talking about a different kind of payment."

I took a quick step backwards, unnerved by the X-rated gleam in his eye. Carlo was a fascinating man, but he was also a disturbing one, and at this moment, he was disturbing my pulse rate.

"What kind of payment?" I asked warily.

"You mean I have to spell it out?" He crossed his arms, tipped his head to one side and flashed his teeth.

I turned away and began to pour boiling water into the communal teapot. When it overflowed onto the draining board, I stopped.

Carlo laughed.

"I don't think..." I mumbled.

"Good. Don't." He came up behind me and put his hands on my shoulders. I felt his lips on my neck.

"What are you doing?" I gasped. I wasn't sure I liked his lips there much. They felt rubbery.

"Taking my payment." He curved a hand around my breast.

I definitely didn't like that. "Don't," I said, squirming away from him. "Carlo, please...."

He frowned. "What's the matter, Lady Janey? I thought...."

He stopped abruptly and I turned to look over my shoulder.

A tall girl with a lot of frizzy blonde hair and a lot more bare leg than skirt was standing in the doorway with her arm around a thickset young man.

"Hello," said the blonde. "Hope we're not interrupting. I'm Arabella Ash. And this is Duncan."

"I'm Janey," I said, remembering last night and trying not to blush. "You weren't interrupting. I was just going."

"You haven't had your tea," called Carlo as I headed for the door.

I didn't care about tea anymore. I just wanted to escape to the solitude of my room. Carlo awed and intrigued me, and I liked him finding me attractive; but today, that grin of his seemed more predatory than teasing and I wasn't sure I was ready to be preyed on.

That uncertainty lasted only until the following morning when I met Carlo coming up the stairs. He was fully dressed, but there was dark stubble on his chin and he looked as if he'd just got out of bed. To my chagrin, he did no more than nod and brush past me. I gazed after him and tried to swallow the lump of disappointment in my throat.

So that was that. Carlo wasn't interested after all. He must have found me too young and dull to waste time on. Oh, why had I refused to let him kiss me? Why, after all my dreams and passionately innocent longings, had I lost my nerve when the chance came my way? Instead of impressing the handsomest man I'd ever met with my wit and charm and poise, I'd impressed him with my countrified timidity. It wasn't any wonder he'd lost interest.

I clumped on down to the kitchen feeling ugly.

In the weeks that followed I did my best to avoid meeting Carlo. Although he was civil enough when our paths did happen to cross, just the sight of him made me feel foolish, and it was easy enough to use the kitchen when I knew he'd be at work. He made no effort to seek me out again, and whenever I wasn't sure of his schedule, I took to eating apples and crackers in my room.

As sanctuaries went, my cheerless bolt-hole wasn't much, but I found myself spending more and more time there. It was safe. Once the door was locked, the outside world couldn't intrude physically, although it wasn't possible to ignore the Ashes' nightly rumbles.

Work was a different matter. I liked working at Inspirational Books. The customers were a quiet, undemanding lot, interested in obscure religious texts or relentlessly positive books on how to live better by thinking uplifting thoughts.

Mr. Reid wasn't a difficult man to work for as long as I said, "Yes, Mr. Reid," "No, Mr. Reid," "I'm terribly sorry, Mr. Reid," depending on the situation.

My Chantersley education hadn't been wasted after all.

One day, after I'd been working at the shop for almost six weeks, I phoned my parents. I'd thought of them often, especially Dad, and written to let them know I was all right. But all at once the need to hear their voices became overwhelming.

"Hello, Jane," my mother responded with a certain wariness. "We got your letter."

"Good. Everything's still all right. Mother, could you call me back? I'm in a call box and I don't have much change."

"Really, Jane. Can't you get a phone of your own?"

"I will when I can. Mother, please...."

"All right. I'll call you in a minute. Your father just came home for his lunch."

So much for maternal concern. I felt a prick of disappointment. Though I hadn't yet forgiven her for John Marlowe, I think subconsciously I'd expected her to faint with joy at the sound of my voice. Instead, she seemed more interested in Dad's lunch.

I gave her the number and hung up, hoping no one else would come to use the phone.

Luckily, Dad phoned me back almost at once. "Janey! How are you? Is everything all right? You're not short of money?"

I was, but I wouldn't admit it. "No, not at all. And yes, everything's all right. What about you? And Mother? How are the fish?"

"Oh, we're muddling along. The shop is doing quite nicely. No need to worry about us. It's grand to hear from you, Janey." He coughed nervously. "You will come and see us soon, won't you?"

Even Dad sounded hurried. But of course, he had to get back to his shop. "Yes, I will," I assured him and hung up feeling a bit like a bird who's been pushed out of the nest and isn't expected to return. Yet I hadn't been pushed. I had left on my own.

It was very odd. I thought wistfully of the days when my greatest worry had been Posy Bantley-Brown's biting tongue.

When I went back to the bookshop, a fat young woman with a sad face came in to ask if we carried any books that would inspire her to lose weight. I left her browsing in the Self-Help section and went to sort a stack of bills into, 'Must pay immediately,' 'Pay if possible,' and 'Will accept further excuses.'

Five minutes later, Mr. Reid stamped through the door carrying a newspaper and a fresh box of cake. He disappeared into his office without speaking and banged the door shut behind him. The fat young woman left without making a purchase.

I went on sorting bills and when I next looked up it was to see the young man who worked at Perilous Pages next door standing on one foot in the doorway pushing his glasses up his nose. He blinked at me from behind thick lenses and smiled the cajoling smile that always made me think of a basset hound desperate for approval.

"Hello, Colin." I darted a wary glance over my shoulder. The door to Mr. Reid's office was still closed. "Okay, you can come in."

"God out, is he?"

"No, he's in the office. I don't think he wants to be disturbed."

Colin always referred to my place of work as "Heaven" and to Ivan Reid as "God." It had made me uneasy at first, but now I took his irreverence for granted.

Perilous Pages, which specialized in adventure novels and thrillers of the John Buchan persuasion, was owned by a gimlet-eyed woman whom Colin called "Her Nibs." Apt enough titles, I supposed—except that there was nothing godlike about not paying bills, or my wages either, unless God was reminded.

Colin grinned at me. "What's he doing? Reading obscene literature, or indulging in acts of gross indecency with the plant life?"

I choked back a giggle and lifted a finger to my lips. "Shh. He might hear you."

"Sorry." He edged inside and shut the door on the chilling end-of-summer rain that was streaking against what was visible of the window above a precarious tower of inspirational books. "Is he in one of his moods then?"

"Mm. An especially foul one. He was growling and stamping his feet when he came in. I expect his football team lost again yesterday."

Colin shook his head. "You ought to get a job in less hallowed circles, Janey. Heaven doesn't seem to suit you very well."

I smiled. "It suits me fine. And there aren't any jobs in less hallowed circles. Not for people who have no degree and no training in anything useful."

"Oh, I don't know. Listen, I have a job for you—"

"No," I said firmly. "I am not going to play bait and switch with June."

June Gunderson worked in the record shop across the street. She was pretty, giggly, and not a bit attracted to basset hounds except as nice, undemanding pets. But Colin read too many of his shop's unlikely men's adventure yarns and was convinced that all he had to do to gain June's slavering attention was pretend to be passionately desired by someone else. Enter Janey Blackman, hired vamp. He'd been pestering me to go into business as his love-interest for over a week now, but I had steadfastly refused to co-operate.

Colin blinked like a sorrowful owl. "Janey, all I want is for you to pretend to fancy me like crazy. Then we can set things up so that June catches us kissing—"

"No, we can't. It wouldn't work. For one thing, I'm not going to kiss you."

Colin hunched his shoulders and managed to look more like a basset hound than ever. "Janey—"

"No," I said.

I liked Colin. He was the sort of man who couldn't threaten my peace of mind. But I didn't want to kiss him. Nor was I especially flattered to know he didn't really want to kiss me.

I slammed a fresh box of bills onto the counter.

"Ssh," whispered Colin. "You'll disturb God." He stuck out his lower lip and looked more lugubrious than before.

"No, I won't. He likes the sound of me working. He only goes in there to eat cake and sulk."

"Janey..." Colin gave me an ingratiating smile. "Janey, do please be reasonable. I'd do it for you if—"

"I don't want you to do it for me. And anyway, I'm the wrong person to ask."

"No, you're not. Listen, all you have to do is kiss me once—"

"I don't want to kiss you. Once, twice or thrice. Neither does June."

Colin's face crumpled like a discarded football. His Adam's apple wobbled and I felt as if I'd kicked a harmless puppy. Heavens, we were both in the same boat. I was no raving beauty either, and boys didn't exactly fall over themselves to kiss me. Carlo had ignored me for weeks.

"I didn't mean it that way," I said quickly. "It's just that..." I hesitated, hating to betray my inexperience, but knowing it was the only way to make amends. "Just that I've never kissed anyone before. I-I'm not sure I'd be any good at it, and—well, you know. Maybe June feels the same."

I could tell he didn't believe me, but he wanted to. In the end he decided to be magnanimous. "I'll teach you," he said, as if he and

Casanova had a lot in common. He left his post by the door and came towards me.

"No," I croaked. "Colin, don't be daft. What if a customer comes in?"

"You're on your tea break," Colin said promptly. "Like me."

"I don't take kissing tea breaks. Colin, go away."

I didn't want him to kiss me. When it came to the crunch, I hadn't been sure I wanted Carlo to kiss me, and I'd found him amazingly attractive. Besides, the first time was supposed to be memorable, not some hasty groping behind the counter with a man whose lips reminded me of a dog's. And what if a customer did come in? It happened sometimes.

Colin kept advancing round the end of the counter. I backed away until my calves slammed up against an open box of books.

I said, "Ouch," a little too loudly just as Colin's hands closed on my shoulders, and I smelled the cheese sandwich he'd had for lunch.

"Come on, Janey." He smiled encouragingly. "You'll like it."

"No, I won't," I said. "And you won't either. I'm not June."

My voice must have risen on the last sentence, because immediately I heard the creak of an executive chair-back and the sound of feet thudding to the floor. "Help," muttered Colin, as he leaped over the counter like a basset hound attempting to be a wallaby.

He wasn't fast enough. Just before he jumped, the door to Mr. Reid's office was flung open and God himself stood scowling on the threshold.

"What's going on?" he demanded, cake crumbs dancing on his bushy, gray beard. "Young man, this is an inspirational bookshop. I will not have lewdness and promiscuity on my premises. Get out. Miss Blackman, you're sacked."

"I'm terribly sorry, Mr. Reid," I said quickly.

"It wasn't Janey's fault, Sir." Colin squared his shoulders and tried to look heroic. "It was my idea." When Mr. Reid only raised his finger and pointed at the door, he added reluctantly, "Janey didn't want to kiss me."

"I don't care what Miss Blackman wanted. Young man, I told you to get out. Miss Blackman, your cheque will be sent to you in the mail."

I doubted if it would. Inspirational Books stayed in business by not sending cheques in the mail. My intestines began to feel as if someone had tied them in a slipknot. I couldn't afford to lose my job. But when I turned to Colin, hoping for further support, he was already slithering through the door. Damn him. I considered heaving half a dozen Powers of Positive Affirmation at his retreating back, but thought better of it almost at once. Mr. Reid would probably make me pay for every one of them.

Would bursting into tears do any good? One glance at my boss's austere, unrelenting countenance convinced me that wasn't likely. He was a religious man, but not a compassionate one, and I had several times heard him carrying on about the lewd and immoral ways of modern youth.

In the end, I decided to salvage my pride since there didn't seem much else to salvage. "Very well, Mr. Reid. I'll just get my bag then and I'll be off. Oh, and in case you need them, I put all today's bills in the In tray. And there are nine boxes left to be unpacked." I pointed at an untidy pile of cardboard on the floor and, with my chin tilted proudly, stalked towards the drawer where I kept my bag.

Mr. Reid cleared his throat so vigorously that a further shower of crumbs descended from his beard. "Just a minute," he said.

I thought fast, something I wasn't usually good at. Timing was of the essence. Mr. Reid, having demonstrated his high moral principles, was remembering belatedly that I was useful to him. On the other hand, there was a matter of face to be saved.

I put a hand over my eyes, sniffed noisily—Allison would have admired my sense of drama—and clutched my bag to my chest as I began a calculated stumble towards the door.

As I reached it, two things happened.

Mr. Reid, in his most sepulchrally godlike voice, said, "Wait. Miss Blackman, justice should be tempered with mercy. I am willing to give you another chance."

And the door opened to admit Posy Bantley-Brown.

CHAPTER THREE

"Posy?" I said, hearing my voice come out high and fractured. "Wha-what are you doing here?"

Posy's smile was ingenuous. "Lovely to see you again, Janey. Actually, I ran into Allison. She told me you were working in town, so I thought I'd pop in to say hello."

"Why?" I asked bluntly, wishing Allison had told her I was working in a coal mine in Brazil. Assuming there were coal mines in Brazil. I wasn't good at geography.

Posy had the nerve to look mystified. "I thought we might have lunch together sometime. When I find a free moment," she added, in case I made the mistake of thinking she really meant it. She patted her perfectly permed curls. "Didn't Allison tell you? I've taken a part-time job doing make-up demonstrations for Sollaby's. It's a rather smart little shop on Bond Street. You may have heard of it."

Of course, I'd heard of it. Who hadn't?

Behind us, Mr. Reid made menacing throat-clearing noises. "Miss Blackman, if you don't mind, there is work to be done."

I began to feel a little lightheaded—either from the result of not being sacked after all, or from seeing Posy again. "Of course, Mr. Reid," I said blithely. "Um—Miss Bantley-Brown has come in to look at some books."

"Ah." Mr. Reid eyed Posy's well-nourished figure over the top of his glasses and said in a voice heavy with sarcasm, "Are you sure you wouldn't prefer something from Perilous Pages next door, Miss Bantley-Brown?"

Posy blinked her false eyelashes at him.

"Would you, Posy?" I asked.

Posy, out of her depth, shook her head.

The opportunity was too good to pass up. "Perhaps a Life of St. Augustine then?" I suggested, feeling as if we'd never left Chantersley and I was finally getting the chance to get my own back for twelve years of sniping and spite.

Her mouth fell open and she began to move backward towards the door. "Thank you," she said, "but—"

"We have several studies of the Reformation too, if you're interested. Or the sermons of Father—"

"No. No, thank you. I'll—er—call again when you're not so busy, Janey." She looked at me as if she suspected me of having either sprouted wings or grown a tail, and backed out onto the wet pavement. It was still raining and a gust of wind blew through the door. I watched her struggle with her umbrella and would have felt guilty if it had been anyone but Posy.

"I said you could keep your job, Miss Blackman," Mr. Reid said sourly. "Not indulge in chitchat with your friends. Count yourself lucky, young lady."

"Oh, yes, Mr. Reid. I do. But Posy isn't actually my friend."

"Hm." He gave one of the boxes of books a good kick and stamped back into his office. Only this time, he didn't shut the door.

I carried on with the bills, reflecting that it was too bad Mr. Reid's one grand passion wasn't something civilized like cricket, instead of an aggressive game like football. The outcome of important matches could be accurately gauged by his temper.

About an hour later, as I knelt on the floor unpacking the cartons of books, another rush of wind swept through the door. It was followed by a large, ambling bear of a man who stood gazing round the shop with a disarming air of bewilderment.

I stood up, wiping my hands on my skirt and hoping I didn't have ink on my nose or cobwebs in my hair.

"Can I help you?" I asked.

The man smiled a lazy, pleasant smile that immediately made me feel comfortable. "I was looking for Posy Bantley-Brown. She said she'd be here." He glanced at a watch with a wide leather band. "I suppose I'm a few minutes late."

"She left an hour ago," I said.

"I'm not that late. She must have changed her mind."

I brushed the back of my hand surreptitiously down my nose. It came away clean but I had rubbed a dormant spot that immediately started to itch. "She may have meant to wait," I said. "I think my boss and I scared her away."

He ran his eyes—nice smoky greenish-grey ones—first over me and then over the books on the nearest tightly packed shelf. "You don't look very terrifying. But I expect you did scare her away if you tried to sell her something like this." He picked out a small, leather-bound volume of Christian poetry. "Or this." He waved an abridged Pilgrim's Progress under my nose.

I giggled. He was funny as well as nice to look at. I guessed him to be in his late twenties—a little heavier around the waist than perhaps he should have been, but still in good physical shape. How on earth had he come to be friends with Posy?

"Did she say if she'd be coming back?" he asked, not sounding as though he cared especially.

"No. She didn't say anything."

"Doesn't sound like Posy." He grinned.

"She's a friend of yours?" I still wasn't sure I believed it.

"Yes. You could put it that way. I'm engaged to her."

Engaged! Posy was engaged? I braced myself against the counter. "But she's only been out of school a few weeks," I mumbled with a singular lack of tact.

He shrugged. "I know. It was all decided in rather a hurry."

It must have been. If Posy had been engaged to this attractive man while she was still at Chantersley, she would have made sure the entire school knew about it—in triplicate.

He must have seen my astonishment because he added amiably, "Not that kind of hurry. We've known each other for years in a manner of speaking. We're more or less neighbours."

Oh. Neighbours. Well, that might explain it. And Posy was rich. Her father was President of Bantley-Brown Sporting Wear. None of us at school had been allowed to forget that she stood to inherit a fortune. Besides, why else would anyone marry Posy?

Even as I thought it, I knew I wasn't being altogether fair. Posy was pretty, and she had a soft, cushiony body that was bound to appeal to some men.

"She never said a word to anyone at school," I said.

"No. Well, we didn't really get past the acquaintance stage until a few weeks ago. Once everything was decided, our families wanted us to wait until Her Ladyship was eighteen before we made it official."

He was talking about Posy as if she were an amusing, if slightly spoiled child. But perhaps that was the kind of woman he liked.

"I see." I was irritated for no logical reason. When a chair scraped on the floor of Mr. Reid's office, I added loudly, "Is there something I can help you with, Sir?"

For a moment he looked startled, but as soon as he caught on, he grinned and replied in an extra deep baritone, "Yes. Thank you. This will do very well." He handed me the book of Christian poetry.

Oh, he was nice, much too nice for beastly Posy.

I thanked him and was just ringing up his purchase when the door opened to admit Posy and yet another blast of wind.

"My umbrella blew inside out," she said crossly. "Oh, there you are, David. You're late."

"Only a couple of minutes." He relieved her of the battered umbrella and propped it up against the counter. "You weren't here."

"Oh. Well, I couldn't wait all day." She started to pout, recollected she had an audience, and tucked her hand possessively in David's arm. "Janey, I'd like to introduce you to my fiancè, David Foley. David, this is Janey Blackman. We were at school together. Remember I told you about her? She was the rebel who always wore odd bits of uniform that didn't match. Didn't you, Janey?"

I picked up a large, flat book that was lying on the counter and thought about smashing it on her teased blonde head. But I couldn't make a scene in front of David. Besides, I was no longer a schoolgirl. Posy couldn't hurt me anymore.

"I wasn't a rebel," I said. "Sometimes my parents couldn't afford the regulation uniform, so I had to make do with something less expensive in the same colour."

There. I'd admitted it. For the first time in my life, instead of allowing Posy's barb to hit home, I had deflected it by admitting the truth—which was that my parents had often had to stretch paychecks to make ends meet.

I put the book down and glanced up. David Foley was shaking his head reproachfully at Posy, who widened her baby blue eyes and looked innocent. *One of her better performances*, I thought—and was tempted to laugh outright. Funny, two months ago I'd have been tempted to disembowel her. Now I couldn't even work up a proper hate. It was deflating in a way. So was the disturbing notion that my mother might have been right about Posy all along.

Except that Posy had David. Gypsy Jasmine hadn't yet managed to upstage her in the marital stakes.

I no longer wondered what had prompted Posy to come into the shop. She wanted to show off her catch of the day so she could watch me looking envious. Posy always assumed everyone coveted what she had.

"Come on, Posy," David said tersely. "Your friend has work to do."

"Oh, but..." She tilted her head and tried a little damage control. "Janey, I didn't realize your family had money problems. I'm so sorry. Now what about lunch? Shall we make it tomorrow?"

She hadn't been serious about lunch, but now she meant to go through with it. Even Posy was bright enough to see that her spiteful gibes had failed to amuse the man she was most anxious to impress.

"I don't take lunch hours," I said.

"Oh. What a pity."

"Sunday?" suggested David, putting his hands in his grey flannel pockets and rocking back on his heels.

"Sunday?" Posy repeated. "Oh, I don't think..." She paused. "My parents are expecting us on Sunday, darling."

"I know," David said. "And your father was saying just the other day that you don't seem to bring home many friends. How about it, Janey?"

His smile was charming and persuasive and Posy looked so cross I didn't hesitate. "Thank you, that would be nice."

"Good."

I nodded, suddenly tongue-tied. David was heaven, but Posy was closer to purgatory—and it had just dawned on me that in a fit of more or less senseless malice, I had accepted an invitation to The Beeches, her big, fancy house beside the Thames. And I had no desire whatever to go there.

I watched Posy lower her carefully mascaraed eyelashes and felt a quick rush of hope. All was not lost. The Bantley-Brown would find some way to avoid having Janey Blackman, who wore bits of uniform that didn't match, to lunch with her social climbing parents.

My relief was precipitate. Instead of trying to put me off, she smiled patronizingly and said, "Lovely. Come about twelve-thirty. You do know the way, I suppose?"

"I'll pick her up," David said, before I had a chance to reply.

Posy's mouth fell open. "But—you'll be with your parents, won't you?" she objected.

"No, I've some business to attend to at the gallery. I'll spend Saturday in town and drive down with Janey on Sunday." He smiled at me. "Where do you live?"

I glanced at Posy. Her mouth was slack, exposing a lot of pink gum, and her eyes were so huge I thought she was going to cry. Briefly, I considered telling her I'd remembered a previous engagement. But when David pulled a pen out of his pocket and raised nice, bushy eyebrows at me, I gave him my address instead.

Posy finally shut her mouth. "Well, all right then," she muttered, in a voice that was lower and more natural than usual. She practically dragged David over to the door.

"I'll collect you about quarter to twelve," he called over his shoulder as she bore him off into the rain.

I nodded mutely.

After that, and much to my relief, the rest of the day passed without incident. Enough had happened in the last few hours to keep me going until Christmas.

By the time I got home that evening I was exhausted, on edge and very wet. My umbrella was somewhere on the Underground.

Not since the day I'd found out my father was not my father had I felt so confused and unsettled, and at the same time, keyed-up and excited. It didn't make a whole lot of sense. There was nothing exciting about nearly losing my job, and I certainly didn't want to go to The Beeches.

In the end, confused and unsettled won the day.

A particularly pungent blast of Mrs. Carmody's smoke assaulted my sinuses the moment I stepped into the hallway. It made my eyes smart, and for a moment, I was tempted to turn tail and run until I remembered there was nowhere to run to. Soon, when the hurt had blurred a little more, I would return to visit Willbury and my parents. But I couldn't bring myself to do it just yet. And I couldn't run to Allison either. She was still living with her father and travelling up to London every day to attend the Lily Pardoe School of Dramatic Art.

I stumbled across the dimly lit hallway in a haze of self-pity and smoke and didn't at first take in that someone was coming down the stairs.

"Allo, allo," said Carlo. "What's this all about? You look as though you thought you won the Pools then found out you didn't."

Was it that obvious something had happened? I shook my head without speaking. Having spent weeks regretting what hadn't happened with Carlo and skulking in my room whenever I thought he might be in the house, I couldn't think of a single thing to say.

"Then what's this?" He came down the last step and touched his knuckles to my cheek. "You've gone all red and bright-eyed."

Damn. I was blushing again and I had to stop. This could be my chance to redeem myself—to convince Carlo I wasn't as boring as he thought.

I gave him a smile that I hoped was brave and mysterious, tossed back the hair he had once admired, and said gaily, "Oh, it's nothing. Bit of a fraught day, but nothing serious."

"What you need is a drink." He dropped a bracing arm around my shoulders.

"Maybe," I agreed without enthusiasm. "I don't usually." Dad always offered me sherry at Christmas, but I didn't like it much.

Carlo laughed as another plume of smoke wafted up from the basement. "Time you started then. How about the Happy Toad?"

I knew the Happy Toad. I passed it every day on my way home from work and usually had to navigate my way around the customers overflowing onto the pavement. It could be fun to go there with Carlo. He smelled kind of musky this evening. But what if I made a fool of myself again?

"I can't afford it," I said.

"My treat."

"Oh, no." I shook my head. "Thank you, but I couldn't." He mustn't think I'd been hinting. He had probably only asked me out of charity.

"Come on, Lady Janey. Don't be such a poker." He smiled at me as if I were a little girl who was dutifully refusing to accept sweets from a stranger.

To show him I was a woman of the world, I started to say, "Well, if you're sure I won't be imposing..." then realized how Chantersley that sounded. "Look..." I tried again. "You were on your way out—"

"That's right. For a drink at the pub. I could do with some company. Come on, Janey, don't be a prude."

Was that how he saw me? "I'm not a prude," I said quickly. "All right, I'll come."

"That's my girl." He patted me familiarly on the rear. "Hurry up and get yourself ready."

I nodded and went upstairs to change into my tightest black skirt. When I came down again, Carlo was lounging against a damp stain on the wall with his hands in the pockets of a new black leather jacket which I recognized as being a lot more expensive than the old one. He looked gorgeous. When he grinned and held out his hand, I took it without hesitation. Instant goose bumps prickled up my arm.

The Happy Toad turned out to be a noisy, crowded watering hole with lots of dark polished wood and light, incomprehensible artwork on the walls. Carlo bought me something called a Pink Lady. I liked it. When he ordered another, I didn't argue.

"What happened to upset you?" he asked. "You looked about ready to collapse when you came in. Like a balloon with a slow leak."

"I'm not that fat," I giggled. Carlo was being nice to me again.

"No." He squeezed my shoulder. "You're just right."

We were backed into a corner by the bar, hemmed in by a noisy group celebrating somebody's promotion. But Carlo's breath on my cheek smelled spicy and warm, and his voice was low and sympathetic. I told him I'd nearly lost my job and he nodded understandingly and bought me another drink.

Half an hour later, when I was on my fourth drink, I discovered that Carlo had two heads, both of them nodding understandingly. So I told him about Willbury and that my father wasn't really my father.

He shrugged. "Never knew my old man. Don't think Mum's sure who he was."

Well, that certainly put my parentage in perspective. Poor Carlo. I swallowed and the two pink lines in front of my eyes merged into the neon fixture above the bar. In a moment Carlo's two faces became one again and everything fell back into place.

"How—um—awkward for her," I said.

Carlo laughed as though I'd said something funny instead of inadequate. "You've a different way of saying things, haven't you? Where'd you get your posh accent?"

I closed my eyes and a propellor began spinning inside my head. "From Chantersley Private School for Girls," I said, staggering a little as I stuck my nose in the air and tried to sound like Miss Barclay.

"You'd better sit down," Carlo said.

He found us a place at a table. "You've got lovely eyes," I said, when I was able to bring his face into focus. "All soft and velvety."

"Have I?" He leaned forward and fixed me with an eloquently scorching stare. I was just coming round to the idea that I rather enjoyed being smoldered at when I started to slide off my chair. Carlo stopped smoldering at once and turned wary. "Hey," he exclaimed, "are you all right?"

"Just-just a little sleepy. And I think I forgot to have lunch."

He nodded. "Right. Better get you home. You'll be no good to anyone dead drunk."

"I'm not drunk. I feel very well," I assured him. "That man in the corner though. He's in a drate of advanced stunkenness, don't you think?" The man in the corner had gone all fuzzy and blurred.

"Christ," Carlo muttered. "Come on, up you get."

He sprang to his feet and jerked me out of my chair. I reached for the remains of my drink, but he pushed it away saying, "Oh, no you don't," and spun me briskly through the crowd and out into the street.

I felt better in the open air. The rain had stopped and it was pleasantly fresh. Carlo put his arm around my waist, and I allowed my head to drop onto his shoulder. He had been so kind to me tonight, and he looked so handsome. If he tried to kiss me again I wouldn't run away.

But when we got home, he marched me straight up to the bathroom. *How had he known I needed to be sick?*

Throwing up had a sobering effect. I waited until I was sure I could stand before stumbling out onto the landing.

Carlo was waiting for me beside Mrs. Carmody's strategic aspidistra. "Better?" he asked.

I nodded. "Much. I feel a bit limp, but I'm all right now."

"I'll make us some tea. And you'd better eat a slice of dry bread."

"Oh, I couldn't...."

"Yes, you could. Don't argue."

He made the tea and I ate the bread because I was still too limp to argue. When I'd finished, he insisted on helping me to my room. I felt very tired and it was nice having the support of his manly arm.

As soon as we reached my eyrie beneath the eaves, Carlo flipped on the light, clicked the door shut and sat me down on the bed. "Right," he said. "Better get your clothes off."

"What?"

"Your clothes. Better get them off. You said you were tired."

"I am. But you're here."

"That's all right." He sat down beside me and began to unbutton my blouse. When I tried to stop him, he held my hand away, went on unbuttoning, and kissed me. I hadn't even seen it coming. Thank God I'd rinsed out my mouth and put sugar in my tea.

His lips were damp. I'd always dreamed of being kissed by a tall, dark man and Carlo ought to have been perfect for the part. I waited for the earth to move, but it didn't. If this was kissing, it wasn't much to get excited about.

"Open up," Carlo said against my cheek.

Now that we'd started I had to find out if it got better. I opened my mouth.

His tongue tasted of beer. I didn't like it. Kissing seemed a very wet business. A little later I realized my blouse was lying crumpled on the bed and Carlo was breathing oddly and pulling at the zipper on my skirt.

"Take the rest of your things off," he ordered, shrugging off his jacket.

"No, don't. " I tried to push him away.

"I'm not going to hurt you," he said impatiently. "I only want to look at you. We needn't go any further."

"But—"

"Come on, Janey. You've nothing to be ashamed of. I'll take my clothes off too, and we'll just lie quietly on the bed."

A spring squeaked in the Ash's flat down below, and I heard Arabella's high-pitched giggle. I didn't think I'd enjoy lying naked beside Carlo. I liked him with his clothes on. But it seemed important to him and I did want to please him, wanted so much for him to like me. Surely it couldn't hurt to do as he asked, and I didn't really mind him seeing my body. Mother had never talked much about sex beyond telling me what went where and saying don't. But Carlo had said we needn't go any further, needn't actually do it—and I couldn't get pregnant just by sleeping in the same bed with a man. Maybe he was right. It might actually be fun…friendly and warm and daringly sophisticated. Anyway, I was too exhausted to put up much of a fight.

"As long as you don't—well, do anything," I said, just to be sure he understood.

"You're a virgin?" He sounded surprised.

"Yes," I admitted, feeling foolish.

His shirt joined his jacket on the floor. "All right, we'll just lie next to each other. Okay?"

He spoke soothingly, as if he were talking to a baby. But I wasn't a baby, and I didn't want him to think of me that way. "All right," I said, feeling very bold and still a little dizzy. "But you mustn't do anything else." It wasn't maidenly virtue speaking. It was craven fear.

Carlo had taken off his trousers. I'd never seen a man naked before, and the idea of that pink protuberance inside me was frankly terrifying. I shut my eyes, deciding on the spot I'd never marry.

"Come on then," said Carlo, tugging at my skirt. When I pulled away, he said impatiently, "I told you nothing has to happen."

He was right there. Nothing was going to happen. And if all he wanted was to lie beside me while we drifted off to sleep....

I pulled my clothes off quickly and slipped beneath the frayed, brown blanket. It wasn't cold in my attic despite the lateness of the season, but the covers added a measure of security.

Carlo turned off the light, the bed heaved, and I felt his warm body collide with mine. I drew away, but immediately he put his hand on my breast.

"Don't," I said, going rigid.

"Don't like that? How about this?" He moved his hand in between my legs.

That was better, not altogether unpleasant. Carlo began to nuzzle my neck. His lips still felt wet, like the water I could hear running down the pipes outside the window.

"Are you mad for it?" he whispered a minute later.

I wondered vaguely why I could hear paper being ripped. My eyelids were extraordinarily heavy. "Mad for what?" I asked drowsily.

He used a word I hadn't heard before. "No," I said. "I don't think so."

He began further frantic activity with his hand.

"Carlo," I said, "I told you I don't want—"

I didn't get to finish the sentence. He was kissing me again, his lips gulping and insistent and his body was lying over mine. I tried to push him off and felt a quick, sharp pain between my legs. Carlo grunted and shuddered on top of me.

Moments later, it was over.

He flopped off me and lay on his back.

"You said you wouldn't," I accused, though I wasn't entirely sure he had. Surely that couldn't be what the fuss was all about.

I ran my hands down my thighs and over my stomach. Everything felt the same.

Carlo propped himself up on one elbow, his face long and pale in the moonlight. "But you can't have thought..." He stared down at me in frank disbelief. "You took your clothes off."

"Because you asked me to."

I hugged my arms around my chest. *Had I been dreaming*? It didn't seem possible that I, Janey Blackman, was no longer a virgin. Was that what had happened? Was all the snickering about something as ridiculous and undignified as that?

I had to be sure. "Was that...I mean, did we—am I...?"

Carlo laughed through his nose. "You really are an innocent, aren't you, Lady Janey? Yes, we did. And no, you aren't. Not any longer."

I stared into the shadows. So it was true. I'd said no, and he'd done it anyway. Technically at least, I'd just been raped.

So why wasn't I having hysterics? I was supposed to mind, to feel violated and angry and desperate because something so—so ludicrous and ordinary had happened. I waited anxiously for the proper feelings to hit me, but they didn't.

I felt none of those things. My strongest sensation was a liberating sense of relief—glorious, overwhelming, unbelievable, mind-bending relief.

I'd had sex. I, Janey Blackman, HAD HAD SEX. And it hadn't been terrifying at all. Next time it might even be as exciting as my books hinted it was meant to be. Only the first time was supposed to hurt. Maybe I'd get married after all. Maybe I'd marry Carlo. I liked being close to him, liked being desirable and wanted, and sometimes when he touched me, I liked that too.

I started to laugh.

"Janey," Carlo was instantly suspicious. "You enjoyed it, didn't you?"

His face hung just above mine, his lips puffed out in a pout. He looked like a little boy who had just lost his favourite marble to a friend.

"Yes," I lied. "I enjoyed it."

He smirked, content in his manhood. "You wanted it, didn't you?"

"No, but I'm glad it happened."

"You must have wanted it."

"Perhaps," I agreed.

I hadn't, but it seemed to matter to him. And I was glad I wasn't a virgin. Even Allison hadn't achieved that. I doubted if Posy had either. Her David wasn't like Carlo. If she said no, he'd be too considerate to force himself on her. And Posy was bound to have said no, if only to keep him on a string. I hugged myself tighter. It was wonderful not to be frightened anymore.

Beside me I heard Carlo's gentle snoring.

I stayed awake, thinking about what had happened and wishing there was someone I could tell.

It must have been around two in the morning before I stopped congratulating myself long enough to think about how babies are made.

A sliver of moonlight lay pale on the wall. The dripping of water down the pipes was steady and restful, and somewhere outside a cat howled its mournful message at the night.

Oh, God. What had I done? I laid an arm over my eyes. There was a reason my mother had said don't do it —a reason that had to do with more than just religion and morality. Look what had happened to her. Oh, if only she had explained more than the mechanics. I'd heard that men think differently than women. Maybe Carlo had honestly believed I knew what I was doing once I got over my maidenly modesty. I should have known, of course, instead of being so trusting and naive. Yet I'd believed him when he told me nothing would happen. I'd had too many drinks and been sick, and every ounce of common sense had deserted me—all because I'd wanted to please a handsome man—as Mother must once have wanted to please John Marlowe.

I turned on my side and touched a hand to Carlo's shoulder. He stirred, but he didn't wake up. If I shook him, he'd probably be angry, but I couldn't wait until morning. I shook him again, and he grunted and dug an elbow into my chest.

The luminous hands on my cheap alarm clock read five to midnight. I closed my eyes. Maybe if I shook him really hard....

I was still planning my next assault when I fell asleep.

~*~

"Carlo," I said. "Carlo, wait a minute."

I had woken to find him once again on top of me.

"Whafor?" he muttered. "Janey...."

I pushed him off, this time without difficulty. "Carlo, what if I have a baby?"

"Huh?" He frowned and brushed a lock of hair out of his eyes. "Not to worry. I took care of it."

Oh. That's what the rustling sound had been. Of course. But it was still too soon for all-out relief. "They break sometimes, don't they?" I whispered, remembering Posy giggling about some unfortunate girl having to fish one of those out with a spoon. Not that it sounded all that likely now that I understood the way things worked.

"It didn't break," Carlo said gruffly. "Come on, Janey. You want to, don't you?"

I wondered if he'd listen if I said no. He hadn't last night. He smelled stale this morning, and there was a nest of dark stubble on his chin. But there didn't seem much point in pushing him away. Besides, the second time was sure to be better. I would like it just like the heroines in my books.

I gave myself to him compliantly. But it wasn't any better. I was only pleased because he was. His enthusiastic groans made me feel very grown up.

When it was over, he kissed me perfunctorily and said he'd see me later.

I got up and had a bath, and by the time I was dressed, there was no time left for breakfast and I was almost late for work. Which, after yesterday, would only have been asking for trouble.

Mr. Reid was behind the counter eating cake when I arrived. My stomach growled indignantly. He looked up, and for the first time since I'd come to work for him, it occurred to me to wonder if there was a Mrs. Reid tucked away somewhere. If so, she didn't do breakfasts—or lunches.

To my amazement, when he saw me looking hungrily at his cake, he asked if I wanted a piece. I guessed it was his way of making up to me for yesterday's tantrum.

"Yes, please," I said eagerly. "Did your wife make it, Mr. Reid?"

He shook his head and glared ferociously at a scratch on the counter. "Don't have a wife. Lost her and my boy twenty years ago."

"Oh, Mr. Reid. I am so sorry." I didn't know what else to say, but I was shocked. Mr. Reid was human. He'd suffered a terrible loss. And I'd thought he was just a grumpy old bear who liked power.

He must have seen from my face what I was thinking, because after clearing his throat noisily and dislodging the crumbs from his beard, he said heavily, "Train crash. Clapham Junction. They were on their way to visit Fanny's mother. The old girl had a fatal heart attack when she heard the news. Just as well, really...we never did get on."

"Oh, Mr. Reid!" He was being gruff and stoical about it, but that didn't mean he wasn't suffering. How could I have laughed at this sad, bereaved man and called him God? No wonder he was sometimes short-tempered. Malnourished as well, if the ubiquitous cake was anything to go by.

"Long time ago," he muttered, and disappeared into his office.

I set to work dusting the shelves and trying to write letters in my head explaining, with more than my usual inventiveness, that payment was in the mail and further large orders would follow. But in spite of my newfound sympathy for my boss, I couldn't keep my mind on his letters for long. Carlo's soft, persuasive voice kept getting mixed up with my creative evasions.

I couldn't wait to tell Allison what had happened.

CHAPTER FOUR

Arabella reached for the kettle that someone had placed on the shelf above the fridge. "You and Carlo an item?" she asked, hitching up the strip of material that masqueraded as her skirt. "Damn that Lavender anyway. Just because she's got arms like a gorilla don't mean she has to store the kettle up by the ceiling."

I laughed. In the few weeks I had known Arabella, I had come to appreciate her directness even when I wasn't anxious to respond to it. "I've never seen Miss Lavender or Mrs. Garcia," I said, deliberately avoiding her question about Carlo. "Do they really exist?"

"Well, they sure as hell aren't ghosts." She swore as stale water from the kettle cascaded over her hair. "Course they only live here part-time."

"Oh. Why's that?" I sat down at the table and waited for her to finish making the tea that I supposed was to go with the two bowls of glutinous brown soup she had already thumped onto a black plastic tray.

It was Saturday evening, Carlo was at work, and I had come downstairs with the idea of making myself something more substantial than cheese and crackers. But Arabella was ahead of me, and there wasn't room for two people to cook at the same time. Not that anything went on in this kitchen that could seriously be labelled cooking.

Arabella paused with her hand on a loaf of white bread. "You serious?"

"About what?"

"Lavender and Garcia. Don't you know about them?"

Obviously, I didn't. "Not much. Carlo said Mrs. Garcia has a husband, so I suppose that means she's divorced—"

"Hah!" Arabella scoffed. "You don't know much, do you? Never mind, just give our Carlo time and he'll fix that. Garcia isn't divorced. She's bi. Has a couple of kids. Lavender's her bit on the side."

"Oh. I see." I didn't really. But years ago Posy had snickeringly passed on some dubious bits of intelligence gleaned from her family's widowed cook, who seemed to double as an expert on the sex life of Homo Britannicus. Mother's embarrassed explanations hadn't included the existence of the likes of Oscar Wilde or Radcliffe Hall.

Just imagine Lavender and Garcia being like that! I was living in a genuine den of urban decadence. Even Arabella was a bit exotic. She sometimes worked as a model for an art school when she'd finished her regular shift at a local cafe. And Duncan worked for a mail order firm that sold books in brown paper packages.

Arabella picked up her tray. "So what is going on with you and Carlo?" she demanded. "By the way, did you know old Carmody listens outside your door?"

"No, but I might have guessed. The stairway always smells of smoke."

"Uh huh. And?" Arabella wasn't easily deflected. "What about Carlo?"

Because she had called me a little innocent, I produced my best woman-of-the-world smile. "What do you think is going on with me and Carlo?" I asked artfully, wanting her to know, but prolonging the suspense just to tease her.

Arabella grinned and the soup bowls tilted dangerously. "That's what I figured. Watch out though. He's a slippery one, is Carlo. Don't let him hurt you."

"I won't."

She nodded and pranced out of the kitchen balancing the tray on her shoulder with one hand.

I poked my index finger at a blob of soup that lay like a jellied eye on the green oilcloth. *Could Carlo hurt me?* He fascinated me, of course, but the truth was I wasn't at all sure what was going on between us. He arrived in my bed each night never doubting his welcome, and I embraced him willingly enough even though our nightly couplings gave me no more than a mild pleasure in giving him pleasure. The loss of my virginity still awed me, and I was anxious to add to my experience.

So far I hadn't. Nor had Carlo taken me anywhere since that first night. Not even to the Happy Toad on his day off. We didn't talk much either, and I still knew nothing about him beyond the fact that he'd never known his father and he worked as a waiter somewhere close to Leicester Square. He wouldn't tell me exactly where.

I lifted my finger and licked the soup off it pensively. Cream of Boiled Socks, not Jellied Eye. No doubt about it, Duncan was in for a treat.

I was grinning as I rounded up Arabella's stale breadcrumbs and herded them into a mound. What did it matter if Carlo hadn't yet given me a chance to show him off? Tomorrow I was going to The Beeches, and because of him I could actually look forward to it. This time I would be the one to flaunt my superior status. Posy might be engaged, but I was a Woman of Experience.

My stomach started to rumble, and I stood up to dislodge the tin opener that had been jamming our ill-fitting cutlery drawer for two days. I might not be much of a cook, but even I could warm up tinned chicken stew.

~*~

David Foley arrived fifteen minutes late to pick me up. By that time I'd been standing outside Number Fifteen for half an hour, unable to face the thought of that charming, cultivated man ringing the bell and being surprised by Mrs. Carmody in full witch regalia—complete with a mystical cloud smoking about her head.

I didn't stop to wonder why it mattered.

"Hello." David sprang out of a shiny white Alpha Romeo, which I was relieved to see wasn't roofless. "Sorry I'm late." He flung open the door and waved me in.

"That's all right. It's not raining."

On the contrary, it was a beautiful September morning—or would have been if there had been anything for the sun to shine on besides grey buildings, black railings and a couple of bedraggled blackbirds in the gutter pecking at a crust of soggy bread.

David glanced at the blackbirds, then at me, and I saw him grimace.

When he saw me noticing the grimace, he said at once, "That frock suits you. Matches the green of your eyes."

Nice save. Carlo never said things like that. "Thank you." I struggled to sound casual, as if men paid me compliments every day.

David didn't drive as fast as I'd expected and he didn't talk much, but every now and then I caught him turning his head my way as if he wasn't quite sure what to make of me.

After a while I said, "What's the matter? I haven't grown a tail or anything, have I?"

"Not that I can see. Does that zip go down very far? Because I think you forgot to do it up."

"Oh!" I put my hand over my shoulder. He was right. I had pushed the zip of my green jersey dress as far as I could from the bottom but I'd forgotten to finish the job.

I squirmed, trying to rectify the situation, but David was driving faster now, and my fingers wouldn't connect with the tab. He watched me fidget for a while then said, "Allow me," and reached behind my back.

His touch was efficient and unexpectedly intimate. Although his fingers lingered only seconds at my neck, I shivered as I mumbled my thanks.

"Cold?" he asked.

No, cold wasn't my problem. I wasn't sure what was, but I felt a kind of restlessness, a dissatisfaction, as if I'd woken from a beautiful dream to find it was all an illusion.

"No, I'm quite warm," I replied. "Is it far?"

"The Beeches? No, about another ten minutes."

We were out of London now, cruising through a series of pretty villages. The trees were beginning to turn colour. I thought of the avenue leading to Chantersley, always the colour of warm copper in the autumn. On Wrenbert Terrace the trees all gave up once they reached a certain height, and any leaves they still bore were mud brown.

"Do you live near The Beeches?" I asked David. "You said you and Posy were neighbours."

"Our families are. I have a flat in town, but my parents spend most of their time in Much Gotham now that Father's given up his directorship of the bank. They're only a few miles from the Bantley-Browns. But of course, we're much less—grand." He hesitated on the word grand, and I wondered what, exactly, he meant. To me he seemed pretty grand himself.

Of course, I'd heard of Much Gotham. It was frequently mentioned with scathing condescension by the more left-wing newspapers as an example of the kind of attractive old town where The Golf Club was the centre of the universe and retired colonels, bishops and judges lurked behind every box hedge.

Thank heaven I hadn't let David ring my doorbell.

"I suppose you've known Posy forever then," I said.

"It seems that way sometimes."

"She never mentioned you." I didn't want to appear suspicious, but it was hard to understand how Posy, who never missed a chance to show off, could have failed to tell us she knew a charming, dishy man who came with connections to a bank.

"Didn't she?" David was non-committal—too non-committal.

"Do you love her?" I blurted. When it dawned on me how gauche that must have sounded, I buried my face in my hands.

"I'm not sure that's any of your business," David said mildly.

My cheeks burned beneath my fingers and heat tingled up my neck and over my ears.

"I'm sorry, I didn't mean..." I sputtered, before subsiding into a hopeless silence. What on earth had made me ask such a personal question? As David had pointed out, it wasn't my business. Perhaps Arabella's outspoken curiosity was contagious.

There was no reason why David should care about my feelings, but my confusion must have touched him in some way, because after an uncomfortable pause, he said, "Sorry. That was uncalled for."

"No. No, it wasn't...."

We came to a pair of wrought iron gates that opened onto a gravelled driveway at the end of which I could just see the roof of a large house. "Look," David said patiently, "I realize it's natural for you to worry about your friend. I'm a lot older than Posy, and I suppose you're wondering..." He paused, then began again on a different tack. "The point is, there are reasons why I think Posy and I will suit. Some of those reasons, I admit, are strictly practical. But that doesn't mean I don't care for her."

"No, of course it doesn't. I am sorry and I do know I shouldn't have asked." His being nice about it only made me feel worse.

David reached over and patted me on the nearest knee. "Don't worry. I over-reacted."

Perhaps he had, but it had been a disgracefully nosy question. Which, come to think of it, he hadn't actually answered. I opened my mouth, then shut it before I could insert my foot in it again.

David pulled the car onto a red brick circle in front of a pink palace of a house with white stone eagles in charge of the massive front door. Serried ranks of chrysanthemums stood sentinel beside the smooth, weedless lawns, and a crazy-paving path led to tennis courts and a covered swimming pool. The Thames was just visible through the trees behind the house.

"Here we are," David said.

"Yes." I scrabbled for the handle, but he was already out of the car and opening my door.

He looked so solemn I couldn't resist inclining my head as I stepped out, saying grandly, "Thank you, James. I'll let you know if I should require your services further."

David blinked, then started to laugh. "You're full of surprises, aren't you?"

I hadn't been. I'd been rather-dull-Janey whom everyone but Allison overlooked. But Carlo had happened since then. Maybe other things were changing as well.

The door of the house swung open before I had a chance to answer, and Posy came tripping down the steps. She looked plump, pretty and pleased with herself in a smart blue linen dress that made the most of her curves.

"Hello, darling," she cooed, trotting up to David and lifting her cheek for his kiss. As soon as he had dutifully delivered it, she turned to me.

"Janey, how nice you could come. You do look sweet in that frock."

That sounded like a compliment but, knowing Posy, it was only her backhanded way of telling me I looked terribly young.

"Thank you," I said. "David tells me it matches my eyes."

Posy's eyelids flickered. "How charming." She smiled up at David. "Well done, darling."

Phony bitch! I waited, expecting to feel a familiar flare of hate. But it didn't come. Posy's malice didn't seem important. I wasn't even certain it was malice. Perhaps it was just Posy, who couldn't help being herself.

As I mulled over this novel idea, a dark-haired woman with a figure like Posy's came twittering down the steps to greet us.

"Come in, come in," she gushed. "I'm afraid Sunday is Jamieson's day off, so we're having to do the honours ourselves. So tiresome. Lovely to see you, dears. Posy, do take Janey upstairs to powder her nose. Now come along, David, your parents are here and we're all having drinks in the drawing room. Isn't it fun?"

She swept us up the steps with her arms outstretched as if she were blessing the multitudes. I glanced at David, who was looking inscrutable, and at Posy, who was looking cross.

"Come on then," she said ungraciously, and led me up a white curving staircase to a gilded gallery that ran around three sides of the hall.

"This is my room," Posy said, leading me off the gallery and opening the door to a large, bright bedroom with white velvet chairs, a dusty pink carpet and a lot of starched pink frills. "Do you want to powder your nose? I have my own bathroom, of course."

Naturally. Posy had everything.

"Not really," I admitted.

"Neither do I." She plumped herself into one of the velvet chairs and crossed her ankles. "I think Mummy wants David to herself."

"Why ever should she?"

"We're buying my ring tomorrow. I expect she's giving him advice."

"But you're the one who'll be wearing it," I said, noting that her ring finger did indeed lack the flashy diamond I'd expected her to favour.

Posy turned pink and tossed her curls. "I know, but Mummy says he ought to buy me something special. Not like that plain old topaz his mother wears. Of course, that's been in the family for ages. The Foley's go back centuries, you know."

So did the Blackmans and the Smiths and the Browns, only nobody cared.

"Does David want to buy you a topaz?" I asked.

"Not necessarily. He did say I should choose something discreet—as well as valuable," she added quickly, in case I should think David wasn't much of a catch after all.

I smothered a smile.

"Of course, it's bound to be absolutely brilliant," Posy assured me. "Don't you wish you were engaged to someone like David?"

I crossed to the window and stared down at the well-kept lawns sloping towards a row of weeping willows along the riverbank—not a mangy cat or a dustbin in sight. "You are lucky," I agreed, though I wasn't really talking about David.

"He's gorgeous, isn't he?" said Posy—who was.

I didn't look at her. "I suppose he is."

"Don't worry," she said indulgently to my back. "You're sure to meet some nice little man in a few years. I expect you'll be terribly devoted."

A man like my father? There were worse fates. But Carlo wasn't a bit like my father.

I turned around and treated Posy to the patronizing smile I'd been practicing all week. "As a matter of fact," I drawled, "I've already met a man. He's not necessarily nice, but he's certainly experienced."

Posy lowered her eyelashes. "Really, Janey. How would you know?"

Come to think of it, I didn't. But Carlo seemed to know what he was doing. "It's not hard to tell," I said with an air of condescension.

Posy tossed her curls. "Janey, honestly. Surely you don't..." She stopped, adjusted the belt of her dress, and started again. "What's his name? Where did you meet him?"

"His name's Carlo. He rents one of the flats below mine. Actually, I met him in the kitchen."

"Oh. You're serious, aren't you?"

"Yes, I am."

She stared, and I held her gaze as reluctantly, she made up her mind to believe me.

"You mean you've kissed him?" she asked.

I laughed as if the possibility that I hadn't was absurd. "Of course."

"Oh. Is that all?"

She desperately wanted it to be all.

I hesitated, but only briefly. Posy had never been known for her discretion, but surely even she wouldn't spill the beans to my dad. Besides, fish shops in Willbury weren't her usual sort of haunt.

"Of course, it's not all," I said, raising my eyebrows to indicate that I couldn't believe she'd actually had to ask.

"Janey! Surely you don't mean...?" The Bantley-Brown mouth gaped most satisfactorily.

"Honestly, Posy." I pretended to cover a yawn. "What do you think?"

She folded her hands tightly in her lap. "You haven't slept with him? You couldn't have."

"Well, there hasn't been much sleeping about it," I admitted with a smirk. There had been, of course. Carlo invariably fell asleep almost as soon as his business was completed. But I had no intention of telling Posy that.

"Janey!" If I'd wanted to, I could have seen her tonsils.

"But surely you and David...?" I put my head on one side and paused archly.

Posy shook her head, pouting and making no attempt to hide her irritation—and suddenly, the thought of those two in bed together did seem ludicrous and unlikely.

As soon as she recovered from the shock, Posy attempted to regain control of the conversation. "I mean to wear white to my wedding," she announced with a small, brittle smile.

"Yes, but that doesn't mean—after all you are engaged." I smoothed back my hair, savouring every moment of this heaven-sent opportunity to display my superior carnal knowledge.

"Yes, but I still mean to wait for marriage." Posy pulled a tissue out of a pink marbled box beside the bed and folded it into a small, fat square. I watched curiosity wage war with her desire to keep me in my place.

Curiosity won. "What's it like?" she asked, in a funny, whispery voice.

Only then did it occur to me to wonder if Posy's preoccupation with sex came from fear. Was it possible that, deep down, she was as terrified as I had been before Carlo?

I collapsed onto the wide white windowsill and looked away from her anxious blue eyes. Here, at last, was the perfect opportunity to avenge myself for all the embarrassment and unkindness I'd suffered at her hands. I hesitated.

The sound of voices in the hallway cut briefly into the silence. Posy squirmed awkwardly on the bed, and I allowed my revenge to slip away.

"It's all right," I said. "Nothing to it. You just have to be there."

"Doesn't it hurt?"

"Only the first time—and not much even then."

"Oh. Do you like it?" She giggled nervously. "You don't sound very excited."

I wasn't very excited, except by my newfound status as a Woman of Experience. "I don't mind it," I said. "It's nice being held and sometimes, I quite like Carlo touching me—well, where he does."

Posy giggled again. "I thought it was supposed to be cataclysmic."

"So did I," I admitted. "Maybe it is for some people. Or maybe that's just in books. Of course, it could be cataclysmic for you and David." It didn't seem likely, but Posy looked so worried I found myself inspired to be magnanimous. The idea of scaring her silly wasn't as appealing as it would have been only a few weeks ago.

"Do you think it will be?" she asked. "Cataclysmic?"

I didn't. David was nicer than Carlo, and just as attractive in his way, but I didn't see how that could make a difference.

"Anything's possible," I said.

"I suppose so."

I felt sorry for her. I, Janey Blackman, actually felt sorry for the Bantley-Brown. "Should we go downstairs now?" I asked, wanting to end this conversation. "Your mother will think I'm having a bath."

Posy shook her head. "Mummy won't care. She'll be too busy sparkling at Jasmine's new boyfriend."

"Jasmine has a boyfriend?"

Posy nodded. "She's sixteen now, you know. Mummy says she looks like Cleopatra."

"She is very pretty." Posy looked sulky, so I added, "So are you," and was amazed to see her face come alight as if she'd never been told that before—which she certainly hadn't by me.

She stood up and said, "I suppose we had better go down," with a smile that held what could have been genuine warmth. "We'll miss out on the sherry if we don't."

I could have lived with missing out on the sherry, but I didn't say so.

The drawing room faced the river. It was a big, warm room that in the hands of different owners could have been a haven of subtle elegance. In Bantley-Brown hands it was a monument to money. Crystal and gilt everywhere, lots of velvet, antique furniture that looked as though it had been lifted from some minor ducal palace, and an enormous chandelier that would have been perfect on the set of *Call Me Madam.*

I stood just inside the doorway trying not to gape, and at once my eye was drawn to a flash of blazing scarlet by the French windows—Jasmine, in something filmy, flowing and very red. A dark man who looked several years her senior was bending down to whisper in her ear. On the other side of the room David, draped against the mantel, was watching her with an appreciative smile.

Posy saw the smile and frowned, and immediately Mrs. Bantley-Brown swept up to us, waved Posy away, and bore me off on a round of introductions.

I hadn't met Posy's father before. He was tall and grey-haired with the kind of face that turns up in wine advertisements looking suave. When he took my hand and said, "Hello there, little lady," I knew at once that Posy's careful accent hadn't come from him. This man made no attempt to sugarcoat his origins. Yet he exuded confidence as if he'd been born to a dukedom—the kind that had no need to hawk the family treasures to make ends meet. A ring with diamonds and a crest sparkled on the middle finger of his right hand.

Mr. Foley was an older, stooped version of his son, with steel-grey hair and David's pleasant smile. Mrs. Foley was slim and long-nosed in a well-cut tweed skirt and fawn twin-set. Her pearls, I assumed, must be real. She shook my hand briskly and said, "So you're a friend of Posy's," as if I came as something of a relief. I wondered what she'd expected.

Conversation in the room was muted, and apart from Jasmine and her escort, no one seemed to be looking at anyone else. I wondered what our entrance had interrupted.

A glass of sherry was thrust into my hand as Posy's mother bustled me over to meet Jasmine and her boyfriend. "This is Martin Radburn," announced Mrs. Bantley-Brown, as if she were pulling a rather classy rabbit out of a hat. "I expect you've heard of his father, Sir George Radburn. Martin's in publishing."

"He'd rather be in Jasmine," muttered Posy.

She couldn't have said that. Not Posy. Not here. Surely, I must have misheard.

I hadn't. Martin Radburn's skin turned from olive to brick, Jasmine glowered, and Mrs. Bantley-Brown, her voice shrill, cried, "Posy, that's not at all nice. I don't know where you pick up such awful things. Apologize to Martin at once."

Conversation ceased. The only sound came from a songbird hidden in the branches of a beech tree.

I stared at Posy. Her normally pale face had turned almost as red as Jasmine's dress, but her full mouth was puffed in a pout.

"I didn't say it to Martin," she protested. "I was talking to Janey."

All eyes swivelled in my direction. "To Janey," Mrs. Bantley-Brown repeated. "Well, I'm afraid that's not the sort of language we expect to hear from Chantersley girls."

Which showed how much she knew about Chantersley.

Mrs. Foley said wasn't it nice the rain had held off, and Posy's lips protruded even further. I guessed she had only made her brash remark to show me I wasn't the only one with knowledge of what went on behind bedroom doors. Unfortunately, she had chosen the wrong place to prove it, because Mrs. Bantley-Brown was looking at me as if I'd just peeled off all my clothes. Did she think I was the cause of her daughter's descent into precisely the sort of vulgarity she had been sent to Chantersley to avoid?

I swallowed. What could I say? That the offending words had been Posy's and not mine? I was still floundering, undecided, when David loped across the room. He pressed his hand down hard on Posy's shoulder.

"I'm sure Posy didn't mean that the way it sounded," he said, directing his remarks, not to Martin Radborn, but quietly to Mrs. Bantley-Brown.

"But did you hear what she said?" Posy's mother, ignoring his cue, spoke in a shrill voice that everyone could hear.

"It doesn't matter." Martin Radburn, his face a dull raspberry colour now, cleared his throat and tugged awkwardly at his tie.

"Posy will apologize anyway," David said. "Won't you, Posy?"

The voice of authority, mild but hard to ignore. It would have made me listen if I'd been Posy. I wondered how she would respond.

Her blue eyes narrowed, became almost catlike, and for a moment I thought she was going to stamp her foot. "Why are you all being so beastly to me?" she demanded. When nobody answered, she shrugged. "Oh, all right. I'm sorry. There. Are you satisfied?"

Mr. Bantley-Brown laughed, made a lot of noise clanking crystal, and offered sherry all around. Martin muttered something unintelligible, and everyone else began talking at once. No one took any further notice of me, so I shifted around to get a better view of David and Posy. He was standing over her looking grim and shaking his head. She looked close to tears.

I thought sourly that if David liked playing schoolmaster to Posy's spoiled little girl, the two of them ought to get along well. Otherwise, their marriage looked destined for disaster.

"Yer dinner's ready," a high-pitched voice announced over the stilted hum of conversation.

A small woman with limp brown hair straggling out from under a cap stood grinning in the doorway. At least, I guessed she was grinning. It was hard to tell, because most of her teeth were missing.

Posy's legendary cook. The one from whom Posy had learned the facts and fictions of life.

Jasmine had told us how Mr. Bantley-Brown had insisted on bringing Cook into the household over Mrs. B-B's protests, because she had been kind to him when he was a child growing up in the East End. His parents had died when he was young—tragically, Posy had said. Of drink, Jasmine had said. After listening to Jasmine's down-to-earth account of her father's origins, we all knew that Harry Bantley-Brown had risen above his roots to make a fortune for himself clothing the golf and shooting set. To his credit, he hadn't forgotten the good-hearted neighbour from less affluent days.

Posy's mother, looking as though she would very much like to forget the widowed cook, hurried over to her and snapped, "Thank you, Cook. Just serve it, will you?"

Mrs. B-B's hopes of impressing Sir George Radburn's son with the Bantley-Brown gentility appeared to be fading fast.

Lunch, in the white and gold dining room, was an odd affair. On the surface the conversation was civilized enough, but at times it seemed no more than a cloak for emotions that ran deeper than disappointment over the weather at the last point-to-point, or irritation with the Labour Party's platform.

To heighten the uncomfortable atmosphere, Cook kept popping her head around the door to ask if everyone had enough, and Mrs. Bantley-Brown kept saying, "Thank you, Cook, that will be all," in a voice that cracked with mortification. Every time this happened, Mr. Bantley-Brown frowned at his wife, said something loud about horses to David's mother, and offered me the gravy. I wondered how often this scene had been played out over the years. Apparently Mrs. B-B had never learned to accept her cook's cheerful eccentricities.

David's father appeared mesmerized by a gilt-framed oil featuring a blindingly colorful garden and two poodles. Noticing, Mr. B-B announced that the picture had cost him a pretty penny.

Martin changed colour several times for no reason and ended up an ugly shade of mottled mud that would have made great camouflage if he'd been on the run. Jasmine sat silently scowling. I reflected that Jasmine was the only girl I knew who could scowl and look beautiful at the same time.

David and Posy sat side by side, not talking.

I thought about the Sunday dinners we'd had at home. They had been plain, but Mother was a good cook, and Dad enjoyed what she cooked for him and said so. The atmosphere around our kitchen table had been comfortable and more relaxed than on weekdays.

The opposite was true in this glittering room with its palatial furniture and undercurrents of social ambition, class distinction and suppressed hostility. The feelings I sensed here were the opposite of comfortable.

I tried to be unobtrusive as I sat quietly consuming my food and absorbing the currents that seethed beneath the commonplace ritual of Sunday lunch. *Soon*, I thought, *I will return to make peace with my parents.* My mother too had suffered from social ambitions, but at least she loved me in her way.

I wasn't sure anyone loved Posy.

Coffee was served in the drawing room, and soon afterwards Martin stood up and said he had to leave. Jasmine jumped up to go with him, and Mrs. Bantley-Brown explained loudly, "They have to be at Radburn Manor in time for tea."

Nobody answered, and not long afterwards, David rose too and suggested a walk by the river. "Coming, Janey?" he asked.

"You and Posy go," I said quickly. "I'm quite happy to sit here and digest."

The corner of his mouth twitched attractively. "Sure?"

"Yes, of course."

"All right. Posy? How about it?"

She nodded, and he took her hand and pulled her out of a gold brocade chair that contrasted prettily with her dress.

They left by the French windows, and when they reached the edge of the lawn he put an arm around her shoulders in a gesture that seemed more protective than physically affectionate. I'd noticed they didn't touch much.

"You should have gone with them, my dear," said David's father. I realized he'd been watching me and flushed.

"Oh, no. I'm sure they'd rather be alone."

He smiled with a puzzling edge of sadness. "Perhaps. In any case, it was thoughtful of you to give them the opportunity. Wasn't it thoughtful of Janey?" He turned to his wife, who was chatting about dogs to a bored-looking Mrs. Bantley-Brown.

"Yes, indeed." Mrs. Foley's smile was automatic.

Posy's mother covered a yawn.

I said that perhaps I would go for a walk after all.

It was peaceful beside the river. I liked watching the ducks dive into the water and send up spray, and I liked the feel of the sun on my skin. I could breath more easily out here.

Far down the path, two figures were standing side by side on the riverbank, heads bent, staring into the water. One was fair, the other unmistakably blonde.

They didn't seem to be touching, or even talking.

Tea was ready by the time I returned to the house. Posy and David came back a few minutes later. They weren't smiling, but they were holding hands.

As soon as tea was over, David said he'd drive me back to town.

We said goodbye and thank you, and Mr. Bantley-Brown told me to come again. Mrs. Bantley-Brown pretended she hadn't heard him.

I was glad. I didn't want to come again.

"That bad, was it?" asked David, as I sank onto the seat beside him and released what I had thought was an inaudible sigh.

"No, of course not. It was—um, nice."

"Nice?" He started to smile, then thought better of it.

"Yes," I said with more conviction. "I enjoyed it." I hadn't exactly, but at least I couldn't complain that I'd been bored.

"Liar."

"I am not lying." I couldn't blame him for laughing at me, but I didn't like it that my feelings were so transparent.

"All right," he said agreeably, "if you say so."

I scowled at a robin pecking a reluctant worm out of a rose bed. From the corner of my eye I caught David suppressing a grin.

"Have you and Posy always been friends?" he asked as we cruised down the driveway.

Posy, Posy, Posy. Always Posy. "No," I said. "Have you?"

"Have I what?"

"Always been friends with Posy?"

Expensive leather creaked as he shifted in his seat to look at me. "Friends? No, though I've known her vaguely for years. The first time I saw her was at her father's wedding. She looked like a sulky Shirley Temple in those days."

"At whose wedding?" I gaped at him. "Did you say her father's? But—isn't Mrs. B-B Posy's mother?"

"Stepmother. Jasmine's her half-sister. Don't tell me you didn't know."

"No. No, I didn't. It must have happened a long time ago."

"Mm. Fifteen years or so, I'd guess."

I watched his big hands on the wheel. He had a red birthmark at the base of his right thumb. If I concentrated on that, I wouldn't need to face the fact that Posy and I had more in common than I'd thought. We had both been raised by people who weren't our parents.

That might go some way towards explaining Posy, but it didn't explain why David wanted to marry her.

"I'm glad Posy apologized to Martin," I said, feeling my way around an answer to the puzzle.

"Are you?"

"Yes, of course. Martin and Jasmine were embarrassed."

"And Cora Bantley-Brown was livid," he agreed.

"I don't see why you put up with Posy," I said, knowing I sounded surly and not caring.

David cocked an eye at me and sighed.

Damn. What was it about him that made me say things I shouldn't?

"I don't put up with her," he said equably. "Her family do. Besides, what would you have me do?" The car made a sound like a cat on tiles as he took the next corner too fast. "Put her over my knee? That sort of thing is rather out of fashion now, I'm told. Or do you know something I don't?"

Flustered, I fidgeted with the strap on my bag and mumbled, "Of course not. That isn't what I meant."

"I'm glad. Sounds exhausting. What did you mean then?"

I bit my lip. "I don't know. Just that the two of you seem so—different, I suppose."

"As in incompatible?"

I grunted non-committal.

"Oh, I don't know. Posy's pretty and uncomplicated. Does it surprise you that I find her attractive?"

"It does rather. Do you?"

"It would be a pretty grim outlook if I didn't." He spoke pleasantly enough, but with a finality that let me know the subject was closed.

I didn't believe him altogether. He was a man, and I could understand his wanting to take Posy to bed—which according to her he hadn't. But I couldn't see him in the role of paternalistic husband to her child-bride. Still, it had nothing to do with me. I wasn't likely to see a lot of either of them after today.

"How are the sales of Inspirational Books going?" he asked as we swept past a crumbling brick church with a blood-red sign on its fence warning passing motorists that sin lurked around each bend in the Road of Life.

"Well enough," I said.

David successfully negotiated another turn without surprising so much as a trace of lurking sin. I told him all about Mr. Reid and the unpaid bills.

He laughed. "Not a very profitable business from the sounds of it."

"No, but I think it could be if Mr. Reid cared enough." I hesitated, then decided I was sufficiently curious to risk another rebuff. "What kind of business are you in?"

David switched gears so abruptly that they squealed. "I run a small gallery on Davies Street. Oriental art, mainly."

Mm. Exclusive. "That must be fascinating," I said.

"You're interested in oriental art?"

I wasn't, but it was too late to back out without looking foolish. "I don't actually know much about it," I admitted, "but I'd like to."

"Would you? Why?"

Ouch. Was he deliberately trying to embarrass me? I fixed my gaze on an overgrown carpet of a dog that was trying to outrun the car. "Well, it just sounds—interesting," I said.

"At the moment, it's a thundering pain in the neck."

The dog fell back and I turned to stare at David in surprise. He was glaring at the passing countryside as if it were a landscape on the moon.

"Why is it a pain in the neck?" I asked cautiously.

"There's a lot of competition and people aren't buying as they used to. Leaves me with a cash flow problem. Partly my own fault, of course. I wasn't cut out to be a businessman. Father wanted me to go into Sotheby's or Christie's, but I preferred to strike out on my own."

"And now you regret it?"

He shrugged. "Not really. The problems aren't insurmountable. Eventually, I expect things will sort themselves out."

"I see." I glanced doubtfully at his uncommunicative profile. In my experience, cash flowed away in direct proportion to one's need. Unless....

Posy. The unpleasant thought thudded into my head. Was she the solution to David's cash flow problems? That would certainly explain their unlikely union. But David was so civilized, so nice. Surely he wouldn't...?

"Actually, I don't quite see," I corrected myself. "What—?"

David took his hands off the wheel. "Of course, you don't," he snapped. "Why should you?"

No reason, but I wasn't without imagination. Posy wasn't my idea of the average man's dream come true, but then neither was dealing in oriental art. My own father was capable of going all dreamy-eyed over turbot and bloaters. It was quite possible David was similarly obsessed over Posy.

I watched the wind from the open window blow golden ripples in his hair, and the car, freed from the restraint of his hands, swung straight for a gruesome purple fence.

David pulled it back onto the road and said, "Look, I'm sorry. I didn't mean to snap at you."

"It's all right." I pinched a fold in my green dress then tried to smooth it. If only this awful drive was over. I shouldn't have come, should have stayed in London, or even gone to visit my parents. Dad was sure to be worrying, even though I'd told him I was all right.

We were silent after that, deep in our own reflections, and when the car drew up outside Mrs. Carmody's, I smiled my relief and said, "Thank you very much."

David smiled back wryly, and I was just thinking what a warm, appealing smile he had when Carlo came whistling round the corner. He looked over his shoulder and waved, and I caught a glimpse of long, honey-blonde hair swinging away down the street.

David, following the direction of my eyes, frowned and said, "You know that chap?"

"Yes. He's my boyfriend." It was more or less the truth.

He nodded and climbed out of the car to help me onto the pavement.

"Thank you," I said again. "It was kind of you to drive me."

"Wasn't it, though?" He slid back onto the seat. "Let me know if I can be of further service."

"Of course, James." I nodded graciously and did my duchess act.

It didn't seem to surprise him much this time, and he laughed and waved a casual goodbye as he drove off.

Carlo came up to me looking Latin. "Who was that?"

"His name's David Foley. He's engaged to a school friend of mine."

"Oh. Some fancy car. What was he doing out with you?"

Was he jealous? If he was, I hoped it was because of me and not the car. "David drove me down to the country," I explained, "to have lunch with my friend and her family."

"Oh, the country," he mimicked, in his idea of an upper-crust drawl. "And did you have a fabulous time in the country, Lady Janey?"

I knew Carlo felt threatened by the difference in our backgrounds. It made me feel guilty, and I was beginning to get very tired of guilt.

"Yes, I had a nice time," I said. "Did you have a nice time with your—friend?"

His shrug was just short of suggestive. "What do you think?"

With a sinking feeling in my intestines, I turned to go into the house. Immediately, Carlo grabbed my arm.

"Don't," I said, trying to shake him off along with my hurt.

"Why? Not good enough for you after your friend with the posh car?"

"David is Posy's friend." My eyes were watering, and only partly because his grip on my arm was too tight.

"What difference does that make?" he sneered.

"I don't know." Once again I tried to pull away, but Carlo wouldn't let go.

"Come on," he said, urging me up the steps. "In you go." I allowed him to lead me through the hall and up the stairs. A smell of frying mingled with the inevitable smoke coming up from the basement.

"What do you think you're doing?" I asked, as we passed the second landing.

"I'm going to show you a better time than he did."

"Then let's go out somewhere. I—"

"Maybe we will—after."

A bedspring twanged as we passed the Ashes' room. "After what?"

"You'll see." We were on the top floor now. "Open your door."

He had too much after-shave on. It made me feel a bit dizzy. "Carlo, listen—"

"No, you listen. Open the door."

I opened it. This was only Carlo after all—Carlo, who had spent the last six nights in my bed. He wasn't drunk, just belligerent, and he had never hurt me. The room smelled thick and smoky and at once I went to fling open the window.

When I turned around, Carlo was leaning against the door looking operatic. Black suited him. I began to feel the faint tingling under my skin that I'd felt once or twice before, although it never seemed to come to anything. Maybe this time it would.

"What now?" I asked. Carlo was already taking his clothes off, and I spoke more for something to say than because I needed an answer.

Not surprisingly, I didn't get one. Carlo took me by the arms, sat me on the bed and started to pull up my dress. I thought about resisting, but only because he hadn't asked. The tingling was growing stronger, and I craved a release whose existence I sensed but had yet to experience.

Carlo touched my breast, and I quivered like jelly waiting to be eaten. Was I, at last, going to find out what the fuss was all about? I turned to him with a hopeful little murmur.

Nothing happened that hadn't happened before.

Carlo laid me on the bed and did what he always did. The only difference was that this time he went on longer and afterwards, he didn't go to sleep. I felt sore and disappointed. Carlo, resting on one elbow, looked down at me as if he'd just conquered the Bastille single-handedly.

"Well?" he asked. "How was that?"

"Fine," I said. *Did he expect me to burst into applause?*

"Only fine?"

I kicked the tangled sheet from around my ankles. He was always sensitive about his performance. "Wonderful," I amended, having no reason to prick his ego.

Carlo flattened his lips, reminding me of a little boy balked of a treat. He often looked like that. "You're about as much fun as an iceberg," he grunted. "That hair of yours is a sham."

I flinched. Was I an iceberg? Was there something wrong with me? I had no way of knowing. But I did know his scornful judgement hurt.

"It's not dyed," I said, deliberately misunderstanding. "It's my real colour."

Carlo made an impatient noise with his tongue and rolled to the edge of the bed. I pulled up the faded brown blanket. Its dinginess was in keeping with my mood.

"Are you leaving?" I asked, as he stood up and pulled on his trousers. "I thought you said we'd go out."

"That was before." He flashed me a full frontal of his very white teeth.

I turned my face to the wall, and a minute or so later I heard the window rattle as the door clicked shut behind him.

There was a fresh brown burn on the shabby wall. Had Mrs. Carmody been lying on my bed? Funny, I didn't seem to care much. Any more than Carlo really cared about me. I was just a convenience. Or was I dessert to follow the honey-blonde main course?

She could be a relative, of course. I sat up, banging my head on the brass bedpost. Did he have relatives? He'd never mentioned anyone except his mother. But the blonde could even be his sister.

I clung to that thought, trying to convince myself I needn't worry. Carlo's nose was out of joint, but he'd be back.

I lay down again, felt something throb, and touched the sore spot on my head where I'd hit the bedpost.

Carlo didn't come back that night.

The next morning, as I was scooping greasy wet tea leaves out of the sink, Mrs. Carmody came puffing into the kitchen in her black sateen dressing gown. "He's gone," she announced with a scowl.

"Who is, Mrs. Carmody?"

I thought I already knew. The tea leaves were staining my fingers.

"Mr. Bozelli. No notice, not a penny of extra rent." She squinted at me through a cloud of putrid smoke. "You know where he is?"

I shook my head and reached for the tap. When the last slimy tea leaf had disappeared, I dried my hands and stumbled towards a chair. But Mrs. Carmody was standing in my way, and when I tried to move around her I collided with a corner of the table.

It retaliated by jabbing a splinter into my rear.

When I let out a howl, Mrs. Carmody said quickly, "No damaging the furniture now."

I couldn't summon enough interest to tell her the furniture had no business damaging me.

CHAPTER FIVE

"What's eating you?"

Colin's flat drawl made me start. Lost in a fog of self-pity, I hadn't heard the door of Inspirational Books give its customary snarl when opened.

"Nothing," I replied automatically.

"You look like spilled milk." He sidled inside but didn't close the door.

"You do have a way with words." Picking up a bedraggled feather duster, I flicked it desultorily over a shelf of leather-bound inspiration and refused to look at Colin in case he saw the red rims round my eyes. "What do you want?"

"Nice to see you too," Colin said. "God awake?"

"He's not God anymore. He's been nice to me lately. And yes, he is awake. At least, I think so. He's gone to an auction."

"Good." Colin slammed the door.

"Why? What do you want?" I asked morosely.

"Luckily for me, not you," he snapped, finally losing patience with my surliness. But he couldn't maintain his ill humour for long, and almost at once a grin split the melancholy arrangement of his features. "I came to tell you June's agreed to go out."

I laid my duster carefully on a shelf. "With you?"

"Yes, with me. Don't look so bloody surprised."

"Oh, Colin, I am glad." I picked the duster up again and waved it at him, momentarily forgetting my own woes. "Really I am. And I'm sorry I was grumpy. What made her change her mind?"

"Not sure. She just came into the shop and asked if I was doing anything tonight. I think she broke up with that d—" He stopped. "That Italian boyfriend of hers."

"Oh." The duster slipped from my fingers. "I didn't know she had a boyfriend. That's wonderful, Colin."

"Yes." He peered at me shortsightedly, his basset face longer than ever with concern. "Is something the matter, Janey?"

"No, I—no, nothing. I'm just tired." I couldn't bring myself to tell Colin that, as of last night, my Italian boyfriend was no longer mine—if he ever had been.

Carlo hadn't taken the trouble to break up with me. He'd just packed up his bags and left. Mrs. Carmody was fit to be tied. I felt as if my face had been stepped on. I had given Carl—well, more accurately, he had taken—something I was supposed to value greatly. Now that I knew how cheaply I'd lost it, contrarily, I wanted it back. A regretful goodbye might not have eased the hurt, but at least I wouldn't have felt so like a toy designed to last only until a newer, shinier model came on the market— in this case, a model with honey-blonde hair.

"Where are you planning to take June?" I asked Colin, mainly to take my mind off myself.

"The Cat's Banana."

"Oh."

I must have looked blank because he went on patiently, "It's a nightclub. In Soho. June says they have a great band, so—"

He broke off abruptly as the front door creaked and a voice behind us rumbled, "One that plays marching tunes, I hope. Good afternoon, young man."

Mr. Reid stood framed in the doorway looking biblical. With his white hair blowing around his face he resembled, if not God, at least one of the sterner Old Testament prophets.

Colin wasn't slow to take the hint. He mumbled, "Good afternoon, Sir," and began to shuffle sideways towards the door.

Mr. Reid stamped behind the counter and watched him go. "Can't keep away from you, can he?"

I returned to my dusting. "Colin?" I said with my back to him. "Oh, Colin's not interested in me. He came to tell me he's got a date with June. She works at the record shop."

Mr. Reid cleared his throat like a racing car engine revving up. "Miss Blackman?"

I jumped, then turned round slowly, wondering if he meant to sack me again. A puff of dust flew up my nose, and I sneezed daintily.

"Bless you," he said.

I gaped at him. "Mr. Reid...?"

"Harrumph." The engine in his throat growled once more, gently but with feeling, then without a word he stalked off into his office.

I shook my head and fetched a step stool with wheels from beneath the counter. There had never been much point in trying to make sense of my boss. It was best just to ignore his moods and think of more important things—like Colin's astonishing success in attracting June. I had been so sure his suit was hopeless but I was glad for him, glad he was happy.

If only bloody Carlo had felt that way about me....

But of course he hadn't, or he wouldn't have walked out on me. What a fool I'd been to imagine he was jealous of David. I'd been a convenience, nothing more, a handy frozen pudding that had never quite thawed to his taste.

Unfortunately, knowing that didn't help a bit.

I climbed onto the stool and rested my head forlornly against a volume of pious poetry. It smelled of old, brittle leather. I sniffed, so busy feeling sorry for myself that I didn't at first notice that the wheels beneath my feet were sliding away. Too late, I grabbed for the bookcase, missed, and tumbled backwards onto what felt like a lumpy cushion with legs.

The cushion turned out to be my boss.

"Wh-what?" I gasped, rolling off him and struggling to my feet. "What happened? Did you move my stool, Mr. Reid?" I clung to the nearest shelf as he pulled himself up with a lot of creaking and 'harrumphing.'

"Accident," he muttered. "No need to get excited."

I wasn't excited. If anything, I was annoyed, and fairly certain my fall had been no accident.

Had I imagined the heat in his hands as they had briefly touched my waist—imagined them brushing across my breasts? I must have. Mr. Reid might not be God, but he was a gentleman. A gentleman who took the teachings of the Bible to heart—and I didn't need to be an expert in the scriptures to know those teachings didn't advocate feeling up the staff.

Pulling myself together, I straightened my skirt and pinned up a stray wisp of hair. When I looked round, Mr. Reid had his back to me and was once again escaping into his office. *Good.* I shook my head and promptly dislodged the comb that kept the precarious edifice of my hair on top of my head.

A family of four came in just then, and for a while I was kept busy searching for devotional literature for two hopelessly unholy small boys. I did my best with little conviction that Grandmother's Favourite Bible Stories would do much good. By the time they left, the afternoon was over.

I was about to close off the cash register when Mr. Reid emerged from his office with pink icing sticking to his beard.

"Leave it," he ordered. "Go home. No need for both of us to stay."

"Yes, Mr. Reid," I said meekly, wondering what was behind this unusual magnanimity. I hoped it wasn't guilt.

For once I was glad to get back to Mrs. Carmody's. The Underground had been hot and airless, and the passengers pressed together as tightly as cigarettes in a pack. Some of them smelled that way too. When I got into the open, the pavements were crowded and the wind blew dirt and rubbish in my face.

I had never thought of Number Fifteen as a place of refuge, but today I did.

In the kitchen, a tall, dark man who reminded me of Nat King Cole was bumbling around opening and shutting drawers. If this was Carlo's replacement, the colour of his money must have met with Mrs. Carmody's approval. I tried, unsuccessfully, to dislodge the lump clogging my throat. So much for my fantasies that a remorseful Carlo would return to beg forgiveness. Now I knew he wasn't coming back.

"I'm looking for a bread knife," the man said. "Is there one?"

"No. There isn't."

"Oh." He looked gloomy.

"You'd be better off buying your own knife," I told him. "The ones in here always disappear."

"I wanted toast with my eggs," he explained, nodding at two leathery looking amoebas in the frying pan. When I grunted sympathetically, he added, "I could cook some up for you if you like."

The offer was meant kindly, but it was too much. Carlo had cooked eggs that first night. Later, he had put his hand on my backside as we walked up the stairs, explaining that Mrs. Carmody thrived on her tenants' immoralities....

"Thank you, it's very kind of you, but I have to go." Choking back tears, I fled for the sanctuary of my attic.

It wasn't until I heard Duncan and Arabella arguing in the hall outside their flat that I realized I hadn't even stopped to find out if the new tenant had a name.

~*~

The train lurched, and I was flung hard against the pie-faced man sitting next to me. He immediately spread his legs so that his fat thigh was angled against mine. As there were no vacant seats in the carriage, I sat in scowling silence and endured. Last year, when that other man had put his hand up my skirt, I had secretly been flattered. I wasn't flattered now, but I couldn't summon up the gumption or the energy to make a scene. What did it matter? Carlo probably behaved the same way on trains.

Were all men lecherous, self-absorbed toads? I thought of Dad, concealing his knowledge of Mother's deception all those years. No, Dad wasn't a toad. Posy's David didn't seem too bad either, although as far as I could tell he was only marrying her because he wanted her in his bed. At least he was marrying her—not like Carlo, who had taken his pleasure and vanished without trace.

That had been just over a week ago. I was used to the idea now. Not happy, but used to it. Indignation was beginning to heal the bruises to my ego, and already I was missing him less, even beginning to believe I hadn't cared for him much in the first place.

And now, at last, I was on my way back to Willbury.

Out of the blue, Mr. Reid had offered me Monday and Tuesday off, which meant I didn't have to be back at work for four days. At this point, I wasn't sure if I was grateful for the extra time or not. After the drama of my leaving, home was bound to be awkward at first.

The man beside me spread his legs wider. He was wearing thick, navy blue trousers that smelled of rain and gin. I watched dirty cotton clouds rushing past the window and tried to pretend I didn't notice the pressure against my thigh. Ten minutes later the train shuddered to a stop outside Willbury, and I hit the platform at a run. For all I knew, this was the gin drinker's stop as well as mine and my reluctance to make a scene didn't extend to being assaulted behind the dustbins off Station Street.

~*~

Number 48 looked exactly as it had on the day I left, except that the sun had shone on my departure, and today the sky was dark with endless rain. I'm not sure why I expected the house to look different—wishful thinking, perhaps, or a private conceit that without me things wouldn't be the same.

Dad flung open the door when I was only halfway up the path, his small mouth beaming a welcome. I stopped, and he came charging out to envelop me in a bear hug. My confidence restored, I hugged him back.

"Janey," he said. "Oh, Janey girl, it's grand to have you back. Here, let's have a look at you." He held me away, oblivious to the rain, as he carefully examined my face. Briefly, his gaze dropped to the jeans that Mother had always refused to let me wear.

"Only in the country," she had said firmly.

A voice that wasn't Dad's said, "You're thinner."

I looked over his shoulder. Mother was standing just behind him, her eyes a little brighter than usual, her cheeks a little fuller, but otherwise looking the way she always had—pale, tired and refined as a faded lace collar.

"I have lost a few ounces," I agreed, smiling enthusiastically because I couldn't quite bring myself to hug her. "Arabella says it suits me. She lives downstairs."

"Makes you look older," Dad said.

"I'll be nineteen soon."

"So you will, so you will. Come on in then." He beamed as if he were welcoming visiting royalty instead of the Prodigal Daughter.

"You're not at the shop," I said, belatedly realizing it wasn't early closing day.

"I took the afternoon off in your honour. Left my assistant in charge."

"You have an assistant?"

"Maryan, her name is. She comes in twice a week. Knows her fish too. Working out well, is Maryan."

He sounded cheerful and assured, as though life in general was working out well. The mild, drooping man I had known all the years of my childhood no longer seemed to exist.

We went inside and I was glad I was spending a few days after all. At least I would have my old room to retreat to. It would have been awful if I'd had to spend my visit seated demurely in the sitting room as if I were a guest in the house that for most of my life I'd called home.

My blue and white room was just the way I'd left it— cluttered with magazines, clothes and books. A dead fly lay on the windowsill, its black body curling to dust. Hadn't Mother bothered to clean then? That was so unlike her that I felt a familiar fluttering of guilt.

My teddy bear still lay on the bed where I'd left him. I picked him up and gave him a squeeze. He felt right in my arms, as soft and familiar as sleep. And why shouldn't I take him back to London? It was nobody's business but mine who shared my bed, and he would be a lot less disruptive than Carlo—more comforting too.

When I went downstairs, I found Mother making rock cakes in the kitchen. Dad, she said, had gone out to pick up a paper.

I guessed he had really gone out to give Mother and me a chance to talk alone. Bless him.

A green oilcloth that smelled as if it had just come out of its package covered the old wooden table in the corner. I pulled out a chair and sat down. Rain beat against the window behind me.

Abandoning the rock cakes, Mother put a cup of tea in front of me and sat too. "Jane..." She pushed at the fine, washed-out hair that long ago had been a shining, silky blonde. "Jane, before you say anything, I want you to know that I do understand why you went away. And I'm sorry. You can't know how sorry." She bent her head and took a quick sip of tea.

"Why? What are you sorry about?" I knew, but I had to make her put it in words.

"That you found out about your father the way you did..." She pushed at her hair again, then clasped her hands in her lap as if she had to force them to keep still.

"Which father?" I asked.

Mother's face crumpled. "Oh, Jane. You're so young...."

A momentary pang of compassion became impatience. I knew I was young, but I was used to Mother being in charge, not halting and indecisive.

"I'm old enough to know I grew up believing in a lie," I said unfeelingly. "And that Dad looked after us and loved us, and that you repaid him by—by...."

To my dismay, I couldn't go on. My chest felt tight and my voice was coming out all shrill and cracked.

Mother, her face stricken, leaned over the teacups and patted vaguely at my hand. I pulled it away.

"You hurt him," I whispered. "You hurt Dad. Why, Mum? Why?"

She pulled a tissue out of her sleeve and blew her nose. "I didn't mean to. I was grateful to him."

She hadn't told me not to call her Mum! Overwrought as I was, I noticed that. "Only grateful?" I asked.

"No. More than that." She brushed the back of her hand across her eyes. "I suppose I was living in a dreamworld all those years."

"A dreamworld?" I didn't understand. Mother wasn't the dreamer in our family. I was.

The rain stopped at that moment and everything went quiet. "Yes," Mother said. "If I hadn't been, I'd have realized long ago just what kind of a man your father is."

"John Marlowe?" I asked, confused, suspicious and afraid of what she might be going to say.

She shook her head. "No. I loved John. I was young then too. But—oh, Jane, I wouldn't have done what I did if I'd known..." She made a funny gulping noise at the back of her throat.

I didn't get a chance to ask "known what?" because the back door banged at that moment and Dad, waving a paper, came beaming into the kitchen.

"Ah, there you are. Any tea left, Edith?"

Mother shook her head. "No. I'll make you some fresh."

I stared from her face to Dad's. *What was this?* In the old days she would have said, "No, Frank, you'll just have to wait until tea time."

Over the next few days I was to discover that the old days were gone—apparently forever. More had changed at Number 48 than Mother's rigid rules about tea.

Dad still treated me as his beloved little girl who needed to be protected from unpleasantness, but apart from that he was truly a different man. Confident, assertive, comfortable in what he was doing—and Mother responded to his assurance with an almost girlish hesitation and a startling willingness to please. Although I could tell she was no happier about the fish shop than she had been when I left, she did her best to hide her disapproval, and Dad seemed satisfied with that.

I wasn't as easily reconciled to this disruption of all my previously held notions. Perhaps it was too soon, the secret of my birth still too raw, but parents weren't supposed to change so radically, nor were they supposed to start eyeing each other like couples did in films just before the music soared and the scene faded out. It was embarrassing, and I didn't like it a bit.

On the evening before I was due to return to London, my embarrassment finally erupted.

Mother had just returned from her job at Curry and Coles. The moment she came through the door, she started bustling about preparing Dad's dinner and fussing because the spinach wasn't fresh. I leaned unhelpfully against the wall and watched her. In the end, and only partly because I didn't much care for spinach, I said irritably, "Oh, for heaven's sake, Mum, what does it matter? You know Dad will eat whatever you put in front of him."

Mother, offended, said, "Yes, I expect he will. But when you're a little older you'll realize there's more to making a marriage work than—"

"Than spinach," I interrupted. "Yes, I've noticed that, and it's positively sick-making."

"We certainly don't mean to make you sick, Jane." Mother, her mouth all pinched, sliced sharply through a bunch of spinach stalks.

"I know." I was immediately riddled with guilt. "Mum—I didn't really mean it. Sorry."

"Jane, I'm sure it's hard for you to accept, but your father and I..." She frowned and sliced briskly, narrowly missing her left thumb. "You see...."

She paused, and I saw quite clearly.

"Yes," I said. "I know. Dad's always adored you, hasn't he? And now you're beginning to love him back."

Mother put down the knife and stood with her palms pressed flat on the cutting board. "Love?" she said tiredly. "Jane, what can you possibly know about love? You—"

"More than you think," I interrupted, conveniently ignoring the fact that for the last week I'd been wondering the same thing myself.

She looked at me, her tired eyes middle-aged and pitying, and the pain I'd been battening down all weekend burst out in unthinking resentment. "I'm not exactly innocent, you know."

"Jane!" Pity vanished, and in an instant Mother became the militant moralist I'd grown up with. "Of course, you're innocent. You don't know what you're talking about."

"Yes, I do." I moved from the door to curl my fingers around the back of the nearest chair. "I'm talking about sex. You know, what men and women do in bed."

Mother closed her eyes. "And elsewhere," she murmured. "Yes, of course you know about that. I told you. And I warned you—"

"You didn't warn me. You just said 'don't'."

I watched the muscles in her throat contract. "That was more than my mother told me," she said, staring at the knife in her hand as if she wondered how it had got there. She put it down and began to twist the rope of cultured pearls around her neck.

"Jane, you have to understand..." Her voice, low and disjointed, played on my conscience like chalk on a blackboard. "You don't know what it was like." As if her legs would no longer support her, she stumbled across the floor and flopped into a chair. "I should have tried to talk to you. Of course, I should have."

"You did, I think. It wasn't enough."

"Not enough? Jane, what are you trying to tell me?" Her naturally pale skin was like parchment, and for a moment I was afraid she would faint.

"I'm not pregnant," I said quickly. "And I haven't got a social disease."

Mother closed her eyes. "Thank God."

"Yes," I agreed.

She didn't seem to hear me. "I know I should have talked to you more frankly. But I was so ashamed...."

Ashamed? What was this? Ashamed was something Mother had always said other people ought to be.

"Of the way I came to have you." She twisted the pearls so tightly they began to form a pattern round her neck.

I winced, and she said quickly, "I don't mean I didn't want you. But talking about—sex, meant remembering. I wasn't much older than you are when I met John. But things were different in those days. I knew nothing, or very little, about how babies are made. I thought if I told you the bare—that is, the facts, and emphasized that you had to wait for marriage—it would be enough." She released the pearls and started twisting the buttons on her blouse. "Oh, dear. I'm not making sense, am I? The truth is, I didn't want to talk about it in case you asked too many questions about your own birth. Besides, I thought you knew...I mean, girls watch films now and read the papers. They know about babies and—and social diseases. Don't they?"

Carlo had thought that too. He had refused to believe I hadn't known what I was getting into when I innocently agreed to take my clothes off. He said this wasn't the eighteenth century and girls today weren't that gullible.

He was wrong. I think most of us at Chantersley were dreamers. We knew as much, or more, than our mothers did about the risks of unprotected sex, but we didn't relate the misfortunes of others to ourselves. And we certainly didn't understand the hormonal needs of the male sex. We were far too absorbed with our own.

But Mother understood, and she hadn't told me.

"We may know about babies," I said bitterly, "but that doesn't mean we know about men."

Mother stopped tormenting her buttons and dropped her hands into her lap. "No. I suppose not," she agreed. "Jane—do you want me to tell you about your father? About John?"

"No," I said. "He's not my father. Dad is. Do you want me to tell you about my lover?"

I don't know why I said it. It wasn't bragging. I was still angry with her, of course, and in a way irritated by her efforts to make amends. Or maybe, deep down, I needed someone to blame for Carlo. But if I had imagined for a moment the effect my words would have on my mother, I'd have zipped up my lips and sealed them closed with tape.

Mother's parchment skin turned nearly transparent. She clutched at the edge of the table and tried to stand. "Jane, no. No, you can't, you mustn't, you haven't..." Her body began to sway gently.

"Mother?" I don't know what I'd expected, but certainly not this. "Mother, are you all right?"

She opened her mouth, but no sound came, and the green oilcloth began to slide off the table where she was gripping it.

"Mother?" I repeated, frightened now. "Mother, it's all right, really. I didn't mean...."

There was no point finishing the sentence because her eyes had glazed over and she couldn't hear me.

I think I screamed as she slid off the chair and crumpled to the floor in a rustling heap of green oilcloth. But I'm not sure what happened after that.

I remember standing over her prone figure thinking how small and old she looked, even though she was only forty-three. Dad told me later that when he arrived home from the shop, brisk young men in uniforms, who told him there was no need to worry, were loading my semi-comatose mother aboard an ambulance.

So I must have done something right.

~*~

Late that night when we left the hospital, Dad's pale eyes were misted with tears.

"Oh, Dad." I dropped my head onto his brown tweed shoulder. "Dad, I'm sorry. It was all my fault."

"Nonsense." He removed my damp face gently from his neck. "We can't hold you responsible for this, Janey. Entirely my doing, I'm glad to say."

I stared at him. There was a funny, wry twist to his mouth. "Dad? You look pleased," I exclaimed.

Dad threw back his shoulders and grew a foot taller in front of my eyes. "I am pleased. The doctor said your mother's going to have a baby."

I caught his arm to make him stop. Two nurses pushed past us, giggling. Tires squealed somewhere in the night. "Dad! You're not serious? You can't be."

But when I looked at his face I knew he was. His mouth was stretched so wide I expected his teeth to fall out.

~*~

"They're keeping her in overnight for observation," Dad explained to me for the third time. "But the doctor said everything looks fine. He doesn't know why she fainted."

We were sitting at the kitchen table shovelling in some baked beans we'd found at the back of the cupboard, and I was trying to look pleased instead of stunned.

I knew why Mother had fainted. But I was beginning to learn that there are times when not telling the whole truth and nothing but the truth is the best and kindest thing to do.

Mother was having a baby. I still didn't quite believe it. At first the thought had seemed positively indecent. Then I'd looked at Dad's face, all soft and proud and filled with wonder, and I couldn't stay disgusted for long.

It was my fault she'd fainted though, but in some way, Dad's happiness helped assuage the guilt.

"Babies are beautiful," he said, spearing a bean. "I didn't think I'd ever have another."

Another? Oh, Dad. Determined not to cry, I sniffed loudly.

~*~

Mother came home the following morning. Both Dad and I had expected her to be weak and in need of rest. However, from the moment she walked into the kitchen and discovered two saucepans hanging on the wrong hooks and an unauthorized bean on the floor beside the cooker, she took over as if she'd spent the night at the Ritz instead of The Hepzibah Crump General Hospital.

"You'll need some help," I said grudgingly. "I'll call Mr. Reid and ask for the week off. I'm sure he'll understand."

I wasn't sure, but I had to do something to make amends for putting her in hospital.

Mr. Reid had been nice to me lately, though I still had the feeling he wasn't entirely convinced that if left to my own devices I wouldn't start stocking his saintly shelves with titles like Sin in Black Lace or Scarlet Garters in the Park.

"The whole week?" Mother said. "It's really not necessary. I wouldn't want you to jeopardize your job." She rather liked me working for Inspirational Books. But I could tell she wanted me to stay.

"The whole week?" echoed Mr. Reid when he answered the phone. He was silent after that, and I waited for him to refuse me. Instead he mumbled, "Hm. Don't know about that. But I suppose, in the circumstances, if you must...."

I assured him I must.

"Oh, very well. But only one week, mind. Without—"

"Without pay," I finished dryly. "Of course."

I was wary of Mother that first afternoon, half-expecting her to collapse on me again. But she showed no signs of collapsing and seemed anxious for Dad to return to work. As soon as he did, she sat me down at the kitchen table where all the trouble had begun, and said, "Now then, Jane. Let's finish what we started."

I didn't want to finish anything, particularly what we'd started, but I was afraid of upsetting her again. "What—um—what did we start?" I asked warily.

Mother twisted her pearls. "Too much, I think. For one thing, you said you didn't want me to tell you about John Marlowe. But are you sure?"

"Quite sure." I didn't have to think about that. Not yet, and maybe not ever.

She nodded, and I guessed she was relieved. "We'll leave it for the present then. But I most definitely do want to know what you've been up to." She fixed me with an eye even more effective at quelling opposition than Miss Barclay's.

I thought of saying I'd changed my mind and would love to discuss my natural father. But that would only put off the evil moment I had so unthinkingly brought on myself.

Might as well get it over with at once.

I took a deep breath, said, "Yes, mother," and told her about Carlo.

When I'd finished, she looked at me with sorrowful understanding. "Do you love him?" she asked.

"Yes. I think so. Or rather I thought so. I'm not sure I do anymore."

"That's good."

I wasn't sure what was good, but at least she hadn't fainted again. "I'll know better next time," I said.

"Yes," she agreed, with a sigh. "We always know better when it's too late. At least you're luckier than I was."

"Am I?" *What on earth was she talking about*?

"You said he took precautions."

Oh. I saw what she meant. "Yes. Yes, he did."

"Well, that's something, isn't it?" She lowered her eyes, her gaze caressing her stomach with a kind of wonder.

"You didn't," I said, with a resurgence of resentment. "Neither time."

She smiled, that proud, dreamy, maddening smile that mothers wear when talking about their children. "No, I didn't. That's why you're here. But this one was planned." She stroked the place where "this one's" cells were rapidly dividing.

"And I was an accident, of course." I gave her an I-don't-care smile.

"Oh, Jane." She raised her hand as if she meant to touch my cheek, then changed her mind and dropped it awkwardly on the edge of the table. "Yes, you were. If only all accidents were as fortunate."

Good damage control, I thought sourly, even though I could tell she was sincere.

Dimly, and with considerable discomfort, I understood that for the next nine months Mother's energies were likely to focus inward. This baby she was having still seemed somehow indecent, but if it took her single-minded attention off me—well, perhaps it wouldn't be all bad.

I gave her a strained smile, feeling light years away from the naive, dreamy schoolgirl who had left Willbury in such haste last July.

Mother returned the smile with a certain sadness, and I stood up to wash the egg-stained dishes we'd left soaking in the sink.

For the remainder of my stay in Willbury, Mother and I maintained a civilized truce. Both of us were anxious to avoid conflict, and I suppose, in a way, both of us were motivated by guilt. Outwardly at least, all was forgiven.

The following Monday I went back to London. It seemed different somehow, as if I'd been away for years. In fact, it had been a week and a half.

CHAPTER SIX

"Ah, you're back," Mr. Reid exclaimed with flattering relief. "Good." He nodded at the door to his office. "Bills are piling up. Better take care of those first. Mother all right?" He added that as an afterthought.

So nothing had changed while I'd been gone. Taking care of bills remained a priority, which meant doing my best not to take care of them. I felt as if I'd never been away.

"Mother's doing very well," I said, and headed directly for the office.

Two days later, as I was putting a new tape in the cash register, Mr. Reid came up behind me and mentioned offhandedly that I'd had a visitor the previous week.

"A visitor?" I stepped sideways because he was standing unusually close, and my elbow caught the edge of the counter. "Ouch," I said.

Mr. Reid cleared his throat. "Large type with bushy hair. Said you were a friend of his fiancée."

David? David Foley? It had to be. Posy was the only person I knew who actually had a fiancé. But I hadn't expected to hear from either her or David again after that curious afternoon at The Beeches. "Was he by himself?" I asked doubtfully.

"He didn't bring a cast of thousands." Mr. Reid was in a caustic mood today. "Bought a couple of books though. Seemed respectable enough."

Good old David. Visiting me at the shop was turning out to be expensive for him. I doubted he would venture in again.

"Did he—um—leave a message?" I asked, wondering what Posy wanted now. Presumably David had been sent as an emissary.

Mr. Reid shook his head. "No. Said it wasn't important."

I shrugged. It was odd that David had come at all, but I was sorry I'd missed him. He was nice. Big and comforting and kind—as well as thick enough to get engaged to Posy. I opened a drawer beneath the counter, then slammed it closed again because I couldn't remember why I'd opened it in the first place. David's face kept getting in the way.

On Saturday I stayed late at work to catch up on the bills I'd missed not paying while I was away. When I arrived home after picking up my usual scant supply of groceries, a familiar car was parked across the street. I watched a pair of endless legs emerge from under the dashboard followed by a large, solid body topped by a head of wavy hair. David, with his hands thrust into the pockets of well-cut grey flannel trousers, strolled across the street to join me. He seemed not to notice I was gaping at him.

"What are you doing here?" I asked, in a tone that was the opposite of Chantersley graciousness.

David's frown was a masterpiece of polite reproach. "I thought we might have dinner."

A light flashed off behind Mrs. Carmody's yellowing lace curtains. I wondered if she'd gone for her binoculars. "Where's Posy?" I asked.

David gave a lugubrious sigh and rolled his eyes at the dark purple clouds rolling in from the west. "When last seen she was reclining on a sofa looking fragile and being waited on hand and foot by her harried Cook."

"Oh. What's the matter with her? And why aren't you waiting on her too?"

"As far as I can gather, her indisposition is strictly a female affair. I was told to go away."

"Oh," I said. "Is that all? Posy always turned green when she got her period at school."

"And there I was trying to be delicate." David shook his head at me, his hair a lovely dark bronze in the waning light.

"There's nothing delicate about Posy," I said, forgetting for a moment that he planned to marry the scourge of my schooldays. When I remembered, I added quickly. "But that doesn't mean you and I can have dinner. She wouldn't like it."

But I would like it very much, I thought regretfully. In a way though, I was disappointed in David. He was the kind of man I'd have expected to spend the evening dutifully at home out of true-blue loyalty to Posy.

"Was that why you came to the bookshop?" I asked. "To ask me out?"

"No. I was in the vicinity and thought I'd drop by."

"Then why are you asking me now?"

"I'm not. At least not in the sense you mean. I'm at a loose end and I hoped you might be too."

"Oh." Why did people always assume I had nothing to do? Hadn't he believed me when I'd told him Carlo was my boyfriend? A blast of wind swept round the corner, lifting my skirt and sending a dustbin lid clattering down the street.

"Don't look so shocked," David said, misinterpreting my frown. "Posy won't mind me giving you a meal. It's your company I'm after, not your body."

Did he have to be so direct? I blushed and hoped it was too dark for him to see. "That's just as well. Because my body's not up for grabs."

"I didn't imagine it would be."

Was he laughing at me? Twelve years of Posy had left me with a very thin skin about personal remarks, even though I'd always pretended not to care.

David caught my arm as I turned away, making my string bag of groceries thump against my knee. "Hold it. Don't run off," he said. "I promise I won't eat you."

His fingers were strong, even through the thickness of my coat—and it wasn't fair of him to suggest I was afraid.

"I know you won't," I said, trying to shake him off as I switched the bag to my other hand.

"Then why not have dinner with me? Don't you want to?"

Well, yes. I did want to. For one thing, David was unlikely to feed me tinned spaghetti for the third boring day in a row.

"I don't have anything to wear," I said, making a last-ditch attempt at resistance.

"If only that were true..." murmured David with a leer in his voice.

It was such an exaggerated, comical leer that I laughed and gave in at once—as I'd wanted to all along. David was no Casanova I rationalized. He wouldn't let Posy down. And anyway, why should I worry about Posy? In all the years I'd known her, she had never once worried about my feelings.

"All right," I agreed. "But not anywhere fancy. I really don't have much to wear."

"There's a pub over on the North Bank that does a very decent line in fish 'n chips. Would that suit you?"

I nodded. "Perfectly. Can you wait a minute while I change?"

He tilted his head, and I knew he was waiting for me to ask him in. I blinked and pretended not to understand. How could I explain that the thought of his privileged nose elevating itself over the disagreeable odours routinely erupting from the Carmody basement was a prospect I just couldn't face?

"I'll wait in the car," he said politely, when the expected invitation wasn't offered.

"Yes. I won't be a moment." I hurried inside feeling like Cinderella just before the ball—except that I was missing a fairy godmother, and the only available prince—well, he wasn't. He was Posy's fiancè.

Lacking the necessary magic, I changed into a neatly cut grey dress, which I hoped would do for David's pub, and decided against fussing with my face. From bitter experience I knew that the moment I succeeded in covering a spot on my chin, three bigger ones would pop up on my nose. Better to leave well enough alone.

David didn't comment on my appearance when I joined him a few minutes later, but his smile was approving, and when he opened the passenger door and waved me in, I took my seat with a confidence that came from knowing I looked nice.

Traffic that evening was light, and about twenty minutes later we pulled up in front of a squat, white building set in the centre of a small garden on the North Bank of the Thames. Fog was creeping up from the river as we walked towards the heavy, oak doors, and the sound of waves lapping at stone had a timelessness about it that made me sad. I wondered what had first brought David here. Crouched in this forgotten corner, it wasn't a place he would have come upon by accident.

The atmosphere inside the pub was in total contrast to its Victorian exterior. Light and laughter and the smell of familiar English food greeted us as we stepped through the door. Immediately, and in spite of the uncurtained windows and chrome chairs that turned out to be more comfortable than they looked, I felt at home.

"This doesn't seem like your sort of place," I said, after David found us a table near one of the bare windows.

"Oh? And what is my sort of place?"

"Big old fireplaces, genuine oak beams, lots of faded antiques and discreet waiters bowing over engraved silver trays."

"Good heavens. Where did that come from?"

"I've no idea," I admitted.

His smile was polite but a little pained, and I gave a nervous laugh, wishing I'd kept my mouth shut. David looked at the menu and said, "Actually, I'm more interested in good food. I've been coming here off and on for years."

"Oh, I didn't mean to sound—"

"Snobbish?" he suggested quietly.

I closed my hand round a serviceable glass salt shaker, determined not to let him see he'd scored a hit. "I don't think I'm that. But people do seem to fall into a certain way of doing things without ever thinking much about it."

"Do they?"

"Of course, they do. For instance, everyone at Chantersley—well, everyone except Allison Campbell—votes Conservative. Or they will once they get the chance to vote. And they all think saying 'pleased to meet you,' or 'pardon,' is a mortal sin."

David grinned and leaned back in his chair. He was very long as well as rather big, and he had lovely ocean-grey eyes.

"And you? What do you think?" he asked.

"About what?"

Somebody behind the bar dropped a tray and swore with predictable triteness. When the catcalls and the noise quieted down, David said, "About voting and saying 'pleased to meet you.'"

"Oh. I'm not sure about voting. But I don't say 'pleased to meet you.'"

"I know. And would you think it awful if I did?"

"No. But you wouldn't." I twisted sideways to avoid the interested gaze of a beefy man at the next table. "Arabella does, though. And Carlo. They live—lived in my digs."

"I see." David looked amused and said he was off to order our fish 'n chips. When he came back, the man at the next table was still staring at me. I put my hand up to my nose to see if I'd developed a new spot. David moved his chair to block the view and handed me a glass of white wine I didn't really want. He'd ordered beer for himself, not the gentlemanly gin I'd expected.

"Is Carlo the boyfriend?" he asked.

So he had believed me, but hadn't cared. "He was," I said. "Not anymore."

"Do you mind?"

The question startled me. *Did I mind?* I had returned from Willbury expecting to be haunted by Carlo—to wake in the night, alone in my bed except for Teddy, and feel emptiness. And sometimes I did, particularly when I heard suggestive grunts and giggles pulsing from the suite down below. But the feeling of aching betrayal had gone—had become something very much like indifference.

"No," I said. "I don't think I do much."

"That's good."

"Why do you say that?"

He shrugged. "I've been in love—or lust—a few times. It can hurt when it comes to an end. I'm glad that didn't happen to you."

"Why did you invite me?" I asked, studying the liquid in my glass as if I knew something about wine.

"I told you, because I was at a loose end. I also thought this might be my chance to get to know you."

"Why should you want to know me?"

He swallowed a healthy mouthful of beer, then fixed his gaze on a point behind my head. "You're Posy's friend."

"Yes?" I wasn't, but there was no need to say so.

David took another gulp of beer and laid his glass carefully over a wet spot on the table. "There are things about her I don't seem to understand."

He wasn't the only one. "I see," I said. "So you thought we could talk about Posy—since you can't be with her tonight."

What a charming prospect. An evening spent discussing the Bantley-Brown. But then what else had I expected besides a break from eating tinned spaghetti?

"If you want to put it that way, yes." David gave me an apologetic grimace. "You seem to be the only friend she has."

"Not really." I tried to be non-committal. It didn't seem a good time to tell him what I really thought of his fiancèe."

"Sometimes she seems very—unsure of herself," David said.

"Does she?" Posy, secure in her own little bubble of self-centredness, unsure of herself? I blinked, then remembered our surprising conversation at the Beeches and decided David could, just possibly, be right.

"Mm." He strummed his fingers on the table, realized what he was doing and stopped abruptly. "She does. Almost as if she's afraid to let her guard down in case I discover what's behind it.

"And what do you think is behind it?" I could have told him there wasn't much, but I didn't.

"Sometimes I'm not at all sure. What was she like at school? Not Shirley Temple, I suspect."

"No. Lucretia Borgia."

He smiled. "A much maligned lady, I think."

"There you are then." I spoke a shade more tartly than I'd intended.

David frowned, first at me, then into his beer. "Sorry. You don't want to talk about her, do you?"

Brilliant deduction. "I don't mind," I said untruthfully. "But you're the one who's engaged to her. You really ought to know what she's like."

"I know she wants to marry me." He wrapped his hands around his tankard and stared into the rich dark brew. "The thing is, sometimes I get the feeling I make her nervous."

If he was right, then Posy was even more of a dimwit than I'd thought. There was nothing remotely threatening about David.

"What gives you that idea?" I asked.

David went on investigating his beer as if he expected it to yield up inspiration. I wondered if I was imagining that the tips of his ears had turned red. "Nothing specific. It's just a feeling I have." He was silent for a while, but when he raised his head, my suspicions were confirmed. His skin was the colour of self-conscious brick.

"Perhaps she's afraid of getting carried away," I suggested airily. Before Carlo, I would never have dared to suggest anything so personal.

"Perhaps. That's not the impression I get."

I wondered what impression he did get.

"Then maybe she's afraid you'll get carried away and not want to marry her afterwards." I didn't believe that for a moment. Posy was just being herself. Making other people squirm was her specialty.

David looked fierce, and I thrust my chin out defensively.

"I'm not that kind of lowlife," he snapped.

"No, of course not." I thought again of the conversation I'd had with Posy in her frilly pink bedroom at The Beeches. I had decided then that in spite of, or perhaps because of, her prurient fascination with sex, she was as scared of it as I'd been before Carlo.

Of course, David hadn't actually said he was talking about sex. But what else would make him go all hot and bothered and bear-like? Anyway, it wasn't up to me to explain Posy, and I was tired of discussing her. I responded to his scowl with what I hoped was a nonchalant smile. "Look," I said, "if you're asking my advice on the seduction of Posy B-B...."

"I'm not."

"Oh."

Our fish 'n chips arrived at that moment, cutting me off before I could put my foot in any deeper. Saved by a halibut! I suppressed a giggle and, seizing the vinegar, began to sprinkle wildly, inhaling the fumes until my eyes began to water. If I kept quiet, maybe my remark would pass without further comment.

It didn't.

As I stared through the window into the bank of fog rolling up from the river, David made a crooked attempt at a tension-easing smile, "Listen," he said, "there's no sense in our sniping at each other."

"Of course, there isn't." I popped a morsel of lightly battered cod between my teeth.

"I'm glad you agree." Again he drummed his fingers on the table. I waited, and after a pause he said, "Just so you know, I wasn't asking your advice on seduction. That's not what I have in mind at the moment."

"Good. I don't think Posy would like it."

David picked up his knife looking poker-faced. "No. I doubt if she would."

He didn't say any more, and for a while I had the disturbing feeling he'd forgotten I was there. His big fist lay curled beside his plate, and when someone bumped into my chair and apologized, without thinking much about it, I reached across the table to lay my hand over his.

His flesh was warm, firm, but I pulled back at once when I felt the skin tighten across his knuckles.

"Why don't you ask Posy how she feels?" I suggested.

"I did," he said gloomily. "If she'd had a fan, I think she'd have fluttered it in my face."

"Oh." I tried not to choke on my wine. Posy had a talent for playing the Victorian miss when it suited her.

David shifted some chips around his plate, but he didn't eat them. "There's something very elusive about my Posy," he said. The wry affection with which he spoke confused me. I honestly hadn't thought he liked Posy much.

"Elusive? Posy?" I exclaimed. Then, seeing his shoulders stiffen, I amended hastily, "I don't think that's quite the right word."

"Perhaps not." He met my eyes and suddenly he smiled. "Look, I'm sorry. I don't expect you to solve my problems for me. I'm not even sure they are problems. It's just that I know women talk to each other—"

"Yes, of course we do. So do men, I expect. But the nice ones don't go around telling other people what they've talked about."

"Ouch." David made a face that made me want to laugh. "That puts me in my place."

"I didn't exactly mean it that way."

"Didn't you? You're probably right just the same."

"I wish I could help," I said impulsively. He was being nice again, and I really hadn't meant to snap.

"I know you do."

It was more than I knew myself. I liked David, but for the life of me I couldn't understand what had drawn him to Posy. He was a modern man with modern attitudes. He was also attractive, intelligent and generally self-assured. So how could he be even remotely smitten with a childish, self-centred creature like Posy—who was currently reclining on a sofa being fragile?

No one had ever permitted me to be fragile. Dreamy, yes. Solitary, often. But never fragile. Mother didn't believe in fragile. Dad didn't know it existed.

"Penny for them," David said.

"Oh, I was just thinking."

"About what?"

I fidgeted with a chip. "About you and Posy."

"But you'd rather think about something else?"

"Maybe."

"All right. Let's talk about you."

"Oh, there's nothing very fascinating about me." I affected a sudden busyness with a thin slice of lemon on my plate.

"Nonsense." David leaned forward. "Is the fellow at the next table still leering at you?"

I had to smile. David was good for the ego when he chose to be. "No, he left. I think he got tired of looking at your back."

"Good. Now tell me about Janey Blackman. How many hearts have you broken?"

I giggled. He didn't mean it, of course, but that kind of teasing I could take. "None," I said. "Although, I used to be madly in love with the waiter in the coffee bar on High Street. I wouldn't have minded breaking his heart."

"But you didn't?"

"No. He never noticed me. I used to go there with my friend, Allison, and some of the girls from school. I'd sit there, speechless, wearing a smile and my best olive-green dress."

I didn't add that Posy had said the dress made me look like an aubergine that had been left to ripen too long in the sun. Or that my mother said the waiter absolutely wouldn't do.

"With me it was our au pair," David said, smiling. "She was French. Totally unsuitable, according to Mother."

Was he psychic? "We have something in common then," I said.

"Mm. What else, I wonder? Where were you born? What do you do when you're not working? And what do like to do when you go out?"

"All that? Are you sure you're not a frustrated private eye?" I couldn't have said that to Carlo. With David it seemed natural to tease.

"Positive. I'm quite content with my choice of careers. But we weren't going to talk about me." He laid his napkin on the table and sat back. "So where were you born?"

"Willbury," I answered self-consciously. "In the Hepzibah Crump Private Hospital. It's a general hospital now."

David chuckled obligingly, and as the eerie sound of foghorns competed with laughter and the cheerful chink of glass, I found myself telling him more. That I had no serious hobbies beyond reading, although I dreamed of one day writing stories myself, that I liked most kinds of music but had never actually danced with a man, and that when I went out, it had usually been to films with my parents.

"What about plays?" David asked.

"Only the pantomime at Christmas. And occasionally the Willbury Rep."

"A postively deprived childhood." He smiled to show he didn't mean it and made a show of glancing at his watch. "It's too late to take in a play. Want to go dancing?"

His mouth curved so attractively that I had a ridiculous and unnerving urge to touch it. Yes, I wanted to go dancing. Very much. But we couldn't.

"No, thank you." I shook my head. "It wouldn't be fair to Posy."

"She wouldn't mind."

Did he really know so little about the woman he planned to live with for the rest of his life? "She'd mind," I assured him. "So would I."

He shrugged. "Okay, then we won't. Would you like coffee?"

An unworthy hope that he might attempt to change my mind about the dancing died a speedy death. "Thank you," I said.

As soon as we finished the coffee, which tasted bitter, I told him I had to get home.

"All right." He put down his cup. "Whatever you say."

Did he have to be so damned obliging? Didn't he know I wanted the evening to go on? As we worked our way around the noisy groups of drinkers crowded between the door and us, I wondered if I looked as irritable as I felt.

David's breath was warm on my neck, stirring my hair as he helped me into my coat.

We skirted a clutch of giggling girls with over-teased hair and walked out into the fog.

"Brr," I said. "It's cold. Spooky."

"Mm." David paused by a low stone wall above the riverbank. Not so much as a glimmer of light penetrated the gloom, and the clammy air smelled faintly of decay. "A splendid night for murder," he said, and put his hand on the back of my neck.

"Don't!" I gave a little shriek and leaped away. The atmosphere was too sinister for jokes.

David laughed softly. "Don't worry. I'm no Jack the Ripper."

I peered at him through the murk. He looked different somehow, taller and less approachable. An illusion created by the fog? "I didn't think you were," I said. "Can we go now?"

"Of course." He took my arm, and when I jumped like a nervous grasshopper, he bent down and peered into my face. I don't know what he saw there, but whatever it was made him frown. "My car's this way," he said, turning me around.

"How did you know I have no sense of—of direction?" I found myself puzzlingly short of breath.

"From the blank bewilderment in your eyes." His voice was dry, not altogether amused. I wondered what had caused him to frown.

He drove slowly through the fog-shrouded streets, concentrating on the road and paying no attention to me. When we reached Wrenbert Terrace he didn't linger, but saw me quickly to the door and said goodnight.

"Goodnight—and thank you," I replied. "It's been a lovely evening. I hope Posy's feeling better tomorrow."

"I'll tell her you sent your sympathies." He waited while I fumbled with my key.

"Yes. Do that." So he did mean to tell Posy we'd spent the evening together. Whatever had made me think he wouldn't?

I didn't look to see if he was watching as I stepped inside and closed the door.

That night I stayed awake for a long time hugging my old teddy bear to my chest. The attic was colder than usual, but it wasn't the cold that kept sleep at bay. I tossed restlessly, twisting the sheets until they were wound around my torso like swaddling bands. It was a good thing Carlo wasn't with me. My tossing would have made him bad tempered. Teddy didn't care. He didn't snore either.

Where was Carlo tonight? I wondered for a while, then decided it didn't matter anymore.

As dawn began to push away the night, I fell asleep. The following morning I was late for work.

Mr. Reid wasn't pleased. "I pay you to get here on time," he snapped, glaring at me over the counter.

Oh. So that was to be our mood today. When I'd first started working for him he'd been predictable—as in permanently grouchy and godlike. Then he'd changed and become almost human after he told me about his lost wife and child. Now—in fact ever since I'd returned from my visit to Willbury—I never knew what to expect.

I closed the door on lingering wisps of fog and started to unbutton my coat.

"Keep it on," growled Mr. Reid.

"Oh. Am I sacked again?" There wasn't much point in protesting, and anyway, I was too tired to care.

He beetled his eyebrows at me. "No. Take this cheque over to Suiter's. Our credit's run out. Maybe the fresh air will wake you up." He handed me a creased brown envelope.

So that was to be my punishment. He knew the air was anything but fresh and that it was a miserable morning to be outside. I took the cheque silently, no longer in any doubt as to the cause of his bad temper. One of our wholesalers was actually forcing him to pay up.

Suitor's was a short bus ride away—or a long walk. But the buses would be crowded today.

I chose the walk.

As I slouched past Perilous Pages, keeping as close to the wall as I could, the door flew open and a hand shot out to grab me by the arm.

"Hey," I protested, recognizing the hand even before I saw its owner's face. "Colin, you've got the wrong woman. I'm not June."

"I know. Come in for a minute."

"I can't. God's being godlike again. He's probably timing me."

"All right, I'll fix it with Her Nibs and take a tea break. Hold on."

He disappeared into the shop and a few seconds later re-emerged wearing a raincoat several sizes too big for him.

"What's the matter?" I asked, as he followed me round the corner onto Charing Cross Road. "You look frazzled." I didn't add that the raincoat made him look like a flasher.

"It's June," he said bleakly.

I couldn't resist it. "No, it's not. It's October."

Colin sighed. "Very funny. Janey, she's pregnant."

"What!" I stared at our twisted reflections in the window of a shop that sold music. Colin's face was grey, and I conquered an impulse to burst into, 'June Is Bustin' Out All Over.' "Congratulations," I said instead.

Colin kicked at a discarded newspaper in the gutter. "It's not mine. The baby's not mine."

I closed my eyes and tripped over a crack in the pavement. "Are you sure? Did she tell you that?"

"No. But if it was mine, she couldn't be sure yet. And she says she is."

"Oh Colin, no. How beastly for you. I am sorry." Poor Colin. After all his dreaming and panting after June, imagine it ending up like this. Now I knew why I'd never much cared for his June. "So you've broken off with her," I said.

Colin, looking sick, shook his head. "No. I think I'm going to marry her. She says she wants to. The thing is..." He stopped, and I wondered what was coming next. "The thing is—do you think I ought to tell her I know? That the baby isn't mine?"

"Colin, yes." There wasn't the remotest question in my mind. "Yes, of course you must tell her."

"Do you think so?"

"You have to tell her," I repeated urgently. "The child has a right to know too."

Colin looked at me strangely. "Yes, I suppose you're right—"

"I am. Believe me. Don't even think of leaving her in the dark." As we started walking again, I asked, "Do you know who the father is?"

"Her old boyfriend." He put his hands in his pockets and hunched his shoulders. "Carlo somebody. I think he must have scarpered the moment he found out she was pregnant. That's probably why she took up with me."

"Carlo somebody?" I narrowly missed colliding with a street lamp.

"Borelli, Bozelli. Something like that. It doesn't matter. He's out of the picture."

Wasn't he though? The long column of the street lamp seemed to waver. It's colour changed from silver to gunmetal grey. Only when it shuddered and returned to normal was I able to carry on up the street, faster than before, with my hands bunched into fists inside my pockets. Colin hurried after me, unaware of the effect his words had.

"When, exactly, did he disappear?" I asked, slowing down to very small steps and carefully avoiding any cracks.

"About three weeks ago, I think. A day or so before June asked me out."

It could fit. It did fit. That was why Carlo had left. It had nothing to do with me. Probably June had been his girlfriend all along, and those nights he'd spent with me were just a side dish. There hadn't been many of them. And of course, that day I went down to The Beeches, June must have told him about the baby. Yes. That had to be it. He'd been mean and angry that night because he was already planning his escape. It all made sense, right from the beginning when Carlo had helped me find my job. He'd seen Mr. Reid's notice when he'd passed the shop on his way to meet June.

Damn Carlo, I thought viciously. *Damn him to hell*—which was undoubtedly where he was headed. I hoped Satan had a toothache the day he arrived and was feeling extra generous with the coals.

"There's no need to cry over me." Colin's glum voice broke into my thoughts. "I think I'll take your advice and tell June I know the baby isn't mine. She doesn't love me, but maybe she will given time."

Colin had always been an optimist.

"I'm not crying over you," I assured him, brushing a sleeve across my face. "This wretched fog is making my eyes smart. Colin, shouldn't you be getting back to work?"

"I suppose so. Are you sure you're all right?" He frowned, wanting to believe me but not convinced.

"Of course, I'm sure. Don't worry about me. And try not to worry about June. It's bound to work out all right."

I put my hand on his arm to show I meant it, even though I thought everything would probably work out all wrong. Poor, besotted Colin, who deserved so much better than flashy, blonde June. I watched him as he slouched off back to work.

~*~

Three weeks had passed, and all the fallen leaves had become soggy brown heaps in the gutters before I became aware of the possibility that June and I might have more than a brief fling with Carlo in common.

I was alone in the kitchen at the time, picking at a mess of overcooked rice mixed with beans. My stomach heaved, and for a few seconds, I thought I was going to be sick.

The feeling passed, but the dawning of revelation didn't. I had felt sick the last three mornings too.

Panic-stricken, I began to count weeks on my fingers.

Arabella, wearing a skimpy black lace petticoat, came hurtling down the stairs when she heard me scream.

CHAPTER SEVEN

"Janey? Janey, what's happened?" Arabella skidded to a stop still clutching an open tube of lipstick. Her lower lip was white and invisible, her upper one a glossy, pillar-box red that looked as if it had been painted on by a child with an unsteady hand.

"Janey?" she repeated, the panic in her eyes narrowing to suspicion when she saw I was neither bleeding nor being murdered. "Did you see a mouse? Is that why you screamed?"

"No," I groaned. "I wish I had. I'd know how to cope with a mouse."

A mouse wouldn't need me to feed it, burp it, clothe it and protect it. I quite liked mice.

Arabella looked at me as if she thought I'd lost a few crucial connectors in my brain.

"It's..." I hesitated. Should I tell her why I'd screamed? I might be wrong, after all. I'd never been very good at math. But what if I wasn't wrong? What if my calculations were dead-on? Then Arabella would know what to do. She was that sort of person.

"I think I might be pregnant," I mumbled, fixing my eye on a particularly tough-looking bean.

"Christ!" Arabella leaned across the table, and a mixture of powder and Rose of Eden wafted up my nose. "Don't you know enough to avoid that?"

"I didn't." I pushed away my tepid rice and beans. "Carlo said he'd taken care of it."

"For God's sake, Janey, you must have known—"

"Yes, yes I did. I mean he did. But I'm not entirely sure about the last night we—well, you know. The one before he vanished."

Things had happened too fast that night. Carlo had been different, less careful, completely caught up in his own needs.

"Bloody bastard," Arabella said. "He knew he was leaving, didn't he? Must've done."

"I suppose so." Yes, Carlo had known. Damn him.

"Right." Arabella hitched up the strap of her petticoat. "First thing to do then is make sure."

"But how?"

Arabella looked at me as if she didn't believe anyone could be so ignorant.

"Don't you have a doctor?" she asked.

"Yes, but I couldn't go to Dr Preston. He's known me all my life."

"Better try the clinic then. What time is it?" She picked up my wrist and peered down at my watch. Her hand felt cold, but she seemed oblivious to her state of undress. "Hm. Too late. You'll have to wait till tomorrow."

"Tomorrow! But—?"

"Won't make no difference now. You got nine months to worry about it if you are." She shrugged. "'Less you decide not to have it."

"Oh, I couldn't do that." I was shocked. Which was odd, come to think of it. I had never particularly liked babies, yet I seemed not to approve of doing away with them. Mother must once have felt the same, or I wouldn't be here. I cast a despairing glance at the green felt skirt flared across my stomach.

"You couldn't?" Arabella was predictably matter-of-fact. "More fool you."

"Arabella!"

"Don't Arabella me, Janey Blackman. Smartest thing you could do."

I felt my eyes begin to sting with useless tears. Arabella saw me blinking and said brusquely, "Don't worry. You could be late for all kinds of reasons. Here, have a cup of tea. That'll make you feel better."

Exactly what Mother would have said. In her view, tea was the answer to any problem less serious than colliding planets. But I didn't see how even the best Ceylon could help me now. I wasn't sure anything could.

Arabella went to fill the kettle while I slumped despairingly over the table wondering if the smell drifting up from the basement meant Mrs. Carmody was trying a new brand of cigarettes or merely cremating her dinner.

The front door banged. Footsteps sounded on the stairs, slowed, came to a stop by the open door.

"Blimey," said a man's strangled voice.

I looked up. Nat King Cole, whom I'd discovered was actually called Zachary Njenga, was standing in the doorway with his gaze riveted on Arabella's black lace back.

"Oh," said Arabella, swinging round. "Sorry. Don't mind me. Bit of an emergency, it was."

"No need to be sorry." Zachary rubbed a fist across his nose and made a supreme effort to shift his gaze from her scantily clad body. "What happened to your mouth?" he asked when he finally noticed her face. "Been drinking Duncan's blood again, have you?"

Arabella's hand went to her lips. She giggled. "I was interrupted in the middle of putting on my lipstick," she explained, wrinkling her nose at him.

"Ah." Zachary nodded. "Okay, if that's your story..." He turned away, grinning, and went whistling off up the stairs.

Arabella laughed. "He's all right, that one. For one of them," she added, remembering just in time that she was in the habit of regarding 'them' with suspicion. "Good thing Duncan wasn't here."

I thought so too. Duncan took a dim view of other men ogling his wife even when she had all her clothes on. Most of their fights were about her modelling job, which was a bit unfair considering she'd been doing it since long before they'd met. She insisted it was an expression of her repressed artistic nature.

"There now," she said, dumping a cracked white teacup in front of me. "That should settle you."

If only it would. I gazed bleakly at the cup and tried not to think about what was going to happen to me nine months from now. My mother and I could conceivably give birth at the same time. The thought was almost obscene. Conquering a hysterical urge to laugh, I swallowed several mouthfuls of strong tea and, to my amazement, actually felt better.

After a while Arabella patted me on the shoulder, told me not to worry, and went back up to her flat. I linked my arms on the table, laid my head on them and stayed that way until Mrs. Carmody stamped in and snapped off the light.

After that I sat in the dark and thought about Mother and John Marlowe. I understood them now, as I hadn't even tried to understand before. But unlike Mother, and unlike June Gunderson, I had no devoted swain waiting in the wings to pick up the pieces of my life.

A long drawn out howl from across the road made me lift my head. The neighbours' mongrel must have got itself locked out again. I felt like howling too. How long did it take to get the results of a pregnancy test? What would I do if...? No, I didn't want to think about that. Except that it was impossible not to. I pressed my back against the chair and ran my hands over the flatness of my stomach. Would it soon be round and swollen like the pale moon hanging outside the window?

From upstairs I heard Duncan growl one of his more inventive obscenities. Arabella swore back. When their footsteps passed the kitchen door, I guessed they were on their way to the pub--which meant I was in for another disturbed night, not that it made a difference.

The moon disappeared behind a cloud, leaving the room almost pitch black. What would it be like to have a baby? Painful? Frightening? They said it often took forever the first time....

"Please, God, don't let it happen," I whispered. "Please. I'll never do it again."

No answer came, as I had known it wouldn't, and I went on sitting in the shadows while the palms of my hands went damp with fear.

~*~

"Hello, Janey. You look as white as I did when I had the flu. But of course, I was much too poorly to go to work."

I looked up from rearranging a table of books that Mr. Reid had decided to put on sale because they hadn't inspired anyone to buy them.

Posy stood in the doorway looking expensive in a smart black mohair coat and just a shade too much makeup. She was smiling the pleased smile she always wore when she knew she outclassed the competition. Not that I was much competition. She was right about my appearance, and I didn't care. Posy was trouble I could do without today.

I had just phoned the clinic. They said they were sorry, but there had been a delay and my results might not be back until Monday.

Today was Friday.

"I haven't got the flu," I told her. "Posy, Mr. Reid doesn't like me talking to friends, so—"

"Oh, don't worry." Posy was indifferent to the demands of a job that wasn't hers. "I won't keep you. I just popped in to invite you over to David's flat."

"Me? Why? When?"

"This evening. For drinks. It'll make a nice change for you."

It would? "Thank you," I said, "but—"

"Oh, don't say no. You must come," she gushed, in her best Lady Bountiful voice. "It will do you good to get out."

I didn't see why, and said so.

"Janey, you're so self-effacing. You know, you'd really be quite pretty if you wore better clothes and made some sort of effort with your face."

"I was born with my face," I said. She would have been laughable if I'd been in any mood for laughter.

"I was only trying to give you a little helpful advice." Posy lifted an offended shoulder and touched a kid-gloved hand to one of the sale books. She withdrew it hastily when it raised a small swirl of dust. "If you learned how to put on makeup—"

"I haven't time."

"Dear me. You must be busy." Her smile was reproachfully sweet. "But not too busy to come out this evening, I hope. Don't tell me you have other plans."

I started to say I had, but she cut me off, saying archly, "You can bring your boyfriend if you like."

It was painfully clear that Posy couldn't imagine plain Janey Blackman having plans more important than her own. And I hadn't, of course, except to spend another dreary evening staring at dirty walls, unable to concentrate on reading or anything else because all rational thought was blocked out by the terrifying reality of the future.

"No," I said, squeezing another book onto the sale table. "No, I don't have other plans." I didn't tell her I didn't have a boyfriend either.

"Good." She beamed. "David's flat's in Knightsbridge. Do you think you can find it?"

"I found Harrods once," I said. "Can you give me directions?"

She did, although she was confused about bus routes, explaining that she usually took taxis.

Surprise, surprise. I didn't.

When a rumbling noise from the back office presaged the imminent emergence of my boss, Posy waved a hasty goodbye and departed.

Mr. Reid, munching orange cake, watched the door close and said mildly, "Entertaining again, Jane?"

I made a show of lining up the books. He'd been in a good mood earlier, but he never called me Jane, and I didn't feel the informality augered well. "No," I said. "She just dropped in to deliver a message."

"I see. Busy social life you lead." Several crumbs fell on the table.

"Not really." I flicked them onto the floor.

"Hm." He put a hand on my shoulder. "No boyfriend then?"

"No. Not anymore." I squirmed, and he let his hand drop.

"I see. You and I have a similar problem then."

"Maybe." I couldn't see that there was much similarity between the problems of a fiftyish widower and a nineteen-year-old possible-mother-of-one. But there was a sad, hungry look in his eyes and I didn't want to hurt his feelings.

"Ah." He caught my hesitation at once. "I was forgetting. You're too young to be lonely, aren't you?"

Did he think only the old could understand what it was like to feel alone? "No. I feel lonely sometimes," I admitted. *What was he getting at?*

"So do I, so do I." His extended sigh was accompanied by a burp.

"You should marry again," I said on an impulse. He didn't answer at once, and I lowered my head and busied myself with the books. Who was I to give advice to poor Mr. Reid, who had woken up one morning married and a father and gone to bed that same night with no wife, no child—nothing but a musty old bookshop and bills?

I had never lost anyone but Aunt Hilda, who had been nice enough but didn't really matter except to Dad.

"I used to think about remarrying at one time," Mr. Reid said, not telling me to mind my own business as I'd half expected. He moistened his lips with a tongue that was startlingly pink in contrast to the grey in his beard. "Decided against it in the end."

I said, "Oh," and dropped a book onto the floor.

As I bent to retrieve it, a young woman in a mud-brown tweed suit strolled in.

"I'm looking for something uplifting for my mother," she announced, in one of those unnecessarily loud voices that always made me want to say, "Ssh."

By this time I was feeling slightly punch-drunk and was tempted to suggest a new bra.

Luckily, Mr. Reid stepped in front of me and took over.

By the time the woman left, clutching several works of saccharine uplift, the hands of my watch were on closing time. I hurried to put on my coat in case Mr. Reid wanted to continue our earlier conversation, which I had found not only personal, but peculiar.

"Well, Jane?" He came up behind me as I pushed my arm into a sleeve. "What do you say to a bite of supper?"

"Um—supper?" I paused with the coat trailing on the floor. What was this? He'd never offered me supper in the past--or anything else that would cost him money.

"Yes. Would you...? Harrumph. Care to join me?"

Join him? Did that mean I'd be paying for my own meal? Even if it didn't, my instincts told me that accepting his offer would not be a bright thing to do. I searched for a way out and found it at once.

"Thank you, but I'm having supper with my friend. That's why she came in." I smiled at him to soften the refusal. As I struggled to find the other sleeve, my coat dropped onto the floor.

Mr. Reid picked it up. His knees cracked as he drew himself upright. "Another time then. I could do with a bit of company for a change."

I didn't answer, but he was holding out my coat, so I took it and tried to edge past him. He put a hand on the counter to block my escape.

Oh, Lord. What now? I didn't want to have supper with him—not tonight or any other night. It wasn't that I didn't like him. In a way, I was sorry for him. But his skin was flabby wherever it showed, he had a slight paunch, and more often than not there were cake crumbs trapped in his beard.

"Excuse me," I said.

He didn't move. "We get along all right, don't we, Jane?"

"Yes, of course we do." I glanced hopefully at the door. "Mr. Reid ...?"

His eyes brightened. "Yes, my dear?"

His dear? Oh, God. "I do have to go home now," I said.

He nodded, and I knew he was disappointed. "Think about what I said, won't you, Jane?"

What had he said exactly? "Yes, I'll think about it," I agreed, taking care not to meet his eyes.

"Good girl."

I ducked under his arm and made a dash for the door.

"Goodnight," I called, as the cold November air hit my face.

Behind me Mr. Reid shouted, "Just a minute, Jane, there's no need...."

I didn't hear any more. Because there was a need, a desperate need to get away.

~*~

I found David's flat without difficulty. Posy had told me he occupied the bottom floor of a Victorian house that had been converted into what she called "elegant bachelor apartments." She must have got the phrase from her stepmother, who sometimes called people's houses "lovely homes."

I hesitated with my hand on the latch of a white, wrought-iron gate set into a laurel hedge. The square, brick house with the turrets looked terribly grand, even in the muted light from a street lamp. It loomed importantly over a long, narrow lawn that, despite the darkness, looked seamlessly weeded and trimmed. No cabbage or brussels sprouts here, I knew at once. No Mrs. Carmody either.

I stared, trying not to feel intimidated. David was kind, not intimidating, and the simple black dress that I'd bought on sale would surely be appropriate to the occasion. If I tried hard enough, I might even be able to enjoy myself and forget about babies and what life would be like as an unmarried mother.

A black cat stalked up the path swishing a feathery tail. A few seconds later, I felt the first gentle drops of rain on my bare head. Squaring my shoulders, I started after the cat. The gate swung shut behind me with a definite click.

I had only just reached the top of the steep steps leading to David's flat when the heavy front door was flung wide. Immediately, the cat picked up its pace, scurried in ahead of me, and disappeared.

"There you are, Janey!" exclaimed Posy. Her cheeks were pink and she sounded relieved. "I was beginning to think you'd got lost."

"I have a fairly good sense of direction," I said. It wasn't true, but there was no reason to let Princess Posy know that.

"Have you really? How clever of you. Do come in. Oh." She directed a slyly meaningful glance over my shoulder. "Where's the boyfriend?"

"I didn't invite him," I replied, stretching the truth.

"Janey, you are a spoilsport. I wanted to meet him," she pouted prettily.

I didn't respond, and after a moment she recovered from her pique and pulled me into a small hallway with a high, corniced ceiling. The sight of a crackling fire on the other side of open glass doors was infinitely cheering as Posy ushered me into what appeared to be David's sitting room. I looked around with curiosity, not sure what to expect of an art dealer's taste in furnishings, and saw that the walls were painted white and hung with a splendid array of Oriental porcelain. Above the fireplace, a magnificent bronze charger featured an owl that gleamed dully in the light from twin Chinese lamps.

At first, I thought the room was uninhabited. Then a low voice asked, "What was that about, Posy?" and a naked male body levered itself up to stare at me over the back of a crimson velvet sofa.

"Janey!" exclaimed David. "What the devil...?"

That should have been my line, I thought dazedly. I took several steps backwards. "Excuse me, I didn't realize..." I looked around at Posy, aghast. "You did say tonight, didn't you? I'm so sorry...."

"Oh, dear." Posy fluttered her hands. "Did I really say tonight? How silly of me." She turned to David, patting at her hair. "Darling, I hope you don't mind. One of us must have made a mistake. I meant to invite Janey for next week."

David said nothing, but when he made to stand up, I backed out into the hall.

He took an excruciatingly long time getting to his feet, but once he straightened I saw that he wasn't naked after all. Dark grey trousers held in place by a wide black belt clung smoothly and discreetly to his hips below the smooth, nearly hairless perfection of his chest.

Thank God. I closed my eyes.

"Posy, what are you talking about?" he asked. "We have no plans yet for next week."

Posy pursed her mouth into a bow.

David narrowed his eyes. "I get it. Janey's been recruited as a chaperone."

I looked from Posy's pink face to David's dark one. What was going on here? And why was I in the middle of it?

"Look," I said. "I'm sorry. I won't keep you. The mistake was very likely mine—"

"It very likely wasn't," David said. "And now that you're here, I think you'd better stay. Right, Posy?"

"Of course," Posy said. When David looked at her as if he were contemplating frying her for breakfast with extra salt and pepper, she giggled and added, "Don't glare at me like that, darling. You'll frighten Janey."

"No, I won't." David turned away to pick up a shirt that was slung over the back of an ebony chair with claws on the ends of its arms. "Janey doesn't frighten that easily." He shrugged the shirt on but didn't bother to do up the buttons.

"She used to," Posy said, just the faintest of frowns creasing her perfectly powdered forehead. "Janey, where are you going?"

"Home. And you're right. I used to frighten, but I don't anymore."

Not true. I touched a hand to my comfortingly flat stomach, seeking reassurance. I was deathly scared at this moment, not of Posy, but of the faceless lump that might have taken up residence in my womb.

"Sorry if I interrupted something," I muttered as I made for the door.

"You didn't," David said shortly. "Not a chance. Take your coat off, Janey."

"No, really. Thank you..." I didn't want to take my coat off. I wanted to escape from a situation that was none of my making, but which made me feel about as welcome as coffee at a tea-tasting party.

David moved around the sofa to block my retreat. He started unbuttoning my coat. "It's the least we can do," he said, "after dragging you all the way here."

"It doesn't matter. It's not far. Really." I tried to stop him unbuttoning, and the moment our fingers became entangled, he drew back without any urging.

"Of course, it matters. What can I get you to drink?"

"Nothing, honestly. I'm fine."

David rolled his eyes at the ceiling. "Come on. Don't be difficult. It's pouring with rain out there. Now take your coat off and stay."

I wasn't proof against that sort of coercion. Not when it came from David and was accompanied by his smile. So I did as he said and allowed him to help me off with my coat. He threw it over the back of the sofa and, taking my elbow, led me to an armchair by the fire. "Sit," he ordered.

I sat. There didn't seem much else to do.

He crossed to a mahogany sideboard and produced glasses and a selection of bottles. "Sherry?" he asked.

"All right. Thank you." What was the point in refusing? He would never let me go until he was satisfied he'd performed his hostly duties.

Posy, smiling innocuously, sat in the armchair across from me and crossed her legs. She was wearing cream-coloured trousers, a cream cashmere pullover and three, slim gold chains. She looked thinner than usual and rather glamorous. What on earth had she been up to, inviting me here without telling David? Although I no longer believed her every action was motivated by malice or spite, there seemed no way to interpret her invitation other than as another of her small, pointless unkindnesses.

Yet she had welcomed me with what I had been certain was genuine relief. It was very odd.

David handed both of us a sherry and stretched himself out on the sofa. "Apologize to Janey," he said to Posy. "That wasn't fair of you, miss."

"It was a mistake. Janey couldn't have—"

"You know damn well it wasn't Janey's fault."

Posy's lower lip trembled appealingly.

"It's all right. I expect we both made a mistake—" I broke off, because David was looking attractively volcanic, and I had a desperate need to scratch an itch on a private part of me. "Would you excuse me, please?" I stood up. "I have to—um—where's the...?"

"Through the door, down the passage, second on the right," said David.

"Thank you." I scuttled out into the hall.

David's bathroom was white and untidy. Two striped towels lay on the floor beneath the towel-rack, a tiled vanity was littered with books, art catalogues, combs, hair and a collection of razor blades. The bathtub sported an award-winning scum ring. It was obvious that David's love of beautiful things didn't extend to his bathroom. I wondered how Posy, who had complained about hair in the washbasins at school, would survive marriage to a man who used his bathroom as a tip. If he was as casual with his belongings in the bedroom, it was likely to be a battleground in more ways than one.

I scratched my itch and felt better. Then I stared at my face in the soap-splattered mirror, saw a spot forming just below my nose and decided Posy might be right about the makeup. After that I wasted more time washing my hands and wrote my name in the soap on the mirror. Only when I could think of no further excuse to delay did I make my way back to the sitting room.

I was still too soon.

David's controlled voice reached me the moment I stepped into the hall.

" ...realize you were nervous. I understand that. Or at least I try to. But I've never attempted to go further than you want me to, and I've said from the beginning that I'm willing to wait until the honeymoon. There was no need to involve Janey just because you've never been to my flat by yourself." There was a pause, and I thought I heard him sigh. "I don't mean to frighten you, Posy, but we're getting married. Sooner or later you'll have to get used to—"

"I know. I know I will. Oh, David..." Posy started to cry. Soft, feminine little sobs that would have done credit to the Victorian miss he had once accused her of imitating.

I stood still, not sure what to do next.

David swore, gently but graphically.

"You shouldn't talk like that," Posy sniffed in between sobs.

"Sorry." Another loaded pause. "Posy, you do want to marry me, don't you?"

"Of course, I want to marry." The sobs tapered off. She sounded sulky now.

"Yes, but do you want to marry *me*?"

Posy made no answer to that, and I couldn't stay lurking in the hall any longer. They only had to look up to see me through the glass.

I pushed open the doors and went to sit by the fire, pretending not to notice the tension sizzling in the air. Posy was perched on the edge of her chair pouting and fidgeting with her neck chains. David was lying on the sofa with his eyes closed. He looked like a convalescent statue. The pose rather suited him, I thought.

Posy looked pleased to see me. "David's cross with me. You're not upset, are you Janey?"

"Of course not."

I wasn't. Anything that took my mind off my own troubles was all right with me, and in a way I was enjoying this understated drama.

For at least the tenth time, I wondered what had possessed David to ask her to marry him.

A spark flew out of the fireplace and landed on the hearth. As it turned slowly into ash, David said quietly, "Well?"

He wasn't talking to me.

"Of course, I want to marry you," Posy said. "I told you I did."

She sounded resentful. For the first time, I started to wonder why she had agreed to marry him.

When David said, "Good," and got up to leave the room, I asked her.

Posy blinked, as if I'd wondered why she bothered to eat. "One has to have a husband," she said.

In this day and age? Even I, who had spent most of my girlhood in a dreamworld, was aware that women didn't absolutely need a husband to have a life. And Posy had no worries about money.

"Why?" I asked.

"Janey! What an odd question. Don't you want to marry and have children?"

"You want children?" Had Posy any idea what she was getting into?

She smoothed the crease in her trousers. "Yes. I like babies. Don't you?"

No. No, I definitely didn't. At least not now, when I might not have a choice. But I couldn't tell Posy that.

"Not much," I said. "But if I did have one, I'd want—well, I'd want to be in love with its father." I had thought I was in love with Carlo.

"Oh, I am," Posy said, so dismissively that I didn't believe her. "David's devoted to me really, and I've never seen him lose his temper like some men." She preened a little. "Daddy's pleased I'll have someone to look after my interest in the shops once he's gone. David is handsome, isn't he, Janey?"

I nodded, speechless.

"And he's from the right sort of family too. One of his cousins is a baronet." She smiled, pleased with herself. "Imagine what those jealous cats at school would say if they could see me with David."

I could imagine. For once they really would be envious. But I didn't think wanting to inspire envy in one's school friends was a very good reason for spending a lifetime with a man you didn't love.

"David's exactly the sort of man I've always wanted," Posy insisted, as if guessing my thoughts. "Just think—I'll soon have a place of my own, away from Jasmine and Mummy. I'll be able to do all the things I want to do without them telling me I can't."

"Yes, but—what about David's wants? I mean you won't exactly be playing house, and if you're nervous about being alone with him—"

"Oh, that'll be all right once we're married." She dismissed this minor disadvantage with a wave of her hand, as if the two of them held divergent views on curtains. "You said so yourself. I'd just rather not do—well, you know, sex—until it's legal. And I'm sure David won't care about the house. He'll want me to do whatever I choose. Janey, it's going to be such fun. You must come and help me pick out material and things."

Why? So she could watch me turn green? In the old days there would have been no question. Now I wasn't sure. Something had changed, but I didn't know if it was Posy or me.

"If you like," I said.

David came back into the room with his shirt buttoned and tucked into his belt. I felt sorry for him, marrying a woman who saw him purely as an escape route— someone to take care of her affairs, give her a house to play with, provide a child or two perhaps, and beyond that let her have her own way.

Still, any man who couldn't see through Posy had only himself to blame if he allowed her to use him like that.

I reminded myself that it wasn't in any way my problem and told Posy I'd better be on my way.

"No, you'd better stay here," David said. "It's pouring out. You can have the second spare bedroom. You'd like that, wouldn't you, Posy?" His mouth looked a bit grim, but I thought he meant it.

"Oh, yes you must," Posy cried. "I'll go and see if everything's tidy."

She disappeared before I had time to come up with a suitable refusal.

"Saved by the bell," David said, lifting a small brass bell from the desk and shaking it briskly. "She's delighted."

"Don't you mind?" I asked. "I thought you wanted—"

"Posy?" He shrugged. "Of course, I want her. And pretty soon I'm going to have her." When I frowned, he said, "Oh, not until we're married. Don't worry, I'm treating her like delicate Limoges instead of the buxom wench she is. We'll work things out."

Because he seemed to have recovered his good humour, I didn't suggest that anyone who could work Posy out had to be a better psychologist than I was. But I thought it. Nor did I argue about staying. It was getting late, rain was besieging the windows, and I was tired. Fortunately, I always carried a toothbrush in my bag.

Shortly after Posy reappeared, I said goodnight.

The small, sparsely furnished bedroom Posy had prepared for me held a chest of drawers and a comfortable bed with a mattress that wasn't full of lumps. I had no nightdress, but pulled off my black dress and stockings and was asleep almost as soon as I lay down.

In the middle of the night I woke up feeling as if my head was about to burst. I switched on the lamp beside my bed. Three a.m. and the sherry had come back to haunt me. I still wasn't very good at drinking.

After lying still and holding onto my ears in a futile effort to stop the throbbing, I got up, yanked on my dress and went into the bathroom to search for aspirin. There didn't seem to be any, so I stumbled around until I found the kitchen, a shoe-box shaped room at the back of the house that was even more littered than the bathroom.

I was standing helplessly by the door, clutching my head and wondering where to start looking when I heard the sound of slippers slapping against tiles.

I jumped as warm hands closed around my waist.

"What...?" I gasped.

The hands urged me towards a white, oval table strewn with the remains of what looked like last week's lunch on leftover day.

"Better sit down," David said, depositing me unceremoniously in a chair.

He swept his arm across a pile of crumbs and removed something grey and slimy that had once, possibly, been a tea towel. Then he sat down across from me and asked, "What's the trouble, Janey? Anything I can do? You've been looking like a bleached turnip all evening."

I wanted to laugh, not only because he'd called me a bleached turnip, but because his hair was standing up in clumps that looked as though they badly needed mowing.

He looked so kind and comical and concerned that I burst into tears instead.

CHAPTER EIGHT

David was wearing an old grey pullover over trousers he had neglected to zip. I took that in the moment he stood up and began to run water into a grease-spattered kettle.

"I'll make you some tea," he said gruffly.

Did everyone imagine all my problems could be washed away on a great flood of tea?

I wiped the tears off my cheeks and said shakily, "Thank you." There was never any point in arguing with people who had their minds set on tea.

"What's the trouble?" he asked, when he'd finished squashing teabags to hasten the release of the problem-solving elixir. "I hope Posy—"

"No, no. It's not Posy." For once it wasn't.

"Then what is it? Or would you rather not say?" He thumped a gold-trimmed china mug in front of me and sat down looking wary, as if he wasn't sure how to handle tears.

I most certainly would rather not say. "I have a headache," I explained. "There doesn't seem to be any aspirin."

David got up, rummaged in a cupboard and handed me a bottle of pills. "Mother's contribution to my larder," he said. "She insisted I keep them on hand. I didn't see the point, but now I see she was right."

Mothers were right far too often. And it just wasn't possible I was going to be one. I took a frantic gulp of David's tea, sat up straight and tried to think positive thoughts along the lines of those promoted at Inspirational Books. It didn't work. I was still panic-stricken.

David gave me a fishy look, and I swallowed one of the pills. "Did I wake you?" I asked. "I am sorry."

"No, you didn't. Nefertiti did. Then I heard you falling over your feet in the hall."

Nefertiti? He couldn't mean Posy. Not even the most besotted lover could compare her blonde prettiness to that of the legendary queen. Besides, I didn't think David was that besotted.

"Who's Nefertiti?" I asked.

"The cat. She moved in two years ago and has so far ignored every inducement to depart."

He must mean the cat I'd glimpsed briefly last night. "Do you want her to leave?" I asked. "Was she a stray?"

"To answer your first question, yes, I did want her to leave—although I've long since given up hope. As for the second, I suppose you could call her a stray. She walked in one night out of the rain, settled herself on my bed and began washing. She's been performing her ablutions there ever since."

"Oh. And she woke you up?" I managed to produce a wan smile. This was a new side of David.

"Mm. Started sharpening her claws on my chest."

I winced. The thought of claw marks on that smooth, perfect surface made me shudder.

David frowned. "Don't you feel any better?"

"Oh, yes thank you," I lied, taking another quick sip of the tea.

"No, you don't."

He saw too much. "Then why ask?" I muttered.

"That's a good question."

"I know." I put my elbows on the table and pressed my fingertips to my forehead. I wanted to cry again. David actually seemed to care how I felt.

I sniffed, made an effort to snap out of my self-pity, and failed pathetically. How on earth was I going to survive the rest of this weekend? The not knowing was driving me wild.

"Janey?" David reached across the table and touched my hand.

I lifted my head. "What?"

"You're crying again."

So I was. "I can't help it," I said. "My head hurts. And—and I think I'm going to be sick."

I staggered to my feet as the sardines I'd had for supper threatened to reappear in all their lemon-soaked glory. Oh, God. I had to get to the bathroom—at once.

David caught me before I'd taken two steps and thrust an enamel bowl up to my face. I stumbled with it to the table and threw up the contents of my stomach.

"Okay now?" he asked, taking the bowl and handing me a cold, wet rag.

"Yes, thank you," I mumbled. "David, I am sorry."

"Don't be." He went to empty the bowl while I wiped the rag across my face. It was greasy as well as cold, but I didn't care.

When David came back he leaned on the table and asked if the sherry was to blame for the return of my supper.

"I think so. But it was very nice sherry," I added quickly.

He sighed, and I felt even more guilty than before. "It may not have been the sherry," I said, not wanting to insult his hospitality.

"What else then? Did you eat something?"

The kindness of his smile was my undoing. That, and the lingering smell of dead sardine. "No. No, I didn't eat anything I shouldn't have," I blurted. "I think I'm pregnant."

David's eyes widened briefly. He was startled, but not desperately shocked. For a moment I even had the mad idea he might be going to say he didn't do it.

What he actually said was, "Awkward."

"Yes," I agreed. "It is." I began to laugh, and once started I couldn't stop. David got up, filled a glass with water and came back to the table looking hesitant. His trousers, I saw with renewed hysteria, were still unzipped.

"Stop it," he said, sounding more desperate than autocratic.

I think it was the desperation that brought an end to my hysterics.

David closed his eyes, then put the glass back on the draining board. "Are you getting married?" he asked, turning to face me.

"No."

"But the father is going to support you?"

I shook my head. "No. He's disappeared."

"I see. So you're not going to have the baby?"

"I—don't know. I think I have to."

"Oh." He sat down again, frowning, out of his depth. But, unlike Arabella, he didn't say I was a fool.

"I won't know for sure until Monday," I said.

"And if you are? Pregnant, I mean?"

"I don't know. I just don't know." I ran my index finger across the table. It left a narrow snail's trail of grease. "I suppose I'll have to tell my parents."

David's facial muscles relaxed. "That's the best thing, I expect."

"Yes. Listen, I didn't mean to burden you with my troubles. I'm sure you have enough of your own." I knew he had. One of them was sleeping in his spare bedroom. "I'd better go back to bed before we wake up Posy."

"I'm surprised we haven't woken her already. She must be a sound sleeper." David didn't sound altogether pleased, and I didn't blame him. Here he was, in the middle of the night, playing father confessor to his fiancèe's friend, while the fiancèe lay oblivious, catching up on her beauty sleep.

I stood up, still feeling queasy. "Thanks," I said. "Thanks for listening to me. And for cleaning me up. I do feel much better now."

"Good." David looked as if he felt much worse.

"You won't tell Posy, will you?"

"Not if you don't want me to." He was puzzled, not understanding why I would tell him and not my friend.

"I may be wrong," I said, by way of explanation.

He shrugged, knowing it was no explanation but accepting that it was all he would get. "All right. Let me know if there's anything I can do."

Did he mean it? Or was he offering polite platitudes, as men of his background were doubtless taught to do?

An unfairly malignant impulse caught me unawares. "You could marry me, I suppose," I said flippantly, and summoned a grin to show I didn't mean it.

David stared at me, blank-faced. "I suppose I could," he agreed, "if I wasn't already engaged to Posy."

I broadened my grin to beyond the space where I was missing a molar and, to my enormous relief, he began to chuckle. Thank heaven. He had taken my proposal for the joke it was.

Still chuckling, in a way that did nothing for my ego, he saw me to the door of my room and went back to bed with Nefertiti.

I fell asleep almost at once. I hadn't expected to, so when I heard a loud rap on the door and saw feeble daylight gleaming through the curtains, I thought at first I was dreaming.

"Breakfast in fifteen minutes," David called.

I struggled up on the pillows. The brass clock said nine o'clock and a smell of frying was seeping under the door. I wrinkled my nose, hating the smell. It reminded me too much of Mrs. Carmody's. But at least it wasn't making me sick.

By the time I drifted into the kitchen, Posy and David were seated at the table, which in the clear light of a rainless winter morning looked cleaner and less suspect than it had last night. Posy was wearing a belted robe in slinky black silk. David was again in pullover and trousers, now discreetly zipped. I felt ridiculous in last night's crumpled black dress, especially when Posy raised her eyebrows and said, "You look a little rumpled, Janey. What a pity I didn't bring anything you could borrow."

I said, "Good morning." We both knew she never loaned her belongings.

"How are you this morning?" asked David, getting up to crack an egg into an unappetising cast iron pan.

"Better," I said. "Um—I can get my own breakfast. Just some toast…"

"You can't start the day on toast." He sounded exactly like my Mother, who had always insisted on sending me out the door with what she called a "good, solid breakfast." This meant a stomach so full of fried food that by the time I'd raced the half mile to school I felt as if I'd swallowed a sack of lead.

"Yes, I can," I said.

"Not in my house." He added bread to the grease in the pan and proceeded to fry it. I tried not to gag and was thankful when he added half a tomato.

"There you are." He slid the entire confection onto an unheated plate and waved me to the table. "Sit down and eat."

I sat down, and he poured me a cup of tea from a squat china pot.

"Isn't he marvellous?" purred Posy, nibbling on a corner of toast. "Of course, I have to keep trim for the wedding, so he daren't insist I eat too much. But you're not getting married, Janey, so you don't have to worry about your figure." She paused to take a dainty sip of orange juice and added offhandedly, "By the way, I've been meaning to ask you to be my bridesmaid. I thought I'd have you and Jasmine."

Vintage Posy. She didn't care if I turned up at the church looking like an overblown balloon, because that would make her appear slim by comparison. I eyed the pale yellow yolks on my plate. In a few months' time I would probably resemble a balloon whether I ate David's breakfast or not.

"I'm not sure I'll be able to be your bridesmaid," I said guardedly, "But thank you for asking."

"Oh, Janey, don't be tiresome. Of course, you'll be able to."

There was no 'of course' about it. And anyway, I didn't want to be her bridesmaid.

"Let Janey think about it," David suggested. "She can let you know sometime next week."

Bless him. He'd remembered my test results were due on Monday.

"I'd rather know now." Posy's lower lip protruded as it often did when she didn't get her own way at once.

"I'm sorry. I really can't give you an answer today."

"Well, when can you?"

There was genuine apprehension in her eyes, and all at once I understood. Apart from Jasmine, she had no one but me she could ask.

"Tuesday," I replied with reluctance. This was ridiculous. I didn't want to feel sorry for Posy B-B.

"Oh. That's all right then. We were thinking of April." As far as Posy was concerned my attendance at her wedding was now assured.

"I'll let you know," I repeated, swallowing a slippery slab of undercooked egg just as a ball of black fur stalked regally into the kitchen. Nefertiti. If only David's cat were a dog. Allison's dog always sat at attention ready to retrieve falling edibles. But Nefertiti ignored me, interested only in staking her claim to a faded corduroy cushion beside the cooker.

David, observing my reluctance to eat, said encouragingly, "You must start the day with protein. It's good for you."

Not wanting to offend, I swallowed a mouthful of soggy fried bread. Would he care that I didn't appreciate his cooking? I'd care if he didn't like mine. Which, come to think of it, he wouldn't. I didn't much like it myself.

"Rib-sticking," I muttered. It was all I could think of to say about fat-soaked bread, overcooked tomatoes and slimy eggs congealing on an unheated plate.

David, undeceived, shook his head at me.

He took me home after breakfast while Posy stayed behind to get dressed. She seemed to have no qualms about sending me off alone with her fiancè. But then why should she? Pretty Posy didn't see me as any threat—because, of course, I wasn't one.

I was frowning as I climbed into the Alpha, rubbing at a spot on my neck that, left to itself, might not have developed into an ugly white blister.

David eyed me uneasily and told me I must try not to worry. He seemed relieved when the time came to drop me off.

~*~

The rest of the weekend was awful. I had nothing to do but dwell on the more terrifying aspects of motherhood—like giving birth, changing nappies, and dealing with all the mewling and puking. I was certain Shakespeare would turn out to be right about that part.

Arabella tried to cheer me up by asking me to a party, but by now I knew better than to accept. She and Duncan always had a blazing row after every party they attended because Duncan couldn't stand her being ogled by other men. I didn't fancy being caught in the crossfire.

On Sunday evening Zachary came into the kitchen and discovered me moping over a bowl of mushy cornflakes. When he casually suggested a trip to the pub, I turned him down and hoped he didn't think it was because of his colour. It wasn't. I rather liked the idea of being seen to be liberal-minded, but I couldn't face the thought of being sociable.

On Monday morning I stopped at the clinic before I went to work.

The results were negative. I wasn't going to have a baby.

The motherly soul behind the desk watched me swaying on my feet and suggested I'd likely had "that nasty virus that's been going around."

I blinked at her, grinning goofily. My baby was a virus. A wonderful, glorious, incredibly beautiful virus.

"Thank you," I whispered to the Deity and anyone else who was listening. "Oh, thank you, thank you."

Out on the street I let out a whoop of relief that sent a flock of protesting pigeons whirring into the air. By the time I reached the steps to the Underground, I was floating like a fugitive from an aquarium newly released to the sea. Now I could swim free from the terrifying responsibilities of motherhood and I wouldn't, after all, have to fall back on the disappointed charity of my parents. I was still Janey Blackman, dreamer extraordinaire—not Janey Blackman, unmarried mother.

"You're late," said Mr. Reid when I pranced into the shop.

"Sorry," I replied, trying to sound as if I meant it. "I had a doctor's appointment." It was mostly the truth.

"You should have told me." He beetled his eyebrows suspiciously. "Are you ill?"

"No. Just a checkup. I'm fine."

I took off my coat and went to hang it up, and as I passed the counter, I grinned. I couldn't seem to help it.

Mr. Reid put out a hand and touched my arm.

The rest of the day passed in a kind of rosy bubble. The world was out there, but it couldn't touch me. I wasn't going to have a baby. I wasn't, I wasn't, I wasn't! I was safe, life was wonderful, and God had answered my prayers.

"Thank you, Lord," I prayed silently. "Thank you for listening. I promise it won't happen again."

My prayer was in the nature of insurance. I wasn't pregnant, but neither was I taking any chance on offending the Almighty. Besides, I didn't want to offend anyone today.

When Mr. Reid accidentally stepped on my foot, I gave him a blissful smile—and he responded by asking me again if I would join him for supper.

Well, why not? It wouldn't hurt me to give him a few hours of my time. I was deliriously happy. Why should he have to spend the evening alone in his flat—listening to the wireless perhaps—and remembering?

"All right," I said, revelling in magnanimity and sentiment. "Where shall we go, Mr. Reid?"

"Harrumph. How about fish 'n chips at my place?"

What was this? A typically Reid-like manoeuvre to save money? Probably. But if I had learned anything in the weeks since I'd left home, it was that I didn't know much about men—especially lonely, almost-old men. It wasn't that I seriously believed Mr. Reid had less-than-gentlemanly intentions, but I had just escaped from one frying pan and I wasn't looking for a fire.

"How about one of the restaurants around here?" I suggested.

"Hm. More comfortable at home."

Maybe. "But you told me you eat at home all the time," I said brightly. "Isn't it time for a change?"

"Having your company will be a change." Mr. Reid ran his fingers through his beard, dislodging the inevitable crumbs.

Stalemate. He wasn't going to take any hint less obvious than an outright refusal to be hijacked to Fulham. "I'd rather go to a restaurant," I said.

"Huh." He hunched his shoulders. "I suppose if you insist...."

"I do," I said, and felt as if I'd stolen a bone from an elderly dog, except that this old dog wasn't going to get the chance to bite.

"It'll be much more convenient." I gave him a conciliatory smile, which made him grunt, "Huh," again.

Later, as we left the shop and headed into the damp November chill, there remained a certain coolness between us, but the atmosphere thawed as the evening wore on.

We ate spaghetti bolognese in a bustling restaurant just off Leicester Square, and although Mr. Reid seemed to have lost the habit of casual conversation, I could see he was making an effort. I did my best to respond, although I wasn't much good at casual either.

We analysed the weather down to the finest grey detail and then, in desperation, I introduced the subject of my father's fish shop. For some reason that caused Mr. Reid to choke on a chunk of tomato. When he recovered, he gave me a basset-hound look that reminded me of Colin and said, "It's never too late to change your life."

"I suppose not." I didn't ask him if he was thinking of closing the bookshop so he could take up selling insurance. It might put ideas in his head.

At the end of the evening, when the bill was presented, Mr. Reid discovered he had only enough cash to pay for his own meal. He didn't believe in carrying much money, he explained, as if not paying for my dinner was a virtue.

I said nothing as I coughed up my share.

The next day he asked me to have supper with him again. I said I had plans for the evening.

A week later he asked me for the third time, and I thanked him and said I didn't think I should.

"Why not?" He leaned on the counter and mashed a stray glob of cake into the varnish.

"You're my boss. It's not right."

"What's not right?"

"Well—you know—having meals with you."

He looked so fierce I put down the bills I was sorting and backed away.

"Don't see it. Know I'm no spring chicken—"

"Oh, it isn't that, but..." I stopped, not knowing how to go on because it was, more or less, exactly that. If Mr. Reid had looked like Dirk Bogarde or Gregory Peck I wouldn't have minded his being my boss— and I'd have been happy to pay for my own meal.

"What is it then?"

I couldn't answer.

Mr. Reid made a growling noise in his throat. I took another step backwards. He moved forward and caught me by the elbows.

I stared at the big hands I'd never really noticed before and found myself mesmerized by the dark hairs crawling like earwigs across his knuckles. "Mr. Reid!" I said. "What are you doing?"

He didn't reply, but his breath burst out in a gust hot enough to stir my hair as he steered me around the counter and backed me into the nearest bookcase. It was one of the tall ones bolted to the wall.

"Mr. Reid," I repeated, emphatically this time, "what are you doing?" This close to my face, his beard was like a wire-wool pad. Any moment I expected to feel it scratch my chin.

"You think I'm old. Too old." He moved his hands to my shoulders. "That's it, isn't it?" There was a hungry look in his eyes, and his voice was rough, as if he had sand in his throat.

"No," I said. "Of course, you're not too old. Just too old for me. Mr. Reid, please let me go." His breath smelled like something the wire-wool pad had scoured. When he didn't let go, I added, "I'll call the police."

"The police?" At once his features went slack and his face became all eyes and beard. I wasn't frightened now—never had been for more than a few seconds. Mr. Reid was a sad, lonely old man, but he wouldn't hurt me.

I was right. Gradually his grip on my shoulders relaxed and he dropped his arms, allowing me to slide out of his reach. He bowed his head then, defeated, and didn't look at me again.

As soon as he had shuffled back behind the counter, I went to pull on my coat and fetch my bag. As I walked towards the door, the smell of age and old leather seemed stronger, as pungent on this, my last day at Inspirational Books, as it had been on the day I first came.

"I won't be back," I said, standing with my hand on the door.

Mr. Reid shook his head. I waited for him to say something, but he didn't. We looked at each other and he shrugged and said he'd send my cheque in the mail.

The ultimate irony. I even laughed.

A faint smile was trembling at the corners of his mouth as I shut the door behind me for the last time, and he raised a hand in farewell. Having nothing to lose, I waved back. Then I went next door to find Colin.

He was full of breezy sympathy. "Bad luck, Janey. Look, if you'll hang on a minute, I'll close up. It's nearly time anyway, and Her Nibs has gone for the day. Let's talk about it over a pint."

"What about June? Aren't you meeting her?"

"No." Colin slammed the shop keys onto the counter, deliberately making them jangle. "She's probably in bed. Had to give up her job. Kid makes her sick all the time."

"My mother gave up her job too," I said. "Dad wanted her to. But in June's case, it could be just a virus. Babies sometimes are."

It was over a week now since I'd had the news that I didn't have that particular virus, but I was still floating on a tide of euphoria. The fact that I'd just lost my job was a minor glitch compared to the lifetime inconvenience of a child.

Colin looked at me as if he wondered what I'd been drinking and went to close up the shop.

As I waited for him, having nothing else to do, I began to study the colourful literature lining the walls. Almost at once the purple cover of a book featuring a man and two snakes locked in improbable combat caught my attention. I steadied my gaze and looked again. Oh. Not only improbable, but suggestive. Snakes couldn't do that, could they?

I asked Colin when he came back, and he said he didn't know, but if they could, he might consider raising them himself.

I giggled. Colin was fun when he wasn't mooning over June.

The pub round the corner was a steamy joint full of thirsty theatre types and gawking tourists. I propped myself in a corner while Colin fetched me a lager and lime.

"I've never had one of these before," I told him, taking a cautious sip. "It's refreshing."

"'Course it is. That's the idea." He put an arm on the wall above my shoulder. "Okay, so let's have all the grisly details."

"What grisly details?"

"You should know. About you and God, of course. Did he try to have you over the counter?"

"No. He didn't try to have me at all. Just pawed me a bit."

"That's what Carol said."

"Carol?"

"Assistant he had before you. Linda was the one before that. God's girls never last long."

I remembered he'd told me that once before, but I hadn't understood what he was getting at.

"Ought to blow the whistle on him," Colin said. "Never know, he could go overboard one of these days."

"Oh, I don't think so. I'm sure he's harmless." I held my drink close to my chest as a checkered shirt pushed past my shoulder. Its owner trailed a smell of stale sweat.

"That's what they all say," Colin said. "Till something happens."

Was he right? I really didn't think so, and I certainly didn't want to involve Mr. Reid with the police. Didn't want to involve myself either.

A roar from a black-shirted group at the bar drowned out my reply, but when things quieted down again, I said, "Nothing's going to happen. Mr. Reid's like a dog chasing after a bus. He wouldn't know what to do with it if he caught it."

Colin shrugged. "If you say so." He rubbed his back along the wall and stared morosely into a foaming mug of ale.

"What's the matter?" I asked. "You look as though you're the one who lost the job."

"That's just it. I might as well have. Janey, how am I going to support June and a baby on my wages?"

Ah. Reality was beginning to rear its ugly head. Poor Colin. I took a healthy gulp from my glass, and said, "Find Carlo. It's his kid. He ought to pay something."

Colin looked at me curiously, and I remembered I hadn't told him about my own connection to the father of June's child. Nor did I intend to. No need to broadcast the humiliating fact that I'd been used.

"The bugger's disappeared," Colin said. "Anyway, June doesn't want to find him."

"Do you?"

"Not much. Rather push his face in than take his money."

I saw his point.

The checkered shirt pushed its way back holding two full glasses of beer above its head. "I want June's kid to be all mine," Colin explained.

As Frank Blackman had wanted me to be his. A familiar lump began to clog my throat.

"Hey!" Colin saw me swallowing. "No need to worry about me. You've got your own problems."

So I had. I laughed weakly. "We're a pair, aren't we? You without money, me without a job. We should go into partnership selling sob stories."

"Not a bad idea," Colin said glumly. "Except I can't even write a decent letter. Can you?"

"Yes, I can. Not the same though, is it?"

"Oh, I don't know. Do you want to write stories?"

"Mm. I wouldn't mind. When I was a child, books were my best friends. I used to think I'd grow up to be a writer."

"Why not try one of the papers then? Or a magazine?"

"With no experience?" Even I, who had gone through girlhood with my nose in a book determinedly avoiding the grimmer realities of life, was aware that these days one didn't just walk into the nearest newspaper or magazine office and ask for a job as a writer.

A giggling brunette jostled Colin's elbow and some of his beer spilled on my foot. "It's worth a try," he said.

"Is it?" I wriggled my toes. My shoe was full of beer. It made a squelching sound when I moved. I bent to pull it off and collided with a cushion that turned out to be the well-upholstered backside of an impressively large lady in pink trousers. "Sorry," I muttered.

The pink lady glared, Colin snickered, and somebody sneezed in my ear.

"I'm going home," I said.

Colin nodded. "Me too." When we reached the street, he said, "Don't lose touch, Janey. Let us know how you get on."

"Yes, of course." I meant it, yet I couldn't help wondering if I would. "You keep in touch too."

"Yeah."

We parted, and I watched him slouch down the street with his hands in the pockets of his too large raincoat. When he reached the corner he stopped to aim a kick at an unsuspecting letter box on the kerb. Knowing I'd seen him, he grinned sheepishly, and waved.

I wondered if kicking the letter box helped.

The following morning, not knowing what else to do, I took Colin's advice and made my way in the direction of Fleet Street. What, after all, did I have to lose?

As I sat on the bus watching the November wind blow dust and litter along the pavements, I tried to imagine myself as the intrepid heroine of one of my novels. I would arrive at the door of, say, the Telegraph, or even the Manchester Guardian, and find that their Top Writer had suffered a fatal heart attack while eating cream buns. The Managing Editor would rush past me tearing out handfuls of hair because he had no one to replace the Top Writer. I, with a soothing smile, would offer to come to the rescue. Not expecting miracles, but desperate enough to try anything, the now hairless Managing Editor would agree to give me a chance. I, of course, would immediately produce a brilliant column on the Budget (for the Telegraph) or The Crisis in Education (for the Guardian). I knew nothing about either, but there was always a Budget and a Crisis in Education.

Naturally, my stunning performance would result in an immediate offer of a permanent, high-paying job.

What actually happened, of course, was that three tabloids with headlines featuring incest, prostitution and the Royal Family, told me that I could drop off a resume if I liked. I didn't try the Telegraph or the Manchester Guardian.

The end of this dismal day found me hunched over a table in a basic little coffee shop round the corner from the worst of the tabloids. The table was none too clean, but the coffee was warm—tepid, anyway—and I was thankful to be out of the wind. It was only as I began to thaw that I noticed the sign behind the counter saying, "Help Wanted."

"Any experience?" asked the long-faced woman who looked me over when I told her I was Help.

"Oh yes," I said. "I've had a lot of experience working with the public."

I think she must have been desperate, like my mythical Managing Editor—because I got the job.

My hours were to be from seven in the morning to three in the afternoon and the wages were as basic as the coffee. But they would pay the rent.

On my way home I stopped to buy a paper. Across the front page, in huge black print, were the words, "Man Killed by Train. Drama on Underground." In smaller letters I read, "Victim found on tracks at Edgeware Road. Believed to have been escaping from police."

Underneath, flashing a familiar come-hither grin, was a picture of Carlo Bozelli.

CHAPTER NINE

Carlo's face continued to grin up at me from the paper. The print beneath it, read many times over, had long since blurred to dancing black ants. Resting my elbows on the kitchen table, I rubbed my knuckles across my eyes. Funny, I knew more about Carlo now that he was dead than I had ever known when he was alive and breathing in my bed.

His mother's name was Maria. No surprise there. She lived in Hammersmith with her three remaining children, all daughters. No father was mentioned. Carlo had been older than I thought. Twenty-seven. He had, for a short time, been a waiter, but had left that job a few days after I met him. It was suspected that his primary income came from the sale of other people's property. Specifically, he and two other men were wanted for questioning regarding a series of break-ins in the West End. It was thought Carlo had met his death while avoiding arrest. Foul play wasn't suspected, but an officer of the law had been on the platform when he fell.

I forced my eyes to focus and tried again to make sense of the dancing words. They wouldn't stay still. A wet patch was spreading over the centre of the paper. I stared at it, not believing. I couldn't be crying. Why should I cry when I couldn't feel? And yet—I ought to feel, surely. Carlo had been my lover. Even though he had deserted me, I should feel something.

"Oh. You've seen it." Arabella's voice from the doorway jolted me from my disconnected thoughts.

"Yes." I looked up. "Why don't I feel anything, Bella?"

Arabella narrowed her eyes and sucked in her Scarlet Passion lips. "You're whiter than hospital laundry," she informed me. "Either you're feeling something or you've gone into shock."

"I am shocked. I must be. Carlo's dead. He was a thief and I didn't even know it." I folded a corner of the paper and pressed it down until it formed a perfect square. "Do you suppose that's why he vanished? Not because of June's baby, but because he was afraid the police would catch up with him?"

"More'n likely. Must say I had my suspicions. He's no loss, Janey. Tell you what—"

"I know," I forced a smile. "You'll make me a nice cup of tea."

Arabella laughed. "You'll do," she said, looking relieved. Footsteps sounded on the stairs, and she casually unfastened the top button on her shiny, mauve blouse.

The footsteps belonged to Duncan. "Oh, it's you," he said, seeing me hunched over the table. "That's all right then."

I wondered what he'd have said if I'd been Zachary.

"Carlo's dead," said Arabella, who wasn't given to wrapping reality in euphemisms.

"Yeah. I saw." Duncan skidded a glance my way, mumbled something crude about the state of his bladder, and backed out as if I had the plague.

"He don't know what to say to you," Arabella remarked, unnecessarily. "I'll just make you your tea then before I get started on his supper."

I'd noticed when Aunt Hilda died that people often treated the bereaved as if they'd committed some unmentionable faux pas. I watched Arabella fill the ancient kettle and went on wondering why I didn't feel bereaved.

Hours later, as I sat by myself in my room, it came to me that I didn't feel anything because Carlo had never felt anything for me. He had used me, that was all. I had fooled myself for a while, but I probably wasn't the sort of person who could love for long without being loved in return.

The wind rattled the window as if it wanted to come in like Peter Pan, and all at once I felt an incongruous stirring of excitement. I, Janey from Willbury, recently of Chantersley, had been intimately linked with the Underworld.

It wasn't until the small hours of the morning, when my imagination was at its lowest ebb, that I was obliged to admit that a man who broke into struggling businesses and a girl who worked in a bookshop hardly ranked in romantic infamy alongside the likes of Bonnie and Clyde.

I thought of Carlo's mother then. She would be sleepless too, but with far more reason than I had. Maria was grieving her son. There was surely no excitement in grief, certainly no romance—only a terrible pain, and a loss that would be there always. I had never known that kind of grief, didn't believe I ever would—but there in the dark, with the wind outside shaking the windows of my mind, I cried for Maria Bozelli.

They were superficial tears perhaps, but at the time it didn't seem so. And with them I said goodbye to Carlo.

~*~

"Pork pie is what I ordered. Not this muck." The man in the cloth cap glared at the plateful of shepherd's pie I'd set in front of him and scratched his nose with his thumb.

"Oh, I am sorry." I wiped my hands nervously down my apron. "You're not the meatloaf then?"

The man sniffed, and I removed the plate hastily and slid it in front of a tired-looking woman drooping over a bowl of soup at the next table.

"No, I'm the meatloaf, dearie. I think this belongs to that gentleman over there." She flapped a veined hand at a long, tall Viking of a man who was reading a newspaper three tables down.

"Thank you," I mumbled. "Thank you very much." I scooped up the plate and hustled it over to the Viking just seconds before he lowered his paper—which came to rest on top of his lunch.

He stared disbelievingly at the gravy-smeared patch spreading over the middle of the sporting section.

"Sorry," I said, for at least the tenth time that day.

He threw me an inscrutable look and, folding his soggy paper, picked up a fork and began to eat.

I caught a glimpse of Clover, the coffee shop's owner, twisting a tea-towel round her hands and moving her lips as if she was praying—which she probably was. I'd only been working for her for three days, but it was already obvious I wasn't cut out to be a waitress. Clover was nice about it, but I knew she regretted hiring me, and that sooner or later she would harden her heart and give me the sack.

I was watching Clover close her mouth and shake her head in apparent despair when a drawling American voice punctured my self-absorbed gloom. "How did a girl like you end up in a place like this? You look more like the office type to me."

For a moment I wasn't sure who had spoken, then I looked down and saw that the Viking had stopped tucking into his now tepid shepherd's pie and was eyeing me as if my answer mattered.

"I used to be the bookshop type," I said. "But that ended, and I needed a job to pay the rent. I'm sorry about your newspaper."

"You already said that." He put down his fork and leaned back.

"Did I? Yes, I expect I did. I'm..." I swallowed, just in time to stop myself from apologizing again.

"Janey!" Clover's carrying voice rumbled from the kitchen. "Here's your pork pie and your meatloaf. Your two beef stews are coming up."

I muttered something incoherent at the Viking and hurried to pick up the two plates before they too turned tepid.

The rest of the day didn't go much better, and I wasn't surprised when at three o'clock Clover called me over and said I could stay till the end of the week if I liked, but after that she wouldn't be needing me anymore.

I told her I understood and went to get my coat off a peg. So much for my career as a waitress. It was a good thing really, I told myself. I hadn't even remotely liked the job.

Still trying to convince myself I didn't care, I drifted out the door in a kind of fog—and walked smack into a man's grey overcoat.

"Hi there," said the Viking I remembered from lunchtime. He steadied me with one hand and held out the other for me to shake. "I was just coming in to talk to you. I'm Kyle Johannsen."

I blinked and accepted the hand. Was I supposed to know who Kyle Johannsen was? When I realized he was waiting for my response, I said hastily, "Jane Blackman." Not Janey today. For some reason, with this man I felt like Jane.

"There's a pub round the corner," he said. "Come and have a drink."

I didn't want a drink. I wanted to go home and brood. But he had a nice smile, and he'd said I looked like the office type. It wouldn't hurt to accept his invitation.

"All right. Thank you," I agreed. It made a change from saying, "Oh, I am sorry."

The pub was closed, as I should have remembered.

"Too bad," Kyle said. "I've been in England three years and I still keep forgetting about your licensing hours."

He didn't say, "Your crazy licensing hours," but I could tell he thought it. When he suggested I stop by his office instead, I was instantly wary.

"What office?" I asked. "It's only half past three."

For a moment he looked puzzled, then he laughed. "Oh, I get it. You want to know what I'm doing on the loose. As a matter of fact, I took some time off to track you down. And you needn't worry, I keep my etchings at home in my apartment." I gazed at him blankly and he added by way of explanation, "Look, if you're interested, there might be a job for you at Ambrosia."

"Ambrosia?" Where on earth did he work? Some fancy kind of brothel?

"We're in health food wholesaling," Kyle said, in a dryish voice that made me think he'd caught the drift of my thoughts. "You know, lentils, yogurt, healthy stuff like that."

"Really?" I turned up the collar of my coat against the wind. "Then what were you doing at Clover's eating shepherd's pie?"

"Escaping from all that militant good health. Look, you're cold. Do you want to see my office or not?" He seized my arm.

"Yes, all right," I said, surprising myself, "if you like."

As he hustled me down the street, I asked doubtfully, "What kind of a job is it then?"

"Answering phones mostly. I'm in charge of personnel so you can have it if you want it. Our current receptionist is being promoted to secretary after Christmas."

"Oh. Thank you. But why me?"

"You have the right kind of face for the job."

"The right kind of face? I thought you said I'd be answering phones."

"You will, as well as manning the reception desk."

I stopped dead, forcing him to stop too. "What's my face got to do with it?" Was he a white slaver or something? Ought I to be running for my life?

"It's cute. You know, wholesome as fresh pecan pie. Just the sort of look our customers like. It gives them confidence in our products."

I didn't see why. And what on earth was pecan pie? I was about to ask when Kyle started walking again and I had to skip to keep up with him.

Two streets further on, he came to a stop in front of an impressive pair of double glass doors.

I hesitated, but in the end allowed him to usher me into a white, spacious office with unusual greenery growing in boxes around the walls. It was nothing like Inspirational Books.

The girl seated at the big polished desk behind the counter gave me a friendly smile, and immediately I felt more secure.

"Well?" Kyle asked. "What do you think?"

"It's lovely."

"Good. Want the job?"

He was serious. He was also too good to be true.

"I don't understand," I said cautiously. "You must be interviewing other people as well."

"Nope. You'll do. I can tell. So—do you want it, or not? I don't bite, you know. Charlotte, tell her I don't bite."

"It's all right," said the girl behind the desk. "Mr. Johannsen doesn't exactly bite. He just makes up his mind in a hurry."

It looked as though I'd have to make up my mind in a hurry as well. Could I really afford to look this unlikely gift horse in the mouth?

"Well?" Kyle raised a rather fetching pair of eyebrows.

"Yes, please," I said. "At least—I think so. If you're sure? I mean, you don't know me...."

"I know you're a lousy waitress."

That was true enough.

Kyle grinned suddenly and I wondered if there was a catch to my good fortune. But when he followed up the grin with a laugh, it was such a non-threatening, free-and-easy laugh, I decided that even if there was a catch, I didn't care.

He introduced me to Charlotte, the girl behind the desk. I liked her at once, and by the time I left Ambrosia Fine Foods I felt as if I were floating on silver clouds.

No more grumpy customers sneezing into their tea, no more serving meatloaf that was meant to be pork pie—and no more long-suffering Clover.

I, Janey Blackman, had miraculously fallen on my feet.

~*~

"Oh, I am pleased, Jane." Mother reached up to place the star on the Christmas tree—a brand new silver one this year—and turned to look at me as if I'd told her I'd won a reprieve from execution. What I'd actually told her was that by an amazing stroke of luck I had landed the job at Ambrosia Fine Foods. I didn't think my news merited quite the look of glazed relief in her eyes, but I knew she'd been horrified when I'd switched from Inspirational Books to Clover's Coffee Shop.

Dad hadn't minded as much. When I'd popped down to Willbury to tell them, he'd said vaguely, "As long as you're happy, Janey," and gone on listening to a programme on the wireless about Running a Profitable Small Business. He was already running one, as I could tell from the new carpets and curtains, but I suppose he enjoyed the validation.

Now it was Christmas Eve. I had arrived home half an hour ago to find Mother decorating the tree and Dad bumbling around hanging ornaments that she promptly removed and placed somewhere else. When I told them about my new job, Dad beamed and sat down in his favourite armchair while Mother stood holding a velvet reindeer and looking as though the Angel Gabriel had absentmindedly paid her a visit.

"How did it happen, Jane?" she asked.

"Sit down, Edith," Dad said. "Doctor said you mustn't overtire yourself."

Mother waved her hand impatiently. "Yes, yes. In a minute."

Dad knew quite well that she was far too keyed-up to sit, but he couldn't stop himself fussing.

I perched on the arm of a chair beside the fire and told them about Kyle and my resemblance to fresh pecan pie.

"Whatever is that?" Mother was immediately suspicious.

I told her I thought it was something good to eat and she seemed to think that might be all right then.

"I'll be answering phones mostly," I explained. "But there'll be filing and some typing as well."

"Well done, Janey." Dad patted the square arm of his chair because I wasn't close enough to pat in person.

"Yes," Mother agreed. "You'll be glad to get away from that coffee shop." She twitched her shoulders in an unconscious gesture of repugnance.

"It wasn't that bad," I said, unwilling to admit she was right.

"This new job's much more suitable, Jane." Mother nodded decisively. "Frank, don't you think so?"

"Already said I did," Dad answered. "Edith, sit down."

To my surprise, Mother did as he said.

Christmas this year turned out to be different from any past Christmas, and not just because I was given a beautiful green tweed suit as well as my usual books. Although Mother hadn't yet put on any noticeable weight, she had that soft, broody look about her that pregnant women often seemed to get—and Dad's attention, instead of being focused almost exclusively on me, was on the pink, toothless blob growing inside her. After dinner we sat around talking and playing cards instead of tidying Christmas neatly into cupboards so that not a hint of our subdued celebration remained. At bedtime, crumpled paper still obscured the new sitting room carpet and glittery string festooned the backs of the chairs. In the kitchen, the dishes had been washed and left to dry.

It had been a happy day. I'd enjoyed it more than any Christmas I remembered, and although I sensed the cord that bound me to my parents was stretching thin, I knew now it would never really break.

Mother and I had established a certain rapport since I'd had the scare about the baby. I hadn't told her about that awful weekend, but I understood, as I hadn't before, what she must have gone through to have me, and just how desperate she must have been when she married Dad. Over the holiday I tried my best to show her I was sorry. Sorry for Carlo, for leaving home so abruptly, and for not understanding that even Managing-Mothers-Who-Know-How-Things-Ought-to-be-Done   can make mistakes.

My visit this time passed amicably and with a quiet kind of pleasure in getting to know my surprising parents, who had somehow, in the course of a few weeks, turned into actual people.

On Boxing Day Posy phoned and put an end to my feelings of seasonal goodwill.

"I hoped I'd catch you," she said, as I sagged against the ivory wallpaper that Mother had always chosen for the hall. "You don't have a phone in that grim little room of yours, do you?"

I replied frostily. "No, I don't. What makes you think my room's grim?" It was, but I had no intention of conceding even that minor smugness to Posy.

"Oh well, of course one reads about these one-room walk-ups...."

I curled my nose at her, which made me feel better even though I knew she couldn't see me. "Does one? As a matter of fact, the house has a lot of character." It had too, if you counted smoke and food smells, Zachary's offbeat music and Arabella and Duncan's nightly high jinks.

"I'm sure it has." Posy's tone was so condescending it made me grit my teeth. "Now, Janey, you will be available for fittings and things, won't you? I—"

"Fittings?" I interrupted.

"Yes, of course. For your dress. You promised to be my bridesmaid."

"Oh." So I had, in a moment of insane benevolence following the news that I wasn't pregnant.

"I've decided on pink," Posy said. "You'll look very sweet."

"Not in pink, I won't. I'll look like the backside of a rainbow."

"Janey, really. It's a nice, pale pink. Jasmine wanted red, but I said no."

No doubt with great satisfaction, I thought cynically.

"Janey?" Posy's voice, faintly tinged with panic, came to me down the wire. "Janey, you're not going to let me down, are you? David said you might want to, but...."

David? I tuned Posy out and gazed blankly at the new brass umbrella stand I kept stumbling over every time I came through the door. David didn't know I wasn't pregnant. I hadn't seen him since that night in his flat.

"No, no. I won't let you down," I promised, as Posy's persistent whine dragged me back to the matter of the moment. "I'll do it. I'll be your bridesmaid."

A dog barked somewhere outside, and as its staccato yaps increased in volume, the only rational thought I was able to hang on to was that at least I wasn't fated to dazzle the assembled congregation by walking down the aisle in matching red hair and dress.

Thank God for sisterly rivalry.

I wilted against the wall and closed my eyes as I listened to her voice gushing warmly, "Marvellous. Of course, I knew you would. Did I mention we're getting married in St. Martin's? At Much Gotham?"

"No, you didn't." I succeeded in pulling myself together.

"Oh, well of course we had thought of St. Martin's in London, but David's family weren't keen. Much Gotham has quite a nice little church really."

"I'm sure it has." I was also sure David hadn't, for one second, thought of a big London wedding. He'd have considered it the height of ostentation.

Posy rattled on for a while about dresses and hairstyles and why the reception was to be held at The Beeches instead of in "that awful little village hall." I didn't take much notice until I heard her say something about popping into Inspirational Books if she needed to get hold of me in a hurry.

That snapped me to attention. I explained about Ambrosia, with a certain regret that I was no longer working at Clover's. Posy would have hated having a waitress for a bridesmaid.

By the time I hung up the phone, a thin sheen of sweat was forming on my forehead. I wiped it off with a feeling of frustration. Why was it that any encounter with Posy, even long distance, could reduce me to sweating exasperation?

Dad, passing in the hall, saw me scowling and said I wasn't to worry, I was bound to be a success in my new job.

His well-intentioned words had the effect of changing the direction of my thoughts and after that I worried about the job.

I needn't have. The first day was nerve-wracking, as I suppose most first days are, but Kyle spent a lot of time showing me where everything was and assuring me I'd soon catch on. He even pretended it didn't matter when I sent half a dozen calls to Marketing when I should have sent them to Sales.

Charlotte, whose job I had inherited, said he hadn't been nearly so nice to her on her first day.

By the third day it dawned on me that all I had to do to earn my pay was answer phones and sound efficient, although occasionally I was asked to dispense advice about vitamins, herbs, and what tonics were most likely to banish spots.

I wished I knew the answer to that one.

Miss Barclay would have been proud if she'd seen me at work—not dreaming, but looking as though I knew what I was doing, and with my hair in a businesslike twist.

In early February, Posy phoned to summon me for a fitting. By then I felt as if I'd been chatting about things like acidophilous, lipotropic factors and food enzymes for months.

She told me to come on Saturday at two, and it took a moment for my mind to switch gears. I almost prescribed her a course of natural vitamins.

"You'd better come for lunch," Posy said. "I'll send David to pick you up."

"No, don't bother. I'll take the bus."

"The bus? I don't think there is one."

"Bound to be," I said firmly. Posy hadn't a clue about public transportation. "Look, I have to go now. There's a call coming in." I hung up on her, as usual feeling irritated, and picked up a book entitled "Herbal Remedies For Colds." I kept it on my desk for the purpose of impressing passing office management with my enthusiasm.

~*~

There was a bus, of course. On Saturday it dropped me off in front of the cluster of cottages that made up the hamlet of Lesser Gotham. A woman in a striped apron was standing on a ladder cleaning her windows.

"Can you tell me how to get to The Beeches, please?" I asked.

She pointed across the fields. "'Bout half a mile, love. You won't miss it."

The sound of traffic was muted as I made my way along the footpath. Beneath my feet, the frosted winter fields were hard and crisp, and I threw my head back, the better to breathe in the sharp tang of fresh country air.

On a morning like this I could believe I'd stepped back in time to the days before motors and car horns blasted their way into the countryside to shatter all the centuries of peace. I imagined I was a farm girl going to

The Manor to look for work...no, not a farm girl. The daughter of The Manor on her way to a tryst with her lover....

I gazed dreamily at a puff of smoke rising above the trees in the distance and found that I'd bumped into a style.

David stood on the other side of it.

He was wearing a waterproof jacket over grey flannel trousers, and with his hands in his pockets and the breeze lifting his hair, he reminded me of one of those magazine models posing as a casual country gentleman. Except that David wasn't posing. He came that way.

My skirt caught on a nail as I clambered towards him, and awkwardly, I turned to yank it free. David held out a hand to help me down.

"Hello," I said. "What are you doing here? Don't tell me you're going to be measured."

He smiled his lovely, slow smile. "By the dressmaker? I think not. No, I came down to see Posy. She asked me to meet your bus in case you got lost. It seems I'm a little late."

According to Posy, he always was. "I'm not lost," I said, miffed. Even I could hardly get lost in the middle of a field.

"I'm sure you're not." He nodded gravely, and I saw that he was discreetly sizing up my figure.

"No," I said. "It was a false alarm."

"I thought it must have been or you wouldn't have agreed to be a bridesmaid." He gave me his straightforward look. "I'm glad."

"Not as glad as I am."

He laughed and tucked my hand into his elbow. "I'm sure that's true. Just as you won't be as glad as I will when this blasted wedding is over and done with."

"Aren't you enjoying the preparations?"

"No. Do women always get hysterical over weddings?"

"Not that I know of. Who's hysterical?"

"Posy, her stepmother and Jasmine. Not necessarily all at the same time, although I've seen it happen."

I shuddered at the image he'd conjured up. "What a horrible thought. Poor you."

We came to the edge of the field where another style put us on the verge of the winding road I recognized from my last visit. Several cars following a tractor trundled around the corner and we waited patiently for them to pass.

"Don't worry about me," David said, kicking at a handy tuft of grass. "I'll live through it."

I almost said I didn't see why he bothered, but there was something about the set of his jaw and shoulders that convinced me it would be wiser to hold my tongue. I had seen enough of David and Posy together to know that this wedding wasn't your standard starry-eyed romance.

"What are you dreaming about?" he asked brusquely. "Come on, we can cross now."

So we could. The tractor had grumbled its way out of sight.

"I was thinking about you and Posy." When David's eyebrows went up, I added lightly, "I'm sure you'll be very happy together."

"Good," he replied, and I had a feeling I'd put my foot in something sticky.

Without further conversation, we continued down the road until we came to the driveway leading to The Beeches.

We arrived just as Jasmine, dashing in a black mohair coat and red beret, came swanning down the steps on the arm of Martin Radburn.

"Hello," I said. "Aren't you staying to be measured?"

Jasmine frowned. She was all daggers and fire when she frowned—and quite lovely. "No. Posy's being ridiculous. Anyway, I look insipid in pink."

The front door opened, and Posy burst out. She too was in a temper, but it didn't do nearly as much for her looks as it did for her sister's. "Jas, don't you dare leave," she screamed. "You know Mrs. Chesney's coming."

Jasmine tossed her head. Martin tucked his chin into his chest and looked miserable, and David and I stood momentarily frozen. Then David cleared his throat, and said mildly, "What seems to be the trouble, Posy?"

Posy put her plump fists on her waist so that her elbows stuck out like the handles of a sugar bowl. "Jasmine won't stay to be measured. She's just being mean."

"Jasmine?" David turned to his fiancèe's scowling sister. "Can't we sort this out?"

"It is sorted out. Martin and I are going out for lunch."

"Look here," Martin glanced unhappily from Jasmine to David. "Why don't I come back later? We can have lunch another day. I had no idea—"

"She only invited you to spite me," Posy shrilled.

"Why, Jasmine?" David asked.

"Because she's a pig. She said I had to wear beastly pink because it's her wedding, and if I didn't like it, I could lump it. She only chose pink because she knows I hate it."

"Did you, Posy?" David shook his head, the picture of masculine bafflement.

"Of course not." Posy lifted a shoulder and began to fiddle with her hair. She wouldn't meet his eyes.

"She did too," muttered Jasmine, less aggressively now that she'd noticed Martin looking at her as if she had something spotty and contagious.

David had much the same look, but his gaze was directed at Posy and he seemed doggedly determined to stand his ground in the face of behavior he couldn't begin to comprehend. "What about blue?" he suggested. "That would suit both Jasmine and Janey, wouldn't it?" He turned to me for confirmation, not sure of himself in this ultra-feminine dispute.

"Yes," I said. "It would. Or turquoise."

"I want pink," Posy said.

David muttered something that sounded like, "What you both want is..." But he saw me looking at him and changed it to, "What we all need is a drink. Agreed, Radburn?"

Martin, looking as if he'd been thrown a lifeline in a very stormy sea, nodded speechlessly. He started to go back up the steps, leaving Jasmine no choice but to follow. David and I walked behind them, barring escape.

We left our coats in the cloakroom beside the door, and at once Posy tried to walk away. But David caught her elbow and held her back while the rest of us made our way to the drawing room.

For the next few minutes we stood about with our hands behind our backs trying to pretend nothing had happened.

"Nice day," Martin said.

"Crisp," I agreed.

"It's a change to see the sun," Jasmine mumbled.

When the happy couple rejoined us, Posy fluttered her eyelashes at each of us in turn and said she'd decided the bridesmaids should wear aquamarine. "Pink is really so much better in the summer," she announced, as if she'd come to that conclusion without coercion. "Aquamarine will suit Janey particularly well."

One in the eye for her sister, I thought, wondering how, and if, Jasmine would take it.

She did. After one glance at Martin, who seemed fixated on his polished brown shoes, she looked directly at Posy and said, "It will suit me perfectly as well. I'm so glad you changed your mind, Posy."

I wanted to ask David how he'd done it, but I didn't get the chance because Mr. and Mrs. Bantley-Brown came into the room at that moment—almost as if they'd waited until they were certain the fireworks had been doused.

"Drinks," said Mr. Bantley-Brown decisively, and I saw both David and Martin heave sighs of relief.

Mrs. Bantley-Brown jangled her bangles and said wasn't it exciting.

"What?" asked Jasmine.

"Posy's wedding, of course. Don't be silly, darling."

Jasmine turned her back on her mother, and I said quickly, "I'm sure it will be lovely, Mrs. Bantley-Brown. Have you decided what you're going to wear?"

It was the right thing to say. Mrs. B-B beamed at me and launched into a description of a dress that sounded as though it would look smashing at a masquerade ball.

Lunch was just as awkward as on the day I'd first visited The Beeches, but in a different way. Posy and Jasmine tried to pretend the other one wasn't there. Martin kept his head down, obviously wishing he was a thousand miles away crawling through a crocodile infested swamp, or somewhere equally unconnected with The Beeches. David was absorbed with the picture of the garden and the poodles just as his father had been on the previous occasion. Mr. Bantley-Brown, looking dour and distinguished, kept throwing fatherly glances at Posy. Only Mrs. B-B and I made any effort to keep the conversational ball in the air.

There was only so much one could say about the weather.

Mrs. Chesney arrived promptly at two. The measuring seemed to go on for hours in a small room Posy called the Regency Room—perhaps because of its striped blue and gold wallpaper. I'd never had a dress made for me before, and I found the whole process daunting, especially as Posy kept telling me my figure needed padding. Jasmine took the opportunity to tell Posy she ought to lose weight.

At that point, Mrs. Chesney dropped a box full of pins on the floor and said she hoped we'd all keep the figures she was measuring. It struck me as the most sensible suggestion I'd heard all afternoon. Later, the dressmaker and I picked up the pins while Posy fluttered about and Jasmine bolted onto the landing.

"You must stay for tea, Janey," Posy said, after a harried Mrs. Chesney had been shown out.

"Oh, no thank you. I have to catch the bus."

"David will drive you."

Yes, he probably would. But I didn't want him to. "Thank you," I said again. "I mean, thank David. But I'd rather catch the bus." I closed the door and hurried down to the hall.

Posy followed me, making a clicking noise with her tongue. "Don't you like David? You wouldn't let him bring you here either."

"Of course, she likes David," Jasmine drawled from the top of the stairs. "She just doesn't like using him the way you do, Posy. He's not your chauffeur, you know." She draped herself gracefully over the banister.

"Don't be silly. You're far too young to understand. David likes doing things for me." Posy, probably wisely, chose to play the superior elder sister now that the matter of the dresses had been settled, if not to her satisfaction, at least not to Jasmine's either.

"Do I?" David said from behind us.

Posy swung round. "Oh, there you are, David." She giggled coyly. "Well, don't you?"

"Sometimes. What do you want me to do now?"

That was not the voice of a devoted swain by any stretch of the imagination. Jasmine smiled maliciously.

"Janey needs a ride back to London." Posy put a hand on his arm. "You do sound grumpy, darling. You needn't take her if you don't want to. Anyway, she says she'll take the bus."

"No, she won't," David said wearily. "It'll be dark before long."

They were talking about me as if I were a parcel—an inconvenient one. "I am taking the bus," I said, pointing my chin. "You needn't bother about me."

"Don't be ridiculous."

I had a feeling David was at the end of his rope but I didn't care. My back was up, and I was determined to have my own way. If it embarrassed them, that was a bonus.

"I am not being ridiculous. Merely factual," I said loftily. "Now— where did I leave my coat?"

Instead of answering, David went into the cloakroom, produced my coat and held it out for me.

I slipped my arms in, buttoned it, and was about to make a grand exit when I remembered I hadn't thanked Mrs. Bantley-Brown for lunch.

"Mummy's gone into Farnham," Posy said. "You may as well stay for tea."

"No. Thank you. I really must be going. Let me know when you need me for more fittings."

David opened the door, and I thanked him and sailed regally down the steps. When I reached the bottom, something soft brushed against my thigh. I looked around and discovered it was the sleeve of his jacket. He was pulling it on as he hurried to overtake me.

"Oh, please," I said. "Do go back to Posy. Really, I'll be all right."

"I expect you will. But if you won't let me drive you, the least I can do is see you to the bus. This may not be the city, Janey, but that doesn't mean we haven't got our share of perverts on the loose."

He was definitely fed up, but whether that was my doing or Posy's, I wasn't sure. Nor did I mean to find out. I liked David, but I hated it that he felt obliged to act as my chaperone.

We walked through the fields in silence as the shadows lengthened and the birds began to settle for the night. I wasn't the daughter of The Manor anymore. I was a very ordinary receptionist being escorted to the bus by the man who was marrying Posy Bantley-Brown.

When the bus came, David said, "Good night," as if he meant, "Good riddance," touched my hand, and slouched away across the dusky fields.

I watched his broad, slightly stooped back until my bus turned the corner. Soon that back of his would be resting on Posy's bed.

As Carlo's had rested on mine.

It came to me then that although I still thought of Carlo often with nostalgia, resentment and a kind of disbelief in the reality of his death, I didn't mourn him any longer.

Maybe I never had.

On Wednesday I came down with a cold—the draining, persistent kind that resists all attempts to relieve it. So much for Herbal Remedies. I blew so viciously into my hankie that my nose bled all over the phone.

By Friday afternoon my eyes were streaming, my skin was the colour of salmon and, according to Charlotte, my face looked like steak on a bun. When I sneezed three times in succession just as Kyle was passing by my desk, he stopped, took a good look at me, and told me I'd better go home.

"Get Charlotte to take over," he ordered. "You look like hell."

I eyed him balefully. How dared he stand there, the picture of Nordic good health, telling me what I already knew?

"I'll be all right," I assured him in martyred tones.

Martyrdom didn't impress Kyle. "Maybe you will, but I'm not having you sitting there scaring all our customers away. Get going. I'll tell Charlotte to move her things to your desk.

"Thank you." I tried not to sound sarcastic. I hadn't been with Ambrosia long enough to risk telling the man who had hired me that I didn't appreciate being compared to a Gorgon with incipient Black Death.

Once outside, the winter air dried up the mucus in my nose so I could breathe, but my head still felt as if it had been wrapped in wet, cold towels and set on fire. I swayed, narrowly avoiding a collision with a passing postman. As I fought to regain my balance, a pinstriped arm swept around my waist.

"For Christ's sake, Jane! Why didn't you tell me you felt faint?"

"I didn't know I did," I replied groggily.

The pinstripes belonged to Kyle Johannsen, the last person I would have chosen to find me staggering down the street like a drunken duck. It wasn't that I didn't like him. I did, in spite of his bossy, take-charge personality. But that was the whole point. He was my boss, and I wanted him to think of me as his indispensable Miss Efficiency—not someone who needed help staying on her feet.

"Come on then," he said. "My car's around the corner today. I'll drive you home."

"Oh no, there's no need...."

He wasn't listening to me. I was being swept along the street like a dead leaf. Then I was in a bright red car with bucket seats and Kyle was asking for my address.

"Please, really you mustn't...."

I stopped to sneeze, and Kyle said, "Baloney. Come on. Where do you live?"

I told him. What did it matter? Maybe I'd be dead by tomorrow. If I wasn't, I'd still have this cold.

"Feeling sorry for yourself?" he asked.

I hunched into my seat and didn't answer.

On the pavement outside Number Fifteen, two women were screaming at each other over the ownership of a child's battered bike.

Kyle didn't even blink. Nor did he react after he made me open the door on the usual odor of stale smoke and wet socks.

He practically carried me up the stairs.

"Better get undressed," he said. "I won't look."

Shades of Carlo? No, he'd have to be pretty desperate to fancy me the way I was now. Besides, he really had turned his back.

I got undressed and slid beneath the blanket not caring anymore that my boss was seeing my attic home in all its grunge.

He put a hand on my head. "I'll call your doctor."

"I don't have a doctor. Even if I did, he wouldn't come. And there's no phone."

"Don't be so damned obstructive. Your landlady must have a phone."

His voice was not raucously American, but it was loud, too assured, and it grated on my ears. "Please don't yell at me," I said. "It's just a cold. I always have bad ones, but I'm sure to be much better by Monday.

He had very blue eyes. They were studying me with a piercing suspicion. I turned my head to the wall. "It's true. Really." I wanted only to wallow in my misery—alone.

"Who's going to look after you?" Kyle demanded.

"Arabella. She lives downstairs." Hers was the first name that came into my head. Besides, she probably would look after me if I asked, which I wasn't going to do.

"Trying to get rid of me?" he asked.

"Yes, please."

He gave a laugh that reminded me of a branch cracking. "I can take a hint. Want me to get you anything before I leave?"

"No. Thank you." I crossed my arms on the blanket and closed my eyes.

"Overkill," Kyle said. "You're not dead yet. All right, I'm off then. Try to get some sleep. And I don't want to see you on Monday unless you're human."

He shut the door with a thud and I listened to him running down the stairs. He was nice, really—for a boss. Couldn't be much older than Posy's David. And he surely was different from Mr. Reid.

That reminded me of the conversation I'd had with Colin the other day. We'd met, briefly, for coffee. He told me Mr. Reid had a new assistant, a man this time. We shared a laugh over that. I didn't laugh nearly as much when he told me he had married June, who was sick a lot of the time and hard to live with. Colin thought life would be easier once the baby was born.

I didn't tell him I'd heard it was always harder once the baby was born because nobody could get any sleep.

Getting some sleep was what Dr Kyle had ordered. I sniffed miserably and shifted my head on the pillow. Sleep didn't come easily when you couldn't breathe and your head felt like stuffed peppers on toast....

I shut my eyes.

Somewhere around noon the next day I was awakened by the sound of footsteps clomping up the stairs. The footsteps were followed by an insistent thumping on my door and Mrs. Carmody's voice yelling, "You in there, Miss Blackman?"

She didn't wait for an answer. Three seconds later her key turned in the lock.

"You're alive," she said, scowling down at me. "Huh. Told him you would be."

"What?" I turned onto my back. "Told who?"

"Some man." She blew a succession of perfect smoke rings. "American from the sounds of him. Pushy sort. Said you were ill."

"Oh. It's kind of you to come up Mrs. Carmody. I have a cold, that's all."

"Just what I told him. Lot of fuss about nothing, I said."

"Yes. Yes, you're quite right," I agreed faintly.

"Told me I'd be liable to prosecution if you turned up dead, he did. I ask you. Making me come all the way up here for nothing."

I coughed and just managed to stop myself apologizing for not being dead.

Mrs. Carmody coughed back then shuffled off saying she'd better call that American before he got all excited and phoned the police.

"I won't have it," she muttered. "Not in my house, I won't. And I hope there'll be no more of it, Miss Blackman."

"No, Mrs. Carmody," I said meekly. "Of course not." *More of what?* Did the old witch think I was enjoying this cold? Or that I'd put Kyle up to calling?

By Monday I felt a lot better—only a cough and a red nose to show for my weekend in bed—and I went back to work prepared to do battle with Kyle for putting me in hot water with the management of Number Fifteen.

He came in late, looking red-eyed and irritable and said at once, "I thought I told you to stay home."

"You said I could come in if I felt human."

"Hm. I'm glad somebody feels human. You've given me your damn cold."

I apologized. It seemed the soothing thing to do.

Kyle grunted and went off to nurse his bad temper in his office.

The following day he didn't come in. I was glad, because Posy phoned three times to talk about fittings, and Kyle didn't like his staff taking personal calls.

The next few weeks were filled with an endless succession of fusses and fittings. I tried to keep them to a minimum, but Posy was incredibly persistent. Her wedding had to be perfect—the kind of wedding people would talk about admiringly for years. After a while, I became so familiar with The Beeches that I hardly noticed its overwrought opulence and began to feel almost at home there. Even Jamieson, Mrs. B.B.'s incredibly superior butler, once or twice cracked a smile when I appeared at the door.

As the wedding day approached, Posy became quieter and less boastful. She was quite pathetically pleased when I assured her she looked thinner and that her wedding dress was the loveliest I'd seen.

Against all the odds, something approaching friendship was sprouting between us. On her side, its basis was need, on mine, a growing sense of compassion—unexpected, but nonetheless real.

Compassion was a much more comfortable emotion than the hostility I'd born her for twelve years.

Without its softening influence, I might never have survived her wedding day.

CHAPTER TEN

"White suits me, doesn't it?" said Posy, pirouetting in front of her bedroom mirror as she smoothed slinky white satin down her thighs. "I wonder what David will say when he sees me."

"'I do', I expect."

This was Posy's big day and she was, for once, entitled to be boringly self-absorbed. But I was tired of her constant need to be told she was the fairest one of all—especially as she actually did look a dream in sophisticated satin and silk. Jasmine and I looked sweetly juvenile in round-necked taffeta with puffy sleeves, and it didn't help much that I knew our dresses had been chosen specifically to score one over Jasmine.

Posy giggled. "You are funny, Janey. Don't you wish you were me?" She did another little twirl in front of the mirror and spun to face me with her arms held wide so I could have the full benefit of her curvaceous figure swathed snugly in bridal white.

"Not really." I sat down on her bed, not caring if my taffeta creased. When two lines appeared between her baby-blue eyes, marring the made-up perfection of her skin, I added grudgingly, "David's sure to be a wonderful husband though."

"Yes, of course. He's devoted to me." Posy touched the stiff folds of her veil. "I wish all those beastly girls at Chantersley could see me now. They'd be so jealous."

Oh, God. She was back on that again. "Would they?" I asked. "Why?"

"Well, I am marrying the cousin of an earl."

A much removed cousin, David had said. But she was right in a way. Our old classmates might not be exactly jealous, but they would probably be dumbfounded that a man like David had chosen to marry the Bantley-Brown.

"I don't think Allison would envy you," I said. "She always said she meant to have affairs with glamorous intellectuals and never bother with marriage."

"Oh, Allison." Posy studied her pale pink nails with over-played absorption. "Did I tell you I invited her to the wedding?"

I felt my lips stretch in a silly O. "No! Posy, did you really? I thought you didn't—well, I mean you and Allison were never exactly friends."

"No, but she came into Sollaby's a few weeks ago, and when I told her I was getting married, I could see she didn't believe me. So I invited her. She's a dreadful red, of course, but I thought it would be good for her to attend a really traditional wedding."

In other words, it would be good for Posy's ego, which I was beginning to realize was fragile.

"And is she coming?" I asked, without much optimism.

"Yes, and she's bringing a guest. I hope he won't be some awful, scruffy little man in a rented suit."

"Why should he be?"

"Well, you know, she is such a socialist."

Just as I was about to say that I didn't think all socialists wore rented suits—and anyway, would it matter if they did?—Jasmine poked a surly head around the door. "Mummy says you're to hurry up," she said. "The photographer is waiting to take pictures." The head disappeared again and I heard Jasmine's heels rap sharply on the stairs.

"Oh, dear," said Posy, casting a final quick glance at the mirror. "I suppose we'd better go down then." Her voice was pitched higher than usual and she twitched at her veil as if its impeccable arrangement could give her a measure of security.

"It'll be all right," I said, thinking I understood the reason for her panic. "David's kind. He'll be very gentle."

A faint blush darkened Posy's Elizabeth Arden cheeks. "Oh, I'm not worried about that. By tomorrow I'll know more about it than you do. I'll be a married woman."

Did she honestly believe marriage made a difference to one's mastery of that? Or was she merely bolstering her courage with self-delusion?

"So you will," I agreed, giving up. "Come on, let's go then." Although there was no sense feeling irritated, I had to conquer a strong desire to tweak her security veil and disarrange her carefully coiffed hair.

The drawing room was full of people when we made our entrance. Family members, I supposed—the kind who turn up for weddings, funerals and free drinks. Jasmine was there too, of course, her full mouth turned down in a sulky curl. Mrs. B-B was astonishing in royal blue silk with diamonds. Posy's father, standing in front of the white fireplace, was stiff-necked in formal attire. He beamed when he saw Posy come in, then swallowed noticeably and said, "You look beautiful. A real princess."

Posy preened, and a couple of aunts in floral prints twittered up to offer their good wishes. They were followed by two red-faced uncles and a lanky youth with duck-tailed hair—a cousin, I imagined.

"Now if we could just have a few pictures on the steps," said a man with a camera round his neck. "The bride with her father, perhaps...."

We shuffled obediently outside. The sun had conferred its blessing on the day and it was pleasantly warm as we stood about waiting for the photographer to finish arranging Posy and her dress to suit the revealing eye of his camera. After that we stood about some more as the shutter clicked and various members of the wedding party were shunted into place around the bride. I had to bite my lip as I watched Jasmine weigh the satisfaction of ruining Posy's wedding pictures against the desire to look beautiful on camera.

The camera won.

When it was all over, Mrs. B-B flashed her diamond watch and said we shouldn't keep David waiting any longer.

I looked at my economy watch and discovered it was almost two o'clock.

"Did you want to be late on purpose?" I asked Posy, as the five of us—myself, Posy, Jasmine and Mr. & Mrs. Bantley-Brown—settled into the limousine to be chauffeured the short distance to the church.

"No, not really." Posy was flustered. "It won't matter though. David's always late himself."

That was true enough. Perhaps she was afraid she would arrive at the church before he did.

If she was, she needn't have worried. When we peeked through the heavy doors leading into the fifteenth century nave, David and Gerald, his best man, were dutifully planted at the altar. David looked marvellous in tails, and from this angle he looked comfortably relaxed. I glanced at Posy. Her colour was high and her eyes bright with a fevered excitement that had the odd effect of making her look clever.

I felt a tight sensation in my chest. Had I been mistaken about Posy all along? Did she really love David after all? And was he just as crazy about her? It ought to be that way, of course....

The organ ceased its prelude and after a breathless pause, began to play the ponderous Bridal March.

I clutched my bouquet of white roses. As Posy didn't have a train for us to carry, Jasmine and I were to lead the procession down the aisle. But just before we took our first steps, I heard Mr. B-B murmur to Posy, "Remember, if he's not up to scratch, you're to let me know."

Posy didn't answer and I wondered what her father thought he could do about it if David wasn't "up to scratch," whatever that meant. I hoped he wasn't referring to the bedroom, a place where fathers of the bride most definitely didn't belong.

We walked slowly, in time with the music, hearing the occasional soft swish of Posy's skirt and our taffeta dresses. When we took our places at the front of the church, the sun beaming through a stained-glass Madonna above the altar was reflected onto the chancel to capture the bride and groom in a blue pool of light. Posy's smile, as she raised her eyes to look at David, was a masterpiece of tremulous adoration. His answering smile was affectionate, casual and only a little like that of a rather large cat anticipating cream.

I didn't think Mr. B-B needed to worry about David not coming up to scratch. When he said, "I do," his voice must have raised hairs on the backs of more female necks than my own.

Posy's "I do" was less certain, more of a breathless squeak. But it didn't matter. When it was all over, she was still Mrs. David John Foley.

Outside in the churchyard, with the tombs of the dead standing sentinel over this rite of passage of the living, I stood in the shade of a yew tree and tried not to weep.

I wasn't sure why I wanted to cry. I didn't think I was sentimental about weddings, and I didn't think my lachrymose state had anything to do with the inscription on a nearby tombstone which read: "Here lies Septimus Blunt, born February 12th, 1844, died March 19th, 1902 at West Gotham Asylum. For fifty-three years a happy inmate."

Poor Septimus Blunt. He might have been happy, but reading about him made me sad, although not sad enough to cry for him, surely. I watched the crowd of well-wishers jostling around the newlywed couple. Posy was flushed and triumphant in the midst of adulation. David seemed mostly relieved. From his point of view, the endless preparations were over and at last he could get on with the business of the honeymoon. I rubbed a hand over my nose, which was itching, and watched him turn his smile on one of the aunts. She put a hand to her breast as if she were about to swoon. I didn't blame her.

The cousin with the duck-tailed hair dashed up to me as I took another surreptitious swipe at my nose and said he'd been told to fetch me for more photos.

"Don't you like having your picture taken?" he asked.

He thought I was hiding from the photographer. "I don't mind," I said. "At least they'll touch up my spots."

He laughed. "Know what you mean. Had a healthy crop of those myself a few years ago."

There was more jostling as the photographer pushed us into place against the backdrop of the ancient stone church. I was arranged next to Posy.

"It's going very well," I whispered. "But didn't you say Allison was coming?"

Posy shrugged. "Oh, who cares about Allison? Mummy says she phoned to say she can't come after all. Don't you think David looks divine?"

I cared about Allison, but I hadn't really believed she would come. And I didn't think David looked in the least divine. His expression as he gazed down at his bride was very much of this earth.

I smiled noncommittally at Posy and toothily at the camera, and before long we were all on our way back to The Beeches where a marquee had been set up on the lawn.

More photographs, now against a backdrop of the house and river. More congratulations and "Doesn't-she-look-lovelys." Then the receiving line and the shaking of endless hands belonging to a blur of unfamiliar faces. Posy's lack of friends certainly hadn't shortened the invitation list.

A breeze came up, the aunts began to shiver, and we returned to the marquee for champagne and speeches.

When Gerald, the best man and an old school friend of David's, proposed a toast to the pretty bridesmaids, most of the guests nodded and looked at Jasmine. I tried not to mind. My chin had always been chronically pointed.

"Where's Martin?" I whispered to Jasmine when everyone's attention returned to Posy.

She glared at me. "Martin and I aren't going out anymore. Not since that first time you came for fittings. I told him I didn't like his attitude."

His attitude? What kind of a dimwit did she think I was? Of course, it was her atrocious display of pique that had frightened him off.

"I'm sorry," I said.

I wasn't especially. It served Jasmine right.

"Doesn't matter to me," she replied with a shrug. "I can do a lot better than Martin Radburn."

She probably could. I turned away and pretended to concentrate on the big production being made over the cutting of the cake. David's large hand remained clamped over Posy's for ages while the photographer snapped picture after picture of the same beleaguered slice being stabbed.

When that was over, everyone drifted into separate babbling groups, and I found myself standing alone and conspicuous in the centre of the tent. A bar, surrounded by a swilling thirsty crowd, was set up on a trestle near the entrance. I didn't want a drink, but at least I wouldn't be noticed in that throng.

A few minutes later, as I was holding up the bar and trying to look as if I were having a good time, Gerald slouched over to talk to me. I suspected he had been dispatched by a well-meaning David to entertain the lonely bridesmaid, but unfortunately, he wasn't the conversational sort. It soon became obvious he was having as awkward a time as I was.

After a while he muttered something about seeing if David needed him and shuffled away.

I hung around pretending to listen politely to a group of red-faced colonels discussing horses and eventually slipped out onto the lawn.

A gauntlet of dedicated cigar smokers had formed an honour guard around the entrance to the tent, but once I'd navigated their cloying brown haze, the air became fresher and scented with spring. Somewhere on the river a radio was playing songs from the hit-parade.

I wandered down to the edge of the water, absorbing the sounds of the night—music in the distance, waves at my feet, and the soft murmur of wind through the trees—all punctuated by the persistent hum of party conversation.

A small boat puttered past as I lowered myself onto the grass at the edge of the water. The sun touching the trees along the riverbank still gave an illusion of warmth and I was able to pretend I wasn't cold. After a while, I closed my eyes.

When I opened them again, feeling the stirring of something that wasn't wind against my temples, I discovered David was sitting close beside me holding a glass. It was his breath that had lifted my hair.

"What are you doing here?" I asked. "You're supposed to be celebrating your wedding."

"So are you." He took a long swig of whatever he was drinking.

"But it's your wedding. David, what's the matter?"

"I did it," he said.

"Did it?" *Did what?*

"I married her."

"Posy? Of course, you did." I twisted around to study him more closely. "David, are you all right?"

His only response, after laying down his glass, was to put his elbows on his knees and bury his face in his hands.

I frowned uneasily at his hunched shoulders. In the distance a boat whistle screamed, and without warning, a sadness, bone-deep and overwhelming, crawled up out of nowhere to cloud my mind. For a short time the cavernous shadows creeping across the river seemed to beckon me, promising a mysterious kind of peace.

Then, because I didn't know, or couldn't find, a way to express what I was feeling, I said to David, "You'll stain your trousers if you don't get up."

He raised his head and looked at me as if I'd told him little green men were coming to take him to Mars.

"Your trousers," I repeated. "You'll stain them."

"Yes. Probably. What about your dress?"

"It doesn't matter. I'll never wear it again."

"You won't?"

"No." I attempted a smile and almost succeeded in banishing the shadows. "I haven't worn puffed sleeves and peasant necks since third form."

"Mm." He cast a vague glance at my rumpled taffeta. "You do look very young. Was the dress Posy's idea?"

"I'm afraid so."

"It would be." His voice erupted so harshly that a feathered denizen of the river gave a disgruntled squawk and swam to safer shores.

I blinked at him doubtfully. "David—you did want to marry Posy, didn't you? You said you did."

"What?" He ripped a fat blade of grass from its roots and began to shred it systematically. "Now that you mention it, I'm not sure I did. I wanted to take her to bed, but I doubt if that's the same thing."

Was he serious, or was that the drink talking? Either way, I was shocked. "It certainly isn't," I said. The boat whistle shrilled again, and I made my voice rise above it. "David, if you mean that, it's—unconscionable."

He threw away the grass and swallowed what was left of his drink. "Is it? Yes, I suppose it would be unconscionable..." His lips stretched sideways in a grimace. "...If that was the only reason I married her. It would also be bloody stupid and unnecessary."

I gaped at him. Had my judgement really been so skewed? Had I actually thought David was nice? I picked up a small stone and threw it at the water. It landed with a satisfying splash.

"You don't love her at all, do you?" I said.

"Love? I don't know. I don't think I thought about it much."

"But that's—I mean, didn't you consider her feelings?" There had been a time when I hadn't believed Posy had feelings. I knew better now. If nothing else, she had a profound craving for admiration, which meant David would be expected to adore her.

He stared into his empty glass. "Of course, I did. I was told she wanted to marry me. By her father. And you know how it is with Harry Bantley-Brown. Whatever Posy wants, Posy gets."

"David!" His bitterness appalled me. Drink might have loosened his tongue, but I believed he meant what he said. "That's terrible. You didn't marry Posy just because her father told you to. You couldn't have."

"Oh, I could." He gave the glass a final gloomy appraisal and set it back down on the grass. "But you're right. I didn't. At the time, it seemed a good idea."

"And now it doesn't?" I shivered as the damp began to penetrate my skirt.

David put an arm around my shoulders.

I realized I ought to shake it off, but it felt right there, comforting— for him as well, perhaps. I knew I wasn't going to move.

"Cold?" he asked.

"A bit. David...."

"I know, I know. I have to go back to Posy. Don't lecture me, Janey. I need this time to myself."

"You're not by yourself. You're with me." Nothing like stating the obvious.

"You're different. With you I feel—peaceful."

Peaceful? It was better than bored, I supposed.

"I'll do my best for Posy," he said. "You needn't worry on that score."

"I'm not worrying. But, David, if it wasn't just a matter of...."

"Bed?" he suggested, when, embarrassed, I allowed the sentence to trail off.

"Yes." I wrapped a loose tendril of hair round my fingers. "You said yourself that would be stupid. So if it wasn't only that, why...?" I stopped again, not sure I wanted to know the answer.

"Why did I marry her?"

I nodded. He would tell me now. There was, after all, no point in hiding from the truth.

David sighed. "I'm not sure you'll understand. How could you?"

"I could try."

"Yes. I'm sure you would try."

"So—"

"So okay. Okay, you win." He waved his free hand at the sky, as if absolving himself of any responsibility for the consequences of telling me what he thought I wanted to hear.

I waited.

A burst of laughter rose from outside the marquee, hung in the air, then faded into the drone of a passing plane.

"Do you remember what I told you about the gallery?" he asked finally. "That we're not exactly in the black and haven't been for over a year?" He paused to massage the back of his neck.

"Yes, but I don't see—"

"Wait. I'm trying to explain. The point is, with the Bantley-Brown name behind me, my creditors will feel more secure."

Oh. He meant with the Bantley-Brown fortune behind him. Was he telling me that Posy's father had bought a husband for his daughter?

"What about your own family?" I asked, because I didn't want to consider the implications of that thought. "Wouldn't they back you up?"

David shook his head. "Perhaps. I didn't ask them. My father is solvent but not wealthy—and he wasn't keen on my taking on the gallery in the first place."

"Why not?" His father had seemed a pussycat to me.

David flicked a gnat off his trousers and studiously avoided my eye. "My father was a banker before he retired. I'm not sure that has anything to do with it, but he regards art as a losing proposition. Harry Bantley-Brown, on the other hand, likes the idea of a son-in-law in something he thinks of as 'cultured'. There hasn't been a lot of culture in Harry's life."

"So he did buy you for Posy." I raked my fingers through the grass. Should I get up and run away? I wanted to, but my limbs didn't move.

David winced. "Harry isn't above using his money to get what he wants. But no, he didn't buy me for Posy. Her name will help the gallery, but that doesn't mean I didn't want her for herself." His thumb dug into my shoulder. I flinched and he immediately became aware of what he was doing and drew away.

"You're talking past tense," I said, wishing I didn't miss the warmth of his arm. At this moment, I didn't like David much at all.

"Yes, I suppose I am," he agreed. "That's not what I meant though."

"Isn't it?" To me, it sounded as if David had realized too late what he was getting into and now was busy trying to convince himself he really did want Posy for his wife.

"Don't worry, we'll rub along well enough." He straightened his back as if squaring his shoulders could give him the strength to carry him through a lifetime of Posy.

"For as long as you both shall live," I muttered, more or less to myself.

David frowned. "Look, I admit it took Harry's prompting to make me really pay attention to his daughter. But when I did—"

"When you did, you saw a way to solve all your problems." I didn't look at him, not wanting to see reproach, or avarice, in the eyes I had always thought of as kind.

After an uncomfortable pause, he said, "It was never that calculated. Things just happened."

"And you let them."

"I suppose I did. It seemed right at the time. We talked about it and Posy knew exactly what she wanted."

Yes, she always had. At least they had talked. That was something. Both of them must have known what they were doing.

"And that was it?" I was still skeptical. "You allowed yourself to be used as some kind of husband-for-hire?"

David brought his face close to mine. I could smell the whisky on his breath. "If I did—and I'm not saying it's true—what's wrong with that? It's been done before. Don't go all sanctimonious on me, Janey."

Sanctimonious? Was I going sanctimonious? No, this was ridiculous. People didn't marry to recoup the family fortunes—not anymore.

Or did they?

"It may have been done before," I said, turning away and wrapping my arms around my chest to keep warm. "But that doesn't make it right."

David made a sound that I think was meant to be a laugh, but it came out as more of a snarl. "It doesn't make it wrong either."

"I suppose not." The deed was done. Why waste time assigning blame?

I couldn't look at David, but I sensed he was looking at me.

"I am fond of Posy," he said, almost pleading with me now to believe him.

"Of course, you are." There was nothing to be gained by telling him I didn't think he was fond of her at all.

He ripped up another blade of grass and I waited, wondering if there was more.

There was. After a while he said, "Janey, this marriage is going to work, I promise you."

"Is it?" I tried to sound neutral.

"It must. We have to stay married."

This was his wedding day and already he was talking about 'staying married.' For money?

"I see," I said, staring into the shadows on the water. One of them reminded me of a vulture with a great, crooked beak.

"Do you? It's not as bad as it sounds, you know. Even Harry Bantley-Brown likes the idea. His daughter gets the man she wants, and he gets a son-in-law he can trust to look after her interests once he's gone."

"Does he?"

"Damn it, of course he does. What do you take me for, Janey?"

When I didn't answer, he answered for me. "A louse? Is that it?"

I watched a small black beetle climb to the top of a blade of grass, which bent under its weight until it fell back to the ground.

"All right," David aimed a fist at the air. "All right. But you have to admit it's not a bad trade-off. Posy gets what she wants, I gain an attractive wife—and my bank manager will no longer pretend to be out when I call."

No, not a bad trade-off. But was he really that cynical? He'd only been married a few hours, and already he was avoiding his blushing bride. He had no business sitting here with me by the river, stinking of whisky and talking of his marriage as if he'd just negotiated a successful business merger. In the soft evening light his face was haggard, as if he hadn't slept for a week. Yet he had appeared relaxed and well rested in the church, not to mention hungry for Posy.

"Have you been drinking?" I asked. Stupid question. Obviously, he had.

"What does it look like?" He picked up his glass and waved it under my nose. "It's my wedding, dammit. Of course, I've had a drink."

"Of course," I agreed quickly. "Listen, it's going to be all right. Really."

I didn't like or respect what he'd done, but I wished now I hadn't been so critical. How could I know what pressures he'd been under? How could I be sure he hadn't done the right thing? Posy thought he had, and from the sounds of it, he'd been honest with her right from the start.

"You know Posy loves you," I said, eyeing his averted profile.

"Does she?"

"Of course, she does. And there's no reason you shouldn't grow to love her."

Had I really said that? Was it possible to grow to love Posy?

David pulled a handkerchief from his pocket and blew his nose. I pulled my skirt down to my ankles and stared glumly at a yellow-bordered cloud.

"You're a sweet girl, Janey." His fingers grasped my chin and tilted my face up. "A very sweet girl. Did you know that?"

The sound of a lusty male voice singing something about love and marriage came to us from the radio on the river. I started to laugh, but it wasn't funny, so I stopped.

"Why did you tell me all this now?" I asked, ignoring the question that I guessed was alcohol-inspired. "You wouldn't before."

"Ah." He removed his fingers. "I suppose, 'till death do us part,' and all that."

"'Till death do us part'? What—oh, I see."

And I did, finally. David was only in his twenties. Death ought to be a long way away. Yet at one time the thought of twelve years of Posy had almost finished me.

I said, "The future—all those years—do they frighten you? Is that why you're here with me when you ought to be with Posy?"

Instead of answering, he stood up and held out his hand. "Come on. We'd better be getting back before they start thinking we've eloped."

"You can't elope," I pointed out. "You're already married."

"So I am," David agreed, so grimly that I wished I'd kept my mouth shut.

"You're bound to feel better once the reception's over," I said when he'd pulled me to my feet. "Once you're safely off on your honeymoon."

"You think sex will solve anything? Don't be naive, Janey."

I wasn't naive. Not any longer, and certainly not about that. It had merely been the first thought that popped into my head. After my months at Inspirational Books, uplifting platitudes tended to trip off my tongue as glibly as an auctioneer's patter.

"Sorry," I said, stabbing my scalp as I pushed a loose comb back into my hair. "I was trying to cheer you up."

He smiled a funny, sad flicker of a smile. "Thanks, Janey. I didn't mean to be a bore."

The shadows on the river beckoned again. I took a step towards them, and the distant electronic voice began to croon, "Do not forsake me, oh my darling, on this our wedding day...."

David caught my hand, put his arm around my waist, and began to lead me in a slow, half-tipsy dance across the grass. For a big man, he moved with a pleasing grace. The smell of whisky became intense, yet it wasn't unpleasant.

I surrendered to the magic of the music.

Then it stopped and the night went uncannily still. "David," I said, "we have to go back. Posy will be looking for you...."

David said, "To hell with Posy," and bent to kiss me.

For the briefest of moments I let him. Then a voice—Gerald's, I think—shouted, "Not to worry, I'll find him for you," and I pulled away and ran towards the house.

David came thundering up beside me, swaying a little. "Sorry," he said. "I shouldn't have done that."

"It doesn't matter. You didn't mean anything by it."

"No. Of course not. Thanks, Janey."

What was he thanking me for now? The kiss? For not making an issue of it? Or for listening to the story of his courtship and providing a sympathetic ear? Either way it made no difference. As far as David was concerned, that kiss had been no more than an unfortunate impulse precipitated by drink and opportunity—signifying absolutely nothing.

It was different for me. But it shouldn't have been.

As Posy came out of the marquee and hurried towards us in a swirl of indignant virginity, I wanted to tear the white veil from her head and consign it, along with her newly signed marriage certificate, to the deepest part of the Thames.

What I actually did was smile, and say, "David and I met on the towpath. We were catching a breath of fresh air."

Posy frowned and said I needn't have taken so long. "I need help changing," she told me crossly. "We're leaving for the Continent tonight."

As if I didn't already know. Paris, Rome, Vienna—Athens....all a wedding present from Posy's proud father.

I stole a look at David, who was being dragooned into the marquee by an officious Gerald. He returned my look briefly and shrugged.

I followed Posy into the house.

By the time she had changed into a blue wool suit with grey trim, the sun had gone down and an apple green cloud shot with gold was all that remained of the day.

~*~

It was after ten when Gerald dropped me off at Wrenbert Terrace. I had been prepared to make my own way home, but he'd insisted it was no trouble to drive me. On the way, and having had one too many drinks, he suddenly became loquacious and asked me out. I thanked him and refused, wishing I hadn't accepted the lift. Gerald was nice enough, but he was drunk. In any case, I didn't want to go out with him.

A woman's scream greeted me as I stepped through the door of Number Fifteen.

It was followed by the thump of something soft hitting the wall. A pillow probably. Items of Duncan's clothing made a different noise. I was becoming quite familiar with the Ashes' missiles.

Mrs. Carmody, cigarette attached to her bottom lip, met me in the hall. "Them two," she exclaimed, glancing at the ceiling. "My Arthur would never have stood for such goings-on."

So there really had been a Mr. Carmody at one time. I'd often wondered, but not to the point of actually asking. I wouldn't have got an answer in any case. My landlady asked all the questions at Number Fifteen. As I mumbled a "good evening" and edged past her, I reflected that the racket coming from upstairs would have meant a call to the police in most households. Carlo had been right. For all her preaching about immorality, Mrs. Carmody thrived on her tenants' 'goings-on.'

"Hey," she said, as I edged past her. "You. Got a message for you. And didn't I tell you no calls? Think I'm an answering service, do you?"

"No, Mrs. Carmody, of course not. I didn't give your number out. Except to my parents for emergencies—"

"Not an emergency," said Mrs. Carmody, blowing half a dozen fat smoke rings in my face. "Your dad said to tell you your mum had a baby." She gave a cackle that only served to heighten her resemblance to a witch. "Bit long in the tooth for that, ain't she? Must be, judging from the looks of you." She gave another cackle and clumped off to her lair in the basement.

I leaned against the wall and closed my eyes. When I finally started upstairs, I realized I'd forgotten to ask the sex of the newest Blackman.

CHAPTER ELEVEN

No fat thigh nudged my knee as the train to Willbury trundled over the tracks this sunny Saturday afternoon. Instead, a fat little girl squirmed against my hip complaining loudly of boredom. Her harried mother, attempting to calm squalling twin boys, did her best not to hear her.

God! Was this what babies grew into? They were dreary enough when all they did was mule and puke. I began to think my visits to Willbury would be few and far between from now on.

My baby brother, who had arrived two weeks early and been named William, was one week old today. I had hinted at time off from Ambrosia on the grounds that my mother needed help, but Kyle had gone all hard-of-hearing, so I'd hastily withdrawn even the hint. I liked my job and had no wish to jeopardize it over a very young relative I still couldn't quite believe had actually had the audacity to be born.

Besides, I suspected Mother would manage just as well, or better, without my help—a conclusion that turned out not to be far off the mark.

The train arrived in Willbury on time. A hopeful start. At least something augured well for this improbable rendezvous with my new brother.

The moment I lugged my small suitcase round the corner onto Willbury Road, the front door of our house shot open and Dad came bustling along the pavement to greet me.

"Janey! Come along then," he urged, eagerly relieving me of my suitcase. "You're just in time for William's next feeding." His voice was pitched loud enough to reach Mr. Cooper, who was digging up his weed patch next door, and Mrs. Gillaby, who was sitting at her window as she always did, waiting for nothing to happen. They both turned their heads to look at Dad, who threw back his shoulders and thrust out his narrow chest as if he'd just produced the heir to the throne instead of William Francis Blackman.

Fascinating, I brooded, as I trudged up the path beside him. News flash of the year. Baby William is about to partake of refreshment.

"How are you, Dad?" I asked.

"I'm very well, very well indeed." He beamed and allowed me to give him a brief hug before hustling me into the sitting room where Mother was ensconced in a brand new rocking chair beside the hearth.

I stopped in the doorway to stare at the red-faced lump in blue flannel that lay in her arms slurping on a bottle.

"There he is, Janey," said Dad. "There's your baby brother. Hasn't your mother done us proud?" He was a small man, but he sounded about twenty feet tall.

I looked across the room at William. My brother? No. It couldn't be true. That downey-haired creature in Mother's arms might be her son, but he had no connection with me.

I allowed my gaze to slide towards the window. The curtains were new, but still a brave yellow challenge to the neighborhood white net. William's advent had done nothing to change that.

Nobody spoke, and I realized my parents were waiting to hear adoring gasps of sisterly admiration. "You're feeding him from a bottle," I blurted.

Their faces told me that wasn't the gasp they'd expected.

Ambrosia's advisory pamphlets all touted the advantages of "natural mother's milk," as if we stocked it in our warehouse. But I'd never thought much of the idea and was relieved to see Mother didn't either.

"I decided a bottle was nicer," she explained. "Besides, William's father likes to take his turn at feeding him. Don't you, Frank?" She smiled at Dad with a fondness that embarrassed me.

William's father, she had said—not *your* father.

"You'll be wanting to hold him, Janey," Dad said with confidence.

No, I wouldn't. But as there was no way to avoid it without upsetting them, I decided I might as well get it over with at once. I held out my arms, a prisoner resigning herself to handcuffs. After a moment's hesitation, Mother lifted the baby, still with the bottle in his mouth, and handed him over to me.

Immediately my brother stopped slurping and started complaining.

Help! The little beast was an unexploded bomb. At any moment he was likely to go off. Appalled, I handed him back to Mother. William, restored to familiar and competent territory, made a satisfied gurgling noise and settled down to suck.

"Better wait till he's finished," Dad said. "Healthy pair of lungs, hasn't he?"

Paternal pride oozed from every pore. He was positively glowing with it. I said, "Yes, he has," and tried to squash the little black demon of jealousy twitching away at my insides.

The demon continued to twitch for the rest of the day and didn't really quiet down until nighttime. It was only then, as I lay in my familiar blue bed and watched the wind blow the curtains into the room, that I was able to acknowledge the true root of my discontent. What I longed for more than anything, with a yearning that had become a painful pressure in my chest, was to have someone as absorbed with me as my parents were with my brother. Only I wanted the absorbed one to be a man.

I stared at the darkened ceiling and imagined it had become a giant screen. On it I saw Posy, all soft and simpering, clinging to David's arm just before they climbed into the limousine that was to carry them off on their honeymoon. Then the picture changed, and they were standing side by side on one of the bridges of the Seine. They looked happy. I closed my eyes, but I could still see them.

By now, of course, with the stresses of the wedding safely over, the two of them were sure to be blissfully in love. David had already had a week in which to enjoy that well-covered body he found so desirable. And surely, once Posy had recovered from her nervous virginity, she would find it warm and comfortable in his arms.

David would be gentler, less selfish than Carlo.

Knowing I could never have what she had, of course I wanted it desperately. How pleased she would be if she knew.

I fell asleep wallowing in a cocoon of nebulous self-pity. The fact that I had little reason to feel sorry for myself only served to increase my discontent.

My weekend at home wasn't a success.

William was exactly as I'd imagined—messy, noisy and wet. The only time I found him tolerable was when he slept, which didn't seem to happen often or for long. I'd heard that newborns slept eighteen hours a day, but whatever genius had come up with that figure hadn't communicated the information to my brother. By my estimation, he slept approximately four hours a night and two, interrupted, during the day. The rest of the time he yelled for food, which he promptly returned. I decided breastfeeding might not be such a bad thing after all. Mother couldn't have asked me to help her if she'd been the bottle. As it was, she kept passing the baby over to me while she bustled around making meals, doing laundry and indulging in all the unnecessary spit and polish that served to distinguish us from our neighbours.

My father, in particular, expected me to be delighted with the baby, and for his sake, I did try to look worshipful.

"Fine-looking fellow, isn't he?" Dad said, every time he came into a room and found me plugging William's protesting mouth with a teething ring or whatever else came to hand. "How does it feel to have a baby brother?"

It felt boring at best, disagreeable at worst. "Fine," I said stoically. "He's very—um—healthy, isn't he?"

Luckily that seemed to satisfy Dad. Mother, I think, knew I was less than enthusiastic, but she had neither the time nor inclination to worry about the grumbling of a supposedly adult daughter who hadn't lived at home for nine months.

"You'll be glad you know something about babies once you have your own," she informed me briskly when I screwed up my nose at the prospect of changing a dirty nappy.

It didn't seem a good time to tell her I had no intention of ever having my own.

On Sunday I took an earlier train home than I'd planned. Thank heaven Monday wasn't a public holiday.

~*~

"Oh, there you are, Charlotte. I wondered where you'd got to." Mrs. Slade, Ambrosia's Accounting Manager, pulled at the lapels of her navy business suit and frowned suspiciously at my giggling friend.

Charlotte, who was leaning on the counter above my desk, gave a guilty start and said, "Coming, Mrs. Slade. I was just telling Janey to hold your calls."

What she had actually been telling me was that one of our healthy products had so affected her new boyfriend when she'd cooked it for him that he'd spent the weekend trying to get her into bed. She winked at me, rapped her knuckles on the counter and trotted demurely off in Mrs. Slade's wake.

I switched on the phones and got down to the business of fielding the usual rush of Monday morning calls.

It was hard to believe I'd been with Ambrosia five months, but already there were pink and white blossoms in the parks, and the spring storms had given way to May sunshine.

At around eleven o'clock, just as the switchboard began to settle down, the peace of my spacious sanctuary was shattered by the slamming of a door. The ferns in their wooden boxes shuddered, my pencil holder fell over on its side, and Kyle Johannsen blazed across the tiles with all systems set on Trouble-for-Someone.

"Where's Harriet?" he demanded, looming over me as if he were searching for something to squash.

I began to collect the scattered pencils. "She phoned in to say she wasn't well. Didn't you get the message?"

"No, I did not get the message. She phoned in sick on Friday as well. And on Thursday. I suppose she didn't mention when she plans to come back?" His nostrils flared dramatically and he began to pace back and forth across the floor.

"No. No, she didn't, I'm afraid."

"You're afraid," he mimicked, stretching his mouth across his teeth until he looked like an underfed vampire. "Harriet's the one who ought to be afraid."

"I'm sorry," I said, offended.

"Sorry? What are you sorry for? You don't have to cope with Joe Murray."

Joe Murray was our Advertising Manager. Harriet was his assistant. She could spell, type, organize a schedule and generally do all the things Joe Murray was incapable of doing for himself. Without Harriet, the Advertising Department had a habit of lapsing into chaos, and when that happened, revenue went down, causing Joe, who was the president's nephew, to complain to his uncle that everyone except himself was to blame.

The President then blasted Kyle for hiring idiots. It was a system, so I'd been told, that had worked predictably and satisfactorily for two years. Satisfactorily for everyone except Kyle, who preferred blasting others to being blasted. He didn't usually blast me though, and I didn't like it.

"Say something useful, instead of moaning apologies," he snapped.

Useful? He wanted useful? My cheeks began to burn and I looked angrily around for inspiration. When I didn't find it, I looked back at Kyle. If he kept this up I might just hand in my notice. He had no right to vent his temper on me.

Then I saw there was sweat on his forehead. As he paced, his long fingers flexed behind his back as if he couldn't wait to wrap them around some unfortunate victim's neck.

Joe's probably. Kyle was an efficient, if frequently impatient, manager who liked a smooth-running office. If Joe had been equally efficient, or if he hadn't been the President's nephew, Harriet's absence wouldn't have a caused a ripple.

I changed my mind about handing in my notice. Kyle was only being swinish because he was under pressure. He'd been quite different that day I nearly fainted.

"I can take over for Harriet, if you like." I heard my own voice announcing quite calmly.

"You?" He stopped pacing and stared at me.

What had I said? Was I mad? Had my brain suffered a power surge, and shut down? I liked being a receptionist. I was good at it. I couldn't take over from Harriet without training, especially with a panicky Joe Murray breathing down my neck.

Lowering my head, I made a production of searching for buried treasure in my desk drawer. Kyle didn't speak, but I could feel him standing over me like some Nordic vulture waiting to swoop down on my remains. I closed the drawer and began to scribble meaningless notes on a lined pad.

The silence continued, but I knew he hadn't left.

The phone buzzed, and I put though several calls. When I'd finished, Kyle was still there, leaning over the counter looking gimlet-eyed, though his nostrils were no longer flared. "Can you?" he asked. "Take over?"

Was he serious? He certainly looked it. I gulped.

"Well," he said impatiently. "Can you?"

Oh, Lord. He meant it.

I waved an arm, stalling for time, and the small cactus on the edge of my desk stabbed a warning dart through my thumb. I squeaked and shoved the thumb into my mouth. Kyle removed it, frowned at a minute speck of blood, and handed me a clean cotton handkerchief. I took it— and all at once I was no longer Janey Blackman, mousey office receptionist. I was the intrepid heroine of one of my Cinderella sagas, the girl who rises from the gutters of London to head a financial empire, win Wimbledon—or save Kyle Johannsen's undeserving bacon.

That heroine always got her start by taking a risk, usually a monumental one. So why shouldn't I work for Joe Murray? It couldn't be much harder than writing letters explaining why Inspirational Books couldn't, or wouldn't, pay its bills.

"I'm sure I can handle it," I said, affecting a confidence I definitely didn't feel. "I've been reading up on some of our newer products."

That much was true. There had been at least two sarcastic articles in the papers recently saying that health food was a dangerous fraud.

Following all the unfavourable publicity, Harriet's absence was probably the straw that had snapped Management's back.

"You have?" Kyle's gaze sharpened. "So what do you think of our new rose hip tonic?"

"I think it sounds—promising. An effective preventative for the more esoteric viral infections." There. That had a nice, intelligent ring to it.

"Stop showing off." Kyle cut me down to size with one stroke. Then he placed both hands flat on the counter and stared down at me as if he were sizing up the finer points of a doubtful workhorse. "All right," he said in the end. "Let's see what you can do. I'll take you up to Advertising. Get Charlotte to cover for you."

He must be desperate, I thought dazedly. *Or crazy. Maybe both.* But then so was I. Along with incompetence, Joe Murray had a reputation for being both irascible and erratic.

I went to find Charlotte, who was delighted to escape the clutches of Mrs. Slade. Kyle's wasn't the only frayed temper around Ambrosia today.

Joe grunted when Kyle told him I was to be his temporary assistant, and asked if I had any idea what the job involved.

"I can spell and write letters," I replied, knowing he could do neither.

"Typing? Shorthand?" he snapped.

"Typing, yes. In my last job. I don't take shorthand, but I write fast." I didn't add that when I wrote fast I frequently couldn't read my own writing.

"Huh!" Joe grunted. "All right. I suppose that will do. For now." He directed a threatening scowl at Kyle.

Kyle said, "It will have to do—unless someone else in your department can take over. Or unless you'd prefer to handle the work yourself."

"No, no. Jane will be fine," Joe said hastily.

I was glad he thought so.

To my surprise, the first job he gave me was to write a succinct half page extolling the virtues of the rose-hip tonic. Lord, did that mean Harriet wrote his copy for him too? Luckily, I had become adept at embellishing the truth during my days with Ivan Reid and was able to come up with a pungent phrase or two casting doubt on the integrity of the tonic's detractors.

Joe's greasy cowlick fell across his forehead as he glanced at it. "Yes," he said. "That will do." His stocky body sagged with relief.

That evening, as I prepared to join the throng of employees jostling through the big front doors, Kyle came up behind me and tapped me on the shoulder.

"Sorry I chewed you up this morning," he said. "Thanks for helping us out of a difficult situation."

From the corner of my eye, I caught a glimpse of Charlotte's open mouth. "It's all right," I mumbled, hanging my head so he wouldn't see my cheeks go pink with pleasure.

Kyle said, "No, it isn't. I'd like to make it up to you. How about I take you out to dinner?"

"What?" My chin jerked up automatically. "Oh, I couldn't. You don't have to do that."

"What if I want to?"

Oh, no. I wasn't getting into that again. Last time I'd gone out with my boss I'd ended up leaving my job. "I can't," I said. "I—um—have another engagement."

He smiled a thin, disbelieving smile. "You're a lousy liar, Jane. I'm only offering you dinner. No strings attached."

I shook my head and examined the shine on his shoes. "Thank you. It's kind of you. But I—er—I have a rule about not going out with people I work for."

"I'm talking about dinner, not 'going out.' And you don't work for me at the moment. You work for Joe."

"Yes, but—you're still Management."

He laughed. "I've been called a lot of names, but never Management. Okay, don't worry about it. Your rule isn't such a bad one."

He didn't care a bit. He'd only asked me because he felt guilty about losing his temper. "It's a very good rule," I snapped, lifting my head to look him in the eye.

Kyle held up a palm as if to ward me off. "I said it was okay. Enjoy your evening, Miss Blackman." He left before I could frame a reply.

He always moved like that—as if he had too little time to do whatever needed to be done.

Charlotte accosted me outside the door. "He apologized to you," she said. "I heard him."

"Yes. He did."

"But he never apologizes to anyone."

"Maybe he's turned over a new leaf."

"Maybe."

I could tell she didn't believe it, and I sensed her eyes on my back, watching me, until I turned the corner.

When Harriet phoned the following day to say she needed further days off, Joe swore with more imagination than I'd thought he possessed and offered me her job.

"Oh, but Harriet will be back," I said quickly. My heroines never took advantage of another's misfortune—unless they were pushed.

I was pushed.

"Rubbish," Joe said. "Harriet is hedging her bets. She's had an offer from some firm that sells fertilizer, and she can't make up her bloody mind if she wants to take it. The job's yours, if you think you can cope."

Who was I to look a gift horse in the mouth? Not an original thought for an advertising assistant but in the circumstances, it fit.

"Thank you," I said. "I'll do my best."

"You bet you will." His bulbous nose quivered and his cowlick flapped up and down as he grabbed the phone to tell Kyle he'd better find the office a new receptionist.

I'd been told Joe Murray's style of personnel management was strictly intimidation and bluster. So far his behaviour had confirmed this.

But at least my new job would pay better.

As the weeks passed, I discovered I was right on both counts. The pay was good, and Joe was impossible. But somehow I managed.

Generally the work involved correcting my boss's atrocious spelling and making sure he kept his appointments, most of which involved golf or extended lunches. Occasionally, I got to write a paragraph or two that somebody had forgotten to produce for our monthly catalogue, and as long as my prose was liberally sprinkled with words like 'healthy,' 'nourishing' and 'natural,' Joe seemed satisfied. Whether our customers were any healthier, I couldn't say, but I liked to think they might be.

Outside of a vague feeling that there ought to be more to life than work and Mrs. Carmody's, I was happy at Ambrosia. I might not have Posy's assets, but I was good at my job and soon I would be better. That was what I told myself anyway. Certainly, my bank account was growing.

"Suppose you'll be leaving us for posher digs soon," Arabella said to me one evening when we happened to collide in the kitchen. "What are you now, some kind of fancy executive?"

"No, some kind of fancy dogsbody. But I'm learning a lot about the food business. What makes you think I'll be moving?"

Arabella threw four strips of bacon into an overheated pan, then started back as grease jumped up and spattered her bare arms. "Damn," she muttered, edging forward to lower the gas. "Duncan hates burnt bacon."

I waited until the grease had settled back into the bacon before asking again, "Arabella, what makes you think I'll be moving?"

"Stands to reason. You're going up in the world. Ought to have an upper crust address to go with the upper crust job." She flicked the end of her nose with her thumb and gave a sniff.

"I don't want to move," I protested, surprised to discover it was true. "I've been here over a year now. It's come to feel like home."

"Even with Old Matthews snorting and coughing in Lavender and Garcia's old rooms? I'd have thought you'd want to get away."

Miss Lavender and Mrs. Garcia had disappeared two months ago. Rumour had it they'd ended the affair when Mr. Garcia had threatened to seek custody of the children. The two ladies had been replaced by a retired janitor with permanent bronchitis.

"Old Matthews doesn't bother me," I said. I didn't add that Old Matthews' wheezing was a lullaby compared to the racket she and Duncan created almost every night.

Arabella shrugged. "Even so. If I was you, I'd want to live somewhere nicer."

"I'd miss you," I said.

She tossed her head and tried to hide a pleased little smirk. "Go on. Why would you miss me? You with your posh accent an' all."

I didn't like being reminded of the difference in our backgrounds. Chantersley attitudes had worn off surprisingly quickly, and I would have felt comfortable with Arabella and her friends if only they'd felt comfortable with me. Most of them didn't, but that didn't stop Arabella from asking me to go along whenever she went somewhere with "the girls." I think she was sorry for me because I didn't go out much.

I'd accepted one or two invitations from male customers I met through work, but the occasions hadn't been memorable. I wasn't bright or witty, except in my imagination, and too many silences had fallen. When they wanted to kiss me, I let them, and that wasn't memorable either. The word got round and pretty soon the invitations dried up. I might be a success in my job, but on the social front I was pretty much a failure.

"I can't help my accent," I snapped at Arabella as she stabbed the bacon with a fork. "Any more than you can help yours. But you're my friend. Of course, I'd miss you."

"Sorry." She flipped the bacon onto a sheet of silver paper. "No need to get your knickers in a twist. Ouch." She shoved a finger in her mouth. "Damn bacon. I think that pig's out to get me."

"Serves you right." Meat had lost its appeal after a month or two at Ambrosia. Now I rather enjoyed the chance to be sanctimonious.

"Not my fault." Arabella was cheerfully unrepentant. "Duncan thinks bacon and chops are made in factories like potatoes."

"But potatoes aren't..." I stopped. Arabella was studying her purple nails. It had always been impossible to tell when she was pulling my leg—almost as impossible as it was to stay annoyed with her for long. Anyway, I didn't want to stay annoyed with her. Apart from Charlotte, who was usually busy with her boyfriend, she was the only close friend I had. I hadn't seen Allison since school, though we'd spoken once or twice on the phone. I knew she was also busy with a boyfriend.

Posy had sent a postcard from Venice saying marriage was "fabulous," but since then I hadn't heard a word. Presumably, she had no need of my friendship now that David was safely in the bag.

I had never had much need of hers.

"You're nuts," I said, grinning at Arabella. "Potatoes aren't made in factories."

"Crisps are. And those dried things you just add water to."

She had me there.

Later, I thought about what she'd said. I probably could afford to move if I watched my pennies. But I was used to Number Fifteen. I had even grown used to the smoke and the nighttime noises—and Mrs. C's refusal to allow me to put in a phone. She threw a fit every time I suggested it. For all she grumbled about taking calls for her tenants, the phone was her personal pipeline to their business.

That was why, when Posy phoned a few days later, she had no choice but to catch me at the office after getting the number from my parents.

"You really should get a phone, Janey," she complained. "You're the only person I know who doesn't have one. I wanted to get hold of you last night."

"How's David?" I asked.

"David? All right, I suppose. Listen, Janey, you must come and see our new house. I've just had the decorators in."

"Where is it?"

"Oh, we've bought the most delightful Elizabethan cottage just outside Lesser Gotham. You must come. What are you doing on Sunday?"

I'd been thinking of paying a duty visit to my parents and grizzly William, who was reported to be teething.

"Nothing," I said, making a snap decision.

"Oh, good. Do come for tea."

"Thank you. I'd love to." It was almost true.

"I suppose you haven't got a car yet?"

"Me? No. I don't have a licence anyway."

"Oh, I just got mine. I'll pick you up at the bus stop if you like. Look out for a rather super Austin-Healey Sprite. Daddy bought it for me."

"How sweet of him." I copied her gushing condescension. "So looking forward to seeing you."

I hung up then because Joe Murray's nose was poking out the door of his office. Like Kyle, he hated to see his staff taking personal calls.

~*~

"Janey! How sweet you look." Posy, wearing a red and white spotted dress and a straw hat that looked only slightly out of place on this warm, September Sunday, swept up to me as I stumbled off the bus. "Where did you find that dear little frock?"

That dear little frock, a brown sleeveless linen suitable for work, had cost me the best part of a week's pay. "Harrods," I replied, before I could stop myself. I'd actually bought it at C & A.

"Oh." Posy was only momentarily discomposed. "I didn't think you shopped at Harrods."

Neither did I. "Oh yes, quite often." I gave a nonchalant shrug, and immediately felt foolish. What was the matter with me? It was over a year since the two of us had left Chantersley. Surely I wasn't still allowing Posy to make me feel defensive.

The Austin-Healey had been newly painted an improbable powder blue. Posy, seated behind the wheel, looked vaguely out of place. I slid into the passenger seat feeling rather like one of the ugly sisters after Cinderella has swanned off with the Prince.

"You look well," I said grudgingly. "Marriage must agree with you." She also looked fatter, but I managed not to add that.

"Oh, yes." Posy waved a manicured hand. "David looks after me quite nicely."

I noticed she didn't turn her head to meet my eyes. When she switched on the engine and pulled self-consciously onto the road, I was relieved to discover she drove with confidence and a certain degree of skill.

Pembroke Cottage, as Posy called her new home, was only a mile from the bus stop. Surrounded by neatly trimmed hedges, its size wasn't apparent at first. But once Posy had parked the car in a double garage in the back, it became obvious that although the house might have been a cottage in Elizabethan times, additions made by subsequent generations had turned it into a sprawling minor mansion. The newest bits looked suspiciously like stage sets.

Posy pointed to an old wooden rain barrel near the kitchen door. "David says I ought to get rid of that. But I think it's sweet, don't you? So full of character."

Not to mention splinters and bugs. "It's definitely old," I said.

Posy looked at me with a certain suspicion and led me around to the front. "Here we are," she said, flapping a hand at the house. "Isn't it charming?"

"Lovely," I said politely. "Much bigger than I expected."

"Oh, I know. David thought it was too big for just the two of us, but I fell in love with it. Don't you adore the rose garden?"

"It's beautiful."

I gazed, entranced, at the carefully pruned trellis of wild roses arching from the front gate to the door. Beyond it, a circular bed had been cut out of the lawn to provide a more cultivated showcase for autumn roses in deep pinks and plums. Their velvet heads waved gently at the sun, infusing the air with a rich fragrance.

"It is gorgeous, isn't it?" Posy said. "I was right to make Daddy buy it for us, wasn't I?"

Ouch. How was I supposed to answer that? "I don't know," I mumbled. "I suppose if David didn't mind...."

"Oh, David! He'd be happy in a barn, provided it was full of beastly animals. Besides..." She touched my arm. "I think we're going to need the extra space."

I stared at her blankly. "Are you? Why?"

"Oh, Janey, don't be so dense. I've only just told David. Can't you guess?"

"Guess? I...Oh!" A bee buzzed past my nose, and the breeze lifted the curls on Posy's forehead. She was smiling as complacently as ever, but I saw now that there was a softness about her, a kind of glow, that hadn't been there before. Not long ago, I'd seen that same ridiculous glow on my mother's face. "You're going to have a baby," I said.

CHAPTER TWELVE

Posy pushed back her hair, a gesture that emphasized the fulsome outline of her breasts. "Of course, Daddy is absolutely thrilled he's going to have a grandchild," she gloated, as she urged me into the house.

"What about David?" I asked. "Is he thrilled?"

"Oh, yes." She busied herself with a bowl of cut roses on a gate-legged table at the bottom of the stairs. "Of course, it means I'll have to have my own bedroom. The doctor says I'm very fragile."

My jaw dropped. She looked about as fragile as a Reuben's matron. "Fragile?" I repeated. "Why? What's the matter with you?"

"I have a delicate constitution. Mother died when I was very young, you know." She gave the bowl of roses a final quick twist and turned to face me.

"Yes, but I heard that was from..." I stopped. What I'd actually heard was that her mother had got tipsy one winter's night and slipped on a patch of ice and cracked her head.

"Mummy had been in poor health for some time," Posy said firmly.

"Oh. Yes, of course. That's what I heard." The lie came easily enough. "You're not—nervous though? About having a baby?" Posy had always been nervous about anything that didn't contribute to her comfort.

She avoided my eye. "No, of course not. I just have to be careful, the doctor says. Come and see the house." She took me by the arm as if she thought I might try to make a run for it.

In fact, I wouldn't have missed her guided tour for anything. Posy's house, in its way, was remarkable and slightly bizarre—a combination of good, old-fashioned comfort and arid decorator's dream.

The marital bedroom, which I was only allowed to glimpse in passing, seemed to be all Victorian lace, frills and tassels. Posy's taste, I suspected. David's study was a matter of books, Buddhas and oriental furnishings with claws. The kitchen, still supported by what looked like the original beams, was blatantly modern. All the latest gadgets and conveniences. I blinked. Did this mean Posy did her own cooking? Was there no ancient cook whose convenience was irrelevant—and who would have hated the gadgets in any case?

"Do you do the cooking?" I asked.

"Me?" Posy was startled. "Well, of course I make breakfast sometimes, but Kathryn comes in from the village to do the rest."

"Kathryn?"

"She's a young widow. Quite good really. Her mother looks after the child."

That explained the gadgets. They probably went a long way towards the successful acquisition of "good help," a subject I'd heard mothers of girls at school discussing ad nauseam on sports days.

"And this is the drawing room," Posy said, opening the final door. "We had a decorator in, of course."

Although she had chosen a decorator with conservative tastes, everything seemed new, expensive and posed. It was as if the room had been arranged as an advertising layout for the Decorators' Bible. Not so much as a cushion was out of place. The pale gold of the pears in the still life over the mantle was picked up in the colour of the walls, and I had a sense that even the magazines on the mahogany coffee table had been chosen to match the decor.

I opened my mouth. Posy waited expectantly for my murmur of approval.

"Did you and David choose the furniture together?" I asked. "Or did your decorator make all the decisions?" It was the best I could come up with on short notice.

"Choose it together! Of course, we didn't. David doesn't appreciate the finer points of design. Just because he grew up with furniture that's been there forever, he thinks we should be equally tatty." She waved at a beige brocade chair that matched the pattern on the excellent imported carpet. "Why don't you sit over there."

It wasn't a question, so I took the chair she indicated, bent down to pluck a dandelion seed from the skirt of my brown linen dress, and asked, "Where is David, by the way?"

"Out walking his dog. He wasn't sure he'd be back in time for tea."

"Oh." I put the dandelion seed back on my skirt, stared at it, then flicked it onto the floor. "I didn't know he had a dog." *Was David avoiding me*? If he remembered what had happened at the wedding—by no means certain in view of his alcohol consumption—I could hardly be surprised that he wasn't here. Any meeting was bound to be awkward.

"He didn't have a dog," Posy said. "Nefertiti was bad enough. But the moment we moved into the house, he insisted on getting a puppy. His parents' dog had a litter and he took one."

"I like dogs," I said mildly. "Mother wouldn't let me have one."

"I don't blame her. Noisy, messy creatures. Of course, it wouldn't be so bad if David would only leave it in the kitchen."

"Doesn't he?" I looked round for some evidence that anything living and messy had actually passed through this room.

"No, he says that as a member of the family it can go wherever it likes. I told him having Jasmine as a member of the family was bad enough, but he wouldn't listen."

She wasn't even trying to be funny. I swallowed a laugh and said, "Does the dog have a name?"

"Blackie," Posy said disgustedly. "He couldn't even come up with a suitable name."

I gave a non-committal grunt that I hoped would get her off the subject of dogs and on to tea.

It did. With an irritable shrug, Posy bounced around and headed for the kitchen. When she came back, she was pushing a trolley laden with tea, flower-patterned china cups and a dainty selection of sandwiches and cake.

"Kathryn doesn't come on Sundays," she explained. "I had to manage on my own."

"Poor you."

Something in my voice must have given me away, because Posy turned red and put sugar in my tea.

She knew I only took milk.

A dog barked somewhere close at hand. Posy frowned, and when I turned to see what had displeased her, I saw three heads moving past the window.

David had arrived with his father and mother.

Posy gave a martyred sigh. "I thought I heard the Range Rover," she said. "He might have told me he was going to fetch his people."

"Perhaps he didn't know," I suggested. "Maybe he met them by accident."

Posy pursed her mouth, and I had a sudden preview of how she would look when she was old—sour and discontented, with baggy folds under her chin. "He knew perfectly well," she snapped. "I'd better go and put the kettle on again."

"Posy put the kettle on, Posy put the kettle on, Posy put the kettle on and made a cup of tea," I hummed.

"Don't be so silly." As Posy flounced out of the room, I half expected her to add, "Off with your head."

I hadn't really meant to annoy her. It was just one of those silly tunes that sometimes come out for no reason.

David was here. I bit nervously into a cucumber sandwich, and as I did so, Nefertiti, the black cat I'd seen at his flat, stalked regally across the carpet, tail twitching, and launched herself onto my lap.

"Hello, cat," I said, as she began to knead her claws into my thighs. "I don't think your mistress wants you playing in here."

Nefertiti was unimpressed.

I was just thinking I'd better detach her from my dress before she shredded it when a sleek black labrador bounded into the room, spotted the cat, and shot across the carpet in pursuit. I dropped my sandwich. The labrador paused to eat it. By the time it looked up, Nefertiti was standing on all fours on my lap, arching her back and spitting venom.

"Stop it," I said helplessly. "Both of you. I'm a guest, not a battlefield."

Posy came back at that moment carrying a fresh pot of tea. "Oh!" she exclaimed. "Blackie, you wretched animal." Raising her voice, she called piercingly, "David, where are you? Your monster of a dog is attacking Janey."

David and his mother and father converged on the doorway in a body and stood there, momentarily paralysed. Nefertiti, still spitting, batted Blackie on the nose, and the dog, with what I hoped was a playful growl, planted both front paws on my knee.

"Hey," I cried. "Just a minute now...."

"David do something!" shrieked Posy.

"Blackie. Down," David said.

Blackie, with a complaining rumble, slid reluctantly back onto the carpet.

"Sorry," David came into the room and bent down to pat the quivering dog.

He wasn't sorry. He was grinning.

"For heaven's sake get him out of here," snapped Posy. "And take Nefertiti with you. You'll have Janey thinking we run a zoo."

"Janey doesn't mind," David said. "Do you, Janey?"

I hadn't seen him since the wedding. He looked taller, harder somehow. But his friendly grin was the same as ever. I said, "No, it's all right. I like animals."

"Quite right. Sensible girl." David's father pushed his way around his son and sat down. "How about a spot of tea, Posy?" He looked hopefully at his daughter-in-law.

David took the teapot from her hands and waited for her to sit down before handing it back with a stiff little bow.

His mother, observing this display of good manners, nodded approvingly.

"I said get that dog out of here." Posy wasn't as easily placated.

David made a brief movement with his head, as if warning her to keep her temper in front of guests. At the same time he gestured to Blackie, scooped the cat up in his arms, and left the room with the dog trotting obediently at his heels.

By the time he came back, Posy was pouring tea in a silence that was just starting to become awkward. Surprisingly, his presence immediately warmed the room.

"This is very good sponge, my dear. Did you make it?" Mrs. Foley asked, in a pouring-oil-on-troubled-waters sort of voice.

"Posy can't cook," David answered for her. "Kathryn made it."

"Posy has never needed to cook," his mother chided him gently. "I couldn't boil water myself when your father and I were first married."

That, of course, was the difference between David's upbringing and Posy's. David's father made a comfortable but unremarkable living. Posy's father was rich.

"You learned though, Mother." David smiled at her.

"Yes, and I learned to enjoy it. But it's not as though I didn't have help."

"Posy has help."

"It's not the same. Posy hasn't been well, have you, my dear?"

"She's pregnant. Not ill," David said, before Posy had a chance to reply.

"Now, David, you know what the doctor said—"

"Yes, of course. She told me." He lowered himself into a gold, wingbacked chair, at the same time throwing Posy a half-smile and a look that to me seemed more cryptic than apologetic.

She shot back a glare that could only be described as malignant and poured his tea and passed sandwiches in silence.

"It's lovely news about the baby, isn't it?" I said, deciding it was time I did my bit to ease the tension.

"Lovely," Mrs. Foley agreed. "We're all delighted. Aren't we, David?"

"Speaking for myself, yes," David replied.

"Delighted. Quite so. Delighted," muttered his father.

Posy scowled.

The afternoon didn't get much better. Eventually, Posy did make an effort to look pleasant, but she didn't contribute much to the conversation and it was left to the rest of us to maintain a facade of civility. It wasn't easy. The friction between the recently wed pair seethed so close to the veneer of polite platitudes that we were all on tenterhooks waiting for it to explode into an outright eruption.

What, I wondered, *had gone wrong?* The two of them had everything a young married couple could ask for. Maybe they weren't crazy in love with each other, but they'd both known that when they married.

I remembered what Posy had said about David having to move to a separate bedroom. Was that what this was about? Sex? I couldn't see the problem myself. David had to be more thoughtful than Carlo. Maybe he wasn't as easy-going as I'd originally imagined, but he had told me he wanted to make the marriage work. So what if the earth didn't move? I wasn't sure I believed it ever did.

The eruption didn't come. How it was avoided I'll never know, but as soon as tea was over, Mrs. Foley stood up and said they must be getting home to feed the dogs. Her husband, following her lead with alacrity, immediately levered himself to his feet. David said he would drive them.

"Would you like to come too, Janey?" he asked. "I can take you back to town if that would help."

"Oh, no I...."

"I'll take Janey. To the bus stop," Posy said.

Ouch. Snow, ice and freezing rain—with a helping of frost to top them off.

"Thank you, but I'd much rather take the bus," I said to David.

He shrugged. "Please yourself."

Mr. Foley patted my hand as goodbyes were said and told me I was a good girl. Not knowing what to say, I smiled. If I'd been a dog, I'd probably have hung out my tongue and wagged my tail.

"You and David have a beautiful house," I said to Posy, as she and the Sprite returned me to the bus stop. "You must be so happy together."

It was blatant fishing, but I didn't think she'd notice as long as I sounded suitably admiring.

"Oh, yes." She swung the wheel a little too far to the right. "Daddy says it will take time to get David used to being married though. There are some things I just can't make him understand."

"Like dogs in the drawing room?" I suggested.

"Yes. And other things."

"But you're both pleased about the baby."

"Of course."

I hesitated, then curiosity won out, and I made up my mind to ask the question that was none of my business. "Do you remember asking me what it was like? I mean about...."

"Janey, why are you gulping like a trout? You mean about sex, don't you? Of course, I remember. You said I'd like it."

Had I said that? I wasn't sure anymore. I waited for her to tell me I'd been right. Posy wasn't the sort to admit that her life was less than perfect.

But to my surprise, she didn't elaborate, and I lost my nerve and let the subject drop.

Seconds later we arrived at the bus stop. I thanked her and scrambled onto the gravel lining the road.

"Do come again," Posy called, as she backed the car into a turn.

"Thank you."

She nodded. "I'll phone. See you soon, Janey."

She didn't wait for the bus to come. Nor did she phone. The rear of the Sprite as it vanished round the corner was the last I saw of Posy for six months.

Once or twice I actually thought about calling her, but when it came to the point of picking up the phone, I couldn't do it. Our friendship, if that's what it was, had always been odd, and in my more honest moments I knew there was only one reason I might want it to continue—a reason that was much better forgotten.

~*~

"Take a message, please," I said to Arlene, the big-eyed pixie who functioned as secretary-cum-gofer to the Advertising Department.

It was mid-February again, and the weatherman was threatening us with snow. In the glass-walled office to which I'd recently been promoted, I was putting the finishing touches to a promotional paragraph on a new pill that was supposed to cure toothache, backache, cuts, blisters and colds. The copy was already overdue when Arlene rang through to ask if I could take a personal call.

Dad, probably, to tell me William had cut another tooth, taken his first step or performed some other miracle of childhood. I told Arlene to tell him I'd call back.

Darkness was closing in by the time I got round to reading the scrawled note she had dumped on my desk. The sky had turned a deep, menacing grey and the promised snow had already begun to fall. At first

I couldn't read what she'd written. But when I held the note to the light, I made out the words: "David Foley" and "Call."

"Arlene," I yelled, poking my head around the door. "What else did he say?"

"Huh?" She was examining her nose in a mirror. "Dunno. Don't think he said anything. Friend of yours, is he?"

"Yes," I said. "A friend." I wasn't sure if it was true.

David had called me. That meant I could call him back.

I hadn't known I wanted to, hadn't allowed myself to think about him much—and somehow six months had gone by. Posy's baby must be due any moment.

It was after ten when I finally got through to Pembroke Cottage from the only call box near Wrenbert Terrace that sometimes worked. By that time, the snow was ankle deep.

"Hello, Janey," David said. "I thought you might have tried earlier and missed me. I've been at the hospital. Posy had a girl this morning."

"Congratulations," I said. Then, realizing that sounded lukewarm, "That's wonderful news, David. You must be thrilled."

He said he was. He also told me there had been complications following labour, which, apparently, had lasted forty hours. The baby was fine. Posy was all right. She had nearly died but now she was out of danger.

His voice was flat, devoid of the relief he must be feeling. I put it down to exhaustion and asked if he thought Posy would like to see me.

"Yes," David said. "I'm sure she would. When can you come?"

"Saturday," I said.

It was only two days away.

~*~

The hospital was one of those forbidding, Victorian structures the mere sight of which must have encouraged generations of patients to give up the ghost and die quietly. Posy, on the other hand, and despite her protestations of fragility, was obviously made of sterner stuff. As I made my way down the corridor to her private room, I could hear her voice, high-pitched and irritable, demanding that "this wretched tube" be taken out at once.

"Don't be difficult, Posy. The staff are doing their best." That was David's voice, resigned and long-suffering.

"I hate having needles stuck in me. I don't see why—"

"Doctor's orders, Mrs. Foley," said a third voice, brisk and no-nonsense. "We want to get better now, don't we?"

"I don't know what *we* want. I want this tube out of my arm."

I paused in the doorway. Posy, in a blue hospital gown, lay propped on pillows in the bed. A plastic tube was attached to her forearm. On one side of the bed a nurse was checking a thermometer. On the other side, David sat in a hard chair gazing at his wife in weary exasperation. I sniffed the medicinal smell of disinfectant. It easily overwhelmed the scent of the flowers lining the windowsill and nightstand.

David looked up as I walked in and briefly, his eyes came alive. "Janey," he said. "It's good of you to come."

Posy said, "Hello, Janey. I had a perfectly awful time. You are lucky not to be married."

"But you have a beautiful baby girl, and I haven't," I answered, knowing that was what she really meant. "Congratulations. I brought you some flowers."

"Oh, thank you. You are kind." She took the flowers and handed them to David without looking at him. "Do find a vase for them, darling. Of course, I've been absolutely inundated with roses."

I'd brought her early daffodils. *Did she do it on purpose?* At one time I'd have been sure of it.

"How lovely for you," I said. "Can I see the baby?"

I didn't want to see the baby particularly but knew I hadn't a hope of getting out of it.

"Oh, David will take you in a minute. She's behind glass."

Like a monkey in a zoo? Or a crocodile? "Don't you want her in with you?" I asked.

"Oh, yes. As soon as I'm able. She's quite beautiful." This statement was accompanied by a smile of genuine maternal adoration untouched by the self-absorption that had always been so much a part of Posy.

"I'm sure she is," I said.

The nurse had already left the room, and David, still brandishing my daffodils, was prowling around the walls looking baffled.

"Really, David, what is the matter with you?" Posy asked. "Can't you even find a vase?"

"I should have brought one," I said. "I didn't think."

"No reason at all why you should." David laid the flowers on the end of Posy's bed and loped out into the corridor.

"How are you?" I asked, appropriating his chair.

"A little weak." Posy heaved a fragile sigh and closed her eyes.

I stared at her pale round face and was forcibly reminded of a pudding.

"Was it very bad?" I asked. "David said you were in labour forty hours."

"Ghastly." She laid the back of a plump hand across her forehead. "But worth it all now that I have Sidonie."

"Sidonie? Is that what you're calling her?"

"Yes. David wanted Jane, but I said that was much too ordinary." She opened her eyes, presumably to see how I took that. "It suits you quite well though, Janey."

Motherhood hadn't changed her that much.

"Thanks," I said.

I thought about asking her what it was like to have a baby, just as she had once asked me what it was like to have sex. But she was bound to exaggerate, and anyway, I doubted if giving birth was something that could easily be described. I asked her about the baby instead, and she was just telling me how adorable Sidonie's little fingers were when David came back carrying a green glass vase.

"Good God, Janey doesn't want to hear about her fingers," he exclaimed with unpaternal horror. "Come on, Janey. Let me introduce you to my daughter."

When he said 'my daughter,' his shoulders went back and his smile was just like my father's when he looked at William.

I followed David into the corridor, past the nursing station and up to a glass wall behind which half a dozen or so babies lay in what looked to me like boxes.

"There she is." David pointed to a hairless little creature lying on her back with her eyes closed and her tiny hands curled into fists.

"She's sweet," I said dutifully.

"She is, isn't she?" Hearing a worshipful note in his voice, I glanced up. He was beaming at the child as if she were a reincarnation of Aphrodite instead of a puckered-up walnut.

"You like babies?" I asked.

"Mm. As a matter of fact, I do."

We stood there for several minutes staring at David's walnut, until another proud father came along with a captive aunt in tow.

"We'd better go back to Posy," I said.

"I suppose so." His lack of enthusiasm was almost an embarrassment.

Posy was half-asleep, and when Mr. and Mrs. Bantley-Brown arrived a few minutes later, I said it was time I went home. As usual, David said he'd drive me.

Posy came to life again at once. "I thought you said you had work to do tonight."

"I'll deal with it later," he said. "Coming, Janey?"

"Yes, but there's no need—I mean, shouldn't you stay with Posy?"

"Oh, don't worry about me," Posy said, with surprising magnanimity. "Mummy and Daddy are here now."

David bent over to kiss her perfunctorily on the forehead. "I'll come back tomorrow," he said, and ignoring his father-in-law's frown, took my arm and led me from the room.

"Doesn't Mr. Bantley-Brown trust us?" I asked.

"Of course, he does. Why do you ask?"

I thought about that. "No reason. David, why did you ask me to come? Did Posy really want to see me?"

He stopped abruptly in front of the nursing station. "I don't know. She hasn't mentioned you since that day you came for tea."

"Then why—"

"I wanted to see you."

I stared at the smooth sterility of the floor. It was gunmetal grey with black specks. In the background, the keys of a typewriter clicked briskly. I couldn't think of a single thing to say.

After a while I felt David take my arm again and propel me gently through the revolving door. Vaguely, it occurred to me that the door didn't fit with the age of the building, but I couldn't keep my mind off his startling admission for long. It wasn't that I hadn't wanted him to make it, but Posy had just had his baby—a baby he obviously adored.

"Janey," he said, leading me, unresisting, across a car park crisscrossed with ridges of dirty snow. "Janey, what's the matter? I didn't mean to offend you."

"You didn't." I collapsed onto the passenger seat of his car. He could have wanted to see me for any number of ordinary reasons.

I waited for him to offer one, but he was sitting with one arm wrapped around the wheel, staring dully at the mist on the windscreen. After a while I asked, "What's wrong?"

He bent his head until his forehead touched the wheel.

"David...."

"I'm sorry." His voice was thick. I'd never heard it sound like that before.

"There's nothing to be sorry for. Is there?"

"I suppose not." He was silent for several seconds and when he spoke again his tone was normal. "She is beautiful, isn't she?"

"Posy?"

"Posy!" He took his arm from the wheel and laid it along the back of the seat. "No, I was talking about my daughter."

"Yes. She is. Beautiful." She wasn't, but it didn't matter.

David shrugged and gazed moodily at my chin. Was it sprouting another spot? "I should never have married her," he said.

I tried not to let my feelings show. "But—you said you'd make it work. That her father—I mean..." I stopped, gripping my hands tightly in my lap. For no reason I could easily explain, I wanted to shake him.

"I know I did. At the time I thought I could. I was wrong."

"Well, it's done now," I said drearily. "You have a daughter, so you'll just have to make the best of it, won't you?"

He nodded and made an effort at a smile that didn't quite come off. "Yes. I intend to. I wanted to see you, Janey, and to show off Sidonie. But I shouldn't have asked you to come. It wasn't fair of me."

What was he saying? It dawned on me then, as if I'd been hit on the head with a sack of wet cement, that it was possible I wasn't the only one who had spent the last year trying to suppress a classic case of lust. At least I supposed that was the correct term for the sensations I so often felt around David. I stroked my hand along the soft leather seat. Was he the reason I had allowed Posy to come back into my life after Chantersley? And was it possible he felt the same way I did?

"Why wasn't it fair of you?" I asked. "Why shouldn't you want to show off your daughter?"

"There's rather more to it than that."

Yes, no doubt there was. But all at once I didn't want to hear it. "David," I said quickly, "I know Posy isn't always easy, but anyone can see she loves the baby. She'll be a devoted mother, and—"

"And she's my wife. Yes, I know. Forgive me, I've been talking nonsense. It must be lack of sleep." He took his arm from the back of the seat and turned the wireless up high. Bing Crosby was crooning something about "love forever true."

On an impulse, I said, "Goodbye, David," and started to open the door.

He caught my shoulder and held me back. "Janey, where in hell do you think you're going? I won't have you taking the bus back to London in the dark."

"I've done it before. And you don't have a choice."

"Yes, I do." The engine roared and the car shot through the gates before I had time to blink. Once we were on the road, David said, "Don't worry. I won't pounce."

"I should hope not," I said primly.

He laughed. It wasn't a happy laugh. But then he didn't strike me as a particularly happy man. Only when he spoke of his walnut of a daughter did I catch a glimpse of the nonchalant suitor Posy had introduced me to eighteen months before.

We didn't talk much on the drive back to London, and David kept the wireless high to mask the silence. After he stopped the car outside Number Fifteen, he was out and opening my door so fast I felt like unwanted mail being dispatched to the dustbin.

A cat howled somewhere in the darkness, and the wind whipping down the street was damp with the kind of chill only February can bring.

"Goodnight, Janey," David said.

I raised my eyes. He looked much too exhausted to pounce. "Goodnight," I said. "Thank you for bringing me home."

He lifted a gloved hand, touched me on the cheek, then slid back into his car and drove off.

I climbed the stairs to my room and, much later, fell asleep staring at the stars.

On Monday, when Kyle asked me if by any chance I'd changed my mind about going out with Management, I said I had.

CHAPTER THIRTEEN

"Jane, don't you think you're being a little unwise? I'm sure he's very charming, but...."

"We're just friends, Mother. That's all."

Mother and I were seated at the kitchen table slicing mushrooms. William was under the table chewing on my slippers. Foolishly, I had just made the mistake of mentioning that Kyle was divorced, something I had only recently discovered myself.

For the past few months he and I had been taking in the odd show together, and once he had asked me to dinner at the Savoy. I'd felt out of place, but Kyle behaved as if the comforts and luxuries of wealth were his by right. Our friendship, as I tried to assure Mother, was purely platonic, not from any inherent virtue, but for the excellent reason that Kyle wasn't that sort of friend. He said he enjoyed my company, and I was glad of the chance to get out. Sometimes I even paid for my own tickets.

Kyle wasn't at all like David, but he was easy to talk to, and he made me feel witty and charming and older than I was. I did wonder sometimes why he showed no interest in going beyond companionship, but because it suited me, I didn't question his unusual lack of carnal intent.

I tried to tell Mother that, but she found it impossible to accept.

"I know that's the way you feel now, Jane," she fussed. "But friendship can so easily become something more complicated. It's not that I think divorce is immoral, but he's already failed at marriage once—"

"Mum! Who said anything about marriage?" I sliced vigorously at a mushroom that turned out to be my finger. When I let out a yelp, William stopped chewing my slipper and started to scream.

By the time he had been silenced with a chocolate biscuit and I had staunched the flow of blood and added a plaster, I hoped the matter of Kyle would be tacitly dropped.

It wasn't. Mother started in again with a tale about a school friend of hers who had married a divorced man and ended up divorcing him herself.

"Lots of people get divorced," I pointed out.

"I know, but it's so hard on the children."

"Children?" I winced. "I don't have any children. And Kyle and I aren't getting married."

Mother ran a finger along the blade of her knife. "How old is he?"

"I'm not sure. About thirty, I suppose."

"Much too old for you. What happened to his wife?"

"Nothing happened to her. He met her when he was in England on holiday and they got married and he never went back to—a place called Duluth, I think he said. It's on Lake Superior."

"But he isn't married to her any longer. He isn't, is he?" She dropped her knife onto the table with a clatter.

"No. I told you. He's divorced. His wife went back to her first love."

"I suppose that means he came over here and swept her off her feet just like all those Americans in the war. Then she came down to earth and realized she'd married the wrong man. Those Americans!"

"Mother! It wasn't like that. Or it may have been, but it wasn't his fault he fell in love—or hers that she fell out of it, I suppose. At least that's what Kyle says. He's very generous. Doesn't seem to hold it against her."

"You be careful, Jane. These very charming men aren't to be trusted."

"He's not that charming. He's awfully bossy around the office. And just because you trusted the wrong man—" I broke off, because Mother's faded face had turned from ivory to a grungy sort of grey.

"Yes," she said. "Yes, I did." She concentrated on slicing the last mushroom and when there was nothing left to slice, touched a hand to her throat and said, "Jane, I know we talked about this a long time ago—but if you should ever change your mind..." Her voice trailed off and she laid down her knife and stared glassily at my bandaged finger.

Ah. Thank God. I had no idea what she meant, but at least we weren't talking about Kyle. "Change my mind about what?" I asked. "William, stop biting my foot. I'm not a teething ring."

"About the possibility of meeting your father. John, I mean." She picked a minute scrap of mushroom off the table and threw it into the colander with the rest. "If you ever should meet him—please don't tell him about the fish shop. It's not that I mind for myself, but I wouldn't want John to think his daughter hadn't been—well, you know—brought up quite as nicely as he might wish—"

"For heaven's sake, Mother. He doesn't give a damn how I was brought up. He doesn't even know I exist. And there's nothing to be ashamed of about fish." I had a feeling I was repeating something I'd heard from someone else—and then remembered I was, and that the someone had been Dad.

"No. No, there isn't, of course, but John might get the wrong idea." She stabbed the point of the knife at the table, then took in what she was doing and laid it down. "As a matter of fact, John does know you exist."

"Mother! You said—"

"I know. But after William was born your father and I decided that for your sake he ought to be told."

I gripped the edge of the table. "For my sake? Did you see him?"

"No. I wrote him a letter. He didn't answer at once, but a week or two ago he wrote back. He wants to meet you, Jane."

The oilcloth beneath my fingers felt stiff and cold. "No," I whispered. "I don't want to meet him. He's never been my proper father. Dad has."

When Mother didn't react, I asked her why she had waited until now to tell me about the letter.

She picked up a fresh slice of mushroom and studied it as if it held the answer to the mysteries of the universe. "It seemed better to wait until you came home. I know you said you didn't want to meet John, but now that we have William..." She stopped, as if aware that she was treading on quicksand.

William? I shook my head. *What had William...?* Oh. Yes. Of course. William would always know who his father was.

"It makes no difference," I said. "He doesn't care about me. He never did."

"How could he, Jane? You said yourself he didn't know you existed. Now that he does, I think he wants to do the right thing."

"I don't need him."

"Maybe he needs you."

"Or sees me as some kind of duty. Did you tell him I don't ever want to see him?"

"Jane, I think you're making a mistake."

I made myself release my grip on the table and folded my hands loosely in my lap. "Then it's my mistake. You can tell him to forget about me because I already have a father. I'm sure he'll be relieved."

"Perhaps." Mother put down the mushroom. She didn't try to argue anymore, and I wondered if, in her own way, she too was relieved that I didn't want to meet her old lover. Contrarily, I was disappointed when she made no further effort to change my mind.

Frowning, I picked up the colander full of mushrooms and carried it over to the sink. There was a lump the size of a tennis ball in my chest.

"Jane, you're not crying, are you?" Mother's anxious voice said from behind me. "I didn't mean to upset you."

No, I wasn't crying. I smeared the back of my fist across my eyes. Why should I cry over a man I'd never known, or wanted to know? A man who had used my mother as nothing more than a convenience while his fiancèe was away.

I made myself turn around and William crawled out from under the table, saw me frowning at him and smiled. It was a big, goofy smile full of trusting affection—and it made me feel small. I was twenty years old. Old enough not to resent a helpless, if terminally messy, infant just because he was the actual son of the only father I knew well enough to love.

I smiled back at him and he chortled and made a beeline for my slippers.

Mother smiled too--with relief, I think.

"I'm all right," I said. Maybe it was the natural order of things for mothers and daughters to drive each other crazy, but I hated the look of anxious guilt that so often blurred the once sharp outline of her face.

"Really, all right," I insisted.

Mother nodded and the tension eased out of her. William grabbed my leg and pulled himself onto his feet. "He'll soon be walking," I said, astonished to discover I found the fact worthy of comment. Lately I'd been learning that a lot of the comfortable certainties I'd held about myself were not quite as certain as I'd thought.

The rest of the weekend passed smoothly. Mother didn't mention Kyle again. Perhaps she had come to the conclusion that ignoring his existence was the best way to make the problem go away. Later, when Dad came home, I heard him telling Mother how pleased he was to see that William and I had become so fond of each other. Mother said of course we were, as if it had never occurred to her that we might not be.

The following evening I was back in my room at Mrs. Carmody's.

It was a warm evening for early March, and as I sat in the hard chair staring into space and not reading the book on my lap, a robin flew onto a branch of the scrubby chestnut tree outside my window. When he opened his throat and began to sing, I laughed out loud and joined him in a rousing chorus of "All Things Bright and Beautiful."

Life, on the whole, wasn't bad. I liked my job, relations with my parents were cordial, and as long as I kept my mind off Pembroke Cottage, there was no reason to imagine the future would lead to anything but the fulfillment of my dreams—whatever those were. I wasn't as sure about dreaming as I had been.

This hopeful optimism, which at one time I thought I'd lost forever, wasn't seriously dented again until Kyle came into my glass-walled office one morning to tell me he was leaving Ambrosia.

Kyle? Leaving? I frowned in bewilderment as the heart I'd thought immune to further shock sank into the sensible flats I usually wore to work.

"Where are you going?" I asked, flipping through my card file in mindless pursuit of a non-existent address. "Back to the States?"

"No. I'm going to work for B & H Nutrition." He smiled and perched an elegant hip on the corner of my desk.

"But I thought...I mean, they don't sell health foods, do they?"

"No." His smile broadened until it almost reached his ears.

"What are you going to do there?" I asked grumpily. "Sell cheese and crisps?"

Kyle laughed. "I hope not. They've hired me to shake up their head office."

"Oh." He was good at shaking up. It wasn't easy to doze your way through a job with Kyle Johannsen at your back prodding and stirring and demanding to know why today's letters hadn't been mailed yesterday.

"You mean you're going to stir up personnel for them?" I said, beginning to get the picture.

"That's the idea."

"But why? You're already doing that here."

"I'm glad you think so." He extended a leg to examine the tip of his glossy black shoe. "But I figure it's time for a change."

"That's the reason you're leaving?"

"Nope. Not altogether."

Why was he being so evasive? It wasn't like him. "Why, then?" I asked, feeling as if I was extracting obstinate bicuspids.

Kyle stopped examining his shoe and looked me straight in the eye. "We've known each other for a while now, haven't we, Jane?"

"Yes, I suppose so," I agreed, puzzled.

"And we work in the same office. You wouldn't even go out with me at first."

"That was because I had a bad experience at the very first place I worked."

I hadn't told Kyle about Ivan Reid. Inspirational Books was behind me, my ex-boss a pathetic embarrassment. But I had come to trust Kyle Johannsen. He didn't make advances, he wasn't Mr. Reid, and we were friends.

"I thought that might be the problem." He nodded, unsurprised. "You were probably right to refuse me."

Oh. So that was it. I should have known, but I hadn't. "You're leaving so you won't have to work with me any longer, aren't you?" I said.

Arlene's high-pitched giggle sounded from the outer office, but she wasn't looking at us and I didn't think she could hear our conversation.

Kyle shook his head and clamped his lips over what looked like the beginnings of a grin. "I wouldn't exactly put it that way."

"What are you talking about?" I turned my back on him and went on fiddling with the card file.

He didn't answer. I waited for almost a minute, then turned round to demand he stop talking in riddles. Not that he was. I knew perfectly well what he meant. I just didn't like it.

"Look," I began. "It's..." I stopped. Kyle wasn't there. Though I hadn't heard him leave, through my glass barrier I could see him speaking to Arlene, who was chewing the end off a pencil and looking defensive. People often looked that way around Kyle.

Damn. I would miss him when he left. Funny, I hadn't known how much he mattered until now.

I watched him shake his head reprovingly at Arlene, but as soon as he looked in my direction, I turned away to take out my irritation on my typewriter.

In the weeks before Kyle left Ambrosia, I came to believe he was avoiding me. He didn't once suggest we go out, and I began to wonder if I'd misunderstood his intentions altogether. Maybe he wasn't leaving so that he'd feel free to make a pass at me. Now that I thought about it, no one but Carlo had ever made a serious pass. Why should Kyle be any different?

On his last day he shook my hand casually and said he'd see me around.

I wanted to spit in his eye. Instead, I smiled vaguely and said, "I expect so," in the sort of tone my mother used when she meant, "Not bloody likely." Not that Mother would ever have been so crude.

Kyle must have been at his new job for about a week when he called to ask if I wanted to see *Salad Days*.

"Can't you find anyone else?" I asked, dropping my pen and making a mess of the copy I was writing.

"Sure I can. I'd rather take you."

"Oh." I wanted to accept, but at the same time, felt I ought to refuse. Because I wasn't sure why, in the end inclination won. "All right," I agreed ungraciously. "If you want to."

"I'm looking forward to it too," Kyle said, making me feel childish for being surly.

Salad Days was fun. Frivolous and only mildly tuneful, but it didn't matter.

As we were leaving the theatre, Kyle suggested we go back to his flat.

"What?" I stopped dead, and the woman behind me walked into my back. He had spoken as casually as if he were inviting me for afternoon tea, but it was nearly eleven o'clock—and I wasn't as gullible as I had been.

"I said why don't we go back to my flat?" Kyle repeated.

"Why?" I made no pretense at courtesy.

"So we can be by ourselves." He smiled without apparent guile. "We never have been, you know."

A man with an umbrella bumped against my shoulder. "It's getting late," I said. "We both have to work tomorrow."

"Don't sound so middle-aged. Come on, Jane. Come for a coffee. Or a drink. You needn't stay long."

"Not a drink," I said, alarmed.

"All right. Coffee."

"Just coffee," I said firmly. Kyle had always been safe, but I was wary.

"Good," he said. "Great. We'll grab a taxi."

Kyle drove an ancient MG that was his pride and joy, but he rarely drove it into the city. His new job must be paying well if he could afford to take taxis out to Richmond where he'd told me he had a flat on the third floor of a solid brick Georgian. "Quaint," he called it.

I saw what he meant. White-painted trim, high, corniced ceilings and a floor that squeaked whenever you thought it wouldn't. Kyle had furnished it in a style my mother would have labelled 'Middle European,' and which Kyle called "New England." Busy, patterned sofas with skirts, fussy white lampshades, and tables with a country-kitchen look. Not a man's room at all. I looked at him in some surprise, and he said with a touch of pride that his mother had come over when he broke up with his wife and that he'd left her in charge of the decorating.

I didn't ask him if he liked it, but I had an uncomfortable feeling he did. My mother would have turned up her nose and called it 'rather odd.'

He went into the tiny kitchen to make coffee. I didn't offer to help because two people couldn't operate in such a small space without colliding with each other at every turn, and I wasn't nearly ready to collide with Kyle.

When he came back, he threw his jacket over a chair and settled beside me on the sofa, stretching a careless arm along its red and brown printed back. I edged away, and he said, "You needn't be afraid of me, Jane."

"I'm not." It was true. I wasn't afraid, but I didn't necessarily trust him either.

"Then why are you trying to meld with the corner of my sofa?"

"I'm not," I said again.

"All right." He nodded. "I guess I get it."

"Get what?" I tried some more melding, but it didn't work.

He shrugged. "You're not interested, are you? I thought you were."

"Interested?"

"In me." His thin smile was a masterpiece of nonchalance.

Damn. I might have guessed he wouldn't be content with coffee and my company. Had guessed really, without wanting to admit it. I fidgeted with the corded corner of a plush, olive-green cushion. "I've never thought about you that way. Not seriously."

"Okay, I'll buy that. So could you start thinking?"

He was being nice. Not all masculine and offended, and not impatient as he'd so often been at work. I didn't want to lose his friendship.

"I could," I said. "Maybe. But not tonight."

He laughed then. "I'll settle for that if I have to. For now."

We finished our coffee companionably, and afterwards Kyle put me in a taxi back to Wrenbert Terrace. I thought about him all the way home. I did like him. A lot. But he wasn't David.

In the end I gave up thinking and decided just to let things take their course. They would anyway.

~*~

On a Monday morning early in June, I was on the phone discussing a project with an advertiser when I heard a kind of murmuring from the outer office, as if a hive of bees were getting ready to swarm. I glanced through my glass barricade, saw the cause of the commotion and let out a gasp. The advertiser stopped speaking in mid-sentence.

Posy, in a tight-fitting mauve dress sprigged with daisies, had swept into the office with a baby in her arms. Her hair, longer than it had been, swung fetchingly over her shoulders, and she had lost just enough weight to look the perfect picture of a fashionable young mother.

I promised the advertiser I'd call back and stood up.

"Posy," I exclaimed, as she swooped between the desks and moved towards me like a ship in full sail. "What are you doing here?"

She gave me the smug smile I remembered so well from our schooldays. "I came to take you to lunch."

Lunch? With Sidonie along? My experience with William had taught me that lunch in a restaurant with a baby was likely to be about as much fun as lunch with a banshee.

"Oh, I don't think so," I said. "I'm awfully busy—"

Unfortunately, Joe Murray emerged from his carpeted inner sanctum at that moment to run an appreciative eye over Posy's well-displayed curves. After that, all it took was one of her winsome smiles to have him eating out of her hand.

"You go along, Janey," he said, after Posy had explained what she wanted. "Enjoy yourself."

I blinked. Joe usually grumbled if I took time off to grab a sandwich from Clover's.

"No, really," I tried again. "It's not—"

"Rubbish. Off you go now. Boss's orders." He turned to Posy and winked.

I tried not to gag and gave up.

"Where were you thinking of going?" I asked Posy as I picked up my bag.

"There's a nice little French place in Pimlico."

"Pimlico! But that's—"

"Quite all right. Take all the time you want." Joe was still hovering behind us. Or rather, behind Posy. I saw his tongue come out to moisten his fleshy lips.

We took a taxi to the nice little French place. It turned out to be one of those restaurants that have a tendency to lurk in old houses where the service is discreet and superior, the portions small and perfectly presented, and the exorbitant bill presented discreetly. The maitre d' didn't bat an eyelid at the baby as he showed us to a table in a corner behind a blue Delpht flower-box containing a lot of concealing vegetation.

"Sidonie will sleep all through the meal," Posy assured me. "My angel is never the least bit of trouble."

"How lucky you are," I muttered, with deep foreboding. "What brings you to town?"

"Oh, I came to order a few things for the christening. Just a small family party." Her blue eyes slid away from mine, and I knew I wasn't to be invited. "She'll be wearing the Foley family christening dress, of course."

"Lovely." I wondered why she'd bothered to look me up. "How's David?"

"David? Oh, busy with work. He's absolutely devoted to the baby. Isn't she adorable?" Posy threw a fond glance at her child who, as her mother had promised, was sleeping peacefully in a blanket on the red velvet seat.

"Adorable," I agreed.

"I knew you'd want to see her. She's so good and sweet. Would you believe she slept through the night right from the beginning? And doesn't she have the most perfect little face?"

I took a quick sip of the wine Posy had ordered and refrained from replying that at least Sidonie didn't look quite as much like a walnut as she had the last time I'd seen her.

"I'm surprised you didn't leave her with Kathryn," I said instead.

"Oh, I couldn't do that. I'm feeding her myself. It's so much better for the baby, you know."

Well, yes. I had heard that, although I wasn't sure I believed it. But Posy breastfeeding? Posy actually putting another human being before her personal convenience? I swallowed my surprise and said faintly, "Yes, I see. You're a very good mother."

Posy turned to adjust the baby's pink lace dress. I watched her bending over the sleeping child. There was a tenderness in the unnecessary gesture, a softness about her I'd never seen before. Perhaps it was true what they said about motherhood—not that I was tempted to find out.

"I do my best," Posy said simply. "Sidonie's the most important thing in my life."

"More important than David?"

"David's a good father." Her voice was flat as she smoothed her daughter's almost non-existent hair. It was impossible to miss the slight stiffening of her neck or the way her voice rose an octave higher and harder when she talked about her husband.

Our waiter arrived then with the soup du jour. After he left, I deliberately turned the conversation away from the Foley family and began to chat of Chantersley and the past. Then we talked about Jasmine and her new boyfriend—a penniless French count, Posy sniffed—and of Allison, who was in Paris with her Hal. Yet all the while we were talking, I had a feeling I had somehow missed some cue I was meant to catch.

At the end of the meal, the waiter placed a red leather folder beside Posy. I reached for it at once. I couldn't really afford it, but I didn't want her to pay for my lunch.

In the end she did though, seizing the bill before I could, and insisting that of course lunch was on her. When I tried to argue, she smiled. It was a masterly performance of Lady Bountiful treating the Little Match Girl to a meal. Not wanting to turn it into rank melodrama, eventually I let her have her way.

Without really understanding why, I went back to work feeling more resentful and unsure of myself than I had since my Chantersley days.

When I arrived home that evening I went at once to knock on Arabella's door, desperate for conversation that would take my mind off Posy and the placid child she and David had made together. But Arabella and Duncan were out.

Sighing, I went into the kitchen, picked up the kettle, then put it down again and kicked the nearest chair.

"Here, hold on there, Janey. I know they're not much, but them chairs are all we've got. What'd it do to you? Shove a splinter up your backside?"

I swung round. Arabella, in shiny red trousers and waistcoat, was standing in the doorway with both hands planted on her hips. Her heavily darkened eyebrows were arched almost up to her hairline.

I gave her a shamefaced grin and smoothed my hands down my dress. "You're back. Sorry, Bella, I've had a frustrating day."

Arabella squinted at me. "What's the matter? People given up eating healthy, have they?"

"No, it's not that." I sat down on the chair I'd been attacking. "Actually, it's Posy. I told you about her, didn't I? She came into the office today with her baby."

"Oh. You want a baby?" Arabella looked at me as if I'd turned green with crimson spots. "I thought you didn't."

"I didn't. I don't."

"Then what—?"

I shook my head. "It's not the baby I want. Arabella, I-I think I want her husband."

Oh, God. Had I really said that? I couldn't have actually put it into words. Words made everything so much worse—real in a way my feelings about David hadn't been before. I tried to lower my eyes but found I couldn't. They were riveted on Arabella's face.

Silence. A puff of smoke drifted past the door. Outside a boy was whistling a piercing, tuneless sound that scraped the edges of my nerves. And just then the tap began to drip. Arabella seemed cemented to the floor, but when her eyes began to blink, she shook herself and came slowly across the room to pull out the other chair.

"Crikey," she muttered, thumping herself down and running her fingers through the blonde halo of her hair. "Bit awkward, that. Think you can get him?"

"Arabella!"

"Well, you said you wanted him."

"Yes, but that doesn't—I mean what would you say if I told you I fancied Duncan?"

"I'd scratch your eyes out." She sat back, crossed her arms and wrinkled her forehead. "Course you'd have to be crazy to want Duncan."

"I'm probably crazy to want David."

"I dunno. From what you've told me, he sounds all right. Got money too."

"Not much. It's mostly Posy's. Anyway, I don't care about that."

Arabella sighed. "You wouldn't."

"Besides, he's married to Posy." I got up, gave the dripping tap a vicious twist and glared at the greasy green wall.

"Hm. Don't like the sounds of her," Arabella remarked to my back. "Serve her right if you pinched him."

"Oh, Bella, I couldn't—"

"Course you could, if you put your mind to it. You're not all that hideous, you know. Think he fancies you?"

I was too much on edge to laugh. "I don't know. Maybe. He doesn't say much, but I'm sure he's not happy with Posy. She doesn't really care about him."

"Why'd he marry her then?"

"I'm not sure. Sex. And maybe business reasons."

"Cripes. You're not serious?"

"I am, actually."

"Sounds like he got what he deserved."

"Perhaps." A silverfish shimmied across the sink, and I hurried back to the table.

Arabella shrugged. "Oh, well. No sense crying over spilled martinis. Think he wants to leave her?"

"No. They have a daughter."

"Mm. Best have him on the side then. Get him out of your system." She scratched vigorously at a red mark between her cleavage.

"Oh, Bella, you are good for me," I giggled. It was impossible to maintain a decent air of gloom around Arabella. She was a tonic without even trying.

"Hm. That's better. Can't stand it when you wander round looking like a turkey on Christmas Eve. Now then, why don't I fetch Duncan and we'll all go to the pub and then the pictures."

"Won't Duncan mind?"

She laughed. "He'll probably say it beats having to eat my cooking. But he'd better watch it. If he gets too cheeky, he knows I'll make him cook for himself. Scares the hell out of him that does. Doesn't know an egg from an orange. He'd starve to death."

"Oh, Bella, what would I do without you?"

"Probably move to decent digs for a start."

She had me there. If it hadn't been for Arabella, most likely I would have moved by now. Mrs. Carmody wasn't the easiest landlady in London, and her smoke wasn't getting any sweeter. Joe Murray had a habit of sniffing my hair and clothes when I walked past him.

Arabella proved right about Duncan. He was happy—or as happy as he ever allowed himself to be—to avoid his wife's high-risk cooking, and by the time the evening ended, I felt better. Not cheerful exactly, but better. The sun would rise over the rooftops in the morning and I would find I had a life to get on with—a life that wouldn't be wholly dependent on David Foley's smile. As for Kyle, I hadn't seen him for two weeks. Maybe he'd moved out of my life.

The following Monday after work, I rounded the corner onto Wrenbert Terrace with my head down and the hood of my raincoat pulled up against an unexpected blast of summer rain. I had almost reached the bottom step of Number Fifteen, and was about to make a dash for dry ground, when a man stepped out of a doorway across the road and came towards me. He said something I didn't catch, and for a moment I paused. Then I saw his eyes and turned quickly away.

They were very pale, of some indeterminate colour, and they frightened me. I'd never seen eyes that hungry before.

I was halfway up the steps when a voice behind me called, "Janey?"

I whirled round, oblivious now to the weather, but when I looked for the stranger, he was nowhere to be seen. A sedate black Daimler had pulled up to the kerb near the spot where he'd been standing.

"Janey," said the driver of the Daimler.

I looked at him properly then, and it was David.

"You've got a new car," I said stupidly. My hood fell back on my shoulders, and I didn't care that the rain was streaming down my face.

"Yes," David said. "More suited to my status as a married man. Or so Posy and my father-in-law tell me." He nodded at the passenger seat. "Are you going to get in?"

Without thinking about it much, I opened the door and scrambled in beside him. "I'm getting your seat wet," I said, as moisture dripped down my raincoat and trickled into the open-toed shoes I'd worn to work.

"It doesn't matter. Who was that fellow?"

"I don't know. He was standing there when I came home from work."

"Hm. You ought to be careful, Janey. He could be trouble."

"I am careful. David, what are you doing here?"

"I came to talk to you."

"About Posy?"

"No. Not this time."

"What then?" I didn't look at him. There was something about the way he was sitting, or perhaps in the way he was gripping the wheel, that made me think I ought to get out. I'd been doing all right this past week. At Ambrosia, whenever I thought of him with Posy, I forced myself to concentrate on work. At home I had begun to write a series of short, romantic stories which I transcribed on my typewriter at work once everyone else had left for evenings of debauchery, the wireless or their current family crisis.

"I want to talk about you, Janey," David said.

I frowned. "Me? Why?"

He didn't answer. Rain splattered the roof of the Daimler, washing over the windows so that the street was barely visible through the glass. When a large, warm hand closed gently over the fist curled tightly in my lap, I stopped waiting for David to speak and raised my eyes.

"Will you come back to the flat with me?" he said.

I had heard the same words before quite recently, but not from David. "Your flat? You still have it?" I asked.

"I kept it on for those nights when I have to stay in town. Will you come?"

"All right."

It wasn't all right. It was all wrong. I knew that, but it didn't seem nearly as important as the need to go with David.

He started the car, and I kept my eyes on his hands as we drove through the downpour to his flat. We didn't talk. In a way, the fact that I was with him said it all.

There was no black cat this time as we stood side by side on the step while David searched his wallet for his key. But the rain had tapered off and washed-out sunlight gleamed around the edges of the clouds, turning the sky a soft, grey marble streaked with gold.

David took my arm and we moved into the warm privacy of his flat.

The air inside was muggy and smelled of soap. I guessed someone had recently been in to clean.

"Does Posy ever stay here?" I asked.

"No. She's never liked it."

"I'm not surprised."

David sighed. "Don't tell me you're about to read me a lecture on cleanliness and order. I have had a cleaning woman in."

"Okay, I won't read you a lecture." I hesitated, not wanting to pry, but in the end curiosity won out. "Why didn't you have her in before? For Posy's sake?"

"She tidies things."

I smothered a giggle. "Oh. I see. You mean you wait until fungus starts forming in the bath and weeds are coming up through the kitchen floor before you do anything about it."

"Not really. Janey, why are we standing in the hall discussing my housekeeping arrangements? Come in. I need a drink."

I could have told him the answer to his question was quite simple. We were standing in the hall discussing his housekeeping arrangements because I was much more comfortable doing that than acknowledging that I was alone with him in his flat, without his wife, for reasons he hadn't yet made clear.

My reasons for being here were equally confused.

I started to explain that I didn't give a damn whether he chose to live in a pigsty or a palace, but he took my hand and I forgot what I was saying.

David drew me into his comfortable sitting room and went to fling open the curtains and raise the heavy windows. Damp, sweet air flooded the room.

"That's better," I said.

"Mm." He slung his suit coat over a chair and made a beeline for the drinks cabinet. "Sherry?"

I perched myself on the arm of the nearest chair, a velvet wingback in dull gold. Dust puffed up as I sat down. "Oh, I don't need a drink," I said nervously.

"Well, I do." He poured himself a stiff whisky. "Sure you don't want one?"

Now that we were actually here, David seemed to be avoiding my eye. I decided I would have a drink after all.

"Thank you. On second thought, perhaps I will have a sherry." Even with the windows open, the room seemed exceptionally hot.

David handed me the sherry in a cut crystal glass and went to stand by the mantel. There was no screen on the empty fireplace, and without one, it looked hollow and unwelcoming.

I pulled on the hem of my yellow cotton skirt in a vain attempt to cover my knees.

"Don't do that," David said. "There's nothing wrong with your legs."

"Thanks." Did that mean there was plenty wrong with the rest of me? It had been months now since I'd sprouted my last spot.

David smiled, and my stomach did its customary somersault.

"Why am I here?" I asked him.

He tossed back a long swig of whisky. "Your friend. Arabella, I think she said her name was. She called me at the gallery."

"Arabella did? But why?"

David gazed gloomily into his empty glass. "She said that you and I ought to put our cards on the table and stop pussyfooting around."

"She—oh, God." I lowered my eyes, tugged at my skirt again then realized I was doing it and stopped. "I doubt if Arabella ever heard of a mixed metaphor."

"A mixed—Janey, I don't care how your friend mangles the language. Do you?" His glass clattered against the mantel as he put it down.

"No. Arabella's a dear, but..." I shook my head, and a pin fell out of my hair. I picked it off the carpet and shoved it back, an operation which gave me a few much needed seconds to think. *Lord, what had Arabella done? Couldn't she have left me to brood in peace?*

"Janey? Look, I'm sorry if I got it all wrong...."

"What did Arabella actually tell you?" I fixed my gaze on the sober dark blue of his tie.

He didn't answer at once and when he did, he sounded different, as if something had caught in his throat.

"She said I should talk to you. That you were moping around like—"

"A turkey on Christmas Eve?" I stifled a groan.

"That's right. She also said I was the cause of your moping and that I'd better do something about it or else let you get on with your life. I told her I'd never tried to stop you from getting on with anything. But she said I had."

"She was wrong. You haven't."

"No. I didn't think so."

The arm of the chair was digging into the backs of my knees, but I didn't move. I don't think I was capable of moving. A dog barked, someone shouted at it and footsteps pounded on the pavement outside the gate. When I looked up, David was standing in front of me. Without asking permission, he removed my glass and pulled me to my feet.

I ran my tongue along my lower lip. David looked at me, then at the glass, and finally laid it on a low table beside my chair. That done, he stood with his arms held stiffly at his sides and his chin at a military angle. There was a funny, shiny look about his eyes.

He said, "I don't want to mess up your life as well, Janey. Was Arabella telling me the truth?"

As well? As well as what? I swallowed, and he put an arm around my shoulders and led me across to the crimson velvet sofa. "Was she?" he repeated.

I didn't know how to answer. Seeing that, he sat me down before seating himself at the far end of the long sofa. There was no risk of accidental touching.

"I don't know what Arabella said." I twisted the corner of a mud-coloured corduroy cushion. "Except about the pussyfooting."

"She asked if I fancied you." He smiled, but the smile didn't last.

"She didn't! She wouldn't..." But of course, I knew she would. And had. "I'm sorry," I said. "I'd no idea. I didn't ask her to ask you. I mean, I wouldn't. I know you don't fancy me. You're married. And anyway, I'm quite different from Posy. She's got a figure, and I'm a matchstick with a chin—"

"And beautiful red hair. Yes, you are too thin. But you're kind. I like being with you. Why wouldn't I fancy you, Janey?"

I picked up the cushion and placed it securely on my lap. David hadn't actually said he did fancy me. "You're married," I repeated. "I know Arabella meant to be helpful. She always does. But you shouldn't have believed her. If you're worried about me, honestly you needn't be. Not at all."

David crossed his legs. "You haven't answered me."

"Haven't I?" What did he expect me to say? That I found him impossibly attractive and wished he felt the same about me? That I had liked him at once and grown to like him better? That I wished he wasn't married to Posy? I could tell him all that, of course, and make a total fool of myself. But he hadn't said he felt the same way. And if, by some miracle, he did...? Even then, what was the use?

"No," David said. "You haven't. Look at me, Janey."

I started punching the cushion, so he leaned across and took it away. "Janey?"

A wide, ugly ladder ran from my left ankle to the hem of my skirt. I stared at it, and David put a finger under my chin and turned my head.

His eyes were such a beautiful green behind the long, dark lashes, and he was wearing such a sad, soft smile that in the end I couldn't stop myself from touching him. I raised my hand and traced my thumb around the outline of his mouth.

He sucked in his breath and caught my wrist. "So Arabella was right," he said. "I was afraid of that."

"I'm sorry." I pulled my arm away and felt colour surging up to stamp my cheeks with shame. I would definitely kill Arabella when I got home. But at this moment it was all I could do to keep my face averted and my tears from saturating the sofa.

"Don't be sorry." I heard David's voice as a persistent kind of hum, adding to my misery and embarrassment.

"But I am," I wailed. "I know you don't feel that way about me. I don't even want you to, and—oh Lord, I wish I was dead." The meaningless phrase from my childhood burst out of me just as it had done when Posy, or sometimes my mother, had made life seem dramatically unbearable. Now, as then, I found myself muttering a quick prayer cancelling my request to the Deity I wasn't sure I believed in— just in case He might actually think I meant it.

"Janey, don't cry. I couldn't stand it if you were dead, so for God's sake—no for my sake—don't even think it." David's arms went around me and gathered me up against his chest. His shirt was silky and a little damp beneath my cheek, yet I felt warm and cared for in a way I hadn't since the day I fled Willbury.

I sniffed noisily. "For your sake?

"Yes. For my sake." He stroked a hand down my hair as if he were soothing a scared child—which, I belatedly realized, was probably exactly what he thought I was. And it wouldn't do. I wasn't a child. The last two years had hauled me, albeit reluctantly, into the convoluted world of adults. This was no time to revert to snivelling adolescence.

I pulled myself away from the comfort and security of David's arms. He didn't try to hold me, yet I felt as if I were a baby chick emerging from the protection of the egg—vulnerable and horribly exposed.

Making myself face him, I pasted on a smile. "I'm so sorry. I don't usually behave like this. I must be coming down with the flu."

He smiled back, the heartbreaker smile that had been my undoing in the first place. "That's the second time I've been likened to a germ," he said.

"What? I didn't say—"

"I know. Posy did. She said I was worse than the plague." He drummed his fingers absently on his thigh. "Janey, don't play games with me, I get enough of that at home. I know you don't have the flu. It's me, isn't it? You were trying not to cry because of me."

When I dropped my eyes, I felt the springs beneath me heave as if he were about to move towards me. Then all movement ceased as he settled back against the arm of the sofa.

Was there any point in lying to save my pride? I looked up. He was frowning, and I didn't want to lie.

I said, "Yes," and started to get up.

He wouldn't let me. "We have to talk about it," he said, holding my wrists.

I stared at him, and after a few seconds, he released me. "That's why I brought you here," he explained. "To talk."

"Yes. About what, exactly?"

He shook his head, slowly, as if he wasn't entirely sure of the answer. "I think," he said, "that what Arabella told me is true—and I want you to know, Janey, that if it wasn't for Posy, then..." He stopped, pulled a handkerchief from his pocket and wiped it round the back of his neck. "You have to understand I can't leave her."

"Of course not." I was shocked. Yet beneath the shock lay an explosive feeling of elation. David, my lovely David, was talking as though he actually wanted me. Not pretty Posy, but me, Janey, with the pointed chin and ridiculous snubby nose. "Of course, you can't leave her," I said, and gave him what I hoped was a saintly smile.

David closed his eyes. "No. But I wouldn't want you to think—Janey, please believe I never meant to hurt you. I've always liked you. A lot. I don't know if that kind of liking is love, but I do know it can't do either of us much good."

I remembered what Arabella had said about having him on the side. I'd be an 'other woman.' There was something mysterious and deliciously evil about that. I had a brief vision of myself as Cleopatra or

Mata Hari, looking sloe-eyed and seductive in black silk and a lot of sultry makeup. Then David opened his eyes and reality intruded. A lot of makeup only made me look like a product of the undertaker's art.

"I suppose it can't," I said. "Do us any good, I mean."

"No." He stood up and walked across to the window. The sun was bright orange around the clouds now, and in the evening light his fair hair blazed almost as bright as mine.

"If it's no good, why didn't you just ignore Arabella?" I asked his back, knowing I sounded sullen and accusing, but incapable of doing anything about it.

"Perhaps I should have. But I wanted to see you again. To explain...I suppose I hoped it would be easier this way. More final."

Final? Did he mean that? All my silly dreams exploded into dust.

"I'll still see you sometimes, won't I?" I was whispering, though there wasn't any need.

David turned his back on the window. "I think Posy knows."

I blinked at him. "But there's nothing to know."

"No. So there isn't. I meant she suspects I'm fonder of you than I am of her."

I felt a twinge of guilt—along with a longing to rush into his arms. "Is she very hurt?"

"Posy? No, just possessive and mean-spirited. As only she can be."

"David!" His bitterness frightened me. "She's your wife. You knew what she was like when you married her."

He reached for the knot of his tie and tugged it loose. "Sorry. I shouldn't have said that. You're right, of course. Posy is a good and devoted mother."

"But you're not happy."

"Me?" He shrugged. "I made my own bed. I've no business to whine about it now. And I hope Posy isn't unhappy. We do have our daughter in common."

From the way his features gentled when he spoke of his baby, I knew she had to be the one bright thread in the dreary fabric of their marriage.

"You have other things in common, surely," I said, suspecting he hadn't really. "What about...?" No. I couldn't ask him that.

Correctly interpreting the sudden rush of colour to my cheeks, he answered anyway. "That doesn't happen. Posy doesn't enjoy it."

Oh. Well, I could understand that—although I had thought—no, hoped—it might be different with someone like David. Perhaps the whole thing about sex being glorious really was a huge hoax that women perpetuated in order to soothe the egos of their men. Yet both men and women wrote the books I read and most of the heroines seemed to like it. At least they never said they didn't. It was very confusing...especially when I looked at David across the room and saw him standing tall and beautiful against the backdrop of the glowing evening sun. When he shoved his hands into his pockets and draped himself against the window frame, I caught myself holding my breath.

"Maybe she'll get to like it," I suggested uncomfortably. I didn't really want that to happen, and I didn't much like talking about this particular aspect of David's marriage. But as I sat slumped against the cushions, watching him, I knew I couldn't bear him to be unhappy. If I couldn't make him happy myself, I had to hope Posy would.

But he was shaking his head. "No. She won't get to like it. She already has Sidonie."

"Brothers and sisters?" I cleared my throat and twisted the collar of my blouse.

"Not unless an Immaculate Conception can be arranged."

A certain dry amusement seemed to have taken the place of his earlier bitterness. I was glad of that. But what could he possibly have done to make Posy so adamant? Carlo hadn't been any prize in bed either, but it hadn't been that bad. I'd enjoyed some quite pleasant daydreams while he was grunting and puffing on top of me.

David must have seen that I didn't understand, because after a slight pause while he pulled the curtains across the windows to shut out the encroachment of the night, he came to sit down beside me. "I shouldn't be talking to you this way," he said. "It's not your problem and it isn't fair to Posy."

"No," I agreed. "It isn't." He was slouched forward with his arms resting loosely on his knees, and in spite of his size, he looked so dejected and hopeless that, without thinking, I put my hand on his neck and began to rub it.

He straightened at once, staring at me with the dazed look of a man who has just awakened in a place he's never seen before.

He took me in his arms quite spontaneously, as if there was nothing else to do.

"Janey. My love," he murmured against the piled up knot of my hair. "I shouldn't have...Oh, God. What in the world are we going to do?"

"What can we do?" I didn't expect a solution, but I hoped.

There wasn't one, of course. "Nothing," he said. "Bloody nothing. That's what I wanted to be sure you understood. None of this is Posy's fault. I can't leave her."

"Because of the gallery?"

"No!" He jerked his head up as if I'd stabbed him. "Not because of the gallery. If that were all, I swear I'd find a way. Don't you see? I can't leave Posy because she needs me. She's a child, Janey, a spoiled, desperately needy child. I was once fool enough to believe marriage would change her. Now I know it won't. But I have to do my best for her, as well as for my daughter. I don't think Posy could handle a child on her own. Not once Sidonie stops being a toy and becomes a person with a mind of her own. As she will soon enough."

Again I heard that gentleness in his voice, the pride when he spoke of 'my daughter.' Father-love. It was an attractive quality in a man. I started to reach for him, then realized what I was doing and clapped my hands between my knees.

"I understand," I said.

"Do you? Do you, Janey?"

"Of course." I lowered my eyes—his were desperately bright and intense—and made an effort to control the tremor in my voice. "Of course, I do. David, I-I think you'd better take me home."

"Yes. Janey, don't—oh God, you're crying."

"No, I'm not." I stood up and blindly turned my back.

David's hands caught me from behind and spun me around so fast I almost fell. "Look at me," he said, standing between me and the sofa.

I looked at him. After that nothing short of a bomb or an act of God could have stopped us from coming together.

David groaned as his lips came down on mine, and he kissed me as if he had been deprived of water for a week and couldn't drink enough to slake his thirst. I opened my mouth, and he filled it with such sweetness I moaned.

"Janey? Janey, darling. What is it?" His voice was rough with a passionate tenderness I knew would break my heart.

I put my hands on either side of his head. His hair beneath my fingers was strong and springy. "It's you," I said. "You're so beautiful. And you taste so good."

I think he laughed then, a gentle, proud sort of laugh, and he kissed me again and drew me onto the sofa where, in a frantic tangle of limbs and laughter, we made love.

It was all I had dreamed it might be. David was different.

And at last I knew what the fuss was all about.

CHAPTER FOURTEEN

It had been so lovely. I knew now why Duncan and Arabella made all the noise. Yet for me quiet ecstasy was better. The act itself was still ridiculous, even brutal in a way, but the feelings that came with it were not. Towards David I felt a gratitude beyond the words I used so glibly in my stories.

Now, lying stretched across my lumpy bed at Mrs. Carmody's, I raised my arms in languorous remembrance.

David had teased me a little afterwards. Doubting myself—Carlo's careless usage had sapped my meagre store of confidence—I had wondered aloud if my skinny body could honestly have given him pleasure.

He had laughed and quoted Shakespeare at me.

I grant I never saw a goddess go;
My mistress when she walks, treads on the ground:
And yet, by heaven, I think my love as rare
As any she belied with false compare.

Then he had pulled the last remaining pin from my hair. "Your crowning glory," he said, running his fingers through the unrestrained tangle. "There's nothing false about this." He touched my nose. "Or this."

"It's too short," I said, smiling up at him as I lay naked on my back on the sofa while my hands explored the beloved contours of his face. "But I like it when you quote poetry."

I knew even then, although I didn't acknowledge it, that my time with David would be short.

When we made love again, as we did very soon, he laughingly asked if I was trying to devour him. Later, he said my red hair had delivered on its fiery promises with interest. He called me his tigress and I basked in his delight and approval. I had surprised him, I think—but not nearly as much as I'd surprised myself.

At around ten o'clock we ate soup and salmon sandwiches washed down by a bottle of red wine.

I spent the night in David's big bed with the black sheets. He said one of his college friends had given them to him as a wedding present, but that Posy had refused to have them on their bed at Pembroke Cottage. According to her, they were obscene. David took them as the joke his friend intended.

It was a glorious June night after the rain, filled with warmth and laughter and the sound of a faraway dance band on someone's wireless that played on into the small hours of the morning. But when I woke from a sated sleep to hear David breathing quietly beside me and saw dawn spreading its pale green promise across the sky, the first needles of guilt pierced my euphoria.

The arm that held me so closely belonged to a man who belonged to another woman.

Posy had been my enemy. Yet for all the times I had wished her dead, or at the very least banished to a hovel on a particularly cold and distant mountain, I had never greatly coveted anything she had—until now. I knew, dimly, that what I had done with David was the ultimate revenge for all those years of childish torment. But I hadn't planned it and had long since stopped wanting to repay her for the hurts of the past. Only children and pitiful grudge-bearers wasted time plotting revenge.

I also knew I ought to feel a great deal guiltier than I did.

Beside me David stirred and murmured my name in his sleep. Very soon now he would leave me. I could scarcely bear the thought.

With a feeling that was something like reverence, I ran my hand across the silky pale hair on his chest. At once he opened his eyes and gave me a soft morning smile.

This time our love had a desperation to it, a clinging, frantic grasping at fragments of a rapture that was rapidly fading. We both knew we might never be together this way again. Midnight had long since struck, but no glass slipper would be left behind to restore my prince to my arms. I was no Cinderella.

Some time later, as we sat at the kitchen table nibbling toast—neither of us had the heart to cook breakfast—I asked David where Posy thought he had spent the night.

"Here," he said. "I often work late, and when I do, I don't bother to go home." He stirred his tea, although he'd done it twice already. "I used to, but Posy didn't like having to keep food hot for me without being certain when I'd turn up. She hasn't much tolerance for lateness. In the end I decided it would be easier just to stay in town."

I heard what he was saying, knew how Posy hated his habit of turning up when it suited him instead of when it suited her. But that wasn't the point.

"We shouldn't have done it," I said.

"Are you sorry?" His big teeth crunched down on a slice of toast.

Nice teeth. White and straight and strong. "No," I said. "How could I be sorry? It's just that—David, it's a terrible thing we've done to Posy. Even if she doesn't really want...."

"Me?" he suggested, wiping his hands on a napkin.

"Mm." I licked my middle finger and began picking crumbs off the table with a mindless concentration that absolved me of the need to look him in the eye. "Doesn't she? Really?" I hated the thought of David making love to Posy, and what I really meant was didn't he want his lawfully wedded wife?

"What Posy did, she did for England," David said wryly. "I tried, and I think at first she was pleasantly surprised. But the novelty wore off, and once Sidonie was on the way, she lost interest."

"How extraordinary."

"You are exceptionally good for my ego, Janey Blackman. It's been feeling a bit battered of late. Thank you." He reached across the table, picked up my hand in spite of the crumbs and kissed it. "And to answer the question you didn't ask, yes, I enjoyed it. But nothing, nothing like the way I did with you—my mistress who 'treads on the ground.'"

How well he understood me. I believed he meant it too. "Will you tell Posy?" I asked.

"Do you want me to?"

"No. There's no reason to hurt her, unless...well, there's just no reason to hurt her." For us there could be no 'unless.' "Would you tell her if I wanted you to?" I asked.

"No, I'd make you do it."

"Coward," I gave an empty laugh.

"Not at all. I know you wouldn't."

That was true enough. "We can't let it happen again," I said. "Not ever. I know people do. For years sometimes. But—"

"But not you? Not me either, I'm afraid." He pushed back his chair. "Although if I ever come within a mile of you, I doubt if I'll be able to keep away."

"You're good for my ego too." I gazed wretchedly at a big cabbage butterfly fluttering past the window as it battled vainly against the breeze bearing it aloft. *Oh, God. Why had I allowed this to happen?* At least, before, I hadn't known what I was missing. Was this what they called lust? Surely that had to be a part of what I felt. Not all though. Not nearly all.

The butterfly disappeared from view, and David said it was time he left for work.

"Me too," I fidgeted with the handle of my cup. "I'll have to wear the same clothes to work as I did yesterday." I didn't care a jot about my clothes. It was one of those meaningless comments people come out with to mask what they're feeling inside.

"Will anyone notice?" David yawned and stood up.

"Yes. They'll especially notice the two buttons missing from my blouse. Have you a needle and thread?"

"Good God, no. There might be a couple of pins. Hang on, I'll look in the bathroom."

I hung on, and when he came back he held several safety pins in his hand.

"Keep still," he said, and I waited docilely while he started pinning me together.

The unexpected intimacy was too much, for David as well as for me. I gasped the moment his fingers touched my skin, and David stopped pinning and closed his eyes. The muscles in his throat contracted, and for a few seconds I thought, or maybe hoped, that we were about to end up entwined on the kitchen floor. But after a pause, David shook his head and managed to complete the operation without incident.

I told myself it was just as well.

He didn't move away at once but gripped the collar of my blouse and stood gazing down at me as if he were trying to fix my features in his mind for all time. His eyes were dark green and hopeless.

"What is it?" I asked.

He bent his neck, nudging my hair with his forehead. "Christ, Janey, I'm sorry." His breath skimmed the top of my nose. "You know, don't you, that if there was a way, any way at all...?"

"Of course," I mumbled.

There wasn't any way. David wouldn't change. Beneath that laid-back exterior was a conscience that some would call weakness. It would never let him desert the two people who needed him the most. I wasn't even sure I wanted him to leave them. His acceptance of obligation was a part of him. Last night had only happened because of an honest desire to set things straight between us.

Well—maybe not only because of that. His lengthy celibacy might have had something to do with it.

I pried his big hands from my collar. "We'd better get going," I said.

"Yes." He didn't move, and I turned my back and began to pile dishes in the sink. Two plates, two mugs, one teapot and a silver spoon. All that remained of our night of loving.

We said goodbye in the Daimler. David parked it in front of the main door into Ambrosia, and I didn't care if anyone saw us. When he touched my cheek and said, "Thank you, Janey," I grabbed his hand and pressed it to my lips. Then I jumped out onto the pavement and collided with Joe Murray.

The remainder of the day was pure hell. Everyone guessed I hadn't spent the night at home, including Joe, who wasn't known for his interest in the private lives of his staff. But even he couldn't avoid noticing that he'd narrowly escaped being catapulted into the gutter by a rumpled Advertising Assistant with an imitation cloudburst streaming down her face.

Those members of the staff who didn't immediately catch on were speedily informed by the others. I wouldn't have minded much if it hadn't been necessary to pin a nonchalant smile on my face and pretend that nothing unusual had happened. I knew if I didn't every amateur nosey-parker in the building would stop by my desk to see what details they could garner. The worst of them would offer me foul-tasting tonics as well, perhaps on the principle that it's difficult to cry and return one's lunch at the same time.

That night I knocked on Arabella's door intending to tell her she had no business interfering in my life. But when she saw the tears welling in my eyes and held out her arms to give comfort, I hugged her and said, "Thank you," instead.

Much later I crawled back to my room exhausted, drained, and desperately missing David.

There was a fresh cigarette burn on the wall. It took a while before I could even be bothered to mutter, "Damn, Mrs. Carmody." Yet once I said it, I knew I was going to survive. I always did. Funny that. Miss Barclay would be surprised if she knew that surviving, not dreaming, had turned out to be what I did best.

When I lay down on the bed, the wonder of David was still with me. Common sense told me it was over, but blind hope wouldn't let me believe it.

I clung to blind hope for the better part of a year.

~*~

Joe Murray parked himself on the edge of my desk and began leafing through the copy I was writing. It was part of a campaign to promote the virtues of a new seaweed soap that Ambrosia hoped would launch us into cosmetics.

Almost a month had gone by since David and I had said goodbye to each other in the Daimler. In a way, I was shocked that surviving had proved less painful than I'd thought. It wasn't that I missed him any less. At night I often found myself twitching and tossing and dreaming of a bed with black sheets. But advertising was picking up again after a slow spring, and I was busy. At home, Arabella could still make me laugh— and deep down I don't think I truly believed that one night was all we would ever have.

"My wife should try this seaweed stuff." Joe rotated his neck inside the collar of his shirt. "Couldn't believe what she used in the last batch of washing. It gave me a bloody rash."

"How perfectly awful for you," I said, overdoing the sympathy on purpose. To the best of my knowledge, Joe's long-suffering wife had never washed or cooked anything to his satisfaction.

He frowned, justifiably suspicious, and when the phone rang he used the interruption as an excuse to play boss.

"Answer it," he snapped. "You're not paid to sit here looking at your nails."

Joe was in a charming mood. But as there didn't seem much to be gained by pointing out that I wasn't looking at my nails, I obligingly picked up the receiver.

I prayed silently that it wouldn't turn out to be Dad calling to tell me William had just finished reading the collected works of Shakespeare or Chaucer. At not quite two, my brother was a normal baby in every way, but Dad was certain he had sired the greatest genius since Leonardo.

"Miss Blackman?" enquired a breezily nasal voice.

I released my breath and turned sideways, away from Joe's fulminating gaze. My caller, though male, was not my father.

"Yes, this is Miss Blackman. How can I help you?"

A horsey chuckle came down the wire. "By sending us another story like the last one. This is Henry Milligan of Women's Corner Magazine.

We'd like to publish your "Liar's End"—with a different title, of course. How would you feel about "Romantic Deception?"

I clutched the receiver and tried to speak. Only a gurgle came out. It had happened. It had really happened. My story was going to be published. After dozens of brusque rejections wishing me the best of luck placing my work elsewhere, someone actually wanted to buy one of my stories. "Romantic Deception?" I didn't like the title much, but they could call it "Sardines on Toast," for all I cared. My story, the beloved child of my imagination, was going to be read by women all over the country—maybe the world. I was Pinocchio the day he became a boy— no longer a fraudulent imitation, but a real writer.

"You just win the pools?" Joe grunted, rubbing his elbow and scowling.

I ignored him. "Thank you," I croaked into the mouthpiece. "That's very good news, Mr..." Oh, God. I'd forgotten the man's name.

"Milligan," he said helpfully. "Henry Milligan." He must have been used to neophyte writers, because he added, "Of Women's Corner. We want to buy your story."

"Oh, yes. Yes, thank you...um..." What was I supposed to say now? I mustn't let him think I was the town fool, an idiot savant who happened to be able to use words.

"We'll let you know the date of publication once it's scheduled." Henry Milligan was brisk now, relieving me of the need to be coherent. "Anything else I can tell you? If not, I'll be in touch again shortly. We'll look forward to working with you, Miss Blackman."

"Yes, of course. Thank you," I said faintly. "Thank you so much."

He hung up before I had the presence of mind to ask what he meant to pay me. Not that it mattered. For the first time since that hellish morning a month ago when I had said goodbye to David and fallen out of the Daimler at Joe's feet, I actually wanted to shout with joy, dance on my desk and throw my arms around anyone within hugging distance.

Something of the sort must have shown on my face, because Joe slid off my desk and sidled towards the door.

"What was that all about?" he demanded from a safe distance. "Did you win the pools? On company time?"

"Better," I replied. "I sold a story."

"A story?" He was suspicious. "What kind of story?"

"A romantic one." I lifted my chin, expecting him to snort.

Instead he glared. "Good God. It's obvious you haven't met my wife. Here, you'd better make some changes in this. I've marked the passages in green." He threw down my Ode to Soap and spun out into the main office, presumably to stir up Arlene now that he'd finished with me.

Left alone, I stared at the reflection of my face in the glass wall. Was that a pink cloud hanging over my head? Without thinking, I reached for the phone to call David. In my mind I could see his face lighting up with pleasure at my news, hear his low laugh rumbling across the miles....

Halfway through dialing his number, I remembered Posy, and replaced the receiver on its stand.

It had been a beautiful dream, a hard one to let go. But after a while I did.

I phoned my parents instead.

"That's wonderful," said my practical mother. "How much are they paying you, Jane?"

"I don't know. I forgot to ask."

"Jane, really! Never mind, at least it's good news. We can do with some today. Old Mrs. Gillaby died in her sleep last night."

I didn't care about old Mrs. Gillaby. I had nothing against her except nosiness, but she wasn't important in my life, especially not today. Selling my story was what mattered.

Trust mother to prick my balloon.

"I'm sorry to hear that," I said, coming back to earth with a thud. Only a minor thud though. Not even Mother could darken my mood today. I, Janey Blackman, was going to be paid for what I'd written. The amount was irrelevant and I could manage very well without a fortune.

It was a good thing I could because, as I found out soon enough, I wasn't offered one.

I would have phoned Kyle next, but Joe was glaring at me through the glass, so I pretended I was going to the lav and snuck down to tell Charlotte instead.

Charlotte was suitably impressed and asked me if I was going to be famous. I told her no—although secretly I knew I was destined to be the next Monica Dickens or Nancy Mitford.

I had to wait until after work to phone Kyle from the call box on the corner. I hadn't seen him since that night at his flat, but he'd called me at the office now and then—not to ask me out, but just to talk. He seemed to know instinctively that I wasn't yet ready to think of him as more than a friend.

"Kyle?" I asked, when a brisk voice on the other end snapped, "Yes?"

"Jane! Hi there." The instant warmth of his greeting hummed reassuringly down the wires. "How are you?"

"Marvellous," I crowed. "Kyle, I've sold a story. To Women's Corner."

"A story? What do you mean?" He sounded wary, not admiring and delighted as I'd hoped.

"I mean I wrote a story, and Women's Corner is going to publish it."

"You wrote it! Well, I'll be...Hey, that's great Jane, really great. Why didn't you tell me?"

"I am telling you."

"I meant before. You never told me you wrote stories."

"Oh. I don't know." I fidgeted with the telephone cord. "I think I thought you'd laugh."

"Why would I do that? No, never mind. How about we celebrate? Champagne, dinner, the works. Whatever you want."

That was more like it. At least Kyle appreciated the importance of my red-letter day.

"Well..." I said, longing to accept, but not sure it was fair to take advantage of his generosity.

He ignored my hesitation. "Right. That's settled. I'll pick you up at seven-thirty. Okay?"

"Yes. If you're sure...."

"Why would I ask you if I wasn't sure? I'm glad you called. Seven-thirty it is." He hung up the phone before I could think of a reason to refuse—not that I wanted to refuse. My reluctance was due mainly to a concern that Kyle might have read more into my phone call than I'd intended.

I stepped out of the call box and was immediately aware of a figure standing in the shadows by Nanji's shop. It moved towards me, and with a shock, I recognized the man with the hungry eyes who had tried to talk to me outside Number Fifteen. So much had happened that day I'd forgotten all about him until this moment.

"Go away!" I said, when he opened his mouth to speak. "Go away and leave me alone."

"Wait! Please...."

His voice was deep, educated, but I didn't wait. Instead, I spun on my heel and ran all the way to Number Fifteen. His footsteps pounded behind me for a while, then stopped abruptly.

When I looked around, he had his back to me and was walking slowly away, a tall, stooped figure in a grey fedora. If he ever came near me again, I would call the police.

Yet in spite of the unpleasantness of the encounter, by the time I scrambled into the front seat of Kyle's MG at seven-thirty, I had almost succeeded in putting the incident out of my mind.

Kyle grinned at me and looped an arm around my shoulder. "You're in a hurry. I suppose I daren't hope I'm the attraction?" I didn't reply, and he shrugged and said lightly, "I didn't think so. So is your landlady after you for the rent?"

"No, of course she isn't." I rose to the bait at once, then saw he was laughing at me and smoothed my palm down the skirt of my mauve summer dress. "It's nice to see you again, Kyle."

"Hm." He wasn't deceived by the evasion. "Is it?"

"Of course. The office hasn't been the same without you."

"I'll bet." Kyle took off from the kerb so fast he left rubber on the road.

"I've missed you," I said, hoping to erase the small crease between his eyes.

"Have you? Is that why you called me?"

"Not exactly." I couldn't lie to him. "I was excited about selling my story and I needed someone to be excited with me."

His brow smoothed out and he smiled. "Of course I'm excited for you. It's great news, Jane. I just wish you'd told me you were a writer."

I knew what he was getting at. If I'd told him, it would have meant I trusted him, felt close enough to him to confide. But the only person I really trusted was David—who had cheated on his wife and wasn't trustworthy. Logic had never had much to do with my emotions.

"I've told you now," I said. There didn't seem much else to say.

"So you have." He patted my knee in a familiar way that wasn't altogether unpleasant. "Where would you like to eat? The Savoy?"

"Oh, no. Somewhere comfortable."

Kyle laughed. "I doubt the management of the Savoy would appreciate that comment. Where then? The nearest pub?"

"I suppose so."

"No good?" He picked up on my lack of enthusiasm at once. "Okay, how about my apartment? It's comfortable, and it does come stocked with champagne."

Oh. I hadn't expected that. But after all why not? Kyle was attractive enough, his flat was comfortable in a baroque sort of way, and maybe...No. I shied away from the thought. Kyle wasn't David and never would be.

"I'm not sure that's a good idea," I said.

Kyle sighed. "Neither am I. But I'm willing to give it a try if you are."

"All right." I knew I ought to ask exactly what it was he meant to try, but I didn't. "If you like."

"Good. Dinner's in my fridge if you're interested. My cleaning lady is also a cook. Tonight she's left me cold salmon and salads. Will that do?"

"Ye-es." I thought about it, then said more decisively. "Yes, on a hot July night that ought to do very well."

Kyle nodded, non-committal.

Forty-five minutes later we were back where we'd left off in his flat, except that this time I was clutching a glass of champagne as I tried to meld with the corner of his sofa.

Kyle, in his shirtsleeves now, raised his glass. "To—what did you say your story was called?"

"'Romantic Deception,'" I muttered, watching the bubbles pop against the side of my glass. When he started to laugh, I added, "It wasn't my idea. I called it, 'Liar's End.'"

Seeing my embarrassment, Kyle sobered at once. "I expect the magazine knows what its readers like," he said consolingly. "So here's to 'Romantic Deception' and the triumphant career of its brilliant author."

I lifted my own glass self-consciously. "It's only a short story."

"The first of many," Kyle said promptly. "Are you hungry yet? I am."

He was doing his best, and I think he was genuinely happy for me. But he'd always had a hearty appetite, which wasn't surprising considering his level of energy.

"Yes" I said, anxious to oblige him. "I'm ready to eat when you are."

We ate the salads and cold salmon, which tasted deliciously of the Scottish springs from whence it came, and afterwards we retired to the sofa with cups of coffee brewed by Kyle in an aluminium saucepan.

"It smells wonderful. You're very domestic," I said. "I can only manage tea."

"That's because you're British."

I thought it was probably because I was lazy and not much interested, but I didn't say so. "Why do you go on living here?" I asked. "Don't you want to go home? To America?"

"Sure, sometimes. But my mother died last year, my brother and I never got along and—well, I guess I've gotten used to the English rain. In Minnesota we mostly get snow."

"All the time?"

"No, only in winter. That's bad enough."

I could see why it would be. "You're happy here then?" I said.

"Most of the time. Like now, for instance." He put down his glass and wound a strand of my hair round his middle finger.

Help! Was that why I was here? To make Kyle happy? I'd thought it was to celebrate my sale. I cleared my throat and tugged my hair out of his reach.

Kyle put a hand on my shoulder and said politely, "D'you mind if I kiss you?"

Oh, dear. I did mind. But he'd been kind, and at the back of my brain I'd known all along it would come to this. I didn't have to go to bed with him, and surely I could manage a kiss.

"No," I said, in a funny, thin voice that didn't sound like mine. "I don't mind."

He took me at my word, pulled me to him and kissed me enthusiastically on the lips.

At first I didn't respond. Then my blood began to heat up just as it had when David kissed me, and soon I was opening my mouth to welcome the intrusion of his tongue. He tasted of the wine we'd had with dinner.

It was a warm kiss, a thorough one, and I let it go on until Kyle took me by surprise and pulled away.

His blue eyes were brighter than usual, but otherwise he showed no sign that he was moved. Perhaps, after his long wait, he was disappointed.

"Well now," he said, sprawling against the arm of the sofa. "That wasn't so bad, was it?"

I shook my head. "No. It was nice."

Kyle let out a dry crack of laughter. "Nice?"

"Yes. You know—I liked it."

"Uh-huh. So did I. Want to try again?"

Compared to Carlo, or even David, he was being incredibly polite and considerate. I ran my hand over the fussily patterned weave of the sofa. "Do you want to?" I asked.

Kyle seized my wrist. "Dammit, Jane..." He stopped. "This is crazy. Of course, I want to."

I was still gaping at him when he dragged me onto his knees and kissed me again. Soon I felt my skirt slide up and then his long fingers were exploring the inside of my thigh. It was a bit as though a dam had burst, and now that he had started he couldn't, or wouldn't, stop.

When his fingers attempted a more intimate investigation, I pushed them away and struggled off his knee.

Kyle, looking hot and rumpled, raked a hand through his hair and said, "Shit."

We stared at each other. "I don't—" I began.

"Okay, okay. I know you don't. You've got 'virgin' written all over you. I'm sorry."

Had I really? How extraordinary. I debated the merits of telling him the truth. But if I did, it would only encourage him. And I wasn't ready for that yet. My body had responded to his kisses, but my heart hadn't.

"No need to be sorry," I said finally.

"What does that mean?"

"It means I-I like you. But I don't want to—"

"Go to bed with me," Kyle finished, in the acid tone he usually reserved for employees caught daydreaming or phoning their sweethearts.

"No," I agreed.

"What are you waiting for? Marriage? The right man?"

Oh dear, he did sound grumpy. "No," I said, making up my mind. "Kyle, I found the right man. Only he belonged to someone else. I-I think maybe given time...."

"Given time I might do as his replacement?"

Not grumpy. Downright bitter. Impulsively, I put my hand on his arm. "No, it's not that. At least I don't think so. And I'm not—not actually virginal. That is—"

"Jane, either you are a virgin, or you're not. There aren't any in betweens."

"All right then. I'm not."

If he could go all bitter and patronizing and impatient, there was no reason I shouldn't shatter his illusions.

Except he didn't look shattered. He looked relieved and a little amused. "What are smiling at?" I asked.

"Myself mostly. You could have fooled me."

"I did fool you, but not on purpose. You never asked me."

"No. It's not the sort of question I usually ask over the ploughman's plate in the pub. 'By the way, Jane, are you a virgin? Because if you are, I'll have to be twice as careful how I go about seducing you.'" He spoke in a silly, mincing voice that made me want to hit him.

"I didn't think you wanted to seduce me," I said. "At least not at first."

"I didn't. Not while we both worked for Ambrosia. Why do you think I changed jobs?"

"Not just for me?" I blinked at him. He couldn't have changed jobs just because of me.

"Not entirely," he admitted. "I told you I was ready for a change. But I won't pretend the hope of taking our—friendship a step further didn't play a part in my decision."

"Oh. But you haven't phoned me for weeks."

"I wanted to give you time to miss me. I guess it didn't work."

"It did," I pushed at a tangle of hair across my eyes. "Sort of."

"Sure. Once you discovered the other fellow belonged to someone else."

"Oh, I always knew that," I said.

Kyle's eyes narrowed alarmingly. "You did?"

Oh, dear. He did sound disapproving. Funny, I didn't want to go to bed with Kyle, but I hated the startled censure in his tone. Perhaps if I explained, he would understand.

He didn't. When I'd finished explaining how empty David's marriage had become and how he was standing nobly by his wife because of his child, instead of nodding sympathetically, Kyle swore.

"For Christ's sake, Jane. You may not be a virgin, but you're sure an easy mark."

"I am not." I wrapped my arms around my chest. "If you must know, I'm not going to see David again."

"Well, that's something." He stood up, bumping the coffee table with his knee and knocking an ornamental ashtray onto the floor. "Look, if it's all the same to you, I'd better take you home."

"You mean you don't want me after all," I said flatly. Funny, the thought of him not wanting me hurt more that I'd expected.

"No," Kyle smoothed a hand over his chin. "No, I don't mean that. What I want right now is to pick up where your David left off. But I won't. Not tonight. So you go on home and get your beauty sleep, and I'll call you at work in a few days."

"Oh. All right."

We said very little on the drive back to Wrenbert Terrace, but after Kyle had dropped me off and I fell into bed in my attic, I knew I wasn't happy with the way the evening had turned out. I was still ecstatic about selling my story, but at the edge of my mind a gnawing mouse of resentment kept reminding me that Kyle had called me an easy mark. I also felt a purely bodily regret that after a promising start he hadn't attempted to take kisses to their logical conclusion. He had nice fingers, longer than David's, fine-boned....

I fell asleep remembering the feel of them brushing softly over my skin.

Kyle kept his promise to phone in a few days but it was only to tell me he was leaving the country.

"My brother's sick," he said. "Polio."

"I'm sorry." I remembered he'd said he didn't get on with his brother. But in emergencies even feuding families drew together—or so I'd read. And this was surely an emergency.

Kyle told me his brother had two small children and a distraught wife. "I'm taking an indefinite leave of absence," he said.

"Will you be back?" I asked, hating the thought of his leaving.

He hesitated. "Yes. I think so. Does it matter?"

"Yes," I said. "It does. Will you write?"

"Maybe."

"If you do, I'll answer," I said.

He laughed. "Good. You should. You're the writer."

So I was. I'd actually forgotten for a moment.

Over the next few months my writing began to bear fruit. I sold five more stories to Women's Corner and another to a teenage magazine. Eventually, I made enough money to buy my own typewriter, a new Remington. But I didn't make enough to live on and my job with Ambrosia continued to pay the bills while I worked on a longer, more involved story of a brief encounter between a young woman who worked in a bookstore and an older, unhappily married man. Most of the time it seemed to write itself.

Kyle sent two postcards, one from New York and another from Duluth, but neither of them bore an address. I wasn't sure if I minded or not, but I thought about him often. Almost as much as I thought about David.

On a windy Thursday towards the end of September, I walked into my room to discover an ashtray full of butts on my bed. As usual the room reeked of tobacco, and I caught myself grinding my teeth. Had Mrs. Carmody spent the day up here—smoking hams or something? Arabella was right. It was time I moved.

After skewering my hair securely on top of my head in an attempt to create a more formidable image, I stalked downstairs to confront my landlady in her lair.

She opened the door her usual crack, and said, "Oh, there you are."

"What?" I was taken aback. Round One to Mrs. Carmody.

"Got a message for you, I have."

A gust of smoke hit me in the face. "Did you leave it in my room while you were there?" I asked pointedly. "I didn't see it." Round Two to me.

Her eyes shunted sideways. "Couldn't find any place to leave it. Figured it'd be safer with me."

"I'll have it then, please." I extended what I hoped was an authoritative hand.

Mrs. Carmody grunted and would have closed the door if I hadn't inserted my arm through the opening. For a couple of tense seconds, I wondered if she'd hit it with a broomstick, but in the end she muttered something that sounded like a spell and told me she'd see what she could do.

After a several minutes and a lot of snorting and rustling, she shuffled back with a torn scrap of paper in her fingers. "Here. You're to phone this number. Some kind of lawyer, he was. Wouldn't say what it was about." Her sharp little eyes regarded me with greedy curiosity.

"The message was for me? Are you sure?"

"Course I am. Think I'm deaf, do you?"

No, I didn't think she was deaf. But what would "some kind of lawyer," want with me? They must have phoned the wrong person. All the same, I took the paper from her skinny fingers, then opened my mouth to give notice.

Mrs. Carmody banged the door in my face.

I lifted my foot, intending to give it a good kick, but in the end I thought better of it. It would be easy enough to slip a note under the old witch's door. In the meantime, I might as well call this lawyer.

He turned out to be a Mr. Albert Norris, of Norris & Norris, Solicitors. But his secretary said he was out and would call me back. I explained that he'd have to call me at the office and she said he would.

The instant I left the call box, an ear-splitting shriek rose above the sound of wind and traffic and I forgot all about Mr. Albert Norris.

"Fire!" screamed a woman's voice. "Fire! Help! Somebody please help. My husband's in there!"

For a moment, I hesitated. Surely I recognized that voice, even at its startlingly high pitch. When it came again, like the scream of a rabbit in pain, I slung my bag over my shoulder and broke into a run.

Arabella, in red slacks and a tight satin blouse, was dancing up and down on the steps of Number Fifteen waving a newspaper-wrapped parcel like a baton. A curious crowd was gathered below her on the pavement. There was no sign of a fire, although the usual fog obscured any view through the basement windows.

"Arabella?" I ran up the steps and took her arm. "Arabella, there's no fire...."

"There is, there is." She shook off my hand and waved the parcel frantically at the door. A corner of the newspaper lifted and flapped up and down in the wind. "Janey, there's smoke. I can't get in."

There was always smoke, but this crisis sounded real. "Did anyone phone the Fire Brigade?" I asked.

"What for?" a man in a dirty brown cap shouted up at me. "She's crazy, she is."

I doubted it. Arabella's feet had always been anchored firmly on the ground.

My hands were shaking as I pulled the key out of my bag and inserted it into the lock.

Arabella clutched at my arm, and the next moment smoke, not black but grey and overwhelming, blew over us in a suffocating cloud. We started to cough.

"Call the Fire Brigade," I croaked at the gaping crowd. No one moved, so I ran down the steps.

"S'all right, love, " said a woman in a striped apron. "The old lady got out. Fair sight she looked too, with her face all black and that white hair hanging in her face. Her and the young fellow took off."

Mrs. Carmody and—Duncan? Or Zachary? And what about Mr. Matthews?"

I hurried back to Arabella, who was standing quite still with a face as ashen as her last name. "Are you sure Duncan's in there?" I asked, holding a hand over my nose as the grey cloud curled around my head. "Mrs. Carmody and someone else got out."

She gazed at me blankly. "He always goes to sleep before supper."

To gain strength for the night's activities? Odd, the inexcusable thoughts that come to mind in a crisis.

"I've got to get him," Arabella said suddenly. "Here." She thrust her parcel into my hands and ducked. I watched in horror as her head was swallowed up by billowing smoke. Seconds later the rest of her disappeared.

I stared at the parcel, stupefied, and coughing uncontrollably now. Fish. I could smell it in spite of the smoke. Fish 'n chips, that's what I was holding. The Ashes' supper. And if I didn't do something at once, they might never get the chance to eat it.

"Arabella!" I threw the fish at Striped Apron and ducked down to follow my frantic friend.

The wooden floor was rough with grit and splinters. I winced and closed my eyes, forcing myself to inch forward despite a taste like burnt cloth in my mouth. But I had only wriggled a foot or two before I felt something clamp around my ankle. Seconds later, I was most forcibly yanked backwards.

"You're not Arabella."

Duncan's voice. I opened my stinging eyes. *Why was he glaring at me?* I gazed up at him, dazed. Of course, I wasn't Arabella....

"Where is she?" he rasped.

"Inside," I gasped, through spasms of coughing. "She went in looking for you."

Duncan swore and I choked and passed out.

When I came to, I was lying on a hard, narrow bed in a room that kept jolting me around. A young man in a white shirt was bending over me, all smiling reassurance. "You'll be all right," he said. "Inhaled a bit of smoke, that's all. Nothing to worry about."

"Where am I?" I'd read that line so often in books it came almost naturally from my lips.

"Ambulance. We're taking you to the hospital. Just to check you over, see. No need to worry."

He was so sure I oughtn't to worry that I began to wonder if I should.

"Arabella...? And old Mr. Matthews?"

"Husband got the other young lady out." His eyes swivelled sideways.

"And Mr. Matthews?"

"Don't you worry, miss. Everything'll be all right."

"Yes, only..." I tried to shake my head, but the ambulance chose that moment to swing around a corner, so I closed my eyes instead. If Mrs. Carmody and Zachary were safe, old Mr. Matthews ought to be all right too....

When I woke again I was in a hospital ward and a nurse was checking my pulse. Arabella was in the bed next to mine. Duncan, still glowering, sat slumped beside her in a green metal chair. When he saw me looking at him, he sat up and smiled.

I'd never seen Duncan smile before. It made a difference. For the first time I had an inkling of why Arabella loved him.

"Is she all right?" I asked.

"Must be. They're shipping you both home in the morning."

If home was still there. "Is Arabella asleep?"

"Uh-huh."

"What happened? How did the fire get started?"

"Cigarette fell out of an ashtray while Old Carmody was in the lav. Silly old cow hadn't bothered to put it out. Sofa caught fire, and she came screeching upstairs like one of them vampires was after her. She and Zach must've run out the front. I broke a window and got out the back. Bella, she'd gone for our supper."

A long speech for Duncan. "You mean you weren't even in there when Arabella went after you?"

He shrugged. "Zach and I went for the Fire Brigade."

"And Mrs. Carmody?"

"Dunno. Think she and old Matthews headed for the pub."

The pub? While her house was burning down? "Was she out of cigarettes?" I asked.

"More'n likely."

That would explain it. "Is the house badly damaged?" I asked.

"Basement's a mess. Whole place smell's like rotten eggs mixed up with sweaty socks. Your attic's all right though, being farthest from the fire, an all."

With luck my typewriter would be all right then. And Teddy. The rest of it didn't matter much.

"I'm not going back there," I said.

"Don't blame you. Bella and I, we'll have to stay with her people till the place is fixed up. Won't be much fun."

I hid a smile. It would certainly put a damper on their nights.

"Where are you going then?" Duncan asked.

Where was I going? To the office in the morning. After that I supposed I'd have to stay with my parents and take the train up to town every day—at least until I found somewhere else to live. Whatever happened, I wasn't going back to Mrs. Carmody's. The fire was just the incentive I needed to make me move.

Arabella gave a small moan and opened her eyes. Duncan bent over her, and when I saw the look on his face I wanted to cry.

David had looked at me like that. It seemed a long time ago.

Someone across the ward groaned, but when I tried to see what was happening, a nurse bustled up and thrust a thermometer into my mouth. Duncan took advantage of my being safely gagged to grunt, "Thanks, Janey. For going in there to save Bella."

Had I really tried to save Arabella? I had a vague recollection of something to do with fish, a lot of smoke, and Arabella's head disappearing. Whatever I'd done must have been pure instinct. But I rather liked the idea of being Janey Blackman, Intrepid Heroine to the Rescue.

The fact that the Intrepid Heroine had been a damned nuisance who had to be rescued herself was not a fact I felt inclined to dwell on.

I didn't go to work the next day. For one thing, the clothes I'd been wearing were ruined, and I couldn't see Joe taking kindly to the sight of me dancing around the office in a sheet.

When Duncan turned up at the hospital in the morning, he brought clothes he'd borrowed from Arabella's mother. I didn't exactly look a dream in a purple and black flowered tent, but at least it was better than a sheet. Poor Arabella shrieked with horror when her husband presented her with a demure blue cotton buttoned to the neck.

As soon as Arabella and I were discharged, the three of us went back to Wrenbert Street to assess the damage. In my case it was minimal and mostly restricted to smell. Old Mr. Matthews hadn't done as well.

A curious bystander told me he had been rescued, comatose, from his room, but died on the way to the hospital.

"But he can't have," I cried. "The ambulance man said..." I stopped. The ambulance man hadn't actually said much. "Are you sure he's dead?"

I desperately didn't want Mr. Matthews to be dead. I hadn't known him well but I'd listened to his snoring every night, and he was a nice old man who always greeted me politely when we met on the stairs.

Mrs. Carmody, who was in the hall arguing with a man from the insurance company, looked over her shoulder and said irritably, "'Course he is. Told him to get out, I did, but the silly old goat wouldn't budge. Said at his age it didn't matter if he died."

Oh, poor, poor Mr. Matthews. I stared at Mrs. Carmody, shocked by her casual attitude to the death her own carelessness had caused. When I was able to speak, I told her I wouldn't be coming back.

In the evening I took the train to Willbury.

~*~

As I rounded the corner onto my parents' street, I had the oddest feeling that a part of my life had never happened. Mother's voice came clearly through an open bedroom window as I walked past the rows of overblown dahlias lining the path to the front door. She was complaining to Dad that she couldn't get the smell of fish out of his coat.

For a few seconds I was back where I'd been nearly three years ago, an anxious adolescent listening to a conversation she was never meant to hear.

Then I remembered that, with very little fanfare, my twenty-first birthday had come and gone.

The moment I knocked on the door, William started to cry. "He's as good as a doorbell," I said, when Mother flung it open.

"Jane!" she cried, forgetting all about the fish smell in Dad's coat. "Are you all right? You sounded very odd on the phone."

"Yes, quite all right," I assured her. I hadn't mentioned the fire when I'd phoned to let her know I was coming. She and Dad would have imagined me cooked to a crisp. Besides, I couldn't bear the thought of telling her what had happened to Mr. Matthews over the phone. In fact, I couldn't bear the thought of talking about him at all, so in the end I didn't.

The next day I returned to the office.

Arlene greeted me with the news that Norris and Norris, Solicitors, had tried to contact me twice the day before.

I'd forgotten all about the slip of paper I'd wrested from Mrs. Carmody. Without bothering to sit down, I leaned across my desk and dialled. Might as well get it over with at once, though I couldn't see what any solicitors' office could have to say to me.

"Ah, Miss Blackman," said Mr. Albert Norris when I was put through. "I have been endeavoring to reach you for two days."

"I was in a fire," I explained, reacting defensively to what sounded like an accusation of loose living.

"I see." He cleared his throat. Apparently a fire was no excuse for being unavailable. "Miss Blackman? Are you there?"

"Yes, Mr. Norris, I'm here."

"Ah. Good. In that case, perhaps you could find time to call in at our offices? To verify your identity, you understand."

"But I already know who I am."

"Harrrumph. Miss Blackman, please." I heard his chair scrape back. "This is no laughing matter."

"Of course not. I'm not laughing, Mr. Norris." I was near to crying because of old Mr. Matthews, and I would soon be screaming if he didn't get to the point.

"Hm. The fact is, Miss Blackman, I have serious news to impart. You are, of course, aware that your father recently..." He made a whistling noise, as though he were releasing air from fat cheeks. "Has recently, ah—shall we say 'passed away'?"

Dad? Dead? The phone slid out of my hand and crashed onto the desk. Three notebooks, a pencil and a box of typewriter ribbons shot onto the floor and clattered above the standard office hum. Dad couldn't be dead. I'd seen him only this morning....

Gradually my heart descended from my mouth. Sanity returned. Of course, Dad wasn't dead...."

I retrieved the phone from my blotter. "Mr. Norris, who, exactly, are you talking about?" I asked.

"Your father," he said, with a touch of impatience he should have stifled when talking to the supposedly bereaved. "John Marlowe."

"Oh." I put a hand over my eyes.

"Miss Blackman? Surely you knew?" His fussy voice pricked at me down the wire.

"No. No, I didn't. I'm sorry."

"No, no, I am sorry, Miss Blackman. I was under the impression you'd been informed." Mr. Norris cleared his throat. "He died last week—of cancer of the throat, I believe."

"Oh." I didn't know what to say to that. I'd never met my natural father. Was I supposed to care that the man who had abandoned my mother was now dead?

A flash of crimson caught my eye, and I looked up to see Arlene hovering in the doorway.

"Are you all right, Janey?" she mouthed.

I nodded. Albert Norris was speaking again.

"Mr. Marlowe gave us to understand you were aware of his precarious state of health."

"No. No, we never met."

"But—you'll pardon my saying this, Miss Blackman—he even mentioned the colour of your hair. And I believe your young man drives a Daimler."

"No, I don't have a young—that is, how could he possibly...? Oh." I sank onto the edge of my desk as the truth hit me like a fist in the chest.

The man with the hungry eyes. He must have been John Marlowe. I tried to remember what he'd looked like, but I couldn't get past the extraordinary eyes that had once so captivated my mother.

"Mrs. Marlowe inherits the bulk of the estate," I heard Mr. Norris explaining. "As well as the business, of course. But as his only child, he has also left a substantial legacy to you. Yes, quite substantial, if I may say so."

What? I wrapped the telephone cord around my fist and waited for the news to sink in. "Um—how substantial is substantial, Mr. Norris?"

"Ah. Not sure we should discuss that over the phone...."

"Mr. Norris...."

I must have injected sufficient authority into my voice to remind him that I was a potential client who would soon be in possession of that "substantial sum." He named an amount.

I gasped and slithered around my desk to sit down. I had no choice, because in this moment of revelation, my perfectly serviceable legs were unaccountably refusing to hold me up.

~*~

That evening I crouched on the edge of the bed I had slept in for eighteen years and wept at last for the father I had never known or wanted to know.

How could I have been so unkind? How could I have refused to let him approach me, that sad, childless man who had given me life? A man who had rewarded my callousness with a gift that would buy me freedom and financial security.

Raising my tear-stained face to the white ceiling, I begged his forgiveness then and promised that from now on I would remember him in my prayers. I didn't say prayers except in times of great crisis, but in these moments of devastating guilt that inconvenient detail scarcely crossed my mind.

A week later I went alone to lay flowers on John Marlowe's grave, and there, kneeling on the damp grass, I thanked him from the bottom of my heart for his generosity and swore that never again would I turn my back on anyone who needed me.

Never, of course, is a long time, but saying the words eased my conscience.

I suppose, at the time, I even meant them.

1958—1959

For this is Wisdom; to love, to live,
To take what Fate, or the Gods, may give,
To ask no question, to make no prayer,
But to kiss the lips and caress the hair,
Speed passion's ebb as you greet its flow,
To have, to hold, and in time, let go!

From *The Teak Forest* by Laurence Hope

CHAPTER FIFTEEN

I was glad I'd thought of buying flowers. Not the artificial lilies that had caused Mother to shake her head in disapproval the only time she'd visited my flat, but real, fresh-cut carnations in pastel pinks and whites. I jammed the long stems into a green ceramic vase and waltzed with it into the kitchen the advertising blurb had billed as compact and convenient. In fact, it was squashed into what had been a large cupboard in the days before the grand old house I lived in had been converted into a warren of flats.

After filling the vase with water, I hurried back to the sitting room.

Allison was coming. At last, after more than three years, I was going to see her again. Funny, I hadn't realized how much I'd missed her casual friendship until she'd phoned two days ago to ask if she could pop in on Sunday.

"I read one of your stories," she explained, when I was too surprised to answer her at once. "It reminded me I've been meaning to look you up. I have this habit of losing track of people, you see. Have you become rich and famous, Janey?" She laughed, as if the idea of me in connection with fame and riches was a splendid joke—which, unfortunately, it was.

I told her I wasn't famous or rich, but I'd love to see her.

John Marlowe's legacy had indeed been substantial and it had come at just the right time. Without it, I might very well have ended up crawling back to my attic at Number Fifteen. So much of my life had changed since leaving school that Mrs. Carmody's had come to seem a haven of familiar discomfort. But the fire, and my father's legacy, had served to shovel me out of my dependable rut.

"You must move to a better address, Jane," Mother had said the moment she heard of my good fortune.

For once, I couldn't disagree with her.

On the surface, Mother had appeared quietly unmoved by the death of her former lover. I had broken the news to her in person when I arrived home from work to find my parents enjoying a rare moment of peace in the kitchen while William slept. Dad was reading the paper while Mother flipped pensively through the pages of Country Life. As soon as they saw me, they knew something had happened, and after one look at my face, Mother said she'd better make us a cup of tea.

I waited till it was ready before telling them.

Mother said nothing, only looked at Dad with blank eyes and began to pour milk into the cups. When she poured it into the sugar bowl as well, Dad reached across the table to take her hand. She stared at their entwined fingers, then gave him a funny, strained smile, as if moving her lips had become painful. I waited for some more obvious sign that she was touched by John Marlowe's death. But perhaps she wasn't, because all she said was, "He owed you something, Jane."

When William began to yell from his cot, Mother left the room.

Dad looked at me, shook his head, and poured himself more tea. Then he leaned over to pat my hand. "I'm glad he left you the money, Janey. I only wish I'd been able to do more for you myself."

Dear Dad. I hugged him and told him he couldn't have done more. Then I made my way upstairs and collapsed onto my bed, where I spent the rest of the evening wallowing in guilt for the way I'd treated John Marlowe.

The next morning I felt better. Guilty still, but better, and by the time I started looking for new living quarters a week later, excitement and gratitude had largely taken the place of self-reproach.

It was Dad who had stood up to Mother and supported me in the matter of the flat. He had pronounced my new home, in a quiet square just west of Sloane Street, "Very grand," and said my furniture was all right with him as long as I liked it. Mother approved the neighbourhood but said the furniture wouldn't do at all.

"What you need, Jane, are a few good pieces, an oriental rug or two and neutral curtains." She spoke as if she expected me to throw everything out the window and start refurnishing at once.

I didn't ask what would make the 'pieces' good, or what the curtains were supposed to be neutral about. All I knew was that I didn't want the conservative, unfashionable furniture she would foist on me if I gave her the chance. I liked clean lines and glass and tranquil blues and greens, and I didn't care if it was fashionable or not.

Mother was quite sure the Queen wouldn't have chosen anything so outlandish. Dad pointed out that as I was the one who would be living with it, the Queen's opinion needn't be taken into account.

Hard to believe I'd been here almost two years. I gazed with satisfaction at the restful coolness of my sitting room, caught sight of a drooping carnation and snapped it off and, still restless, prowled through the French doors leading to my small balcony above the street. As soon as I stepped outside, the heat from the pavement rose up to blast me in the face.

"The joys of London in July," I muttered, narrowing my eyes against the glare as I went to lean over the railing.

No dustbins and hungry cats here, thank goodness. From my vantage point on the second floor I was able to look down on smartly dressed shoppers, taxis, and a group of lost tourists in light-coloured suits staggering beneath an abundance of cameras. In the fenced garden in the centre of the square, two straight-shouldered ladies in hats were walking a brace of portly corgis. I made a mental note to tell Mother about the corgis. She would approve of those. The Queen had them.

One of the corgis sat down to scratch, another plodded into it, a third started to bark and their owners looked as though they were just working up to a heated altercation with furled umbrellas when the phone rang.

It was Allison. Something had come up. Her flatmate, Hal, was being difficult—he usually was, I gathered—and she wouldn't be able to come after all.

Swallowing my disappointment, I agreed that, of course, we'd get together some other time and hung up. At this rate, we would both be old and grey before we met again—if we ever did. I wondered if I minded anymore.

Friendship was a funny thing. You couldn't depend on it. People you thought you cared about so often drifted away when circumstances no longer held you together. Like Colin, whom I hadn't seen for years. And it had been months since I'd seen Arabella. Perhaps that was why I found so much pleasure in creating my own people. They couldn't disappear.

The phone rang again, and this time it was Kyle.

"Doing anything tonight?" he asked.

My mood lifted at once. I could do with a nice dose of Kyle to take my mind of Allison's defection.

He hadn't let me know he was coming back to England. After the two postcards, I hadn't heard a word.

Then two weeks ago, he had walked into my office at Ambrosia.

"Hi, Jane," he said, as if we'd said goodbye only yesterday. "Doing anything this evening?"

"Kyle?" I stood up stiffly, half convinced he was merely a phantom brought on by too many of Ambrosia's natural vitamins. He looked different. Older, which of course he was, but harder too. His boney face was more aquiline than ever. I took a tentative step forward. "Kyle, what are you...? That is, I thought you were still in America."

"I was. Got back two days ago. On the Queen Elizabeth." He put his hands on my shoulders and bent to peck me on the forehead.

"But why didn't you let me know?" I backed awkwardly into a bookcase. "Your brother—"

"Is as much of a fool as ever. But he's better and back at his job. I figured I'd kept the family ball in the air long enough. Now it's his turn."

I sniffed discreetly as a pleasing aroma of masculine cologne wafted up my nose. Not many of the Englishmen I knew had enough confidence in their maleness to use scent.

"Now that you're back, do you mean to stay?" I asked.

Kyle pushed aside my in-basket and settled on a corner of my desk. "That depends. Did Joe tell you he's being made a partner in Ambrosia?"

"No. No, he didn't."

"Well, he is. I've been offered his job as Advertising Director."

"But you don't know anything about advertising," I protested.

"You'd be surprised what I know. Besides, my job at B & H Foods no longer exists. They went bankrupt."

"Yes, but—"

"What's the matter? Don't you like the idea of having me as your boss?"

"It's not that."

It was, of course. Kyle's new maturity made him more attractive than I remembered, and he was bound to be distracting around the office—as well as too dictatorial by half. And that wasn't the only problem. If Kyle and I started going out again....

Oh. All at once I got it.

"We're not going out any longer, are we? So it won't matter if we work in the same office."

Kyle picked up an elastic band and snapped it. "Aren't we? You have a boyfriend?"

"No one special, but—"

"Ah. That's settled then."

"You're not going to take the job?"

He smiled, an enigmatic and mildly annoying twitch of his narrow lips. "Yes, I think I am. For a year or so anyway. Until I've laid my hands on enough capital to start my own business."

"Then we can't—"

I didn't get any further, because Joe came in, and said, "Ah, there you are, Johannsen. Wondered where you'd got to," and bore Kyle off to his office.

So much for the peaceful and productive afternoon I'd had planned. I spent the rest of it trying to decide if I could possibly work under Kyle again in a job I knew more about than he did. John Marlowe's legacy had helped enormously, but it hadn't absolved me of the need to make more of a living than I could possibly earn from writing stories.

When I stepped off the lift that evening Kyle was waiting for me.

"Let's have a drink." He took my arm as I tried to walk past him.

I thought of refusing, but I was glad to see him again. By the time I'd made up my mind to go with him for old times' sake, we were already outside the local pub. I'd forgotten Kyle's habit of sweeping everything before him like a tank brigade.

The pub was noisy and crowded, but Kyle pushed his way to a corner, propped me against the wall with instructions to "stay put," and went to fetch our drinks. When he came back, he found me fending off the advances of a beefy young man who smelled like the dregs from the bottom of a beer barrel.

"Sorry, pal, the lady's taken." Kyle pushed him away without apparent rancor.

I cringed, expecting a fight to break out. But the beefy young man only shrugged and went to lay siege to a scared-looking blonde holding up a corner of the bar.

"Thanks," I said offhandedly, not wanting him to get the idea I really was 'taken'—at least not by him.

Kyle nodded. "Pleasure's mine. Well, Jane?"

"Well, what?"

"What have you been up to since I left?"

"Working," I said. "Writing. Moving. Visiting my parents."

"And?"

"That's about it."

"No glamorous men in your life?"

I wished I could tell him there were. But although I'd been out with men occasionally when they asked and enjoyed myself sometimes, I'd met no one who could take David's place. "No," I said. "Not really."

"Good. That means you're free this evening."

"I suppose so."

Kyle drained half his lager in one gulp. "That's what I like about you, Jane. Your enthusiasm."

I laughed. "Sorry. You're a bit of a shock."

"Am I? You'd better get used to me quickly then, because I'm starting back at Ambrosia next week."

"Oh." I slumped into the corner and spilled half my wine over my shoes.

"Steady." Kyle grabbed my arm. "I'm not that bad, am I?"

"No, of course not. It's just—"

"That I'll be your boss again?"

"Well—yes."

"It's awkward, I agree. But at the moment, I don't have a lot of room to manoeuvre. I need a job, so we'll just have to be discreet."

I wasn't sure I wanted to be discreet. Not with Kyle, and not with Arlene looking on. But, oh, it was good to see him, and I didn't want to give up what had once been a warm and undemanding friendship.

"Drink up," Kyle said, making it unnecessary for me to answer. "I'm getting hungry."

I drank up and we went to my favourite Italian restaurant and talked the night away. It was good to have someone I could talk to again. I hadn't realized just how much I'd missed Kyle's easy companionship.

The following night we went out again and talked some more—about Duluth, where he'd grown up, and about our families and the books we'd been reading. Kyle favoured factual tomes about the war, whereas I preferred John Buchan, Daphne du Maurier and the romantic regency novels of Georgette Heyer.

On the third night, I invited Kyle up to my flat for a cup of coffee. He hadn't once tried to kiss me since he'd been back, but remembering the way we'd parted, I had a feeling he was working up to something. Even so, I risked asking him up.

He did kiss me—and to my surprise, the blood in my veins rose to a very pleasant simmer at once.

The following week, Kyle moved into Joe's office at Ambrosia.

"Help," whispered Arlene. "I'll never get any work done with that backside of his parading around all the time."

"You'd better," I said. "He's Torquemada incarnate on people he catches slacking off."

All the same, I knew what she meant about his backside. It was definitely distracting.

Two days later I cooked Kyle spaghetti in my flat. It was the one meal I could count on to turn out right. Afterwards he helped me with the dishes and asked me to go to bed.

"Oh," I said, gripping the edge of the sink.

"Oh?" He tossed his tea towel onto my narrow draining board. "Oh? Jane, you do like me, don't you?"

"Of course, I do."

"But not enough?"

It was a question to which I had no satisfactory answer. I had known he would ask sooner or later, but I hadn't known how I would respond.

"Maybe," I said, knowing it wasn't much of an answer.

"But not tonight?"

"No."

"We've been here before, Jane."

"I know. I'm sorry. I will think about it."

Kyle shrugged and left without kissing me goodnight.

After he'd gone, I sat on my kelly green loveseat and tried to work out what was wrong. I did enjoy being with him. Sometimes I even tried to pretend he was a loose-limbed, lanky version of David. But he was sharper-edged, less patient, more determined to get what he wanted than David had ever been. At the moment he wanted me—something the spotty schoolgirl inside me still found hard to believe. So why, given that my nights were often restless, and my body craved a release more explicit than torrid kisses, couldn't I accept Kyle as a substitute for David?

Perhaps I was afraid of being disappointed.

I tried not to wonder if David was solving similar frustrations with a reluctant Posy. He was a man after all, and she was his wife. It was only too likely....

Kyle too would soon look elsewhere. He was neither a saint nor a eunuch and there were plenty of women in London who wouldn't be immune to ice blue eyes and long legs.

How would I feel if he gave up on me? It shouldn't matter, of course.

David would always be the love of my life.

~*~

I went out onto the balcony after Kyle's phone call and watched a young man in shorts and a business haircut watching a tall brunette climb into her car. The air was still steam heated, but black clouds were building castles above the rooftops. We were going to have an angry sunset and maybe thunder.

When Kyle picked me up at eight, the atmosphere was sultry and so was he. I hastily suggested a film. I'd be safe in a darkened theatre, safe from the intimacy I guessed he had in mind. Unfortunately, the film I chose was a revival of *Roman Holiday*, which left me feeling all sad and lovelorn and romantic.

He kissed me the moment we reached the door of my flat, and I almost responded to the question in his eyes with a fervent, "Oh yes, please."

I didn't though, and shortly afterwards he left, looking angular and frustrated.

"I'm sorry," I called after him as he ran down the stairs.

"Sure you are," he muttered and banged into the wall.

The thunder came in the middle of the night along with rain. I didn't much like thunder. As a child I'd believed it was the voice of God warning of impending catastrophe, and in those days catastrophe had meant Posy Bantley-Brown finding another chink in my admittedly flimsy armour.

Yet when she phoned me, exactly two days after the summer storm, I didn't even think to blame the thunder.

"Hello, Janey. Can you come for tea on Saturday?" She spoke in what I'd long ago dubbed her Lady Posy voice.

Just like that. What was it about Chantersley girls that made them pop out of thin air after years of indifferent silence and carry on as if they'd seen you yesterday in class?

"I don't think—" I began.

"I'm asking Lady Cawton," Posy interrupted. "And one or two others. All members of the Conservative Club." When this failed to elicit a gasp of admiring acquiescence, she said a shade irritably, "I hear you're an author now, Janey. It is true, I suppose?"

Oh. So that was it. How typically Posy. Now that I was an "author," someone who might impress her county friends, she was keen to re-establish a connection.

"Yes," I said. "I've sold a few stories. But I'm afraid I can't..." A bird's beak tapped against the window and I stumbled to a stop. Did I really want to pass up an invitation to David's house? Would he be there? Was there a chance I might see him again? If only I could ask. But of course, I couldn't—and of course, he wouldn't be there. Posy was certain to send him off on some errand while she entertained Lady Cawton and the Ladies of the Club. Not a bad name for a rock-n-roll group, that. I giggled with a touch of hysteria.

The bird—a sparrow, I think—cocked its head to one side and flew away.

In the end I accepted Posy's invitation to tea even though I knew it was flirting with disaster.

~*~

"Janey!" Posy clapped her hands in affected delight. "What a flamboyant car. It doesn't seem you somehow. I imagined you driving something more—"

"Conservative?" I suggested, slamming the door behind me as I alighted onto the Pembroke Cottage driveway. "Grey?"

Posy frowned and eyed my ancient and unpredictable red Triumph with a certain suspicion. "It's very red, isn't it?"

"Yes, it is. I've always wanted a flashy red car. I thought it would go nicely with my hair."

She attempted a small, peevish smile, not sure whether to believe me or not. We'd come a long way since Chantersley days, Posy and I.

"Your garden does look sweet," I said, with a condescending wave at the flowerbeds. "How lucky for you the sun came out today."

Posy narrowed her eyes. They weren't as blue as they had been and small folds of flesh had developed at the edges of her mouth. I smiled guiltily. What was the matter with me? I'd already helped myself to her husband. There was no need to pretend her glorious garden wasn't glorious.

With an effort to inject sincerity into my tone, I said, "I've always loved roses," and bent over to sniff the nearest bloom. It smelled heavenly, warm and drugging amid the summer hum of bees. My uncharitable antagonism dropped away like an overblown petal. "A garden is one thing I miss about London," I told her, not bothering to mention that cabbages, not roses, had featured largely in the garden I'd grown up with. It was hard to be convincingly nostalgic about cabbage.

Posy's features relaxed into their usual complacence. "It is rather lovely, isn't it? And Sidonie adores flowers. Do come along, Janey. Everyone's waiting to meet you. I would have sent Kathryn to fetch you in, but she's taken Sidonie for a walk." Posy took me cosily by the arm and urged me up the crazy paving path to the front door where a purring Nefertiti ran up the steps to wrap her silky black body around my legs.

"Beastly cat," said Posy. "Don't you dare come in while I'm entertaining. Shoo, shoo."

Nefertiti gave an indignant meow and scooted into the hydrangea bush beside the door.

Loud female voices with clipped vowels reached us as we stepped into the hall. From the sounds of it, a post mortem was being carried out on last week's point to point.

"You don't ride, do you, Janey?" Posy asked.

"No. I don't."

"Sidonie will, naturally."

I rejected the idea of enquiring how one rode 'unnaturally'.

When we paused in the entrance to the drawing room, the post mortem droned to a halt. I shifted my feet awkwardly as four pairs of eyes skimmed briskly over my yellow summer dress.

Mane needs trimming, coat too pale, flanks on the skinny side, legs passable, I imagined them thinking to themselves.

"This is Jane Blackman," Posy announced into the sudden silence. "She writes those stories for Women's Corner that some of you have read."

I knew at once that she hadn't read any of my stories.

A beefy woman with grey hair twisted into a plait around her head fixed Posy with a formidable stare and said, "And some of us haven't."

"Well..." Posy coloured. "So little time, you know. Jane, you haven't met Lady Cawton, have you?"

"Of course, she hasn't. That's why you asked us to tea. Marjorie..." Lady Cawton turned to a woman in a fluffy white cardigan who reminded me of a sweet woolly lamb. "Here's that author you wanted to meet. Sentimental sort of stories, if you ask me. No horses in 'em."

The lamb stood up and took my hand. "Don't listen to Laura, my dear. They're charming stories. I cried all night over that scene where Rosemary told Edward she couldn't marry him. Then in the morning I discovered I'd got it wrong and that she was going to marry him after all. Percy says I need new glasses. He was terribly cross." She smiled impishly.

"Thank you. How kind," I murmured taking to her at once, but not knowing how to respond.

"Come and sit beside me," she said.

"Do you ever write about horses? Or golf?" asked a tall woman with the beginnings of a moustache. "I'm partial to Agatha Christie myself." She held out her hand. "Faith Farnsworth."

"How do you do." I took the hand cautiously, in case her grip was as hearty as her voice, then took a seat next to woolly Marjorie. "No, actually I know very little about horses."

The stunned silence that followed this shocking admission was broken by Posy's fourth guest, a plump brunette in her thirties, who giggled and said she didn't either.

"Nonsense, Pamela. You have an excellent seat." Lady Cawton directed her penetrating gaze at Pamela's plump bottom. "Now then, Posy, what about some tea?"

"Of course." Posy, flustered, reached for the milk jug and seized the teapot instead.

"Milk for me," said Lady Cawton. "Don't hold with that heathenish American custom of taking tea straight."

"Like whisky," I said, and was skewered by a glare from Posy.

When tea had been poured to Lady C's satisfaction, we ate sandwiches and toasted teacake while Her Ladyship held forth about the disgraceful behaviour of the Labour candidate at last night's meeting in the Town Hall. "Unions," she said darkly. "They're at the bottom of it."

She didn't say what the unions were at the bottom of and no one seemed disposed to ask. To my relief, no one said anything further about my horseless stories, although Marjorie did occasionally look up at me and smile.

Inevitably, the conversation turned to golf.

"You play, of course," said Faith Farnsworth, turning to me just as I took a substantial bite of teacake.

"No," I said, trying to push the teacake into my cheek. "Actually, I don't."

The silence was brief this time, almost as if they'd expected me to let the side down. I glanced hopefully at the clock on the mantel. Ten to five. Was it too early to escape without appearing rude?

Seconds later the matter became academic as the drone of conversation was cut off by the kind of high-decibel shriek that only the very young—or perhaps the very deaf—can generate.

Pamela put her hands over her ears. The rest of us winced and flicked our eyes at Posy.

Her mouth had fallen open. As I watched her close it, I was reminded of a turbot before it landed on the slab at my father's shop. Yet, in reality, she was only immobilized for a few seconds, and when she jumped up and hurried into the hall, I followed her, mumbling something about seeing if I could do anything to help. Even a screaming child seemed preferable to another round of conversational golf. As I left, Lady Cawton was replaying the ninth hole.

"Sidonie's lungs sound—healthy," I said to Posy.

"Her lungs? Oh, yes." For once she spoke without stopping to consider the effect of her words on her audience. "She's terribly sensitive though. So easily upset. Kathryn isn't always as careful of her feelings as she should be."

If the appalling noises coming from upstairs were anything to go by, I suspected Kathryn's feelings might also be in need of tender, loving care.

Posy ran up the stairs with arms outstretched. I hadn't seen her move that fast since the days when we'd both done our best to avoid catching lacrosse balls and being chosen to play on the school's team. I followed her more slowly into a room featuring pink ducks on creamy white walls.

"Darling!" she exclaimed. "What happened? Why is my baby crying?"

A fair-haired child with totally dry eyes hurled herself across the carpet at her mother.

"This won't do, Kathryn." Posy scooped up the child and glared at a woman in her late thirties who was standing with her back to the window. "You know Sidonie mustn't be upset."

"She wanted to climb out the window, Mrs. Foley. I couldn't let her do that," the woman replied. She didn't add, "unfortunately," but I couldn't help wondering if she thought it. The petulant pout on the little girl's lips was so like her mother's that I felt an immediate bond with the housekeeper.

"Now Kathryn, you know how highly-strung Sidonie is. I've told you before she needs to be treated gently." Posy dropped a kiss on the blonde curls tickling her chin.

Kathryn smoothed her hands down a smart blue overall. "If you'll pardon my saying so, Mrs. Foley, gently isn't what she needs at all. She wants a firm hand, that one, not her own way every time she screams." Kathryn had evidently been pushed beyond the point of tact.

"Really, Kathryn." Posy lowered Sidonie to the floor, but kept a hand on her daughter's head as the little girl clung like an incubus to her leg. "You know Sidonie has a delicate nature. I've told you before—"

"Yes, Mrs. Foley. And I'm telling you that little miss is spoiled rotten. If you don't do something about her, she'll grow up without a friend in the world."

"Nonsense. You people have no idea what children need."

"'You people,' Mrs. Foley?" There was an edge to Kathryn's voice. "Now what would you be meaning by that?"

"Well..." Posy flapped her free hand at the housekeeper. "I suppose it's not your fault you went to the village school, but...."

"Posy," I interrupted, sensing Kathryn's imminent explosion. "Didn't you tell me Kathryn's a mother too? She must know about looking after children."

"You don't know anything about it, Janey," Posy dismissed me with a toss of her curls. "Now then, Kathryn—"

"That's all right, Madam. You've no need to say any more. I may not have been to a fancy school, but I do know when my work isn't valued. I'll be handing in my notice, if it's all the same to you." She whipped off the blue overall to reveal a neat figure in slacks and a checked shirt. "I wish you joy of that little hellion."

"Now Kathryn, there's no need—"

Kathryn wasn't listening. With her head held proudly, she stalked out of the room and slammed the door. Seconds later we heard her sandals slapping down the stairs.

I glanced at Posy's brick red face and narrowed, angry eyes. Then I lowered my gaze to the floor, embarrassed, although the scene had been none of my making.

"Wretched woman," Posy muttered. "Our old cook would never have dreamed of behaving like that."

"Your old cook was born over sixty years ago," I pointed out.

"Yes, and I hope you're not trying to tell me this sort of thing is progress." Posy detached Sidonie from her leg, and at once the child started to whine.

"It probably is, you know," I said.

Posy puffed out her cheeks, and when I guessed she was about to tell me not to be so red, I changed the subject. "Listen, it's none of my business, but your guests...."

"Oh, dear. Yes, Lady Cawton..." She glanced down at the snivelling Sidonie, then looked hopefully at me. "Janey, would you mind...?"

"I'll have to be getting home now," I said quickly. "Thank you so much for tea. I'll just go and say goodbye, shall I?"

Her hopes of using me as an unpaid babysitter thwarted, Posy preceded me down the stairs with the incubus wrapped around her neck.

As soon as we reached the drawing room, I took my leave of Lady Cawton and her cohorts and headed for my beloved flashy car.

In a way, I felt sorry for Posy, but there was no doubt she'd brought her troubles on herself. Sidonie struck me as a textbook example of the results of over-indulgence. I wondered if David was equally indulgent.

David. I'd been trying not to think about him, and by this time had almost succeeded in squelching dreams of an unexpected encounter in the hall or a chance meeting behind a stand of golden rod.

There had certainly been no sign of him, so quite possibly he was still in London. Although, surely, he must come home on weekends, if only to see his beastly daughter. I paused to bury my nose in the velvet petals of a pale orange rose. Now that I thought about it, if Sidonie were mine, I wouldn't make much effort to see any more of her than I had to. It wasn't the child's fault, of course—not really.

A dragonfly swooped past my nose, making me jump, and I gave up trying to define the psyche of that unlikeable little girl. It was her father I cared about. But David wasn't here, and in a few minutes, I would be miles away from Pembroke Cottage.

The dragonfly swooped back and I tumbled into my car. Where was David likely to have hidden himself if he was trying to avoid tea with the Ladies of the Club?

The answer came to me almost at once. Although Nefertiti had briefly been in evidence, the dog, Blackie, had not. Nor had I once heard him bark.

That had to be it. David was out walking his dog.

I started up the car and drove down the road until I came to the edge of Gotham Woods. The woods were the perfect place to walk a dog. I slowed to a crawl.

After that it took me only seconds to make up my mind. Pulling the Triumph onto the gravel beside the road, I switched off the engine and settled down to wait.

Twenty minutes later, just as I was telling myself I'd been a total fool, a black snout emerged from behind a tree trunk. Behind it came a wriggling black body attached to a madly revolving tail.

Behind the tail came David.

CHAPTER SIXTEEN

He was thinner, his walk aimless, as if he neither knew nor cared where he was going. The laugh lines around his eyes had become lifelines. At least that was how it seemed to me when David came tramping out of the woods in a patched tweed jacket and fawn trousers.

He didn't see me at first, but Blackie did. The dog couldn't have remembered, but that didn't stop him from bounding up to me, quivering with delight at the prospect of greeting a playmate.

"Hello, Blackie," I whispered, leaning out of the window and bending down to kiss the soft, black snout. It didn't matter that his paws were scrabbling at my paint work.

When I looked up, David was only a few paces away. He held a broken branch in one hand and was slashing at the buttercups growing through the roadside gravel.

"Don't," I said. "They're pretty."

His arm stilled and he took a step towards me. "Janey?"

I blinked and swallowed the lump clogging my throat. David hadn't changed after all. It was still the same for him as it was for me.

Pushing Blackie gently away, I climbed out of the car onto the gravel, and David dropped his branch and took me in his arms.

We stood there, holding each other, unaware that time was moving on, barely aware of the occasional passing car. It was Blackie who brought us back to a world that didn't belong to us alone when, bored by our inattention, he began to bark.

We pulled apart gradually, still lost in the glow of emotions that had miraculously survived our years apart until the ribald hoot of a car horn made us jump.

Blackie, determined to be noticed, put his paws on my chest and licked my face, and I threw my arms around him and rested my cheek on his shiny, black head.

"Oh, Blackie," I whispered. "Darling Blackie."

"He's very badly behaved," David said.

"Yes." I smiled and raised my eyes. "He is, isn't he?" We both knew Blackie behaved exactly as David wished.

"Janey..." He turned away and bent down to pick up the branch. "Janey, I'm sorry. I don't know what to say."

"There isn't much to be said." I wondered if I sounded as hopeless as I felt.

"I know." David didn't turn to face me, but stood with his head thrown back as if he were studying the clouds. After a while he said, "These last couple of years have been hell."

"Have they?"

"Yes. God, yes." He rubbed a hand round the back of his neck. "But you—have you been all right? Happy? I hoped you'd find someone..."

"Did you really?"

"What do you think? No. Of course, I didn't." He hurled his branch at the trees with such savagery that it cracked in two the moment it hit the nearest ancient oak. Blackie ran after it, barking.

I feasted my eyes on David's back and the familiar veined thickness of his neck. Was it really possible to feel this helpless? Even when I'd thought I might be pregnant, there had been something I could do, something to hope for. If only I could have had David's child...

"I don't need anybody else," I said brusquely. "Why should I? I'm self-supporting."

"Yes, I heard you're a writer now. Congratulations."

"Thank you."

He nodded. "I'm glad for you. But that isn't enough, is it? You deserve more."

"More?"

"Yes. Everyone needs someone to..." He shrugged. "Someone to love, I suppose."

Sex? Was that what he meant? I wished he would look at me.

"Do you," I asked, "have someone?"

He turned round then with disconcerting speed. "I have a daughter."

The last time I'd heard him say that his voice had sung with pride. Now it was flat, as if he were saying, "I have a house."

"Yes. I just met her," I told him.

"Lucky you."

That didn't sound like the voice of a proud father. "She's pretty," I said, because if beastly Sidonie were mine I'd be in need of all the reassurance I could get.

"Yes. Thanks to Posy, she's also the infant from hell."

I laughed doubtfully. "She'll improve." When David only sighed and shook his head, I asked, "Did you know I was coming to tea?"

He nodded. "Mm. Posy told me."

"Oh. Did she also tell you not to show your face?"

"No. That was my decision." A ladybird landed on his arm. He didn't bother to wave it away.

"She doesn't know, does she? About us?"

He held out a hand as if he meant to touch me, then changed his mind and let it drop back to his side. "At one time I thought she did, but I was wrong." He glanced in the direction of the woods. "I'd better round up Blackie. He's not very bright, I'm afraid."

"Yes. You'd better." I stared, transfixed, at a small purple flower fighting for a place among the buttercups. I didn't dare blink my eyes. "Goodbye, David."

He made no answer and I was already turning away when I felt the breeze lift my hair. Only it wasn't the breeze. It was David's breath on my neck as he moved around me to lift up my chin.

"It's no good, is it?" he said. "I can't, Janey. Not any longer. Not after seeing you again."

"Can't what?" I whispered. His face was so close I could see the deep pores in his skin.

In the storybook world of my dreams he would have answered, "I can't live without you any longer." What he actually answered was, "I want you, Janey."

My dreams took an unforeseen detour. "What, exactly, do you mean?" As if I didn't know!

He frowned and let me go at once. "Isn't it obvious? God knows, I've tried to make things work with Posy, but..." He shook his head and didn't attempt to go on.

Oh, he had, had he? Well, my bed had been singularly empty too. "And did you have much success?" I asked, trying to sound unconcerned and not succeeding.

David winced. "I wouldn't call it success. Janey...will you meet me somewhere? Soon. In town?"

"For what purpose?" I made an effort to keep my voice level even though my palms were curling into fists.

"Just to talk. Please." He smiled and his lips were as beguiling as ever, his teeth just as even and white. My resentment subsided in helpless defeat.

"All right. You can come to my flat." I gave him the address. "Let's go and find Blackie."

The dog was deep in the woods dragging something green and mouldering from beneath a gorse bush. On closer inspection, it was either a lace from an old boot or a dead snake.

"Drop it, Blackie," David said.

Blackie dropped it and we returned to the road.

I was already in my car when, faintly but with chilling clarity, we heard the shriek.

"Posy," we said in unison.

We stared at each other. "Is she all right?" I asked.

"I doubt it. She only makes a racket like that when she's thoroughly worked up." David was more bored than concerned.

"If she's worked up..." I didn't finish the sentence. If Posy was upset, it might be because someone in one of the passing cars had told her that her husband was kissing strange redheads by the side of the road. "I'd better go," I said, when Posy screeched again.

"No." David took my arm and gestured at the Triumph. "It could be Sidonie. Will you give me a lift? It'll save a few seconds."

Bored, but still dutiful, I thought, as I helped him heave an indignant Blackie into the cramped backseat. After that I slid behind the wheel and drove the short distance back to Pembroke Cottage.

A peculiar silence hung over the aromatic garden. The bees must have been buzzing, the birds singing, but when Posy came stumbling down the driveway to meet us, the only sound I heard was the uneven crack of her heels against the paving.

David leaped out of the car and grabbed her arms. "What's the matter?" he demanded.

Posy shook her head.

"For heaven's sake, woman...."

"Sidonie. It's Sidonie. I can't find her. I only went to answer the phone. David, what if—?"

"Isn't she with Kathryn?" David was impatient, still not really perturbed.

I eased myself out of the car and helped Blackie to climb over the seat. When he ran to the nearest flowerbed and started digging up roses, nobody made any attempt to stop him.

Posy, with increasing panic, was explaining to David that Sidonie had been missing for half an hour, that she had shouted herself hoarse and looked everywhere—

"You can't have," he interrupted. "She must be somewhere. Come on, we'll all have a look. Janey will help. Won't you, Janey?"

"Of course."

"Right. You take the back and the garage. Posy, you take the front. I'll have a look around the house."

"I've already searched the house," Posy moaned.

"That's precisely why I'm checking it again. You could have missed something."

She nodded, looking white and defeated. Then the three of us went our separate ways.

~*~

I saw the small, muddy sandals the moment I climbed the back steps. They were sticking out of the rain barrel Posy had shown me on my first visit to Pembroke Cottage. It was partly screened by a section of box hedge and hadn't been immediately visible from the ground.

Dear God! I stared in horror, not wanting to believe. Fear clenched my stomach. My legs wouldn't move. In the summer heat, I was frozen with fear.

Those were Sidonie's sandals. The white straps were attached to the soft pink flesh of her ankles. But how...? She couldn't have fallen in. The barrel had a lid, I knew it had.

I tried to scream, knowing I must get help. But at first I couldn't. Then a ghastly shriek shattered my eardrums, and once I realized it came from my own throat I was able to move, to jump off the steps and run panting up to the barrel. How could such a little girl have climbed so high? There was no ladder that I could see. But I had to reach her. It might not be too late. What could I...? Ah! The hedge. It was higher than the barrel. That must be how Sidonie had done it. Only I was heavier....

Holding my breath, I grabbed for the top of the hedge and tried to pull myself up. Twigs and leaves came away in my hands. Oh, dear Lord, there must be something...I ran around the other side of the barrel and discovered that, in my panic, I'd overlooked steps of a kind. Just two rotting blocks of wood, one higher than the other, but they would do. I leaped onto the top one and reached up to grasp Sidonie's ankles. They felt warm. Alive. And I couldn't be sick. Not now. Save it for later. I pulled, my chest aching with the strain. Then someone was behind me, shoving me aside, and a man's hands were gripping Sidonie's waist. A series of cracks split the air as the rotting lid that had held the little girl captive gave way to superior force.

I collapsed against the barrel, aware that Sidonie was stretched out on the ground, but afraid to look.

When I did pluck up courage, the first thing I saw was that her hair was wet. The second, that David had her on her stomach and was trying to push air into her lungs. I walked away and was sick into a border of marigolds. After that I went to find Posy.

She was fluttering about near a tall rhododendron bush and calling out for Sidonie in a shrill, panicky voice.

"We've found her," I said.

Posy took one look at my face and screamed. It was a horrible sound, like nothing I'd ever heard, and she went on screaming until I took her by the shoulders and shook her. "Don't," I said. "Please don't. It won't help."

Posy gasped and managed to splutter out, "Is she—is she...?"

"I don't know. She fell into your rain barrel. David's trying to revive her."

I expected her to scream again, but she didn't. Instead, she took a long, gulping breath, stared at me as if I were an envoy of the devil, and began to run like a panic-stricken duck with her plump bottom jiggling and her arms flapping at her sides like misshapen wings.

As soon as she was out of sight, I dashed into the house to call for help, half expecting Lady Cawton to sail out of the drawing room demanding to know what the fuss was all about. Luckily, Posy's guests were long gone.

When help did come, it was in the form of police and an ambulance.

I didn't go with them to see if Sidonie was all right because I couldn't face the horror I might see.

For the next half-hour I sat on the steps of Pembroke Cottage while blurred figures in uniform moved back and forth across my field of vision. I heard voices issuing orders, but none of them was directed at me, and I made no effort to return to reality until I became aware that an unusual quiet had descended on the garden. The shadows were long on the grass and the ambulance had left with Sidonie. So, I supposed, had David and Posy. What had been going on while I sat in my catatonic state?

I could have moved, but I didn't. It was easier to sit quietly, listening to the blessed silence. After a while it was broken by the sound of vigorous shaking, and seconds later Blackie came dancing out of a flowerbed with a wreath of pink blossoms around his head. I led him into the house and discovered a bulky policeman in the hallway taking notes.

"The little girl—will she live?" I asked him.

"Don't know, miss. She's breathing. Father brought her around." He bent down to peer into my face. "Are you the young lady who found her?"

I said I was, and he said that was good, because he had a few questions to ask me. "Expect you could do with a cup of tea," he added kindly.

I didn't even realize I was laughing until I saw him look at me as if he was thinking fondly of men in white coats.

~*~

On a rainy Saturday afternoon late in August, David finally came to my flat. By then I knew Sidonie had survived, but that was all I knew. Her father hadn't said much over the phone and Posy hadn't contacted me at all.

"Nice," David said, settling into my green reclining chair.

"What is?" Having him here, so close, yet in a way as distant as ever, made me jumpy. I turned to fidget with the curtains.

"Your flat. It's restful and—well, nice. But not untouchable. Posy doesn't like me sitting on what she calls the 'decor.' Makes life difficult at times." He spoke with a dry resignation that, for the hundredth time, made me wonder what had possessed him to marry a woman to whom he was so obviously unsuited. It couldn't be much fun for Posy either.

I went to mix us gins and tonics. When I came back, finding no excuse not to sit down, I perched on the edge of the sofa and began to shuffle the magazines scattered across the coffee table into a further state of disorder.

"Janey," David said, "won't you look at me?"

I had no choice then but to meet his eyes.

He lifted his glass and smiled. "I've never thanked you properly, have I? For finding Sidonie in time."

I discovered I was over the shock of that awful day when it occurred to me that if I were David, I wouldn't necessarily count finding his brat of a child as any kind of favour. An unworthy thought that did an injustice to David. But I thought it just the same.

Something of the sort must have shown on my face, because David said, "I know. But she is my daughter."

I saw then that, even in repose, he looked drained, with a weariness that went deeper than the healthy fatigue that comes from hard work or hard play.

What had it been like for him in the weeks since he'd nearly lost his child? When I'd last seen him he had seemed sad, older, not at peace with himself or his life. But now I sensed that some decision had been made.

"Of course Sidonie's your daughter," I said. A gust of rain spattered the window. "How is she?"

"Superficially, she seems to be all right. A little quieter, but that's all to the good."

Remembering Sidonie's ability to make noise, on that point I had to agree. "Was she badly hurt?" I asked.

"No. The barrel wasn't full, thank God. Her head was barely touching the water. But there were splinters from the lid in her face and upper body.

"But no lasting damage?"

"Probably not. The doctors say it's too soon to tell. There could be psychological damage."

He looked so careworn I didn't have the heart to tell him that Sidonie's psyche struck me as remarkably tough. As David had pointed out, she was his daughter.

"I'm sure she'll be fine," I said bracingly. "Children are very resilient." I'd read that somewhere, and it seemed the right thing to say.

"Yes. I expect so." He tilted the recliner and closed his eyes as if he meant to take a nap. I cleared my throat. He must realize there were matters that needed settling between us, and I had no intention of tiptoeing around the flat while he slept off a bad marriage that would still be binding when he woke.

"Why did you come to see me?" I asked, deliberately raising my voice.

David sighed and opened an eye. "Because I said I would."

"I didn't ask you to."

"I know. You did your best to discourage me."

I picked up my drink and listened to the cool chink of ice against glass. "Yes, I suppose I did. But you're here now. Don't you want to talk?"

He didn't answer until he had tipped the chair forward and had a drink in hand. "Not immediately. There's something I want more." His self-deprecating grimace left me in no doubt as to the nature of the something.

"Oh." I crossed my legs and allowed myself the bittersweet pleasure of admiring his manly body sprawled in my chair as if it belonged there. He did look lovely, and that endearing little half-smile had always done me in. Of course, I wanted him. As much as he wanted me. But it wasn't as easy as that. If I gave in to desire now, I could end up with a lifetime spent sharing the man I loved with Posy Bantley-Brown.

No, that was wrong. She was Posy Foley, and she would be sharing him with me, which was even worse.

"We can't," I said.

David heaved another sigh. "I'm afraid you may be right." Still holding his glass, he stood up and slouched across to the window where I couldn't see him.

"So why did you come?" I asked his empty chair.

"Because I want it all, I suppose. I'm tired of loving honour more than you, dear."

To my astonishment, I had to suppress an absurd urge to giggle. "I thought the hero of that poem was going off to war."

"Yes, well that's the way it feels." Another burst of rain hit the window and after a pause, he said heavily, "Makes no difference. I can't leave them, Janey. Posy's been a wreck since the accident. She insists that what happened was everyone's fault but her own, of course, though I'd several times asked her to get rid of that damn barrel. She said it was sweet. Now she's become so nervous and over-protective she'll end up smothering Sidonie if I'm not around to provide some sort of balance."

"What about your parents? Or hers? Can't they help?"

"My mother tries. Her father tries. It doesn't do a damned bit of good. Posy watches over our daughter like a gaoler. She won't even let her go to the lavatory by herself. She's had bars put on all the nursery windows, and she locks Sidonie's door at night. The only time she's allowed out of her mother's sight is when I'm with her. And that's only because Posy hasn't yet found a way to tell me I've no right to take charge of my own daughter."

I heard a series of thumps, as if David was banging his head against glass.

"Posy's had a shock," I said. "Perhaps she'll get over it in time."

"Yes. Perhaps. In the meantime, I can't leave her." The banging stopped. "I'm sorry, Janey."

"Why? Why are you sorry? I never asked you to leave her."

"No. No, you never did. You've been wonderful. Wise and generous and kind. Maybe when things are more settled—"

"Maybe when things are more settled you can visit me? No, David. Even if you mean it, which I'm not sure you do, I don't want to be an 'other woman.' What happened between us—well, it happened. And it was beautiful. But now we have to stop dreaming and get on with our lives."

Was this really me, sounding so gallant and self-sacrificing? I swallowed, not sure whether it was laughter I was gulping back or tears.

The green reclining chair still showed a faint impression of David's body, and a moment later, he resumed his place there.

I knew now he would never leave Posy. Not just because he was a man whose basic instincts were honourable, but because more than he needed me, he needed to be at ease with himself—which he wouldn't be if he left his wife and only child. David was used to being liked, and likeable people didn't run off with redheads from the wrong side of the Willbury tracks. His parents would be horrified as well, and David valued their good opinion.

No, he wouldn't leave Posy. He might think he would, but in the end he wouldn't. And he'd make a lousy part-time lover for the same reasons. He would always worry about being found out and causing hurt. Ironically, to me, as much as to anyone else.

It was all academic anyway. This redhead from the wrong side of the tracks didn't mean to be available any longer.

David was nodding as if he'd read my thoughts. We had always been on the same wavelength.

"Unless you can die when the dream is past—" he said softly. "It is past, isn't it, Janey?"

"Yes." I blinked back the moisture in my eyes. "But neither of us is going to die. You have your family. I have my writing and my job—and my friends."

David nodded. "I know. And one day, soon, you'll meet someone who can give you what I can't."

I shrugged and put on a brave smile. "We'll see. Is that what you want? You said it wasn't."

"Did I? Yes, I suppose I did. But it's time to move on, isn't it? For both of us." He leaned forward and traced his thumb gently around my mouth.

With all my will, but much against my heart,
We two now part.
My Very Dear,
Our solace is, the sad road lies so clear.

His smile was soft and sad, and there were tears in his eyes as well as mine. But something in his voice, or perhaps in the way he cocked his head, made me think he would look back on this moment of parting with a measure of relief. Not that his sadness wasn't real. He wasn't cut out for duplicity. But between him and Posy there had always been some inexplicable tie. His need for me was probably more physical than emotional.

I gained strength from that thought. Strength enough to push his hand away and stumble to my feet.

"You mustn't touch me," I said.

"No." He stood up too, this big, tall man who made my flat look small. I thought of all the years when I wouldn't see him. Posy would never ask me to Pembroke Cottage again. I would be a reminder of her culpability.

"Will you be happy?" I asked. I thought, in his own way, he might be now he'd accepted that he couldn't 'have it all'. David wasn't a man who could live long with despair. In the end he would make the best of what life sent his way. But I hoped, just once before we parted, he would say he loved me.

"I'll try to be, Janey. For Sidonie's sake. You be happy too."

I waited but he didn't say he loved me.

There must have been tears on my face because he took out his handkerchief, looked at it, and began dabbing helplessly at my cheeks.

I took it from him and blew my nose. "Will you send me a photograph?" I asked. "Please."

"Yes. I'll see if I can find one." He didn't ask for one of me, and I blew my nose again.

"Keep the handkerchief," he said, patting me on the shoulder.

I looked at it, damp with my tears, and tried to laugh. "I can see why you wouldn't want it," I choked.

David took a step towards the door, hesitated, then came back and took me in his arms. "Thank you, darling Janey," he said before he kissed me goodbye.

It was a short, rough kiss, and I returned it. But I didn't try to stop him when he left.

CHAPTER SEVENTEEN

The door closed quietly. I listened to David walking down the stairs, heard him stumble on the landing, and when I guessed he must have reached the street, I went onto the balcony to watch him drive away. It didn't matter about the rain washing over me in swollen grey billows, or about the cotton dress clinging to my body like wet silk.

David's car jerked away from the curb, and I caught a last glimpse of his unruly fair hair. I watched until he was out of sight then squared my shoulders. Now all I had to do was accept the loss of my love with noble resignation, as if I were the tragic heroine of one of my more melancholy romances. It seemed as good a way as any to hold off grieving. The grief, I knew, would come later when I thought of all the years that lay ahead.

In the evening Kyle arrived to take me out to dinner. I'd forgotten he was coming.

"Oh God, I can't go out tonight," I greeted him.

"Why not?" He brandished a big box of chocolates, moved me aside and shoved the door shut with his foot. "Are you sick?"

"No. I just don't feel like it."

"Not good enough." He bent down and peered into my face. "Your eyes are all red."

"Are they? Perhaps I've been rubbing them."

"Or perhaps you've been crying. What's happened, Jane?" He glanced round the room, saw the empty gin glasses and said, "You've had a visitor."

"Yes. David Foley. He's the husband of an old school friend. Posy. I think I told you about her."

I knew I'd told him about her, in four-part harmony.

Kyle's too-thin lips almost disappeared. "You sure did. And about her husband. What was he doing here? Or is that a totally dumb question?"

"No, it's not dumb. I think he came to say goodbye."

"Goodbye?" Kyle's eyebrows shot up to meet his hairline. "What the hell do you mean? I thought you told me that was all over.

"It was. But something happened, and I saw him."

Kyle was looking murderous, so I backed away and added with false nonchalance, "Don't worry, it's still over."

"Why? I suppose he's going away."

"No. Just home to his wife."

He lifted the box of chocolates as if he wasn't sure whether to put it down or use it to hammer me over the head. "Are you saying what I think you are, Jane?"

"I don't know. Probably."

"And that's why you don't want to go out? Because you're carrying a torch for that two-timing bastard?"

"He's not a bastard."

"Right. But you're in love with him."

"I'm trying not to be. Kyle, I'm sorry. It really is over."

Kyle swore with a trans-Atlantic inventiveness that astonished me. Then he tossed the chocolates onto a chair and said, "How long has this been going on?"

"I told you. It hasn't. Not for over two years." I began to sidle past him towards the sofa. He had gone all hawk-like and threatening, and although I'd never known him to be physically violent, I was well acquainted with his legendary temper.

He caught my arm as I edged past him. "How do I know you're telling me the truth? That you won't go off and poach some other woman's husband?"

I made a half-hearted attempt to pull away. *Poach*? He was making the most memorable night of my life sound cheap, sordid—which it hadn't been, whatever he thought.

"It was only one night," I told him, resenting the scornful bitterness in his voice. "I didn't plan it."

"So are you saying you regret it?"

I shook my head. "No. Not yet. But in time maybe I will."

Kyle swore some more and curved his hands around my shoulders. His cologne was muskier, more earthy than I'd remembered. When I tried to shrug him off, he kissed me. At first, with the taste of David still on my lips, I resisted. Then it dawned on me that Kyle in a filthy temper kissed exceptionally well. We had exchanged other embraces, but this was different.

In the end I returned his kiss with a kind of desperation, dreaming he could make me forget.

We went on kissing while he began a tentative exploration of parts of me he hadn't touched before. I should have pushed him away, but I didn't, and when he lifted his head I saw that his normally sharp features were blurred with desire. For me.

"You win. We needn't go out," he muttered.

Help! What had I let myself in for? "It's all right," I said. "I wasn't thinking. Just wait while I put something on." I had something on, but it was only my comforting blue bathrobe.

"No need." Kyle slid his hands purposefully down my back. "You're already overdressed."

He had nice hands, longer and bonier than David's. But I couldn't give him what he wanted—not tonight.

"Don't," I said at last, wriggling out of his grasp and tugging awkwardly at the belt of my robe.

"For God's sake, Jane." Kyle yanked at his tie as if it were a noose around his neck. "I've waited over three years."

He hadn't. He'd been gone for two of them. "Is that all you're interested in?" I asked, unfairly. "Sex?"

"If it had been, do you think I'd have hung around this long? While you, apparently, were hankering after a man who wasn't free."

He had a point. "I'm sorry," I said. "I can't."

"Can't or won't?"

"Won't, can't—does it matter?"

"That's it? That's all you've got to say?" He gave me an icy blue glare that might have been intimidating if I'd been in any mood to be intimidated. "In case you haven't noticed, miss, I'm not some fawning little lap dog with nothing better to do than wait until you decide to pat me on the head."

"No," I said, thinking of Blackie who wasn't a lap dog either. "I know you're not."

"Right," he snapped. "Even I can take a hint when it's shovelled on with shit."

"Please, Kyle." I held out a hand to detain him. "Don't...."

He ignored me, turned his back and slammed out the door. A few seconds later the front door slammed as well.

As soon as the echoes of his going died down, I slumped into the recliner, tipped it back and gazed with bleak disinterest at the ceiling. It needed a fresh coat of paint.

Poor Kyle. It wasn't his fault his timing had been terrible. I ought to feel guilty. In a way I did, but caught up in my own misery, I couldn't bring myself to care very much about his. Not that I believed he was miserable exactly. More like furious and frustrated.

The following morning I awoke with a head that felt as if it had been pounded full of nails. The sun shining through the bedroom window hurt my eyes. I squinted and discovered a beetle crawling up a bright beam of light on my chest of drawers.

Perfect, I thought. Exactly suits my mood.

Swinging my feet to the floor, I chivied the beetle into a plastic glass from the bathroom and tipped it out on the balcony. After that, and as the nails in my head began to rattle, I climbed back into bed. There didn't seem much else to do.

Would there ever be? At this moment it didn't seem likely—and yet...I'd got along well enough without David for two years.

Yes, replied the pragmatic side of my brain. But always as a dreamer whose dream wasn't past. Now it is.

The rest of Sunday was hell. As the permanence of David's leaving sank in, I found myself beginning to hate Posy, not for her unkindness as a child, but because I couldn't take possession of her husband. I knew that my feelings were inexcusable. I also knew in a disconnected way that wallowing in self-pity could change nothing.

I tried closing my eyes against the insistent good cheer of the sun, but Dad phoned to tell me William had said "efficacious," and after that I had no hope of getting back to sleep.

Once the nails assaulting my head were well and truly pounded, I survived the day by writing twenty gloomy pages of my novel. Towards evening, I threw them all out.

It wasn't until after work on Monday that I realized I had to talk to Arabella.

Kyle hadn't spoken to me all day except to criticize my copy. He said my writing hadn't been up to standard lately and that I'd better shape up if I wanted to keep my job. At first I thought that was his way of getting back at me for refusing to go to bed with him. But when I complained about his unreasonableness to Arlene, she told me he was only speaking the truth. My copy had been slipping badly this past month.

This past month? I thought about that. It was just about a month ago that I had sat in my car watching David and Blackie emerge from

Gotham Woods. Then Sidonie had fallen into the barrel, and since then my mind had rarely strayed far from the inhabitants of Pembroke Cottage.

By the time five o'clock rolled around my copy had become so unfocused that even I couldn't pretend it was brilliant prose. I began to give serious consideration to a slow climb up Tower Bridge followed by a rapid descent into the Thames. But I didn't like heights, and when Kyle stalked past my office looking as if he'd rather enjoy it if I took a nosedive, I settled on Arabella instead.

It had come to me, as I sat hunched and puffy-eyed at my typewriter, that a dose of Arabella's down-to-earth realism could be just the medicine I needed.

~*~

"Oh," said Mrs. Carmody, in answer to my knock. "It's you."

"So it is," I agreed, ducking as a cloud of smoke threatened to engulf me. "Hello, Mrs. Carmody. I see you've recovered from the fire."

"Insurance," she replied with sly glee. "New carpets and curtains. Settee too. Brown velvet and lace. Matches my mother's lace lampshade, it does."

My mother would have shuddered. "Oh. How nice," I said. "Um—is Arabella in? I mean Mrs. Ash?"

"Don't ask me. Shouldn't think so. Been awful quiet up there lately."

"Can I check, please?" If Arabella was in, and it was quiet, that meant Duncan was probably out.

"Suit yourself." Mrs. Carmody shuffled sideways, firing a parting salvo of smoke. I sneezed and headed for the stairs.

The place hadn't changed in spite of a fresh coat of grey-looking paint. The landing still creaked in the same spot and there were the same long scratches down Duncan and Arabella's door.

I knocked and waited.

No one answered at first, but I heard what sounded like somebody swearing, followed by a thump as something—feet perhaps—hit the floor. Then more swearing and thumping until at last, the door was dragged open.

"Bella! You are in!" Relieved, I stopped holding my breath. "I'm sorry to barge in on you like this, but...

" I stopped, the rest of my speech swallowed in astonishment. This vision in a pink satin robe and fluffy slippers was Arabella all right, but not the svelte and brassy siren I remembered.

Arabella laughed. "Sight for sore eyes, aren't I? Never mind, little buggers'll be popping out soon. Doc says I'm going to have twins."

"Twins? C-congratulations. That's, um—"

"A bloody disaster, that's what," Arabella interrupted cheerfully. "Not to worry. Mum says she'll look after them while I'm working. Have to work, won't I? Got to keep food in their mouths."

"Duncan...?" I said faintly.

"Oh, he's working too, and he'll have to wangle a bit extra on the side. We'll manage. Got to move out of here though. Old Carmody says she doesn't want no kids."

"Can she throw you out? Legally?"

"Dunno. Don't make no difference, wouldn't stay anyway. She'd assphyxiate them with her bloody fags. There. How's that for a word?"

I laughed for the first time in days. "Oh, Arabella, you are good for me."

"So's castor oil. Well, don't just stand there. Come on in."

I followed her into the flat. A huge bed took up most of the main room, which was littered with odds and ends of food, clothing and newspaper. Through an open door I could see that the smaller room, which was supposed to be Duncan's study, was stacked floor to ceiling with packages in plain brown wrappers. No doubt Duncan's illicit contribution to the family coffers.

Arabella heaved her bulk onto the bed. "Want some tea?" she asked, predictably.

"No thanks. Can I make you some?"

She gestured at a teapot and a cracked cup and saucer on the floor. "Just had a cup. What brings you by, Janey? It's been ages."

"I should have come before."

"Yeah, you should have."

"You haven't been my way either," I pointed out, perching myself on a straight-backed kitchen chair with uneven legs.

Arabella shrugged. "Haven't been anywhere to speak of. Too much of me to lug around these days."

So that was it. And I'd thought she'd been avoiding me because my improved circumstances made her feel out of place. I should have known better. There wasn't much that could seriously discombobulate Arabella.

"I'd have come if I'd known," I assured her.

"Not to worry. You're here now." She grinned companionably.

"Oh, Bella." Her cheerfulness was my undoing, and it shattered the remnants of my pride. "Bella, I'm so miserable."

"Here now." She pushed herself upright and leaned over her stomach to peer into my face. "What's the matter? That boss of yours giving you a hard time?"

"Yes, but it's really not his fault. It's David."

"Oh, him. Didn't work out, I suppose. Can't say I'm all that surprised. Best to leave them married ones alone."

"Well, of course it is." I frowned, trying to remember. "Didn't you once tell me I ought to have an affair with David?"

"Mm. And did you?"

"Not really. Just one night."

"Blimey. That bad, was it?"

"No, it was wonderful."

"Oh," Arabella nodded sagely. "I get it. Guilt. Spoils everything, don't it?"

She had always had a knack for getting to the rotten root of the matter. "Yes," I admitted. "His. And mine too, I suppose. He'll never leave them, Bella. He doesn't really want to."

"Do you want him to?"

"I don't know. No, I suppose not. He wouldn't be happy, so I wouldn't either."

"Well, then. That's that, isn't it? Never mind. Lots more fish in the ocean."

"I don't want fish. I want—"

"What you want is to stop feeling sorry for yourself, kiddo. Won't help none, you know. Think about all the good stuff. You've got a fancy place to live, you've got family, you've got a job, you like writing them fairytales of yours...hell, one day you could even be famous. What do you need a man for?"

Put like that, I didn't. But I wanted one. Specifically, the one I couldn't have.

I sighed. "Same thing you do, I expect. It feels so—so marvellous. Being in love, I mean."

"Is that what you call it? Huh. Could have fooled me. But if you're talking about plain old sex—hey, with hair like yours you can't miss. Bound to be all kinds of men chasing after you."

"I think there's more to it than hair," I replied, making a face.

But as usual she was right. I did have plenty to be happy about, although that wasn't what I wanted to hear. And one day I would be happy. Yes, and famous. Why not? It was only a matter of making up my mind.

What about David? the same mind disloyally replied.

265

Oh yes, David would always be there, a memory of love and lust gone awry. But already I could feel myself letting him go. I didn't want to. Not yet. But it was happening whether I wanted it or not.

As for 'plain old sex'...well, there was always Kyle. I wasn't in love with him, but I liked him, liked being with him most of the time. We were more than friends, and sometimes when he kissed me....

Hadn't I once read somewhere that Samuel Johnson said that when grief is fresh, any attempt to divert it only irritates? It was true in a way, but I couldn't be irritated by Arabella. And surely there had to be some truth in that dreary old cliche about the healing powers of time....

I made an effort and smiled. "Thanks," I said. "Thanks for the vote of confidence—though I'm not sure I want men running after me."

"'Course you do."

I shook my head. "You know, just now, when you were talking about all the good stuff in my life—you forgot something."

"Me? Forget something? Never." She threw up her hands and rolled her eyes at the ceiling. "All right, I'll bite. What did I forget?"

"You forgot to mention yourself. You're one of my very best things, Bella."

She didn't answer, and at first I worried that she thought I was mocking her. But when I heard a sniff and turned to look more closely, I saw that she was rubbing her eyes.

"Go on," she said gruffly. "I bet you say that to all the girls."

Dear Arabella. My mother would disapprove of her most heartily, but Mother didn't know what she was missing. To me, at this moment, Arabella was one of life's dearest mercies.

Duncan came home a short time later looking hungry in more ways than one. We chatted for a few more minutes and then I left.

As soon as I got back to the flat, I phoned Kyle.

He was curt at first, not trusting me, but after we'd been talking for a while his voice softened.

When I went into work the next morning, a dozen crimson roses graced my desk.

~*~

Summer was late the following year, but it came in the end.

Almost eleven months had passed since I'd last seen David, and today crimson roses graced my windowsill, filling the flat with their warm, sweet scent. I stretched lazily as I sat at the small desk in my bedroom sorting through a pile of letters and bills.

There was a mildly caustic note from Mother accusing me of being, "Out with that boyfriend of yours, I suppose," every time she'd tried to phone lately.

My parents had met Kyle and liked him, though Mother still tended to grumble about his long-ago divorce. "You may be interested to know," her letter went on, "that we've finally moved into our new house." The fish shop had been doing so well that Dad had at last been able to buy Mother her coveted house on the "good" side of town. "William," she added, "has his name down for Tonbridge. That's where Mrs. Featherstonhaugh from The Grange sent her sons."

I smiled and started on the rest of the mail, which consisted of a postcard from Allison who was in Paris on a buying trip and still hopelessly attached to her Hal, three requests for donations, two bills, a cheque from Women's Corner and a letter postmarked Much Gotham.

I stared at this last, frowning over the unfamiliar writing, but could elicit no further information from the envelope. In the end I was obliged to slit it open.

Inside were two neatly typed pages. Whoever had sent this letter wanted to be certain I could read what she wrote.

Except that the sender wasn't a she.

The signature at the bottom of the second page was David's. I'd never seen his handwriting before.

Several minutes passed before I found the courage to lift the pages from my lap, spread them carefully on the desk, and begin to read:

Dearest Janey,

Forgive me for once again intruding on your life.
Best, I think, if I go straight to the point.
Posy left me a month ago. She took Sidonie with her and has asked for a divorce. She plans to marry Sir Rupert Hawkridge, the psychiatrist I persuaded her to see after Sidonie's accident. Posy is much recovered, I believe, and I'm relieved to say she no longer treats our daughter like a porcelain doll.
Sir Rupert, along with his knighthood, has an impressive pedigree and an estate in Scotland. Posy tells me she finds him irresistible. Her decision, I think, may have been prompted by Jasmine's recent marriage to a French count.

> *Janey, my dear love, this means that soon I'll be*
> *free. If you don't want to see me, I'll understand. I*
> *know I hurt you deeply in the past and, as I've found*
> *out, a lot can happen in a year. But if you still care for*
> *me, please don't leave me in suspense. Pick up the*
> *phone, and I'll come to you whenever and wherever*
> *you tell me.*
>
> *Believe it or not, "I have been faithful to thee,*
> *Cynara, in my fashion." I always will be.*
>
> *Yours in love and hope,*
> *David.*

Oh, no. I stared at the words blurring before my eyes. No, this couldn't be real. Not now, when it was much, much too late. He said he'd been faithful, but he hadn't. Not to me, the mythical Cynara of his fantasies, and not to Posy, who was finally about to achieve the exalted status she had always believed she deserved. It wasn't his fault, it had just happened that way, but....

I folded a corner of the letter, pressing it down with my thumb, then unfolded it and smoothed the paper out.

I couldn't deny that David would always have a place in my heart—and I did still care for him in a wistful, nostalgic sort of way. But I couldn't go back. Thanks to time and Arabella—now the mother of placid twin boys—I had survived the loss of my love and grown beyond it. By placing one foot in front of the other, tentatively at first, and then with confidence, I had allowed the pain to heal to the point where I was able to tread lightly and with laughter.

I no longer worked for Ambrosia. It had become awkward once my friendship with Kyle turned physical, which had happened not long after I said goodbye to David. When I was offered a job with a magazine called The Metaphysical Mind, I accepted it.

I still wasn't sure what a metaphysical mind was, but that didn't stop me from writing about it.

When I told Kyle I was leaving Ambrosia, he heaved a sigh of relief and said, "Thank God. It hasn't been easy keeping my mind on work with you around. I was wondering how I could fire you without breaking your heart."

"Without getting yourself banished from my bed, you mean," I scoffed without rancour.

"No, actually I was thinking of asking you to marry me."

"And now you don't have to," I said.

He laughed. "Oh, I don't know. I still may. Would you say yes?"

"No. Not yet. I'm waiting for you to grow up."

Not surprisingly, that had ended with Kyle rolling me onto the bed so he could prove to me exactly how grown up he was.

I was comfortable with Kyle, both in and out of bed. Unlike David, he wouldn't dream of quoting poetry at me, but he was rarely dull, and I'd grown used to his volatile temper. His rages never went deep. Much more importantly, he made me laugh.

I was comfortable with other parts of my life as well. I liked my new job, my short stories continued to sell, and the book I'd been writing forever was almost finished—as was my ill-advised addiction to David Foley.

I picked up his letter and ran it back and forth through my fingers. When a shrill whistle sounded from the street, I jumped. Two dogs began to bark, and I thought I recognized the voices of the corgis. There were five of them now. Sighing, I traced my finger over David's name. I had loved him too, in my fashion. Loved him and handed him my heart. But he had given it back. It was mine now. If I gave it again—as maybe I already had—it would be to a man who would keep it.

I reread the letter and felt sad for David. He had, I think, loved Posy more than he knew. Certainly he loved his horrid little daughter. But I couldn't fill the vacancy in his life. He would have to do that for himself.

I put down his letter and went into the sitting room. A bright-eyed seagull landed on the sill and watched me as I picked up the phone.

When David answered, I told him I was sorry.

He was silent for several seconds before he said, "I'm sorry too, Janey. More than you'll ever know. But I promised you I'd understand, and I do."

After that we spoke, awkwardly, of Posy and Sidonie and the gallery and my job, and when there was nothing more to say we wished each other well and said goodbye. The seagull flew off, its wings silver-white against the sky.

I was crying when I hung up the phone.

Kyle arrived a few minutes later, saw my face, and enfolded me in the comforting security of his arms.

"What is it?" he asked.

"David."

He held me away, his fingers gripping my elbows, and glared into my eyes. "That bastard? Again?"

"No," I said. "Never again."

"You said that before."

"And I meant it. He's free to marry me now. I turned him down."

"You didn't want to," he accused. "You're crying."

"I know. I'm not sure why. But it isn't because I turned him down."

"Isn't it? Are you sure?" He pulled me towards him and laid a hand on the back of my neck.

"Yes. I'm sure. It's over, Kyle. Really."

He stared down at me as if he expected to read the truth in my eyes—as perhaps he did, because after a while he said, "Good," and ran his hand possessively down my spine. "You'd better marry me then. It's the only way I can think of to keep you away from that two-timing creep."

"Maybe I will," I said, not bothering to defend David's honour.

Kyle's fingers traced a path through my tears. "When?"

"Not today. Not tomorrow either."

"I'll wait then. But not forever."

"No," I agreed. "Not forever."

Taking that as acquiescence, Kyle picked me up and carried me into the bedroom to seal the promise I hadn't yet made in the usual way.

~*~

In September I took a few days' holiday and went down to Willbury to admire my parents' new house.

Dad had developed a potbelly. Mother, queening it in, "such a nice part of town," was in her element. William was as predictably obstreperous as ever and a thoroughgoing pain in the neck, but neither of my parents seemed to notice.

On Monday, after breakfast, I went for a walk. It was instinct, I suppose, that set me on the road to Chantersley, yet when I reached the familiar wrought iron gates, I hesitated.

"Old Girls' Day," had come and gone; I hadn't been near my old school since the day I left—so what was I doing here now? I had no real business on the grounds. But as I turned away, I heard the off-key echo of girlish voices raised in song.

The lure was irresistible.

I walked down the familiar driveway and the remembered words came to me quite clearly.

Lord, behold us with Thy blessing
Once again assembled here
Onward be our footsteps pressing,
In Thy love, and faith, and fear;

My footsteps pressed onward, not in fear, but in curiosity and nostalgia, and perhaps a kind of faith. So many of my dreams had been nurtured at Chantersley. It was fitting I should be here today to celebrate what the children inside undoubtedly mourned as an ending—of their holidays and freedom in the sun.

For me it wasn't an ending. In spite of a few yellowed leaves heralding the approach of autumn, today was a beginning.

Keep the spell of home affection
Still alive in every heart;
May its power, with mild direction,
Draw our love from self apart....

I smiled as a small, grey squirrel darted across my path. That very morning I had seen the spell of home affection draw my mother's love from self apart when she kissed Dad goodbye and said she hoped the new line of kippers would do well. There had been a time when Mother would have sniffed at the mention of anything so plebeian as kippers.

Break temptation's fatal power,
Shielding all with guardian care,
Safe in every careless hour
Safe from sloth and sensual snare;

Temptation's fatal power? David? Yes, that power was broken. As for 'safe in every careless hour,' well, that was asking a lot. So was safety from sloth, and I rather liked sensual snare. But I would do my best to 'do as I would be done by,' try to heal more than I hurt....

I hadn't always felt that way, especially about Posy. But I wasn't shy little Janey anymore. I was Jane. Mother had been right after all. And the best part of my life lay ahead.

I gave a little skip and called to the solid Victorian building where I'd spent twelve long years of my life, "Watch out world! Jane Blackman is about to take you by storm."

This time my foot hit no inconvenient pebble and I remained proudly confident and upright—until I thought I saw Miss Barclay peering through a window and decided it was time to beat a confident retreat.

~The End~

About the author of A WOMAN OF EXPERIENCE

Kay Gregory was born and educated in England. Shortly after moving to Canada as a teenager, she met her husband in the unromantic setting of a dog club banquet. He was a blind date who filled in when the man she was supposed to meet came down with appendicitis. Kay and her husband now make their home near Vancouver, B.C., where they have two grown sons and a mini Australian Shepherd called Riley who believes it's his job to herd anything that moves.

At various times Kay has co-habited, more or less willingly, with dogs, hamsters, gerbils, guinea pigs, rats and ferrets. Over the years she has had more jobs that she can count: Everything from removing the roe from dead herring to packaging paper bags—the bags won and she lost the job—running a health food bar, cleaning offices and working in a variety of offices as a not-very-efficient secretary. Once, when asked what she did for a living, Kay replied, "I don't know. Mostly I change jobs."

Now the author of over twenty-five novels, Kay says, "Writing books is definitely the best job I've ever had, and it's one I don't plan to change."

Escape the Past by K. G. McAbee   Fantasy
Can they escape their pasts and find a future in each other's arms?

The Anonymous Amanuensis by Judith Glad   Regency
Regency England is a man's world, until one woman writes her own rules...

No More Secrets, No More Lies by Marie Roy   Contemporary
Secrets, lies, and consequences. What consequences does Sydney Morgan pay when all secrets are exposed?

The Dragon's Horn by Glynnis Kincaid   Fantasy
Three Dragons. Three Immortals. One Choice. But what will they choose? Will they rescue their loved ones, or fight to redeem the world?

The Binding by PhyllisAnn Welsh   Fantasy
He's an Elf Lord trying to save his people. She's a fantasy writer trying to save her sanity. Chosen by the gods to rescue an entire race, they first have to save each other.

Dream Knight by Alexis Kaye Lynn   Medieval
Do you believe in the power of dreams?

Allude to Murder by Emma Kennedy   Suspense
Balkan smuggling conspiracy entangles two Americans

Mating Season by Liz Hunter   Contemporary
One lucky sailboat captain + His fetching first mate + Hurricane Season=Mating Season!

Unlawful by Dorice Nelson   Medieval
Butchery tainted their first encounter... Enslavement separated them... Deception and deceit reunited them... Thus began their struggle of courage and conquest...

Saranac Lake Requiem by Shel Damsky   Historical
Gabriel Levine never dreamed that he would find a new life, true friendship, love, and mortal danger.

Angels Unaware by Priscilla A. Maine   Historical
Is Rebecca's faith strong enough to sustain her through the most trying battles, and help her stand strong in the midst of her adversities?

Enchanted Cottage by Linda Bleser   Paranormal
A story for women who may feel their youth slipping away, but not their zest for life, their taste for adventure, or their ability to recognize and appreciate the power of love—at whatever stage it enters their life.

A Fine Impersonation by K.G. McAbee   Fantasy
Can an incompetent actor take the place of a prince? He can...if he lives long enough to try!

The Choosing by PhyllisAnn Welsh   Fantasy
An extraordinary tale of love, villains and magic!

Apology for the Devil by Stewart Thomas   Thriller/Intrigue
American Secret Service Agent Lia Blaine and Major Robert Garrick of the elite British Special Air Services find themselves thrown together into a violent maelstrom of corruption and treachery which leads up into the White House.

For Baby's Sake by Maralee Lowder   Contemporary Romance
When Rich Jones enters the diner the only thing he wants is a hearty meal and a chance to see his favorite waitress, Anna. What he doesn't expect is a surprise "gift" that will alter his life forever.

Guarder Lore by Shawn P. Madison   Science Fiction
When a terrorist plot rocks the U.E.N. and thrusts the Guarder Squadron into public view, a history of the ultra-secret is sanctioned for the first time. Now one man, a historian who barely believes the myths himself, discovers the truth behind the legends.

The Last Light by Ana Salazar   Regency
Small and pale, Grace Radbyrne is a timid vicar's widow, burdened by a seemingly impossible dream. Damian Ward, Duke of Carisbrooke, is a bitter man, damaged by betrayal. Failing to locate her missing brother alone, Grace agrees to become Damian's mistress in exchange for his assistance...a devil's bargain only love can break.

The Scent of Stone by Savannah Michaels   Paranormal
Tintagel Castle, secret caves, and a tantalizing scent cause havoc on two unwilling lovers. Shawn Corrigan and Darcy Brannigan find themselves in over their heads as a love potion created in 500 AD affects their lives and hearts. Throw in the magic of Merlin and his delightful sidekick, Aili, and you'll never look at a stone the same way again.

Too Many Spies Spoil the Case by Miles Archer   Mystery
Hard-hitting, quick thinking and an irreverent mouth propel Doug McCool through a tight action thriller with plenty of bodies dropping, bullets flying and, of course, too many spies. Join the hippy detective as he takes you on a tour of San Francisco in the mid-70s.

Married by Mistake by Laurie Alice Eakes   Regency
To protect Stormy from the machinations of her guardian, Dante claims she is his wife and she is by Scottish law. But danger stems from unexpected and far more dangerous sources than Stormy's uncle.

Tyrant Moon by Elaine Corvidae   Fantasy
He had vowed to do no harm. She was born to kill. Can a dying mage and a barbarian warrior put aside their differences long enough to stop a rogue wizard...before time runs out for them both?

Surviving the Novel Experience, An Author's Handbook by K.G. McAbee & A.A. Aguirre
An essential handbook for both established and aspiring authors.

The Scottish Thistle by Cindy Vallar   Historical
Rory MacGregor protects her people with cunning and Second Sight. A warrior bound by honor, Duncan Cameron weds her. Will their union survive deposed royalty, vindictive clansmen, and bloody rebellion?

Yorkshire by Lynne Connolly   Historical
When Rose Golightly accompanies her family on a visit to their cousins in Yorkshire, she doesn't expect a run down house...and the love of her life.

Why Ask for the Moon? by Elizabeth Taylor George   Historical
Why has Iris Montgomery abandoned a life of ease for a moment of bliss in Kian McKitterage's arms? Can their love survive life's most difficult challenges?